# A

# RIVER

## *of*

# CROWS

S̲HANESSA G̲LUHM

TouchPoint Press
*Relax. Read. Repeat.*

A RIVER OF CROWS
By Shanessa Gluhm
Published by TouchPoint Press
Brookland, AR 72417
www.touchpointpress.com

Hardcover ISBN: 978-1-956851-57-1
Softcover ISBN: 978-1-956851-58-8

TouchPoint Press books may be purchased in bulk or at special discounts for sales promotions, gifts, fundraising, or educational purposes. For details, contact the Sales and Distribution Staff: info@touchpointpress.com.

Editor: Kimberly Coghlan
Cover Design: Aleksandar Milosavljevic

First Edition

Library of Congress Control Number: 2023932707

Printed in the United States of America.

To my parents, Shannon and Tammy McClain, for all those Friday nights spent eating pizza in front of the TV watching the *TGIF* lineup. Those were the days.

If men had wings and bore black feathers,
few of them would be clever enough to be crows.
—Henry Ward Beecher

# Prologue

I've heard about angels, a tunnel, and a bright white light, but all I see are crows—smears and smudges of crows circling above the water. The same water I've swum in, fished in, and studied beside will be the water that will soon flood my lungs. This river has been a part of me for so long, it's only fitting that I soon become a part of it.

I push against the hands that hold me under, then try pulling instead. I claw and thrash, but it's not enough. I've always been a fighter, yet somehow, I already know this is a fight I can't win.

When they find me—*if* they find me—they will say I slipped. No one will pay. No one except me, even though many are guilty. But the crows see my killer's face. The crows see all they've done. And a crow never forgets.

The water is choppier now, and my panic rises with it. My body craves oxygen. My legs kick beneath me; my arms rise above me. The hands push down with more force. Everything is futile. My mouth opens, and water floods my throat, burning into my lungs. My legs stop kicking; my arms stop flailing. I close my eyes as my body becomes limp. The hands above me feel me stop resisting but only shove me down further, as though my surrender is a trick. I can't blame them for thinking that.

But this is no trick; this is the end. I open my eyes once more. The crows are still there, waiting. I fall asleep and dream of them diving into the water, lifting me with their talons, and laying my lifeless body on the riverbank. Like a bird, I am flying, hovering above my body, watching this funeral-like ritual when one crow, the largest one, flies up toward me. He zips ahead, and I follow. With a clarity that only comes in dreams, I know he is here to guide my soul into whatever comes next.

# Chapter 1

*Houston, Texas, 2008*

Sloan Bevan took her time clearing her desk. The building was empty, but unlike most of her colleagues, she didn't have anyone to rush home to. She already missed the sounds of laughing students and paper being torn from notebooks. There was nothing sadder than a silent classroom.

Sloan thought about the fifth graders who had filled these empty desks just hours ago. She could usually say with confidence she'd prepared them for middle school but worried this year that her disaster of a personal life had seeped into her classroom.

Picking up a few folders from the desk, Sloan glimpsed the papers she'd been avoiding for three weeks now, *Final Decree of Divorce*. Even after five months of going through the process, reading the words still hurt.

She and Liam married in 2000. The same year she started teaching. Sloan approached her marriage the same way she approached the start of her career, with unbridled optimism. It was hard to remember the feeling now, eight exhausting years later.

Sloan knew she needed to sign the papers and put all this behind her. Liam certainly had. Of course, he'd put their marriage behind him *during* their marriage—the moment he met Megan Cooper, to be exact.

As much as Sloan hated Megan, she couldn't place all the blame on her—even if she was a homewrecker. No marriage is unraveled by pulling a single thread. Just like no family is. Sloan understood that all too well.

Sloan was a child of the '80s, and growing up, she never considered a world without shopping malls or Saturday-morning cartoons. Never gave thought to a time before she existed, when her parents lived separate lives. She'd been an only child once but remembered little from those two years. In every memory, her brother was there. As a girl, it was impossible to imagine a world unlike the realm of her childhood. It was just as difficult to imagine a different future. Sloan never dreamed of a world where MTV aired more television shows than music videos—or where she carried a computer in her pocket.

She never thought her parents would again live separate lives or that she would become an only child once more. Never expected the river she'd learned to swim and fish in would be the river that claimed her brother's life. And never in a million years would she have guessed her father's hands would hold Ridge under the murky water at Crow's Nest Creek until he stopped breathing.

No, she didn't see any of it coming.

Sloan's phone vibrated in her pocket. She drew in a long breath. The number was not Liam's, but seeing it made Sloan's heart skip just the same: Noah Dawson. Her voice cracked as she answered.

"Hi, Sloan. It's Noah," he said, his voice barely above a whisper.

Sloan cleared her throat. "Oh, hey." She tried to sound like she didn't already know it would be him on the other end of the line. Tried to sound like somewhere along the way she'd deleted his number from her phone, forgotten it entirely.

"Sorry to bother you, but have you checked your voicemail? Cedar Grove is trying to reach you. Caroline left."

Sloan shot up from her chair. "What do you mean she left? She can't do that."

"She can, Sloan. Everything since the psychiatric hospital has been voluntary. She's in a private facility."

Sloan paced across the classroom, staring down at the carpet dotted with orphaned pencil stubs, erasers, and a few sparkly hairbands.

Her mom seemed to like the home. She hadn't complained about it. Not that Sloan had called her much or ever asked for her opinion. Sloan had given up the hope that anyone or any program could help her mother, but at least they had kept her safe and fed. What was she supposed to do now?

"I can help," Noah said as if he'd read her mind. "She's back at the house. I can turn the utilities on and bring down the old furniture from the attic. My mom's gonna pick up some groceries too."

"Yeah, thanks." Sloan looked around the classroom. "I have some work to finish up. Mandatory meetings tomorrow, but I can be there Saturday. Let me know what I owe you."

"Well, I've always wanted an explanation."

Sloan tensed. "Noah. Don't."

"Hey, I'm kidding. Don't worry about it. I'm sorry all this is happening. First, your dad's release date was set, and now this. I wish . . . I wish I could . . ."

Sloan choked back tears. She couldn't cry to Noah. Not anymore. "I've gotta go. I'll be in touch."

She ended the call before Noah had a chance to say anything else. She grabbed the box of tissues. Empty. She threw it across the room and wiped her eyes across her sleeve. Then she grabbed a pen and signed the divorce papers.

Dad was getting out, Mom was getting out, and Sloan was getting out too.

As soon as Sloan passed the sunbaked *Welcome to Mallowater* sign, it felt like an x-ray apron had dropped on her chest. Mallowater was only half a day's drive from Sloan's home in Houston, but it was also a lifetime away. She'd left this backwater town the summer after graduation and hadn't looked back.

Sloan noticed the population marker was almost too faded to see now. It read 38,375, but Sloan was certain that number decreased every day.

There was nothing much special about Mallowater, Texas. Towering pine trees, scattered crops of wheat and cotton, nearly lost in weeds, old rotting barns in forgotten fields, shredded tires and beer cans littering the road, and of course, crows. Crows on every fence post, crows dotting telephone wires, crows at Easthead River. With so many crows at Easthead River, no one even called it by its name. It was always Crow's Nest Creek.

And Crow's Nest Creek had swept away twelve years of happy memories.

Sloan's phone rang from the passenger seat. She flipped it over and saw the number. Liam. Her breath caught. He deserved to be sent to voicemail, but she couldn't bring herself to decline his call.

"Hi, Sloan. How are you?"

How was she? What kind of cliché question was that? She was terrible. "I'm okay."

"My lawyer said you dropped off the papers. Thanks for signing them."

Sloan sank in her seat. It was over. It was *really* over. "I didn't think I had a choice."

"Don't start that, Lo." Liam exhaled into the phone. "This isn't all on me."

Sloan gripped the wheel. "Don't call me Lo. You have no right to call me that. And it *is* all on you, Liam. You and Megan, that is."

"Leave her out of this." Liam raised his voice. "I wasn't perfect, but I *never* cheated."

"Right. Guess it's normal to have 3 a.m. conversations with coworkers."

"Come on. You never trusted me, not from the start. You were always waiting for the other shoe to drop."

Sloan gave a wry laugh. "And drop it did."

"Believe whatever you want, but Megan had nothing to do with this."

"So, you aren't seeing her?" Sloan's tire hit the road's shoulder. Silence.

Sloan yanked the car back onto the road. "Are you seeing her?"

"Yeah, I am *now*. She's been a friend and—"

"Enough, Liam. I signed the papers. Tell me when the house sells. I got everything out I needed."

"Sloan, wait." Liam lowered his voice. "I heard you were going to Mallowater."

"Who told you that?"

"Take my car," Liam said, ignoring the question. "That Chevy is on its tenth life. And we can find someone to help with your mom."

"Wow. Guess good news really does travel fast."

"Don't be like this, Sloan. You shouldn't have to do this alone."

Sloan's eyes flooded with tears. No, she shouldn't have to do this alone, but she *was* alone. Completely alone, again.

"Goodbye, Liam." She ended the call and threw the phone onto the floorboard. The road blurred through her tears. Liam always said her eyes were prettier when she cried. That they brightened to emerald green, like a sky changing colors during a storm. With all the crying she'd done recently, they had to be glowing like the Emerald City by now.

Sloan riffled around in her purse, searching for the cassette. It would only make her feel worse, but she needed it. She carried the tape around like an alcoholic stashing an emergency bottle of whiskey. Sloan's hands shook as she slid it into the tape deck, the only part of the old clunker that somehow still worked perfectly. Keith Whitley's "I'm Over You" began right on cue. Of all the songs to start on. When Sloan couldn't stop her tears fast enough, she pulled over to the side of the road and sobbed. She could pretend it was for Liam, but these tears were really for the first man to break her heart, Jay Hadfield, her father.

# Chapter 2

*Mallowater, Texas, 1988*

Sloan Hadfield cared little for crows. So, while her mom and brother talked birds, Sloan opened her copy of *The Egypt Game* and tried to ignore them.

"Is it time for the night roosts again?" Ridge asked. He sat across from Sloan—floppy blonde hair obscuring his eyes as he studied the tattered bird encyclopedia in front of him.

As Mom stirred hamburger meat around in a pan, the spicy aroma of paprika tickled Sloan's nose. "Pretty soon. It's almost fall, and breeding season is over," her mother answered.

Sloan said a silent prayer Mom wouldn't go into any more detail about crow breeding. She already knew more about birds' mating habits than any twelve-year-old should. Daddy said her mom was once a brilliant scientist, the kind that studies birds. Said she gave up some fancy internship to come to the middle of nowhere Texas to be with him. Seeing as how Sloan's father worked as a traveling salesman for the Fuller Brush Company, that part of the story never made sense to Sloan. Why didn't Daddy move to New York to be with the woman he loved? Didn't people in New York need toilet brushes and kitchen degreasers too?

"What's your favorite bird, Sloan?" Ridge asked.

Sloan kept her eyes on her book. "The phoenix."

"That's not an actual bird." He pushed the book towards her. "You can look in here."

Sloan shoved the book across the table. "When's dinner going to be ready?"

"Soon." Mom tossed Sloan an apple from the counter. "Have this while you wait."

Sloan caught the apple, then dropped it on the table and resumed her reading. Ridge reached across and grabbed for it. "Hey!" Sloan snatched the fruit back up. "That's mine."

"You weren't even going to eat it." Ridge's face reddened to the same shade as the apple.

"Yes, I was!" Sloan chomped into the fruit. "Get your own."

"Both of you, stop." Mom pressed the meat down with a wooden spoon, and the grease sizzled. "Do you realize how lucky you are to have one another? Have I ever told you about the special relationship between brother and sister crows?"

"No." Ridge turned his chair away from the table and toward his mother. "Tell us!"

Sloan rolled her eyes. *Here we go again.*

Mom approached the table. "Well, in most bird species, once the bird leaves the nest, that's it. They go off and find their own way. But not crows." Mom's eyes brightened. "Crows stay with their family for years, sticking around to help protect younger siblings. They even help bring the momma bird food for the baby." She raised her eyebrows at Sloan.

Ridge slowly turned back to the table. "Sorry I tried to take your apple, Lo."

Sloan looked back at her book but felt her mom's eyes boring into her.

The screeching sound of the screen door granted Sloan a reprieve. She jumped up, dropping the book on the floor. "Daddy!"

"Lo! Come give your old man a hug, will you?" Sloan charged and wrapped her arms around her dad's chest. He smelled like aftershave and pine. He lifted the bill of her Detroit Lions cap. "I missed the game Sunday. How are the Lions looking this season?"

Sloan grimaced. "Well, they only lost by one touchdown."

He shook his head. "I don't know, Lo. I think we may need a new team to root for." He handed Mom his briefcase, kissing her cheek. "Hey, we're missing one. Where's my boy?"

"Hi, Dad." Ridge waved from the kitchen doorway.

Daddy walked over and ruffled Ridge's hair, then stuck his head farther into the kitchen. "Something smells delicious."

"Tacos," Mom said.

"Perfect! That's just what I've been hungry for. There's not a restaurant in the entire state of Texas that can hold a candle to your cooking."

"Want me to take your coat?" Sloan asked.

"Sure thing." He kicked off his shoes and walked to the radio. "Let's dance, Caroline."

"Dinner's on the stove, Jay."

Daddy turned the dial until the baritone voice of Ricky Van Shelton filled the living room. "Come on. One song."

Mom wiped her hands on her denim shorts. "Oh, fine, but not a word if the meat's black."

Sloan watched her parents sway, lost in their own private world. Mom was wearing a pink tank top, and her blonde hair cascaded just past her bronzed shoulders. She was tall with long legs, just like Sloan. But unlike Sloan, the long legs suited her. She was always graceful in her movements.

Daddy leaned in and whispered something into Mom's ear. It sounded like, "I'm sorry." Sloan hoped this didn't mean he had to leave again tomorrow.

Mom pulled back. "Sorry for what?"

"That we don't have everything we dreamed of."

"Oh, stop it, Jay Hadfield. What more could anyone want than this?"

He leaned in to kiss her, and Sloan turned away. Sometimes it was gross how affectionate they were. However, it seemed more and more parents were getting divorced, parents of her classmates, parents of the neighbors. Sloan was glad that would never happen to her mom and dad—glad they still loved each other.

Daddy sang along as they continued to dance. He had the deep voice and Texas twang of a country singer, but mom said he couldn't carry a tune.

After the song's last notes played, Mom tried to pull away.

"Oh, come on, one more," Daddy said. "Listen, it's Keith Whitley."

"Nope." Mom laughed as she wriggled free from his arms. "Dinner's burning."

"And it's almost time for our show," Sloan said, reaching for the remote.

Daddy held up a hand. "Not yet." He turned the radio volume up. "It's a sin to turn off the radio in the middle of a Keith Whitley song."

Sloan rolled her eyes and tried to look annoyed, but she couldn't stop smiling. Tacos were cooking, *Who's the Boss* was starting, and best of all, Daddy was home.

"Please, Mom. Just one chapter," Ridge pleaded. "I won't be able to fall asleep without it."

Sloan sank into her pillow. Ridge and his routines. Her brother was an enigma. He was smart for a ten-year-old, gifted even, yet he still couldn't fall asleep without a bedtime story.

"Not tonight, Ridge." Mom switched off the lamp between their bed. "It's after ten and a school night."

Sloan burrowed under the covers. "Not to mention, we're about five years too old for bedtime stories."

"Oh," Ridge said as if that had never occurred to him. Sloan hadn't meant to hurt him. He'd always been so sensitive. Ridge sat up in bed. "Now that I'm learning all about birds, do you think I can ask for a parrot for Christmas?"

Mom sat on Ridge's bed. "Pets are a big responsibility. And what makes you want a parrot?"

"They can talk."

"Well, so can crows."

"They can?" Ridge's voice rose an octave higher.

"You can train them to. Crows speak better than parrots and can mimic sounds and voices uncannily."

"Can they mimic snoring?" Sloan came out from under her pillow. She hated sharing a room with her brother. Not like she had any choice, but he could be especially annoying after ten on a school night.

Mom stood. "Very funny. But it's late." She kissed Ridge on the forehead and blew a kiss at Sloan. "Sleep tight."

Sloan flopped to face the wall. She was almost asleep when she heard Ridge stirring. "Go to sleep," she said without turning around.

"Sorry. Just have one question." He flipped the lamp on. "Do you ever wish Mom and Dad would get married?"

"Not usually at 10:30 p.m.," Sloan said but rolled over to face him. "It's the eighties. Moms and dads don't have to be married."

Ridge's brow furrowed. "But I want them to stay together forever."

"They will. They aren't old-fashioned, Ridge. Mom said they don't need some piece of paper or ring to prove they love each other. Plenty of moms and dads sign pieces of paper only to rip them up." Sloan scooped up a stuffed animal from the floor by her bed. A blue jay named Blue that Ridge used to carry around everywhere. She threw it at him. "Now go to sleep."

Ridge dropped the bird on the floor before flopping down on his pillow. Sloan knew if she hadn't teased him for sleeping with it a few months ago, he still would be. "Night, Lo. I love you."

"Love you too, dummy." Sloan reached for the lamp but froze at the sudden crash across the hall.

Ridge jolted up. "What was that?"

"I'm not sure," Sloan said, but every muscle in her body went rigid.

Tears filled Ridge's eyes. "It's happening again."

"Maybe not," Sloan said, but her mother's wild scream confirmed their fear. It *was* happening again. Twice now in one month. Sloan jumped out of bed. The floor felt even colder than usual. "Let me handle this. You stay put."

"But—"

"No buts! Do as I say!" Sloan realized she was yelling, too, further frightening Ridge. "It'll be okay. I promise." She grabbed Blue off the floor and handed him to Ridge. "If you go, it'll only make things worse. Do you understand?"

He nodded, squeezing Blue against his chest.

Sloan walked into the hallway, closing the door behind her.

"Jay, wake up!" her mother cried.

Daddy was talking too, but his words made no sense. It was all gibberish.

Sloan cracked the door to her parent's room. "Mom?"

"Go, Sloan!" Mom pleaded. "Call Walt!"

Sloan pushed the door the rest of the way open. Her parents were on the floor between the bed and the window, Daddy on top, pinning Mom to that cold, cold floor.

"Daddy, stop!" Sloan stepped into the room. Her father didn't get up but looked over his shoulder at Sloan. His normally sparkling eyes dull, his wavy blonde hair drenched in sweat.

"Sloan, no. Get the phone. Call Walt," Mom repeated.

Sloan ran for the phone in the hallway. She misdialed twice before she steadied her hand and called Walter Dawson.

"Hello?" a sweet, sleepy voice said.

"Mrs. Dawson, it's Sloan. We need Walt."

That seemed to wake up Doreen Dawson. "Walt, wake up," Sloan heard her say. "Is it your daddy again, Sloan? Are you okay?"

Sloan still heard her mother crying and her dad mumbling. She turned back down the hallway and noticed her bedroom door open. She hadn't left it that way.

Sloan felt like she was moving in slow motion back down the hallway. She peeked into their room, but Ridge was gone. She saw the camouflage sheath on his bed and winced. Their father gave Ridge that hunting knife—a knife he had refused to use until now, apparently.

She turned toward her parents' room and watched Ridge tiptoeing toward their parents. His grip was so tight on the knife that his hand was white. "Ridge, no!"

Ridge dropped his hand to his side. His lips and chin trembled.

"He's choking her."

Sloan looked across the room. Ridge was right. Their mom kicked and thrashed as she tried to force their father's hands from her neck.

Before Sloan could figure out how to stop her dad, Ridge jumped on his back, hitting and screaming. Sloan watched Ridge and her mom try to fight off Daddy, but they were no match for him. She realized she wouldn't be either, but she couldn't stop thinking about Ridge's knife, just inches from her foot. Could she use it if she had to? *Hurry, Walt. Please hurry.*

Her father climbed to his feet. Ridge was still on him, pounding his fists. In one swift motion, Daddy raised up higher, throwing Ridge behind him. Sloan screamed when Ridge hit the wall. It was a thud so terrible, she'd remember it forever.

Her mom screamed, too—a sound almost as loud as the crash. It seemed to stun Daddy, who moved away from her, blinking rapidly, and rubbing his head.

Mom charged for Ridge, who had sat up. "I just bumped my head," he said. "It doesn't hurt." He flashed a smile at Mom, but Sloan noticed blood in his shaggy, matted hair.

"Is he okay?" Sloan's voice shook.

"I think so," Caroline said, examining her son.

"What's going on?" Daddy stood behind them, his voice still thick with sleep. "My god, Ridge. What happened?"

Outside the window, a motorcycle roared. The sound of salvation. The sound of Walt.

Sloan met Walt at the door. He was still in his pajamas, the white of his tee-shirt contrasting against dark brown skin, his gray flannel pants not quite concealing the gun tucked into them. "What happened, Sloan?" He pushed past her into the house. Though he was a small man, Walt had a commanding presence and unexpected strength, as he'd proven the last time he had to restrain Sloan's sleepwalking father.

"It's over." Sloan surprised herself by throwing her arms around Walt. "But Ridge hit his head. Can you help him?"

"Does he need an ambulance?"

"No!" Sloan backed away. "You can't report this, Walt. They'll arrest Daddy. It was just one of his nightmares. From Vietnam. Like last time. You understand, right?"

"Hey, hey." Walt's voice was calming. "I understand. Remember, I fought in the war too? I promise I'm not gonna let anything happen to Ridge or your dad, either. Understand?"

Sloan nodded, wiping her snotty nose across the sleeve of her nightgown. As thankful as she was for Walt, as much as she wanted to believe his words, she somehow knew that he'd never be able to keep this promise.

# Chapter 3

*Mallowater, TX, 2008*

As if the Keith Whitley tape wasn't enough, Sloan stopped at Crow's Nest Creek before going home.

Mud squished under her brown Doc Martens as she climbed the steep ridge. She had run up this incline ten thousand times but wasn't as surefooted now.

Sloan's shirt clung to her back, and her hair was already frizzing. "We're in for another hot summer," the friendly postal worker told her yesterday. As if there was a different kind of summer here in East Texas.

The water moved slowly today, trickling around massive boulders in the middle of the wide river. It was the kind of sound that soothed people, the peaceful noises they played when getting a massage or trying to fall asleep. In a few more months, it would be difficult to hear the water over the sound of the crows. *That* was a sound *nobody* could fall asleep to.

Not much about the river had changed. Sloan's favorite climbing tree still stood; its limbs just as gnarled as she remembered them. If she closed her eyes, she could still see a pink glittery Easter egg in the crook of a branch, the last one she'd found the year they hunted eggs here.

A moss-covered fallen tree trunk she remembered was still here too. How many times had she, Ridge, and Noah balanced on it? The same trail still cut through the tall, pinecone-littered grass—the one made by animals visiting the water's edge. Bits of tinfoil and leftover plastic baggies from picnics still littered the bank.

Sloan peered into the creek. Minnows flashed beneath the surface and brought back a memory. She was a toddler wading in the ford of the river, holding hands with her parents, splashing and singing "Ring Around the Rosie." They were laughing. They were happy.

Hard to believe this peaceful place was the site of her brother's death. Of course, the water hadn't been peaceful that day. It had rained for weeks, and the creek raged. But the creek didn't take Ridge's life. Their father did.

Sloan closed her eyes to stop her tears. She inhaled, breathing in wet earth and rotting bark. Now was no time for a panic attack.

She sat down and touched the water. They'd never found her brother's body, just a shoe, a piece of his torn t-shirt, and the god-awful green beanie he loved so much. And, of course, his blood. "Where'd you go, Ridge?" Sloan asked her reflection.

A crow cawed loudly from a tree. Sloan wondered if her mom had been out here yet to look for nests, wondered if she even cared to anymore. Sloan stood. Only one way to find out, and she couldn't put it off any longer.

The outside of the house looked foreign, not at all resembling the home of Sloan's childhood. The crusty white paint was peeling, and at least half a dozen shingles were missing from the roof.

Clearly, the last renters hadn't taken care of the place. Walt had tried to tell her that, but she'd been too wrapped up in her own life to care.

Sloan knocked on the warped screen door. It seemed silly to knock on the door she'd barged in and out of for nineteen years, but this wasn't her home anymore. She didn't have a home anymore.

Sloan held her breath as the door scraped open. And just like that, she was face-to-face with the woman she hadn't faced in thirteen years.

Her mom held the door open, the other hand on her hip. Well, aren't you going to come in?" There was no hint of emotion in Caroline Radel's voice.

"Hi, Mom," Sloan said, stepping through the threshold. It looked even smaller inside than she remembered. Growing up, Sloan had always been a little embarrassed by their home. Her friend Jenny lived in a nice house in town. It wasn't a mansion, but it had an entryway, two bathrooms, a dining room with a table that sat eight, and a never-ending hallway to summersault down.

Three steps into Sloan's home, and you were already in the middle of the living room. A few more, and you'd find yourself in the kitchen, so crowded that one side of the four-seater table had to be pressed against the wall when not being used. A glance to the left before entering that tiny kitchen would reveal a compact hallway crammed with two bedrooms and a single bathroom. It was the kind of house where the back door was visible from the front—the kind of house not built for summersaults. It was a marvel that any of them could keep secrets in a house this small.

At least it looked better on the inside than on the outside. A pungent smell of lemon polish and window cleaner permeated the stuffy air. Sloan opened the window by the front door.

"Did Walt and Doreen clean the place up?" Sloan noticed a few unfamiliar paintings hung on the walls and a framed photo of Sloan and Caroline on the mantle next to a ceramic collection of owls. "And decorate?"

"Well, somebody had to."

Sloan looked at her mom. Like the house, Caroline had seen better days. Dark bags settled under her eyes, with deep-set wrinkles around her mouth, and her once silky, almost white-blonde hair was coarse, ash-gray. Both Sloan's parents once had beautiful blonde hair. Sloan's was always a darker blonde, the color of dirty dishwater. Nothing about her physical appearance had been quite up to par with her beautiful parents. She was like the copies that came out of the ancient photocopier in the teacher's lounge at her school. You could sort of make out the original, but it was mostly a grainy mess.

"I certainly haven't been able to clean, seeing as how I just broke myself out of the nuthouse. The one you locked me in and never even visited."

"Considering you hardly ever even took my calls, I didn't figure a visit would go over well," Sloan said.

"What did you expect? That I could just forgive you for abandoning me? Not a chance."

Sloan threw up her hands. "Yet I'm supposed to forgive you?"

Caroline rolled her eyes. "I was always there when you were growing up."

"Physically, maybe, but—" Sloan rubbed her forehead. "Whatever. It doesn't even matter. All that matters is now. What's the plan?" she snapped. "How will you survive? Pay for your meds?" It was a mistake to try to reason with Caroline, but Sloan wouldn't take the blame for this. She'd worked her ass off to assure her mom got the best care possible. All it took was her mom's signature to throw it all away.

"I don't need meds, Sloan. I never did. Two days clean, and I've never been better," she said, lighting a cigarette.

Sloan rubbed her face, refusing to engage further. She looked into the void of her mom's eyes and tried to remember who she'd once been. The woman who had put her children's shirts in the dryer every winter morning so they'd be warm, the woman who sat through hours of Chutes and Ladders, the woman who had loved Sloan so well. "Okay, Mom. We'll figure it out."

Caroline flicked cigarette ash on the floor. "Walt and Doreen will help me. And their boy . . . what's his name?" She smirked.

Sloan stomped on the ash. "You know his name. He brings you Whataburger every Sunday."

"Not *every* Sunday." Caroline took another puff of the cigarette. "He's married. To one of the Sullivan girls. The real pretty one."

Sloan stiffened. "Vickie. Yeah, I heard."

"The one that got away, eh?" Caroline punched Sloan's shoulder.

"No, Mom. Not the one that got away. The one that grew up and made a life, just like I did."

Caroline grabbed a blue Solo cup to tap ash into. "That's right. You got married too. Or so a little birdie told me. I certainly wasn't there to zip up your gown."

"We didn't have a wedding," Sloan said. "Eloped in Vegas."

"Vegas. Trashy, trashy."

"Well, when your dad's not available to walk you down the aisle, you might as well let Elvis do it."

Caroline's eyes roamed down to Sloan's hand. "Are you getting your ring cleaned?"

Sloan jerked her hand back. She'd only quit wearing the ring a few weeks ago, her empty finger a constant reminder of everything in her life that was missing. "It didn't work out."

Sloan's mother blew out a breath. "Well, hell. I tried to tell you, girl. You can't trust a man. Not any of them, not ever. I figured growing up with that sonofabitch Jay Hadfield as your daddy might've taught you that. But you're like your momma—gotta learn the hard way."

Sloan's heart clenched at the sound of her father's name. She walked into the kitchen. "How are you on groceries?"

"The Dawsons brought me a few things. I can make do."

Sloan stepped into the pantry. It had always been full growing up. They were never rich, but they always had enough. Sloan remembered her mother's obsessiveness about the order of the pantry. After they bought groceries, Caroline would take everything out of its box and put it into plastic containers. Cereal had white lids, crackers blue. Labeled cans for flour, sugar, coffee, and tea. Canned goods in rows, spices organized alphabetically. "You'll learn soon enough, Lo," her mom once said when Sloan asked her why she bothered. "There is so very little this man-made world allows women to have control of. The pantry is one of them, so I figure I might as well take advantage." Sloan didn't understand then, but she did now. She understood a lot more now. Like what led her mom to knock all those orderly cans to the ground that long-ago night. She understood why she'd taken the time to remove each lid off its plastic container and fling its contents across the floor. She even understood why her mother had lied to her about why she did it. "I'm just missing my daddy," Mom had told her. Sloan's granddad had died a few months before. Sloan missed him too. So much that she understood the need to break something. So, she'd gone to bed without even realizing that night had been the beginning of the end.

Sloan drove an hour to Tyler for groceries. Mallowater only had one grocery store. She might have found everything she needed there but would have found plenty she didn't need too. Plenty of eyes boring into her, plenty of questions she didn't want to answer. She could be inconspicuous in Tyler. And it afforded her another couple of hours that she didn't have to be locked inside that tiny house with her mother. Sloan wondered how she'd get through a week, much less an entire summer. She needed to get Caroline back in that home, and fast.

Sloan took her time at Wal-Mart. She didn't have a list, so she wandered down every aisle, trying to guess what her mother might eat. Halfway down the cereal aisle, she paused, trying to decide between something sensible and something chocolate, when someone stopped behind her. *Not Noah,* she thought. *Anybody but Noah.*

She grabbed a box of Cocoa Puffs and continued to walk. The person behind her moved too. Sloan sped up. By the time she reached the end of the aisle, the other cart had stopped again. She laughed at herself for being paranoid. Other people needed cereal. Noah wouldn't be in Tyler. Still, she couldn't stop herself from turning to make sure.

She saw the red hair first, made even more vivid under the bright fluorescent lighting. Sloan's blood and all its heat settled in her face. She stood frozen, staring at Felicity as Timbaland's "Apologize" blared through the store's speakers. As much as she hadn't wanted to see Noah, this was worse. Of all the stores in Tyler, of all the aisles.

Felicity's oversized, cartoon princess eyes grew even wider as she stood staring back at Sloan. She opened her mouth, then closed it again, like Sloan was a sea witch who'd stolen her voice.

Sloan pulled at her purse with shaky hands. Once she had it, she took a step backward and then froze. The entire store spun.

"Sloan? Are you okay?"

Sloan didn't even realize she had unstuck her feet until she found herself running out of the store. She fumbled with her keys to unlock her car door, praying it would start the first time. She let out the breath she'd been holding when the engine roared to life. Coming to Tyler had been a mistake with *them* living here. She guessed there really was no place for her to hide anymore.

# Chapter 4

*Mallowater, TX, 1988*

It surprised Sloan to find her dad waiting for her in the school's office. "What are you doing here?"

He smiled that megawatt smile Jay Hadfield was famous for. It lit him up, making his blue eyes sparkle. How could a man with a smile that big and eyes that blue ever choke anyone?

"Thought I'd bust you out of here early today."

Sloan looked down the hallway. "What about Ridge?"

"Another time. I wanted to talk to you alone. How about a dipped cone and a drive?"

"Okay." Sloan pointed at the lined sheet on the counter. "You gotta sign me out."

Sloan should have been thrilled to miss school, to spend time with her dad alone, but the air was heavy with anticipation of the difficult conversation she sensed was awaiting her.

"Mom said you had a meeting in Longview today." Sloan kept

her eyes out the window as they pulled out of the school parking lot.

Daddy turned down the radio. "Meetings can be moved. Work can wait."

"Oh." Sloan took in a breath. "Is this about last night?"

He nodded. "I get you don't want to talk about it, Sloan. You and I are a lot alike. We're forgetters, you and me, just want to move on. That's not always a bad thing, but I'm sure you have questions about what happened. This was the second really bad one." He touched her shoulder. "I bet you're a little scared."

A single tear leaked from Sloan's eye. She closed her eyes to stop the rest. "I'm not scared now, but it was scary then."

"I bet." Daddy tapped the steering wheel. "Remember how I told you I fought in Vietnam?"

"Yes," Sloan whispered. "That's why you don't like fireworks. Why you have bad dreams."

"It's more than bad dreams, baby. I saw some terrible things. I *did* some terrible things. Things even an old forgetter like me can't forget."

"Will you ever get better?" Sloan asked.

"Maybe. Your mom thinks I need to see a doctor, and I'm going to. I've always had bad dreams, but this is the second time I've attacked your mother." Daddy tugged at his ear. "You understand, I'd never hurt her, never hurt any of you, not if I was thinking straight."

The tears in her father's voice broke Sloan's heart. She took his arm. "Of course you wouldn't; we all know that."

He wiped his eyes. "In better news, I've been looking at that lot behind us. I'm thinking of making an offer and building us a new house."

Sloan raised her eyebrows. "With three bedrooms?"

"Four rooms at least," Daddy said in the voice he used to sell furniture polish. The voice that didn't sound like his own. "Two stories, with a wraparound porch." He pushed his shoulders back. "You and Ridge can have the upstairs rooms, and I'll build you both balconies to read on."

Read. *Crap*. Sloan had reading homework, and she left her book at school.

As if Daddy had read her mind, he glanced to the backseat at her backpack. "Mom said it's report-card day."

Sloan rubbed a hand over her face. "Yeah. I was hoping you might talk to her about my grades again."

"How bad?"

"I don't know."

"Yeah, you do. Out with it."

"C in Math and Spelling. D in Science." Sloan slammed her back against the seat. "I know what you're going to say. That I can do better. But I can't! I'm not smart like Ridge. I'm the oldest in my class because I had to take second grade twice."

"Hey, hey! That's enough of that talk." Daddy pulled into the Dairy Queen parking lot. "You repeating second grade paid off because now you're a great reader. What's your reading grade?"

"88," Sloan said.

"88! That's terrific."

Sloan crossed her arms. "Yeah, but Ridge makes straight A's."

"Okay, so Ridge is gifted. That's great, but he's got his own issues. Ridge has a hard time . . ." He tilted his head. "He has a hard time relating to normal folks. It's hard for me to relate to him, and he's my son. Ridge will face social challenges you never will. You know how the kids pick on him."

Kids *did* pick on him. If only he'd quit being so babyish. Sloan got suspended in third grade for punching a boy who emptied Ridge's lunch box in the trash, replacing the food with an empty baby-food jar he'd found on the playground. Daddy had taken her out for ice cream then, too, come to think of it.

Daddy reached into her backpack and dug out the report card. "Let's see here. B in reading, A in social studies, and S in conduct. What's that stand for?"

"Satisfactory."

"Ah, then what's this say here?" He turned the report card toward her, pointing at the last grade.

Sloan leaned forward. "S+," she said. "But it doesn't matter. It's art."

"Why shouldn't art matter as much as math and science? Your mother will be thrilled."

"No, she won't." Sloan pushed down the report card. "Not when she sees the C in Spelling. She's made me study with her every week, but it's not helping."

"You're an artist, Sloan Hadfield. Nobody gives a shit if an artist can spell or not. We can't all be scientists like your mom. Somebody's gotta create paintings. Somebody's gotta sell toilet brushes."

Sloan giggled.

"It's true! So, what do you say the artist and toilet brush salesmen celebrate this S+ by going inside for our ice cream?"

"Sure!" Sloan unbuckled. Her Cs no longer mattered, nor did the forgotten reading book. Daddy had fixed it all with the promise of a dipped cone and a four-bedroom house.

Sloan couldn't help but notice how Mom was never quite the same after the night Daddy threw Ridge. Then there was the night she destroyed the pantry. She was missing Grandpa, Sloan told herself. But then why had she stopped cooking Daddy's favorite dinners on the nights he came home? Why had they stopped dancing?

Sloan opened the front door quietly in case her mom was napping again. She napped a lot these days.

Mom and Ridge were talking quietly in the kitchen, whispering almost. Sloan stepped closer to eavesdrop but bumped into the coffee table. "Ouch!" she grabbed her leg.

Her mom rushed into the living room. "Sloan, when did you get home?"

"Just now," Sloan said, rubbing her knee.

"Oh. How was art club?"

"Pretty good." This was a first. Her mom never asked about her art. "I drew you a picture today," Sloan said.

"Oh?"

Sloan pulled the sketchbook out of her backpack. The edge of the page ripped as she tore it out.

Mom looked at the picture. "It's a crow."

"Yeah." Sloan bit her lip. "I'm not good at birds yet. I need more work on feathers."

"No, it's great. Thanks." She set it on the couch. "Ridge, your sister's home. Why don't you both head to the river?"

"Do we have to?" Sloan's stomach growled. "When's dinner?"

"Leftovers tonight, so you can eat when you get back. Ridge wants to watch the crows."

Sloan groaned. "It's not even November yet."

"Some come in October," Mom said. "I'd go with you, but Libby is stopping by. I need a girls' night."

"What? Libby's always over. You had a week of girls' nights."

"Yes, and she's leaving in two days, Sloan. My one friend in this desolate town is moving in two days." Mom raised her voice. "Following her husband to a new job—giving up everything—and I can't stop her."

Sloan wanted to tell her mom that she was sad Libby was leaving too. With no grandparents left, Libby and Vince Turner were the closest things she and Ridge had to extended family. But she saw the tears in her mother's eyes, and she suddenly wanted to leave. "Come on, Ridge; let's go."

"Can Noah come?" Ridge stood in the doorway.

"Yeah, whatever," Sloan said. Ridge smiled, but Sloan sensed something off about him. He looked pale. Sick, almost. "Get your jacket," Sloan told him. "You aren't wearing mine this time, no matter how much you whine."

"See you in a few hours." Mom rubbed her head like it ached.

Sloan started for the door but stopped at the couch, seeing the crow picture tossed where her mom had left it. She crumbled it into a ball and dropped it in the wastebasket on the way out the door.

"Race ya in," Sloan told Noah as she propped up the kickstand to her bike. Noah dropped his bike and ran for the water, shedding his backpack halfway down the embankment. Sloan followed, kicking off her shoes and peeling off her socks and jacket, losing only by seconds. The green water was colder than she expected, and it stung.

"Mom didn't say we could go in," Ridge called from the bank.

"Come on." Sloan swam farther out, the soil-like scent of the water giving way to a less pleasant fishy smell. "Your clothes will dry."

Ridge shook his head. "It's too cold."

"Don't be a chicken," Noah called.

Ridge was undeterred. He climbed off his bike and sat in the grass, looking up into the towering trees. "Be quiet, or you'll scare them away."

"Fine." Sloan swam back to the bank. Someone would probably recognize her and tell her mom if she went any further.

Noah followed Sloan out of the water. Even though he was Ridge's friend, it was always Sloan's lead he followed. Noah was eleven, smack in between Sloan and Ridge in age, but he and Sloan were in the same grade since she'd been held back. At least they had different teachers this year. Last year in fifth grade, all her friends teased her about how Noah followed her like a shadow.

"There's a blanket and snacks in my backpack," he said.

Of course there was. Sloan never had to worry about needing anything when Noah came along. He was a model boy scout if there ever was one.

Ridge and Noah spread the blanket while Sloan looked over the creek at the deepening blue sky. A few crows flew overhead. The first sign of a night roost.

Sloan looked at her brother. He smiled for the first time since arriving at the creek. "They're coming," he said.

Ridge's excitement grew as the number of crows did. Sloan still couldn't believe her mom hadn't come. She lived for these night roosts. Something wasn't right. Sloan shivered, and she wasn't sure if it was the fault of her cold clothes, or something more.

By the time Noah handed out the Grape Squeezits and Fruit Wrinkles, even more crows had arrived. Thousands swarmed in from every direction, converging like it was some sort of summit. They flew over the creek in winding formations, mirroring the water's graceful and wild movements. A river of crows.

The birds grew louder. Sloan couldn't hear the flowing water or chirping crickets over the flapping wings and angry caws as the birds jostled for position in the surrounding trees. Sloan knew from her mom why crows roosted together at night—protection, warmth, better access to food—but why here? What had brought so many to this creek?

Sloan turned. Her brother's mouth was wide open, but he'd stopped shoving fruit snacks into it. He stared into the sky, transfixed by the show.

The creek grew quieter as the birds settled. The branches bent under their weight. Ridge grabbed Sloan's hand. His eyes were full of tears. Tears over birds? Man, he was strange.

"Thanks for bringing me here, Sloan," he said. "I love you just like a crow loves his sister."

"I love you too. Now stop being weird." She shook her hand free.

Noah wiped grass off his pants leg. "We better get home." He always worried about getting home on time. Sloan supposed that was natural with a father on the police force.

"Can't we stay a little longer?" Ridge asked.

"No." Sloan stood. "It's almost dark." She looked up at the trees dotted black with birds, feeling like an intruder in their home. "We'll come back another time."

"No, we won't," Ridge argued.

Sloan held up her pinkie. "Here, I'll pinkie swear on it."

"It's fine." Ridge jumped up and tugged at the blanket. He was careful when moving his bike from the tree it rested against, careful not to disturb the crows.

"Hey, look!" Noah pointed to the sky. "A shooting star."

A second star flashed in Sloan's peripheral. "And there's another one!"

"Wow!" Ridge lowered his bike and walked to stand beside Sloan and Noah. "It's a meteor shower. Mrs. Baker told my class about it. We have to stay."

Neither Sloan nor Noah argued this time. They all sat back down for another half hour, watching the lights paint the sky, coming in from all directions, just like the crows.

"We should make a wish," Sloan said. "Before it's over."

Ridge spoke first. "I wish for another night like this one."

Sloan would have normally rolled her eyes at her brother's sentimentality, but something about the night felt special, magical even. And of all the wishes in the world, Sloan couldn't think of one better.

# Chapter 5

*Mallowater, TX, 2008*

Sloan's heart still raced after she unloaded groceries. She'd had to stop in Mallowater for them but didn't even mind the stares or whispers. Anything was better than seeing Felicity.

Sloan turned on the television. Even PBS was better than the quiet. It surprised her when she flipped the channel and was met with more than just static. Noah, she realized. He'd not only turned the utilities on but also the cable. She needed to pay him back. Yet, she could never truly pay him back, could she? Noah and his parents had taken care of her mom all these years since Sloan escaped. Sloan only wrote the checks that allowed her mom to stay at the mental health residential facility and made the occasional phone call.

Sloan realized Noah thought her a coward for running away, but he didn't understand what it had been like to live with Caroline Radel alone all those years. Sure, he'd tried to be there for Sloan during that time; but he couldn't really understand—not when he had a normal family to go home to every night.

Sloan turned up the volume when a breaking news story flashed on the screen. *Human remains found outside Jefferson.* Sloan dropped the remote. As much as she said she wanted Ridge's remains found, she also held her breath every time these stories made headlines, always praying it wasn't him.

"The remains have been identified as Logan Pruitt," the newscaster announced. "Pruitt disappeared from Longview in 1986 when he was eleven years old."

Sloan vaguely remembered the name, a cautionary tale from her mom to always be aware of her surroundings, to distrust strangers. There were cruel rumors that Logan's parents had ties to a Satanic cult.

"Though little evidence remains, there is hope DNA will be recovered to identify a suspect in this tragic case," the reporter added.

"What's he talking about?"

Sloan jumped. "Geez, Mom. When did you come in?"

"Just now, through the back," Caroline said.

Sloan glanced at her watch. "It's already eight."

"Well, excuse me, warden. I was at the creek visiting my crows." Caroline flopped down on the couch beside Sloan. "Whatcha watching?"

"Do you remember Logan Pruitt? The boy from Longview that went missing?"

"Yeah. Awful story."

"They found his remains. In Jefferson." Sloan grabbed the remote and muted the TV. "Anytime I see a story about remains being found,

I always think of Ridge." Sloan avoided her mom's eyes. "I mean, I know it's crazy. He was washed out to the gulf, but still."

"What the hell are you talking about?" Caroline asked.

"Since they found no remains, it's just hard. No closure or whatever."

"There *aren't* remains." Caroline's tone was sharp. "Ridge is alive."

Sloan's stomach hardened. "No, Mom, he's not. Dad . . ." Sloan could never bring herself to put the blame on who she knew deserved it. "Ridge is gone."

"Then who was I talking to at the creek?"

Sloan rubbed her forehead. "That's not funny, Mom."

"I'm not making a joke. I was talking to Ridge."

Sloan jumped from the couch. "Stop, Mom. Enough with the games. Ridge is dead."

Caroline squinted like she couldn't make sense of Sloan's words. "Your brother is alive. He's *always* been alive."

Sloan sat outside the police station for thirty minutes before going in. She couldn't avoid Noah forever. And while she was picking at scabs, she might as well tear off this one.

"Good morning!" She tried to make her voice sound chipper as she approached the front desk, but she could never get chipper quite right. "Is Detective Dawson in?"

"Do you have an appointment?" The woman behind the desk didn't look up from her magazine.

"No. I'm an old friend and—"

"Sloan?"

She turned, and there he was. Being this close to Noah Dawson still caused a physical reaction in Sloan, like they were high school kids passing in the hallway, biding their time until they could sneak away to make out in the parking lot.

His cologne smelled earthy, like burning pinecones. He and Sloan had tossed them into the fires they built those late nights at Crow's Nest Creek.

"Hey, Noah." Sloan wondered if she should hug him. Shake his hand? Run out the door and never look back?

"Sloan. Wow." He looked at her like he'd seen a ghost. She supposed to Noah that's exactly what she was. "Umm, welcome home." He patted her back, then looked around to ensure no one had seen her. "Did you need something or—?"

"Yeah." Sloan tensed her shoulders. "Do you have a minute?"

"For you? Always," he said. "Follow me."

Doors buzzed, keys jingled, keyboards clacked, and police radios squawked as Sloan walked down the hallway to Noah's office. She kept her head down. The fewer people that recognized her, the better.

"You got your dad's office. Still smells the same. Like old coffee." Sloan sat in a chair on the other side of Noah's desk. "How is he . . . your dad?"

Noah smiled. Sloan tried not to stare, but he looked even better now. The dark smooth skin and perfectly squared jaw were just as she remembered, but he was bigger now, his black polo strangling his biceps and tight against his chest. And the beginnings of a mustache suited him. Sloan allowed herself to look into his eyes; they had always been his best feature. Not only their deep brown but the inner smile that seemed to reflect from them. Sloan had never seen kinder eyes.

"Dad's real good. Fishing a lot, enjoying retirement. You should stop by and see them. That would make their day."

"For sure." Sloan looked down at the threadbare carpet. "I need to thank them for all they've done for my mom and for handling everything with the house." She let her eyes rise to meet his. "And you. I wanted to thank you."

Noah stood and walked to the coffee pot on his windowsill. "We're glad to help. It's the least we could do." He held up the pot of coffee. "Want a cup?"

Sloan shook her head. "No, pretty sure I'm the one who's done the least that can be done."

Noah kept his back to her as he filled his cup. "Well, you needed to get away." Frustration laced his voice.

Sloan rubbed her hands on her thighs. "It was complicated."

Noah sat back down in his chair. "I know. I know." Some warmth had returned to his voice. "I'm sorry we weren't able to talk her into staying at the home."

"Well, thanks for trying. She's worse than I thought, Noah. She's claiming Ridge is still alive. This is going to be an interesting summer."

"You're staying all summer?" Noah's coffee cup hid his expression. "What about Liam?"

"It didn't work out."

Noah set down his cup. "Sorry. I hadn't heard."

"It's fine." Sloan noticed the photo on Noah's desk for the first time. A casual family portrait taken in front of an ornate Christmas tree. A beautiful wife and two children, a boy and a girl, wrapping paper strewn around them. She wasn't sure whether she should be happy for or insanely jealous of Noah's picture-perfect life.

She picked up the photo. "Beautiful family."

"Thanks. Hudson just turned four; Julianne is two."

"Sounds like you've got your hands full," Sloan said because that seemed like something normal people would say.

"They're both pure energy, for sure. But I work so many hours; it's Vickie you should feel sorry for."

Sloan looked at the photo again. Looked at Vickie's beautiful smile, beautiful husband, and beautiful Christmas tree. No, she didn't feel sorry for Vickie. Not at all.

"So that's why you're here?" Noah reclined in his chair. "To say thanks?"

"Thanks and sorry," Sloan whispered. "Sorry for running away like I did."

"Sloan, I already told you. We were glad to look in on Caroline."

"I'm not talking about Mom." Sloan's mouth felt bone dry. "I'm sorry for running out on you."

"Oh." Noah let out a breath that rattled his lips. "That."

"I was miserable in Mallowater." Sloan saw hurt spread across Noah's face. "I mean, everything was miserable except for you. You and your family saved my life all those years."

"We were friends." Noah spun a pencil on his desk.

"Most friendships don't come at such a cost," Sloan said.

"What's that supposed to mean?"

Sloan shifted in her seat. "Your poor dad was dragged through the mud for standing by us. We were outcasts."

"You were victims," Noah said, emphasizing each of the words.

"For five minutes." Sloan huffed. "Long enough for Mom to start throwing rocks at windows and climbing on other people's roofs."

Noah made a steeple with his fingers. "I think most understood the grief changed her. I don't think anybody could blame her."

"*Everybody* blamed her!" Sloan's eyes filled with tears. "Everyone except for your family. And because of your proximity to us, you all became outcasts too."

"Oh, come on."

"It's true." Sloan's nails dug into her palms as she clenched her hands. "That's why your dad never made chief."

Noah drew in a frustrated breath. "The only thing that kept Dad from being chief is the color of our skin. Don't put that on your family."

Sloan unclenched her fists. "It was probably both. But hopefully, you'll get the chance your dad never did. You're young and an accomplished detective already. Things are different now, after all."

"Things are different, but not *that* different," Noah said.

"Oh. I just thought Obama winning the primary was a positive sign."

Noah smirked. "This ain't the White House. This is Texas."

Sloan nodded. "I see."

Noah met her eyes. "Look, Sloan. I've loved you since we were kids. I always figured you'd move after graduation. That you'd go off to college and leave me behind. But I never imagined you'd do it in the middle of the night without so much as a note."

Sloan swallowed. "I left a note."

"Not for me."

"I mentioned you," Sloan said. "And I called."

"Two weeks later." Noah scrubbed his hands over his face. "Sorry. You came to apologize, and I'm dragging it all back out."

"It's okay." Sloan knew she deserved worse. "I was a coward. I didn't know how to say goodbye." Her eyes retraced their path to the picture on his desk. "Things worked out better for you, anyway. You've got a nice family, and I'm a nice train wreck."

"Stop, Sloan. I always hated that about you. Your self-deprecation."

"And I hated your blunt honesty." Sloan allowed herself to grin. "I still kinda do, actually."

Noah returned the smile. "It's good to see you, Sloan. I'm glad you're back. If there's anything else I can do—"

"I saw her," Sloan interrupted.

"Saw who?"

"Felicity." Bile rose and stung Sloan's throat. "Yesterday in Tyler— getting groceries. I saw her."

Noah pulled at his collar. "Damn. Did she recognize you? Did y'all speak?"

"Yeah, she did, and yes, she tried, but I ran," Sloan said.

"Imagine that."

Sloan cocked an eyebrow. "Come on; you can't blame me for that one."

"How did you even recognize her? It's been so long."

Sloan looked away. "That *People* magazine article," she said, leaving out the night she had gotten drunk and stalked Felicity's Myspace. Not one of her finer moments.

"Oh yeah. I was hoping you missed that one."

Sloan wished she had. Not only had she seen it, but she'd also bought it and still had it. She couldn't bring herself to throw it away. How many hours had she spent looking at it? Obsessing over it. Studying Felicity. Studying them all.

"She's a kindergarten teacher," Noah said.

"Kinder? Well, she's definitely crazy then," Sloan said. An attempt to lighten the mood.

"They aren't bad people, Sloan." Noah's voice softened. "No matter how much you want them to be."

Sloan squirmed in her chair. She wanted to argue but had no argument.

Noah glanced at his watch. "Hey, I'm really sorry. But I've got a meeting at ten."

"Right." Sloan shot up from her chair. "Sorry."

Noah walked around the desk. "Don't apologize," he said. "And don't be a stranger, either." She caught another whiff of his cologne as he stepped closer. "It's great to see you, Lo."

*Burning pinecones, rising smoke, a sky full of blue-white stars, a single sleeping bag.* The memories rushed back.

Before Sloan could say anything, Noah wrapped his arms around her. She wanted to resist, to keep her arms stiff at her side, but she sank into his body.

Sloan was familiar with that rush of desire from a new relationship. The overwhelming attraction that lights every single nerve ending on fire. The way you can physically crave another human being. She was just as familiar with the comfort that can only come from a long-term relationship. The complete freedom of knowing you can be yourself and someone will love you at your worst. The shared memories and history that emotionally bond you to another human being.

Now, Sloan realized that only with Noah Dawson was she capable of feeling both simultaneously.

She squeezed tighter, and so did he. She'd tried to avoid coming home, but here she was, back in Mallowater. She'd tried to avoid Crow's Nest Creek, but it was her first stop after pulling into town. And she'd tried to avoid Noah Dawson, only to be back in his arms. He and everything else in this godforsaken town were magnets. They'd been pulling her back since the moment she left.

But Sloan wouldn't stay in his arms. She wouldn't do what had been done to her. With all the strength she had, she let go.

"I need to go." She avoided his eyes.

"Sloan . . ."

"See you around," she added, grabbing her purse and charging out the door.

# Chapter 6

*Mallowater, TX, 1988*

Sloan didn't touch her breakfast, even though Daddy had cooked it. His breakfasts always tasted better than her mom's. It even smelled different. Daddy cooked the bacon in the skillet instead of the microwave, and grease hung in the air for hours afterward.

But even with the greasy bacon on her plate, Sloan didn't have an appetite. This was all so unfair. Why did Ridge get to go fishing, leaving her stuck here with Mom?

Sloan looked at her brother. He didn't look any happier about this arrangement than she did.

"Why the long face, Lo?" Daddy asked, shoveling shredded potatoes into his mouth as he read the morning paper.

"It's not fair." Sloan pushed her plate away. "Why can't I come?"

"Sloan!" Her mother slammed the fridge door. "Drop it."

"It's alright." Daddy winked at Sloan. "I'm off all week. We'll do something special, too. Ridge and I need some man-to-man time."

"All packed." The cooler lid slammed down, and Sloan's mom jumped like she hadn't been the one to drop it. "You've got plenty of water, snacks, and sandwiches for lunch."

Sloan glanced back and forth between her parents. "You're staying till lunch?"

"We're staying till the sun goes down," Daddy said. "Takes time for the fish to bite."

"But it's November! Isn't it cold?"

Mom laughed. "It's supposed to get up to the 70s. If you think this is cold, try a New York November."

Sloan knew there was no way Ridge would leave at sunset; he'd want to watch the crows. He'd talk Daddy into it. She had to think fast.

"Promise you'll be home in time to watch *21 Jump Street*."

Daddy looked up from his paper and raised an eyebrow. "You hate *21 Jump Street*."

"No, I don't." Sloan looked down at her lap. "It's okay."

He tussled Sloan's hair. "Alright. Deal."

Sloan grabbed for the syrup. It wasn't perfect, but it was something.

"Would you look at that?" Daddy reached under the table. "A penny. Who would so carelessly leave their money on the floor?"

"It's just a penny, Dad," Sloan said, mouth full of pancake.

Her father's face twisted in mock surprise. "*Just* a penny. Well, I'll have you know, Sloan Celeste Hadfield, you can take a penny, drill a hole in it, and then you've got a washer you can sell for a dime. That's nine cents profit if you've already got the drill, which we do right over in the garage."

Sloan caught her mom rolling her eyes as she walked toward the table. As much as Sloan loved this dreamer side of her father, she figured they wouldn't be poor if any of his ideas were good.

"Are you sure you've got enough bait?" Mom asked.

Daddy stood. "Relax, Caroline. We aren't going to Jupiter. Sit down," he insisted, pulling out a chair. "Eat. And don't worry about cooking dinner tonight. Spend some time with Lo. Order a pizza." Daddy grabbed one end of the cooler. "Sloan, help me load this."

Sloan took the other end of the bulky red cooler and helped her dad lug it out to the truck.

"Are you sure I can't go?" Sloan tried again.

He shut the truck bed. "Come on, Sloan. You and I can do something Tuesday. I'll even let you miss school. But spend time with your mother today. She's been sad. Your granddad died, then the Turners left. Libby was her only friend around here. Not to mention, you and Ridge are growing up; you don't need her as much as you used to."

"Well, she should get back to writing her bird book."

"That's a great idea," Daddy said. "Your mother graduated top of her class. Sometimes it must seem like she's stuck here, but she can still get back to her passion. God knows there are plenty of crows to study. You should encourage her."

"Mom won't listen to me."

"Probably not," Daddy agreed. "Then how about you just promise to do one thing that makes your mom smile or laugh today?"

Sloan groaned.

"One thing." He crouched and held up a finger in her face. "One."

Sloan pushed his hand down. "Fine. One."

Daddy turned. "Here, hop on. I'll give you a ride back up to the house."

"I'm not a kid anymore, Dad."

"You're still *my* kid. Come on, hop on. We'll shake that grim mood off ya."

Sloan was too old for these silly games, but she hopped on his back anyway. Daddy charged up the lawn, jostling her from side to side. She laughed despite herself. It was impossible to be in a bad mood around Jay Hadfield. No wonder he sold so many cleaning supplies.

Sloan glanced at her watch as her dad set her down. Almost 10:00. *21 Jump Street* came on at 7:00. Nine hours tops, and she'd see him again. If Ridge came home bragging, so what? Her turn was coming. She'd spend today planning everything their day would entail.

She passed her mother and Ridge hugging goodbye and grabbed a pencil from the hallway before going into her room and slamming the door.

Daddy and Ridge were late. Sloan could tell her mom was worried by the way she paced across the living room, chewing her nails and checking the clock. Yet, when Sloan suggested they go out to the creek to find them, Mom told her to stop being ridiculous; they'd be home soon.

Not soon enough, Sloan realized as the music to *21 Jump Street* began. Mom opened one of the pizza boxes. "Don't let it get cold."

Sloan closed the box. Ridge had talked Daddy into watching the crows with him. And Ridge was the baby, so he got whatever he wanted. It was easy to blame her brother, but Daddy had made the promise. Of course, she hadn't kept her promise either. She hadn't even tried to make her mom smile or laugh all day. She'd spent the entire day in her room except for lunch—a lunch Mom didn't even eat with her. She'd made Sloan's sandwich, then gone out to the back porch to smoke another cigarette. Daddy wouldn't be happy about that. He hated when Mom smoked, and she rarely did it when he was in town, but lately, she didn't seem to care. And she wasn't even trying to hide it tonight, didn't bathe herself in perfume.

"Well, if you won't eat, I will." Caroline grabbed a pizza slice and sat on the couch next to Sloan. They watched the first fifteen minutes of the show, but Sloan was too angry to pay attention to the plot.

During the first commercial break, the door burst open.

Daddy charged into the living room, his eyes wide and wild, his brow covered in sweat. Sloan noticed a small red scratch under his right eye. *Not another episode*, Sloan thought. She'd never seen her father have one when he hadn't been asleep.

"Jay?" Mom jumped up, the paper plate from her lap falling to the floor. "What is it, Jay?"

Daddy glanced down the hall. "Is Ridge here?"

"What do you mean is Ridge here?" Mom's voice shook.

"Oh, God." Tears filled his eyes. "Call the police, Caroline."

"Where's Ridge, Jay? Where is he?" Mom's face had gone pale.

Daddy crumpled to the floor, rubbing both hands through his damp hair. "I don't know," he cried. "He disappeared."

"What do you mean?" Mom screamed. "Jay, where is our son?"

Daddy stayed on the floor, but he raised his head. "We fished, and I started feeling strange. The next thing I remember is waking up. Ridge was gone. I searched, Caroline. Nobody saw him. I hoped he'd come home."

"Maybe he's with the Dawsons," Mom said. "I'll call."

Sloan's chest clenched. Some kids may wander off, visit a friend and not tell anyone, but not Ridge. Not ever.

This had to be a terrible nightmare. Her dad shaking on the floor, her mother screaming into the phone. Sloan wanted to do both, cry and scream.

She needed to do *something*. Go comfort Daddy. Go tell Mom to stop yelling. She's hard to understand when she's yelling. But Sloan only sat, sinking deeper and deeper into the couch as the commercial break ended and *21 Jump Street* started again.

The search parties began. Police officers, state troopers, local volunteers, and even the National Guard joined the search. There were

police dogs and helicopters. From her back porch, Sloan heard strangers call her brother's name repeatedly. "Ridge! Ridge! Ridge!"

*Where'd you go, Ridge?*

Sloan's family didn't sit down for dinner; they didn't go to bed. Her dad walked every inch of the creek and would have done it a dozen more times had the police not taken him in for questioning.

Two days passed. Sloan lost all sense of time. All sense of place. All sense of normal.

The shrill ring of the phone drew all their eyes toward it. There was hope with every ring of a phone, with every ring of a doorbell.

"I'll get it." Sloan headed for the phone. Noah was supposed to call back before bed. He listened to everything his father said, everything that came in on the walkie.

"Hello." Sloan gripped the cold phone. "Hi, Libby. Yes, ma'am, she's right here." Mom was already behind her, taking the phone.

Sloan walked back to the couch and sat next to her father. His eyes were red and his hands trembling. "I'll go search again," he mumbled.

"Not tonight, Daddy." Sloan took hold of his forearm. It seemed smaller. She hadn't seen him eat since that Sunday breakfast. "You need to sleep. Really sleep. And when you wake up, we can make breakfast together."

Daddy grabbed his jacket. "When Detective Johnson comes back, tell him I'll be home in an hour."

Mom didn't even glance up when Daddy slammed the door. "No news, Libby," she said. "Still nothing." Sloan watched her mom wipe her eyes. She was strong. Somehow, she'd be okay. Daddy was another story.

Sloan tapped her mom's shoulder. "Can I go to the creek with Daddy?" she whispered.

Mom nodded and shooed Sloan away.

By the time Sloan put on her shoes and jacket, Daddy's truck was gone. Sloan hopped on her bike and rode as fast as she could.

It was dark when she arrived at Crow's Nest Creek, and a few people were still searching. The crows rested quietly in the trees, and Sloan couldn't help but be jealous of them—all at peace, all in their homes, with no frantic searches for a missing baby bird.

She found her dad and walked beside him. Even with only the light of the moon and his small flashlight, Sloan saw tears fill her father's eyes. "They aren't gonna find him, Lo."

Sloan swallowed. "What do you mean? They have to."

"They would have already." Tears dripped off her dad's face. "This entire town has walked this creek for two days. Divers started searching the water today. He's gone."

Sloan felt her own tears, hot behind her eyelids. "Don't give up."

Daddy stopped walking. "Detective Johnson's acting different today. It's like he thinks I did something to Ridge."

"You didn't." She took his hand, trying to ignore the scratches, just beginning to scab over. "You'd never hurt him."

"I *did* hurt him, Sloan. And your mother."

"Well yeah, but that wasn't *you*. It was one of your episodes."

Her father met her eyes. "Who's to say this wasn't?" Daddy scrubbed his hand over his scruffy face. "I'm not who you think I am. I've done some terrible things."

"You mean in the war? Mom says everybody in war does terrible things. That Vietnam was a huge mistake and—"

"No, Sloan, not the war." The harshness of her dad's voice made her jump. He took a deep breath. "I'm sorry. I just need you to remember that no matter what, I love you. I love Ridge. I love your mom."

"We love you too." Sloan wondered why he was talking like this. It seemed like he was slipping away, like he'd never be the same, like nothing ever would. "Can we go home, please?"

"I feel like he's here," Daddy whispered. "Here with the crows. I don't want to leave him."

Sloan reached out her hand. "It's late, Daddy, too dark to ride my bike. Help me put it in your truck and take me home."

"Not now, Sloan."

Sloan couldn't believe her dad was going to let her ride home this late. But of course, she couldn't believe anything from the past two days. Two days. It was Tuesday. Sloan realized she had one more card to play.

"You promised, Dad. You promised Tuesday was our day."

He raised an eyebrow at her. "What?"

"You said we would do whatever I wanted Tuesday."

"Come on. That was before—"

"It doesn't matter," Sloan interrupted. "It's my day, and this is what I want. I want to go home. I want us all to sleep in our beds. I want to wake up and cook breakfast with you." She choked back a sob and stood taller. "Now, come on."

Her dad looked confused, even a little angry, but he pulled out his keys. "Alright," he said. "Let's go home."

Mom was still on the phone with Libby when they arrived, but Sloan saw to it that Daddy climbed into his bed before getting into her own. Within fifteen minutes, he was snoring. Sloan got up to shut her door and noticed her mom was off the phone and had passed out on the couch. Sloan covered her with a blanket, locked the front door, and turned off the light. Somehow, this felt like a step in the right direction, like a turning point. Maybe tomorrow would feel different, look different after they'd all slept.

# Chapter 7

*Mallowater, TX, 2008*

Sloan knelt to pick up another penny from the ground. This was the fourth one she'd found in two days. It was irrational for pennies to trigger her, but they always had. One dumb memory of her dad finding a penny the morning her family fell apart, and she'd never looked at one the same. They'd always make her think of her father.

Jay Hadfield always bragged he was named after Jay Gatsby. When Sloan read *The Great Gatsby* in high school, she saw little resemblance between the two, aside from the ambitious farm boy beginnings and tragic ends.

Of course, this wasn't the end for her father. Sloan understood that now. He was getting out and only fifty-nine years old. Maybe he'd used his time to come up with an idea or invention that was worth a damn. Or, if not, he could always write a tell-all book. Somehow, he'd come out on top.

For the hundredth time since arriving back in Mallowater, Sloan wondered if she should visit her dad. If she was going to see him, she needed to do it now, before he got out. At least in prison, a visit would be controlled. The last time she'd seen him, she was a girl, still convinced he hung the moon. But she had sent him that letter right before she got married. The one telling him to quit reaching out to her. But even then, she didn't get everything off her chest; some things needed to be said in person.

The clock on the mantle chimed. Caroline would be back from the creek anytime. She spent most of her days there but always came home for dinner.

Sloan flipped on the television. She hadn't missed the news since the body of Logan Pruitt had been found. They kept repeating the same things over and over, but Sloan still tuned in. She remembered when her life was reduced to a news story, remembered how it felt to have reporters camping outside her window. Now, she was no better than the people who had sat in front of their televisions each night and watched her life fall apart.

But tonight, an unfamiliar man was on screen, one Sloan hadn't seen interviewed yet. He was thin with small, haunted eyes and dark, floppy hair.

*Breaking news*, the words across the screen scrolled. *Arrest made in the murder of Logan Pruitt. Edward Daughtry, of Dallas, Texas, taken into custody. Dylan Lawrence, an alleged victim of Daughtry, joins us.*

Dylan Lawrence avoided looking at the camera and spoke so softly that Sloan had to turn up the TV to near-max volume.

"So, you went missing from Mallowater in 1992, but your disappearance was never reported?" the journalist asked.

"It was complicated," Dylan said. "After my mom died, I got pretty messed up into drugs. Dad and I got into a fight, and I left."

"But he never called the police?"

Dylan sucked his already hollowed cheeks in. "Let's not vilify an innocent man, okay? I was strung out. He looked for me, but I was sixteen years old. What was he supposed to do? This isn't about my father. This is about Logan Pruitt. This is about the other boys."

Sloan's stomach churned. Other boys?

"Can you tell us if Logan was alive in 1992 when Eddie abducted you?"

"Don't answer that," Sloan heard an off-camera voice say.

"Can you tell us why you and these boys were taken? There are rumors about a child sex ring around Mallowater."

Dylan looked off-camera, perhaps at his lawyer. "I cannot speak as to the specific details of the crime." Silent tears fell from Dylan's eyes.

The interviewer reached across and handed him a tissue. "I understand this is difficult to discuss, Mr. Lawrence. Why now? Why have you decided to speak out about your abduction? Not just to the police, but to the media?"

Dylan brushed his hair out of his face. "Because it's time," he said. "It's past time. If I had told the truth a long time ago . . ." he stopped talking and turned his entire body from the camera.

"I think we're done," came the off-camera voice again, but Dylan held up a hand.

"No, I want to say this." Dylan angled back toward the camera but kept his head down. "I knew what Eddie was doing, and I didn't tell. That's my fault. It's on me." Dylan poked himself hard in the chest.

"I'm sure you were scared," the reporter lowered her voice. "And you were a child, yourself."

Dylan raised his head and looked into the camera. "But now, I'm not. I'm a thirty-two-year-old man, and I'm not scared now. It's time for Daughtry to pay."

Every muscle in Sloan's body went rigid. A child sex ring? Around Mallowater? What if Ridge . . . ? Bile rose in her throat as she stared into Dylan Lawrence's haunted eyes. *No. No. No.*

Caroline charged in the door, jostling Sloan from her trance. "Sloan, I have to tell you something."

"About Dylan Lawrence?" Sloan asked. "I just heard him on the news. Oh, Mom, you don't think . . ."

A sheen of sweat glowed on Caroline's brow. She pulled out her handkerchief and wiped it away. "Dylan who? No, Sloan, this is about Ridge. I told you he's alive, but I haven't told you the entire story. It's time now, Sloan!" Her words fell out of her in a frantic mess, like bees shook loose from their hive.

Sloan turned down the thermostat. "You're sweating and sunburned. You shouldn't be outside so long."

"He's alive, Sloan! I've talked to him at the creek three times now. He never tells me when he'll be back."

"And where at the creek do you meet him?" Sloan worried about what kind of scene her mother made when she believed she was talking to Ridge. The river was crowded in summer.

"At our old campsite. Honestly, Sloan, where else would he be?"

Sloan tugged at her hair. "I don't know, Mom. In the water? In the sky?"

"Both, Lo." Mom spread her arms out and tilted like she was soaring. "Ridge has wings now. He can fly in the sky and swoop into the creek. My boy always wanted to be a crow, and now he is."

Sloan shut her eyes tight as her mother continued her mock flight around the living room. *She can't help it*, Sloan reminded herself. *Nobody chooses to be crazy.*

Just then, Dylan Lawrence flashed into her mind. No, Ridge wasn't at the creek. He wasn't a crow, but that didn't necessarily mean he was gone.

Sloan had just put Caroline to bed a few hours later when the phone rang. She snatched it up before the second ring.

"May I speak to Sloan?" the voice was unfamiliar.

Sloan folded her legs up under her. "Who's this?"

"Felicity."

The name rang through Sloan's head like a cymbal crash.

"Please don't hang up," Felicity said.

Sloan wanted to do more than hang up. She wanted to throw the phone across the room.

But somehow, her body had become petrified stone.

"I'm sorry about the store," Felicity said. "I just wanted to talk."

Sloan gripped the phone tighter. "I have nothing to say to you."

"Have you been watching the news? Logan Pruitt. Dylan Lawrence."

"Yeah, a little." Sloan tried to sound indifferent, as if those two names hadn't been on a constant loop in her head all evening.

"Don't you wonder, Sloan? You *have to* wonder. It happened right around the same time as—"

"Don't say his name." Sloan clenched her teeth. "Don't act like you care. Like you loved him."

Felicity cleared her throat. "I know Dylan. I mean, I know who he is. He's a music teacher there in Mallowater. I emailed him and told him I'd like to talk."

Sloan shifted in her seat. "And?"

"And he's agreed to meet with me. I'll do it alone, Sloan, but I'd like you to come."

"What about your family?" Sloan spat out that last word.

"They think I should leave well enough alone. But I can't. Something's not right here. I think deep down, under your anger, you realize that."

Heat burned in Sloan's cheeks. "You know nothing about my anger."

"Of course I do." Felicity's voice sharpened for the first time in their conversation. "I got hurt too. We all did."

"Don't call me again." Sloan ended the phone call and then yanked the cord from the wall.

# Chapter 8

*Mallowater, TX, 1988*

The police called off the search on day six of Ridge's disappearance. Sloan returned to school on day eight. Mom said they needed to get back to some "sense of normalcy." Like anything could ever be normal again.

Even her school didn't feel right without Ridge in it. No one seemed sure how to treat Sloan. Even her friends avoided her. Only Noah met up with her at recess and waited for her after school to board the bus. He walked her home from the bus stop every day, even though his house was closer.

So, when Sloan spotted Noah's mom waiting for them at the bus stop Friday afternoon, she sensed something was wrong.

"What's going on?" Sloan asked as soon as she stepped off the bus.

Doreen reached her hand out. "You're coming to our house today. We'll have a snack and watch some tv."

Sloan backed away. "Nope. Tell me what's going on."

"I will," Doreen said. "Once we get home."

Tears stung Sloan's eyes. "They found him, didn't they? They found Ridge?"

"I said we'll talk about it at the house." Doreen looked around at the parents and students, now watching the scene.

Sloan didn't care who watched. "Tell me!" she screamed.

Noah took a step forward. "Come on, Sloan. Let's talk and walk."

Sloan wasn't walking anywhere. Not when Doreen was keeping something from her. Sloan took off running. Doreen called for her, and Sloan heard Noah's footsteps, but they'd never catch up with her; Doreen had asthma, and Noah was slow.

A KBWS news van and two police cars sat outside Sloan's house. The news van door slid open just as Sloan made it to her yard. "Start recording!" A voice inside the van instructed.

Sloan struggled to walk a straight line to the door. The ground seemed to shift. They *had* to have found Ridge. That's why the cops were here. Why the news was here.

When Sloan pushed through the screen door, she was shocked to see her father on the ground, pinned by two policemen. Walt stood above them, shaking his head. "Let me go," her father screamed as he thrashed.

"Daddy?"

"Stop fighting, Jay. Your girl is here," Walt said.

Her father stilled, and Sloan barely heard the clink of the handcuffs over her beating heart.

"What's she doing here?" Mom emerged from the hallway and

took Sloan's hand. "Why would you do this right when she gets home from school?"

"I'm sorry, Caroline. I asked Doreen to—"

"Oh, you're sorry?" Mom lurched towards Walt. "Sorry for what? For arresting Jay in front of his daughter?" Caroline took another step, so she was right in Walt's face. "Or that you didn't give me a heads up that this was happening? You are supposed to be our friend."

"You're making a mistake, Walt." Daddy was standing now. An officer holding each arm.

"I sure hope so," Walt said. "Let these men take you to the station. Just be honest, and we can clear all this up."

Caroline jammed her finger into Walt's chest. "Don't talk to us like a cop."

The door scraped open. "Sorry!" Doreen struggled to catch her breath. "She ran off." Doreen pulled the string on the blinds. They closed with a loud whoosh. "Media's out there," she said.

"What happened?" Sloan finally found her voice. She didn't even recognize it.

"These gentlemen need to take your father. So, we'll let them do that; then we'll talk."

An officer peeked out the blinds. "Another news van from Tyler just pulled up. We gotta get him out of here before this turns into a full-fledged circus. Goddamn vultures."

"Let's get this over with." Walt stepped in front of the officers. "Don't make a scene, Jay. It won't help anything."

*It's already a scene*, Sloan thought.

Daddy kept his head down and hurried to the patrol car. Sloan slipped past her mom and ran outside. A reporter yelled something, but Sloan couldn't make it out. Everything sounded like she was in a tunnel. A tunnel with no light to guide her out.

"The family would appreciate some privacy," Walt said.

An officer pushed down Daddy's neck to cram him into the police car.

"Easy!" Sloan pleaded. "Don't hurt him!"

Sloan wedged herself between the car door and her father just as the officer went to slam it. She winced as the door cut into her back.

The other officer pulled the door open and grabbed Sloan by the shirt. "Come on, kid; get back inside!"

"Take your hands off my daughter!" Sloan turned and saw her mom standing in the doorway. "I'll have your job."

"Let her go," Walt said. "Let her hug her father."

"It's gonna be okay. Lo, I promise," Daddy told her. "Now, go inside with your mother."

"Come on, Sloan." Noah reached into the car and took her hand. "Dad can fix all this."

Sloan was fairly certain Walt couldn't fix anything. If he could, why wasn't he?

"How does it feel to know your father is being charged with your brother's murder?" A reporter's voice rose above the noise.

"Goddamn it!" Walt yelled. "She's a child. What is wrong with you?"

"They're trash," Mom yelled again. "All of you are trash!"

Cameras clicked, a microphone screeched, and everyone was yelling. Sloan saw black in her peripheral. The tunnel was narrowing. She needed to get back inside but knew she'd never make it. So, she let it close in on her.

Sloan blinked several times. She wasn't lying on the lawn, but on their couch. Her head hurt, and she was freezing despite the heavy quilt draped across her body.

"She's awake." Mom sat down at Sloan's feet as Sloan pushed herself up. "Not too fast." Mom held up her hand. "Does anything hurt?"

Noah ran into the room and leaned over Sloan. "Are you okay?"

From the corner of the room, Walt cleared his throat. "Go back into the kitchen, Noah. Give us a minute."

"What happened?" Sloan rubbed at an ache on the base of her skull.

Mom pushed a stray hair out of Sloan's face. "You passed out."

"No! What happened with Ridge? Why did that woman say Daddy was being charged with Ridge's murder? Did they find his body?"

Mom scooted in closer. "No, but there were signs of struggle. There was blood."

"Ridge's? How can they be sure it's his?" Sloan asked.

"They found a piece of his shirt, his beanie, and a shoe."

"Where?" Sloan asked.

Mom looked down. "In the water."

"No." Sloan shook her head as if she could make her mom's words fall out. "No!"

Mom put her arm around her. "I'm so sorry."

"What if someone else hurt Ridge *and* Daddy? How do they know what happened?"

Mom glanced at Walt. There was venom in her eyes. "You want to take this one, Walt? Since you're the one who arrested him?"

Walt knelt beside Sloan. "Do you know what PTSD is?"

Sloan shook her head.

"Well, it's what your daddy has. It's a sickness caused by the war."

"The bad dreams?"

Walt handed Sloan his handkerchief. "Yes. We think that's what happened here. A witness came forward. Saw Ridge playing around 3:00, and your Daddy was asleep. I don't think your dad knew where he was or what he was doing. Sometimes terrible accidents happen, but even with accidents, there are consequences. There are laws."

Sloan couldn't bear the thought of her daddy in some jail cell with bank robbers and murderers. He was a good man. He couldn't help having PTSD any more than Doreen could help having asthma.

Walt stood. "I'll make sure he's taken care of. Make sure he can talk to you soon."

"Can I talk to him right now?" Sloan asked.

"No, not today," Mom said. She stood up and walked toward the window.

There were a few minutes of silence. Walt kept opening his mouth and closing it like there was something else he wanted to say.

"What, Walt? What is it?" Sloan asked.

"Something is going to come out," Walt finally said. "But I want you to be strong."

"What's going to come out?" Sloan couldn't imagine how this could get any worse.

Walt rocked on his heels. "Caroline, why don't you come sit down and talk to Sloan?"

"No," Mom said, her back still turned. "I think she's had enough trauma for one day."

They held a small funeral for Ridge. Only Sloan, her mom, Libby, and the Dawsons were in attendance. Mom said she didn't want the media attention, and they couldn't trust anyone. Sloan understood. Boy, did she understand. Because, as it turns out, she couldn't even trust her own father. Still, it seemed wrong there weren't more people mourning her brother.

Libby stayed in Mallowater for a few extra days. She cleaned the house, cooked, and froze food. Sloan even saw her hand Mom a check. "Take it," she insisted.

Caroline shook her head. "I can't."

"Vince insists. Don't be stubborn. It's not just about you. You've got a daughter to care for, and you've lost all your income. Give her a nice Christmas."

Sloan was glad when Mom took the check. It hadn't occurred to her how they'd make money with Daddy in jail.

"Everything is going to be okay. I promise," Libby said as she hugged Sloan goodbye.

Sloan held on tight. She didn't want to let go. Right now, it felt like Libby Turner was keeping everything together. Sloan was sure it would all crumble once she left.

"Can't you and Vince move back?" she asked.

"No, sweetie. Vince's job is in Louisiana. But you can call anytime. You have my number, right?"

"Mom does."

Libby grabbed a sticky note by the phone and scribbled her number. "Now you do too. Call anytime."

"Thank you." Sloan tried to compose herself. She hated sounding like a baby, begging and crying. But there was something so motherly about Libby. She had always been different from Mom, making cookies with Sloan and Ridge and taking them shopping for things Mom said were a waste of money. Mom always said Libby liked to spoil them because she didn't have any children of her own. When Sloan had once asked why, Mom told her, rather matter-of-factly, that some people just couldn't have children.

"Why can't they adopt one?" Sloan asked.

"They're too old. Who's going to give a baby to a couple of forty-seven-year-olds?"

Sloan had never thought of Libby being older than her mom, but she saw it now. Saw it in the cracks around Libby's eyes and mouth. Saw it in the mature way Libby and Vince carried themselves. Of course, their money helped with that too.

But now they were gone, and Sloan was back at school, like everyone just expected life to move on.

"Do you want to hang out at my house again tonight?" Noah asked as they walked to the school bus.

"Mom won't let me. Not two nights in a row. I don't see why it matters. Not like she notices when I'm there."

Noah didn't appear to be listening. His eyes passed Sloan to a petite woman with strawberry blonde hair standing outside her car, staring at them.

"A reporter," Sloan said. She could smell them now. "Wait here." Sloan stomped over to the car. "You can't be here!" She made her voice boom. "What station do you work for?"

The woman's brows crinkled. "I'm not a reporter." Her voice was polished with a hint of a Southern drawl.

"Who are you then? Why are you staring?" Sloan asked.

"Your father asked me to come."

Sloan swallowed hard. "He what?"

The woman rubbed at her arms as if she were cold. "Jay made a lot of mistakes, but he loved Ridge; he loves you."

Sloan noticed a little girl in the backseat changing the tape in her Walkman. She looked like a first or second grader, but Sloan had never seen her at Golden Oak Elementary. And with the poofy red hair, she'd be hard to miss. Sloan turned her attention back to the woman. "How do you know my dad?"

"It's best you ask your mom if she'll take you to visit," the woman said, rifling through her purse. "But if she says no, here's my number." She handed Sloan a folded piece of paper.

"Sloan, come on!" Noah yelled, running toward the bus lane. "They'll leave without us!"

"Think about it," the stranger said. "Think about seeing your dad. You have every right not to, but you can't imagine how sorry he is."

Sloan took the paper. "I need to go, or I'll miss the bus."

The woman smoothed down her dress. "I'm sorry. I can drive you home."

Sloan looked into the backseat. The red-headed girl made eye contact and lifted her hand in a wave.

Who were these strange people? Friends of her father's or not, there was no way Sloan was getting into the car. She sprinted for the bus, making it just in time.

"What the heck, Lo? Who was that?" Noah asked as she plopped in the thinly padded seat beside him.

While Sloan caught her breath, she glanced out the bus window. The woman was still standing there, still watching her.

"And what is that?" Noah pointed to the paper in Sloan's hand.

"Nothing." Sloan wadded the phone number into a ball and shoved it into her backpack. "Just another reporter trying to get a story."

# Chapter 9

*Mallowater, TX, 2008*

Three days later, Sloan still couldn't shake her phone call with Felicity. She lay in bed staring at the ceiling, a million questions jostling in her brain. Had Felicity already met with Dylan Lawrence? Did she learn anything about the crimes of Eddie Daughtry that could make him a suspect in Ridge's disappearance? Would she even call Sloan if she had?

Sloan pushed the covers off and turned on the bedside lamp. Her copy of the final *Harry Potter* book sat on her nightstand, dogeared at chapter twelve. She just hadn't been in the mood for magic since being home. But that was okay. She had one more piece of reading material tucked away in the bottom drawer of her nightstand.

Sloan had taken little from the house when she and Liam split up, packing only the necessities and burning the rest in an epic backyard bonfire. Well, not everything. She'd kept the Keith Whitley tape, the 4X6 picture of her once happy family, and the *People* magazine article from 2000. Each of these items made her feel like shit. They should have been the first to burn, but she couldn't toss them into the flames. That would be like letting go of a part of herself. It was as if each item were a Horcrux in which she'd hidden a fragment of her soul. Destroy them, and what would be left of her?

Sloan opened the bottom drawer and stared at the magazine's cover. The picture still punched her in the gut, just as it had eight years ago in that checkout line. She was still a newlywed in 2000, with a nice house and a handsome husband who loved her. She'd worked so hard to bury her past, but there it was, rising up from the magazine display like a four-headed- snake.

Sloan had grabbed the magazine and slammed it face down on the conveyor belt. Her heart was racing, and her hands were sweaty as the cashier took her time swiping each item. *People* had reached out to Sloan for an interview. She turned them down. She'd turned down every interview request, and so had they. What had changed their minds? Money, she figured.

Sloan had sat in her car for half an hour reading every word of the five-page spread. She knew she should be used to making headlines. Her family had been tabloid fodder before. But now the story was old news, or it had been before this hit the shelves.

Sloan hated remembering that day at the grocery store, but here she was again tonight, clenching that same magazine in her hand, staring at Anna, Brad, Kyle, and Felicity on the cover.

Anna wore a plain white dress and sat, prim and proper, on a chair. Khaki-clad Brad and Kyle stood behind her, strong hands on their mother's delicate shoulders. And sitting on the ground in front of

Anna's chair was Felicity, looking underdressed in her floral tank top, flared jeans, and chunky platforms. Her hair was burnished copper in the photo, not the clown wig red Sloan remembered when she was a girl. Her bangs were pulled back with butterfly clips, like she'd just stepped out of a Delila's catalog. None of them were smiling.

Next to their posed picture was a separate snapshot of Sloan's father from inside the prison. He'd aged so much. Maybe the time in prison was responsible, or possibly grief over what he'd done. But it was easy to appear remorseful for a photo op. The sadness on his face didn't quite reach those sparkly blue eyes. Those lying blue eyes.

The caption was underneath the photo of the somber-faced family and the snapshot of her bright-eyed father. The one that still hurt her to read all these years later.

*Jay Hadfield's Family Speaks Out*

# Chapter 10

*Mallowater, TX, 1989*

The trial began in April. Sloan wasn't allowed to attend, so all her news came from Noah. And the latest news was that Mom sat on the prosecution's side. Sloan wanted to ask why, but it was impossible to even talk to her mom nowadays without it turning into a fight. Maybe Mom's seating choice had to do with who sat on Daddy's side of the courtroom. "His legal wife," Walt had once called her. The term, the thought of it all, made Sloan's stomach hurt.

There had to be an explanation. Maybe Daddy had once married this other woman, his "legal wife," but that didn't mean they were a family.

Sure, her father worked a lot. That's because he was a charismatic salesman. He had clients all over Texas. He often lived out of suitcases in hotel rooms, but this was his home.

But then Sloan thought about the special days, the Thanksgivings, the Christmases. Daddy never spent the full day at home. He was often absent in the morning, coming in from a late-night meeting somewhere across the state. Or, if he was there when they woke up, he always had to leave before dinner to drive somewhere for an early morning meeting the next day. Sloan's family waited on him to open gifts or moved up dinner so he could carve the turkey. Sloan hadn't considered it before, but were late-night business meetings on Christmas Eve normal?

She needed to see her father and question him, but she'd given up asking to visit him after Christmas. Her mother was a grenade, and asking that question would pull the pin.

But today, the need for answers and the need to talk to her father felt like its own grenade inside her belly, waiting to explode.

"Mom?" Though Sloan had worked up her courage all week, the word came out as a whisper. "Mom!" She repeated louder.

"Yes," Caroline answered, but she didn't stop washing the dishes—didn't even turn her head toward Sloan.

Sloan bit her lip. "I'd like to visit Daddy."

Mom froze at the sink, body stiff.

For at least a minute, neither spoke, neither moved. The scalding water hissed as it filled the sink. Finally, Mom turned it off. "What was that?"

"I said I want to see Daddy."

Mom pressed her hands against the counter. "Why would you want to see him after what he's done?"

"That's why I want to see him. I want an explanation."

"What's there to explain?" Soapy water flung off Mom's rubber gloves as she spun around to face Sloan. "He's got another family. A wife. One he married long before I met him."

"Will he live with her? When he gets out of jail?"

Mom grinned. "Yes, I suppose *if* he gets out, he'll have to. Of course, it's not looking good for him." She turned back toward the sink, picking up a bowl from the counter, still full of leftover milk from the cereal Sloan had eaten for dinner. Cereal for dinner had been a normal occurrence since November.

Sloan started to leave but caught a whiff of the overflowing trash can. It was Daddy's job to take it out, or Ridge's when their father was gone. Sloan supposed she'd be the one doing it now.

Mom kept clanging dishes around in the sink, ignoring Sloan fighting with the trash bag. "Can I get some help?"

Caroline sighed. "You're thirteen, Sloan. You should be able to handle the trash."

Sloan gave it another tug, and the bag came out, the trash can toppling over on Sloan's feet. She kicked it away. "You're right. I am thirteen," Sloan said. "Can't I decide for myself who I see?"

Mom's head snapped toward Sloan. Her normally light green eyes now brighter. "No."

"Why, Mom? I have a right—"

"You have no rights!" Mom raised Sloan's cereal bowl from the suds and slammed it on the tile. Sloan jumped away from the shards of glass. "You've always suspected your Daddy hung the moon. I can't say I'm surprised you refuse to accept the facts."

"What facts? How would I know any facts?" Sloan screamed. "You never talk to me."

"The fact that he's a liar and a murderer. Now, you listen to me,"

Caroline said. "I didn't do enough to protect your brother, but I *will* protect you, Sloan."

"Protect me? But Mom—"

"Enough!" She pounded her fist on the counter. "This conversation is over and over forever. Do you understand me?"

"No." Tears spilled out of Sloan's eyes. "I don't understand you at all."

Her mom answered by picking up another dish, a white dinner plate, and slamming it onto the floor. "Get out of my face! Get out of my kitchen!"

Just a moment ago, Sloan had been so angry she would have looked for something to break too, but she'd traded the anger for fear of this stranger smashing dish after dish. It reminded Sloan of the night her mother destroyed the pantry. So, she ran into her bedroom, barricaded the door, and turned up Keith Whitley as loud as she could.

Sloan glanced around the visiting area. She'd never been inside a prison before, never expected she'd ever be in one, especially not to visit her dad.

She considered turning and running out, but she'd come too far. She'd pulled that crumpled paper out of her backpack and called her father's friend. She'd let this stranger drive her here today, lying to her mother about an after-school art class.

Sloan wanted to remain stoic. Daddy had lied, and she wouldn't let him off the hook for that. But when she saw him approaching, cuffed hands and legs, it took her back in time to that November day in her front yard, and she couldn't hold back the tears.

As soon as they freed his hands, he hugged Sloan tight and kissed the side of her head. "Your hair's lighter," he said.

Sloan touched her head. "Yeah. I tried lemon juice, but Doreen gave me some stuff called Sun-In. It works better."

"Well, it looks great," he said as they took their seats. "I've waited so long to see you. I begged your mom and sent letters. I tried, Lo."

"Mom's real mad," Sloan said. "Is it all true? Do you have a wife?"

Daddy's shoulders curled forward, and his chest caved in. "Yes."

"You're not separated or anything? You lived with her too?"

"I'm so sorry. I can't say how very sorry I am."

Sloan pulled her shirt collar over her mouth. He was with her all those Christmas mornings while they waited for him. "Does she live in Mallowater?"

Daddy shook his head. "They live in Tyler."

*They. They.* Not only a wife. Sloan hadn't let herself consider the rest. "So, you have other kids?" Sloan leaned back, creating more space between them.

"Three. Kyle's the oldest. You came next. Bradley was born right before Ridge, and my youngest, her name is Felicity June."

Sloan's head pounded. Nothing in her life made sense. Her brother was gone, but she still had siblings. She wasn't the oldest. She had a sister—a *half-sister.*

Daddy stretched out his hand. "I'm sorry, Lo, but sometimes you can't help who you love."

Sloan wrung her hands under the table. "So, you love them both?"

"Yeah." Daddy retracted his hand. "When I met your mother, there was electricity, Sloan. A connection."

"So why didn't you get a divorce?"

"It's not that simple. Just because I had this connection with your mother didn't mean I stopped loving my wife. She was my high school sweetheart. She stood by me through all the mood swings and nightmares." Tears choked his voice. "She's still standing by me. I don't deserve her."

Despite Sloan's anger toward her mother, she suddenly felt protective of her. Mom wasn't less than Daddy's wife just because she wasn't standing by her man.

Sloan crossed her arms. "Who do you love more?"

Daddy's brows pulled in. "I love them both. It's always been different, separate. Chemistry versus history. I get that it sounds awful. It *is* awful, but I can't help how I feel. Someday you'll understand that."

Sloan hoped not.

"How is your mom?" He bit down on his lip. "Does she ever talk about me?"

Sloan stared at her shoes. "She says you're guilty." She raised her head to meet her father's eyes. "Are you?"

He flinched backward as if she'd hit him. "No, baby. I mean, if I did something, I don't remember, but I just can't imagine doing that to your brother, no matter what kind of nightmare I was trapped in."

Sloan couldn't imagine it either. Or maybe she just didn't want to. She *had* seen him hurt Ridge.

"Do you have plenty to eat? Are the lights still on and everything?" he asked.

"Yeah. The Turners gave mom a big check."

Relief washed over her dad's face. "Good, good. How's everything else?" he asked. "How's school and art?"

Sloan shrugged. "Fine, but I'm ready for summer. Keith Whitley has a new album coming out in August. It's called *I Wonder Do You Think of Me.*"

Daddy smiled. "I like the sound of that."

"I've been saving my allowance for it." Sloan's voice grew louder. "If I bring it here, can you listen?"

Daddy's expression dulled.

"What's wrong?"

"Nothing." Daddy rubbed the back of his neck. "I just hope I won't be here come August. The trial should be over in a week."

"Oh." A week. Sloan hadn't realized it was moving that quickly. "Maybe we'll be able to listen to it at home."

"Home," he repeated. "Now I really like the sound of that."

Jay Hadfield's defense rested on Monday, May 8th. Sloan heard it on the radio. She didn't want to be alone, so she packed a bag and walked to the

Dawson's. Later that night, the jury reached a verdict. They only deliberated for two hours. Walt wouldn't say whether that was good or bad.

It had once been normal to spend the night at the Dawson's. Normal to camp out on the trampoline, but it was weird without Ridge. It was weird for a lot of reasons. Something had shifted between her and Noah. Something that made her insides wiggly when he smiled at her. Something that made Sloan feel uncomfortable taking her shower that night. Like she shouldn't be naked inside the same house as Noah Dawson.

As Sloan sat at the Dawson's table the next morning for breakfast, her mind was on the courtroom across town. Sloan had never been inside a courtroom, but she'd seen plenty on TV. She imagined her father on one side, next to his lawyer. His legal wife behind him, while her mother sat across the aisle behind the prosecutor. And off to the side was a jury. Twelve people who held so many futures in their hands. Futures they had dictated in less than two hours. The verdict had to be innocent, Sloan assumed. No one would decide to take away a daddy in two hours. "Not guilty," they'd say. Daddy would be out in time to listen to Keith Whitley's new tape with her. Sloan would mow lawns and buy concert tickets.

Sloan excused herself from the table to brush her teeth and comb her matted hair. She turned off the water when the phone rang. She stepped quietly out of the bathroom and into the hallway where Doreen stood, back turned, phone pressed against her ear.

"You're kidding," Doreen whispered. "I'll talk to her, but you tell Caroline to get herself here soon."

*Guilty,* Sloan realized. She had gotten it all wrong. Her dad would not see her grow up. He wouldn't be coming home. Either those twelve people had gotten it all wrong, or her father had really killed Ridge.

A weight pressed down on her chest, robbing her of breath. The hallway was too hot. She stepped back into the bathroom and splashed her face with water, fighting the tunnel that wanted to swallow her again.

Sloan didn't pass out this time. She fought against the darkness and made her way to the couch where Doreen held her hand and delivered the news Sloan already suspected. Then Doreen and Noah sat next to her while she sobbed. She didn't fault them for their silence. There was nothing to say.

Of course, that didn't stop Walt from trying when he arrived home an hour later. "He can appeal it, Sloan. This isn't the end."

*But it was,* Sloan thought. Appeals required lawyers. Lawyers cost money. Maybe Daddy's first family was rich, but if his second family's finances were any indication, Sloan doubted it.

Mom didn't arrive for two hours. If she was upset about anything, she showed no sign of it on the car ride home.

"Aren't you even a little sad?" Sloan asked.

"Yes, I'm sad," Mom said but pulled off her sunglasses, revealing clear, dry eyes and mascara without the slightest streak. "I'm sad your brother's gone. Sad your father lied to us all these years."

"But you're not even crying."

"What good does crying do?" Mom pulled sharply into their driveway.

With the car in park, Sloan heard the faint song on the radio. Keith Whitley, she recognized. The lyrics suddenly took on a more personal meaning. She was no stranger to the rain either. Not since November, anyway.

Sloan wiped her eyes again with the handkerchief Walt had given her. "How can you be so cold?"

"I don't expect you to understand any of this, but one day you will," she said, echoing Sloan's father's words. "I need you to trust me. Soon everything is going to make—"

"Shhhh!" Sloan reached and turned the radio knob. "There's breaking news."

"Oh, Sloan, don't listen to the news for a while. You don't want to hear what they say about your father."

"If you're just joining us, there is sad news today in the country music world," the deejay said. "Rising star Keith Whitley was found dead in his Goodlettsville home around noon today. We will keep you posted on this breaking—"

Mom killed the car, and the radio stopped. "Come on. Get in the house. I didn't see any reporters, but that doesn't mean they aren't here."

But Sloan couldn't move. Had she heard right? Was her dad guilty? Was Keith Whitley dead?

"Suit yourself." Mom climbed out of the car and slammed the door.

Once her mom entered the house, Sloan allowed herself to cry, to scream. She cried not just for her Daddy now, but for Keith. Sloan wondered if his wife and little boy felt just like she did now. Wondered how many lives in the world were simultaneously crashing down with her own.

When the car got too hot, Sloan reached to crank down the window and spotted the cameraman in the bushes beside their home. She wondered how long he'd been there. Wondered what pictures he'd taken. She didn't care. She and Daddy would never see Keith Whitley in concert together. They'd never even lay on her floor and listen to his new album together. Keith was dead, and it felt like every dream Sloan had was gone with him.

# Chapter 11

*Mallowater, TX, 2008*

Sloan's eyes jerked open to complete darkness. Her heart pounded, and her pillow was drenched in sweat. It took her a minute to anchor herself in the present, to accept she was safe in her bed.

In her dream, she'd been a teenager shopping at Leo's Drug Emporium with her mom. No matter which aisle she ventured down, the same man followed her. He was thin, wearing a Chicago Bulls baseball cap, but his face was featureless. A face that only makes sense in a dream.

Sloan had ventured away from her mom to check out the latest issue of *Seventeen Magazine*. She hadn't even picked it up before a hand clamped over her mouth and powerful arms pulled her backward.

Sloan sat up in bed and grabbed her water bottle off the bedside table. Her hand shook as she took a drink. *Just a dream*, she assured herself, but certain images had been so vivid and the terror so unsettlingly real. It took Sloan a few more minutes to figure out why.

It wasn't *just* a dream; it was a memory. Sloan remembered the papery cardboard smell of the store that day as Leo stocked a shelf near the cash register. She'd been wearing her new cropped denim jacket and scuffed white Keds. They were too small and rubbed against her heel. She remembered the man's clammy hand over her mouth, remembered her thrashing heartbeat. She knew she needed to fight but felt paralyzed.

But her mom had fought. The stranger almost had Sloan to the door when her mother appeared out of nowhere. Caroline screamed, hit, and bit. She slung her purse at the man, and its contents flew across the dingy tile floor. Hot pink lipstick, Juicy Fruit gum, a blue checkbook holder. Sloan remembered staring at those items on the floor long after the man had let her go and run out of the store.

There had been no other customers in the store, only Leo. "I set off the alarm," he'd told Sloan as he knelt beside her. "Police will be here soon."

But Sloan didn't remember talking to the police. She didn't even remember talking about the incident at all. Was this one of those repressed memories she'd learned about in her child psychology class? Or simply a bad dream brought on by all the talk of kidnapped children and sinister criminals?

There was no waking her mom now, not after she'd taken her Doxepin. Or rather, after Sloan slipped it into her nightly tea.

There was only one other person to ask. If this had happened, Sloan would have told Noah. Or, at the very least, Noah would remember his dad talking about it. By being quiet, Noah learned a lot, especially in the home of a police officer and hairdresser.

Sloan turned on her cell phone. 11:30. Late, but not as late as she expected.

She typed out a lengthy text only to delete it and type it again. At this rate, she wouldn't get it sent until midnight. She finally settled on simple:

*Do you remember a man grabbing me at Leo's when we were kids?*

Sloan laid back on her pillow but kept the phone in her hand. Even though she'd turned the ringer up, she checked the screen every few minutes, as if she'd somehow missed the notification chime. He could already be in bed. The Noah she knew would never go to bed before 2:00 am, but maybe the Noah she knew didn't exist anymore.

Sloan tried to remember more details of that day, tried to recall the man's face, but she couldn't. It was only the denim jacket, too-tight Keds, *Seventeen Magazine*, and hot pink lipstick on the floor.

If it was a memory, someone had tried to abduct her, just like they'd abducted Logan Pruitt and Dylan Lawrence.

The phone chimed. She shot back up in bed to read Noah's reply:

*What are you talking about?*

She responded with all the details this time and waited. Ten minutes later, the next text came in:

*If that happened, you never told me.*

Sloan sagged against her pillow. Was she going crazy? Losing her mind like her mother had always been her greatest fear.

*Ok, thanks. Sorry to bother you,* she typed, but deleted the sentence and tried again. *Can you check the police reports tomorrow?*

This time, the response came instantly. *I'll need an idea of when it happened.*

Sloan tried to guess how old she might have been. The memory of looking at the *Seventeen Magazine* suggested it wasn't long after her father had gone to jail. She'd gone through a phase then, trying to makeover herself—highlights, glittery purple eyeshadow, and that expensive denim jacket. As if the advice in some magazine would help her become a different person with a normal life.

But if it had been so soon after Ridge disappeared, why didn't anyone assume the two events could be connected?

*Niki Taylor*, Sloan remembered. Niki Taylor had been on the magazine cover she'd been reaching for. She opened her phone's web browser and searched "Niki Taylor Seventeen Magazine." The image popped up right away. Sloan zoomed in on the date.

*August 1989. And while you are at it, can I get copies of the reports from Ridge's disappearance?*

*I'll see what I can find.*

*Thank you.* Sloan typed. *I appreciate—*

But another text popped up on her screen, interrupting her response.

*Don't contact me this late again.*

Sloan pressed her lips tight. Noah was supposed to be her friend. But then again, this could have waited until morning.

*Sorry*, she typed, but then deleted it and read his text again. The ever-polite Noah hadn't even prefaced his request with the word *please*. Sloan gathered that any text, even an apology, wasn't welcome right now.

Sloan flopped back down into her bed. She hadn't told Noah about that day at Leo's. She'd never talked to the police, yet she remembered a magazine, a real magazine, she'd reached for in August 1989.

Something was going on in her hometown. Her name had almost been added to a growing list of lost children. Dylan Lawrence. Logan Pruitt. Ridge Hadfield?

Sloan needed to talk to Dylan, even if that meant going through Felicity.

She walked into the living room and plugged the phone back in long enough to get Felicity's number off the caller ID. She decided to send the text now. She didn't need to give herself any time to sleep on it and wake up convinced none of this was real.

*This is Sloan,* she typed. *Sorry to text so late, but have you met with Dylan yet? If not, I'd like to join you. Text me tomorrow and let me know. Thanks!*

Sloan deleted the exclamation mark and hit send.

The response came immediately. *Good timing, Sloan! We are meeting tomorrow at noon for lunch at Applebee's in Tyler! I can pick you up!*

A sour taste filled Sloan's mouth. She'd put up with Felicity in a public place if that meant talking to Dylan, but no way would she tolerate being stuck in a car with her for an hour each way.

*Meet you there,* Sloan typed and then turned off her phone.

Sloan drummed her fingers on the steering wheel the entire drive to Tyler. It should have been the thought of Dylan Lawrence, and whatever information he might hold, making her jittery, but it was mostly the thought of interacting with Felicity.

Sloan remembered again the first time she'd seen Felicity, in the backseat of Anna Hadfield's station wagon, the day she'd shown up to Sloan's school. She remembered the girl's big red hair, smooshed down by the headphones connected to her Walkman. At the time, Sloan hadn't thought much about the electronic, but ever since she learned it was Felicity in the backseat, it had been eating at her. Felicity was in the second grade and had a Walkman. Sloan was in sixth and had begged Daddy for one the entire year.

Obviously, their father had given his best to his real wife and his real wife's children. Sloan and Ridge got the table scraps.

Real wife. The phrase still made Sloan's blood pressure rise. Anna Hadfield, Daddy's proper wife. Sweet, naïve, stand-by-your-man, Anna Hadfield. It had taken Sloan an embarrassingly long time to realize this woman taking her to visits at the prison was her father's wife. Anna was so plain, such a contrast to Sloan's vibrant and beautiful mother, that it made no sense the same man loved them both.

It struck Sloan now how much she hated Anna Hadfield. How she still blamed her for things that couldn't possibly be her fault.

And she couldn't find it within herself to think any better of Anna's children. There was Kyle, a loan officer at Tyler National Credit Union. Brad, four years younger, had his own law firm. Then, of course, little Felicity June. Daddy always called her by both names.

Like his little wide-eyed, freckled face baby girl was too precious for only one.

Sloan hated Felicity most of all. Probably because she was a girl. Like Sloan wasn't sufficient, so Daddy needed to try for a better daughter.

What bothered Sloan most of all was that somehow Anna and her children had come out of the event unscathed. Their community rallied, cooked meals, and set up a donation account at the bank. All the stigma and all the judgment had fallen on Sloan and her mother. Jay's illegitimate kid and his mistress. No one except Noah's family stood by them. Even Libby and Vince Turner stopped calling, eventually. Sure, her mom was nuts, but even as a teenager, Sloan recognized how crappy it was for her mother's only friend to turn her back on her after all she'd been through.

Sloan was so wrapped up in her memories, she almost missed her turn at Applebee's. Car horns wailed as she hit the brake and turned too wide into the parking lot.

Inside, the restaurant was crowded and loud. Silverware clinked, couples laughed, children screamed, sports fans cheered, and Sloan's ears rang.

She spotted Felicity and Dylan in a corner booth. Felicity stood to wave her over. She was wearing a bright pink top with white pants. A chunky turquoise necklace hung around her neck. She looked like she was here for a blind date, not a meeting that might bring terrible news.

Sloan avoided greeting Felicity and turned her attention to Dylan. "Hi." She extended her hand. "I'm Sloan."

Though Dylan stood to introduce himself, he didn't raise his eyes to meet hers. She felt for him. This couldn't be easy. Not the media attention and not this strange meeting with two sort-of sisters. Sloan wondered how much Felicity had told him about their unique situation.

Sloan wanted to cut to the chase. To get to details about the kidnapping. Timelines, locations, other boys, but that's not how they did things in Texas. For a state that touted everything was bigger here, people sure seemed to like small talk.

"So, Felicity tells me you're a music teacher?"

"Yeah." Dylan smiled slightly. He had a long thin face with small sleepy eyes and high sharp cheekbones that left deep hallows on both sides of his face. "At Mallowater Middle School."

"He's a musician himself," Felicity chirped up.

Dylan's cheeks reddened. "I play a little guitar."

He had an unusual voice to match his appearance. Quiet and raspy, like Sloan's teenage crush, Christian Slater. He even had that same '90s heartthrob hairstyle, mid-length, messy, and parted down the middle.

"Oh?" Sloan took a sip of her water. Getting to the harder questions was going to require a harder beverage.

"Yeah, I play guitar and write the occasional song." He spun his straw around. "What about you?"

"I don't write anything," Sloan said.

Dylan laughed. "That's not what I meant. What do you do for a living?" He made eye contact for the first time in the conversation.

"Sorry. I teach fifth grade." Sloan felt heat in her cheeks. "In Houston."

"So, we're all educators." Felicity's singsong voice rose above the noise of the restaurant. "Small world."

Sloan didn't want to talk about education. She wanted to talk about Ridge. She hoped Felicity might take the lead in this conversation since she had arranged this lunch. Since she "knew" Dylan, but obviously, this was all going to be on Sloan.

She flagged down the server, and they made their orders. After Sloan took her first gulp of a Long Island Iced Tea, she gathered her courage. "So, I'm not sure what Felicity has told you, but my brother disappeared in the fall of 1988."

"Yeah, I remember the case. I mean, I remember it happening." Dylan wrapped his hands around his coffee cup. "I hate to have to give a disclaimer, but my lawyer would flip if he knew about this. I'm not supposed to discuss this without him present. I want to help you both, help your dad if I can. I mean, the truth matters, but this can't leave the table."

"Of course not," Sloan said. "It won't."

Dylan nodded. "Alright then. Ask away."

"When were you . . . taken?" Sloan barely got the words out.

"February 1992." His eyes stayed glued to the tabletop.

"The police believe our father killed Ridge, but it's never added up," Felicity said. "They never found a body. There were no leads, but now, hearing about Eddie Daughtry, I wondered if Ridge was also a victim."

Dylan swallowed. "I don't remember a Ridge. But Daughtry gave everyone fake names."

Sloan dug a picture out of her purse. "This is him. A few months before."

Sloan felt the booth shift as Felicity sucked in a breath. Dylan studied the photo, his face giving nothing away.

"I'm sorry," he said, handing it back. "I don't remember him."

Sloan sank back into the booth. Ridge was gone. Why was she torturing herself?

"How many boys did Eddie take?" Felicity asked.

Dylan rocked in his seat. "I only knew Logan, but there were others who would come and go."

"Come and go?" Felicity asked.

"It's not like in the movies where we were chained up in some dungeon." Dylan drummed his fingers against his coffee cup. "The chain was heroin for me. For some boys, it was arcade money. For others, it was fear he'd hurt their family."

"I read a few nights ago that Logan Pruitt was riding his bike home from Movie Time Rentals when he was abducted," Sloan said. The image was seared in her mind. The Huffy bike turned sideways on the street; a plastic VHS case opened beside it. "So, did Eddie just look for opportunity, or did he seek out certain boys?" Sloan was more comfortable asking questions now. The alcohol was doing its job. Giving her courage. She wondered how Dylan could tell his story without the help of it.

"Opportunity, I assume. He seemed to go driving a lot, looking for kids." Dylan let out a hard sigh. "When I was twelve, someone in a Luke Skywalker mask assaulted me on the way home from trick-ortreating. He told me he'd come back and kill me if I ever told. I never told. But he still came back."

"It was Eddie?" Felicity covered her mouth.

"Yeah." Dylan glanced behind him to ensure the empty booth next to theirs hadn't been filled. "Four years later."

"How old are you now?" Sloan asked.

"Just turned thirty-two."

"We're the same age," Sloan said. She didn't have to do the math to determine the year they turned twelve. Halloween 1988. The week before Ridge disappeared.

"But you two didn't know each other from school?" Felicity asked.

"We moved here when I was eleven, and I went to Saint Christopher's," Dylan said.

"Oh, so you're Catholic?" Felicity put her elbow on the table and rested her chin in her hand.

"No, just painfully shy. Mom figured a private school would be easier for me."

Felicity opened her mouth again to speak, but Sloan beat her to it. She needed to steer the conversation back on track. "So, after that Halloween, you didn't see Eddie again for four years?" she asked.

"No, not till I started on the white stuff. Got hooked by a friend, and Eddie was his dealer. He seemed like a cool guy. After my dad kicked me out, I met him to get a hit. He offered his couch for the night." Dylan bent his neck, letting shiny strands of hair cover his eyes. "I got in his car, and it was *the* car from that Halloween night. It all came back. I panicked, he hit me with something, and I woke up a few hours later in Eddie's attic. Logan was there. He'd been there a long time."

Sloan shuddered. "What did Eddie look like then?" she asked, still trying to recall the face of the man who grabbed her in the drugstore.

"Like he does now. Just a little thinner and with more hair."

They stopped talking as the server approached with their food. Sloan had stared at Eddie's mugshot on her computer last night, and it had produced no memories. As hard as she tried, she couldn't put his face, or any face, on her attacker. "I have this memory," Sloan said once the server left. "Of someone trying to grab me at the store."

Dylan rubbed a sugar packet between his fingers. "In my eight months, I never saw a girl. Eddie liked boys."

The vodka sloshed around in Sloan's stomach. She needed to eat her chicken fettuccine but had lost her appetite.

"I'm so sorry this happened to you, Dylan," Felicity said.

"Thank you. The whole reason I'm speaking out is that there are other victims. I want justice for them. I want justice for your brother. Just because I don't remember seeing him doesn't mean Eddie wasn't behind it."

"Was Eddie a Satanist?" Felicity's eyes widened. "That was the talk after Logan's kidnapping."

Dylan smirked. "I think Satanism was the talk of the eighties. But no. No rituals or anything like that went on. Not surprised people assumed that, though. My old man swore every tape I bought had secret satanic messages if played backward."

"Oh gosh, I remember." Felicity giggled. "My grandma made us stop using Proctor and Gamble because she was sure their man in the moon logo was a horned devil with 666 in his beard."

"How did you escape?" Sloan asked. If it were possible Ridge was one of Daughtry's victims, it was also possible he'd gotten away too.

Dylan chewed and swallowed a bite of his chicken strips. "I got clean. Flushed the drugs. Eddie used his victims to make money, including selling us for a few hours here and there."

Sloan squeezed her eyes shut. And she thought she'd had it bad growing up.

Dylan traced a crack in the table. "The guy I met with was drunk; he passed out. I emptied his wallet and just walked out of the hotel." He shook his head. "It's unbelievable when you think about it. I just walked out. Just got on a bus. Just walked in my front door like I hadn't been in hell the past eight months."

Felicity placed a hand over her heart. "And he never came back for you?"

"No. I was getting too old for Eddie's tastes. I hoped if I kept my mouth shut, I'd be fine. But I still got a gun and learned to shoot. Always looked over my shoulder. Still kinda do."

"And you didn't tell anyone?" Sloan asked.

Felicity nudged her under the table.

"I'm sorry. I didn't mean—"

Dylan met her eyes. "It's okay. No, I never told a soul till they found Logan. I worried Eddie would hurt Dad, so I told him I'd hitched a ride to Oklahoma and had been living with a friend." Sloan saw tears forming in Dylan's eyes.

Felicity seemed to notice, too, because she reached across the table and took his hand. "You're so brave, Dylan. Thank you for sharing your story, but we've asked enough for one day. Let's talk about something else."

Sloan wasn't ready for this conversation to end. Even though Dylan didn't remember Ridge, too much didn't add up. There were too many coincidences. The timing, the town, the man who'd tried to take her. "Would Eddie remember if he took Ridge?" she asked.

"Sloan!" Felicity was still holding Dylan's hand. Sloan couldn't tell if this was an attempt at flirting or if Felicity June really was as sweet as everybody claimed.

"You can't trust Eddie to tell the truth," Dylan said. "He's denying everything. Plus, he's got a lot of connections, and I wouldn't want to put you in danger." He pulled his hand away from Felicity's. "I probably shouldn't have even met with you in public, but I figured you may be creeped out if I suggested my house."

Felicity reached across Sloan to grab the check. "Well, I hope we don't get you into any trouble with your lawyer."

"Let's meet again," Sloan said. "Privately."

"Yeah, absolutely." Dylan reached for a napkin. "Do you want my number?"

"I've got it," Felicity's said. "I'll *for sure* call you."

Sloan shook her head. Felicity was actually flirting with this poor man.

"Sounds good." One corner of Dylan's mouth raised when he smiled, and it occurred to Sloan that he didn't mind the flirting. She needed to get out of here.

SHANESSA GLUHM | 101

"I should get going." Sloan slid out from the booth. Dylan started to stand, but Sloan waved him down. "You guys stay, though. Nice meeting you, Dylan."

"You too." Dylan slowly lowered himself back onto the booth.

"Dylan and I will work out the details for our next meeting, and I'll text you. I'm thinking dinner at my apartment." Though Felicity was speaking to Sloan, her attention was still anchored on Dylan.

Sloan forced a smile. She didn't like Felicity, didn't like being the third wheel, but she'd do what she had to do to get to the bottom of all this.

"I'll be there."

# Chapter 12

*Mallowater, TX, 1989*

"Can Sloan stay for dinner?"

Sloan held her breath, waiting for Walt and Doreen's response. She caught the look they exchanged and knew the answer before they said a word.

"Let's give Sloan time with her mother," Walt told Noah. "We've kept her away all week."

Noah stared at the floor. He wasn't one to fight with his parents; plus, they were right. Sloan had been here all summer and had probably worn out her welcome.

She grabbed her backpack. "I'll see you later, Noah."

"Wait." Walt held up his hand. "It's not that we don't want you here. It's just that your mother . . . well, she needs you right now."

Sloan struggled with the backpack. "Mom doesn't even talk to me."

"Caroline is grieving," Doreen explained.

"She hasn't even cried."

Doreen took Sloan's hand. "Grief comes in stages. And denial is the first one."

Sloan freed her hand to swat away a tear. Maybe she cried enough for her and her mother both. "And what's the next stage?"

"Anger, I think. But not everyone goes through them in the same order."

Anger. Sloan understood a little about that. But even though her father deserved her resentment, much of her anger was focused on her mom. Her mom who believed Daddy had killed Ridge. Her mom who expected Sloan to believe it too.

"Do y'all have groceries?" Walt asked, already reaching for his wallet.

"Yeah, we're good," Sloan said. Caroline hadn't been to the store in a while, but food was still in the pantry. And though her mom claimed to be looking for jobs, Sloan hadn't seen her fill out a single application in the almost three months since the verdict. Not that anyone in town would hire her anyway. No one would even look at them.

"Noah, walk Sloan home," Doreen said.

"No, it's okay," Sloan said. "You guys are about to eat."

"I have time," Noah said too eagerly.

Sloan said a half-hearted goodbye to Doreen and Walt before letting Noah lead her out the door.

"Sorry you can't stay," Noah said.

Sloan kicked the gravel. "Your parents are right. I can't avoid Mom forever."

"You can avoid her all Saturday afternoon, though," Noah said.

"Saturday?"

Noah's face fell. "My birthday. You're still coming, right?"

His birthday. Sloan had forgotten. She thought back to Noah's birthday party last year. How she'd promised Ridge she'd go with him but backed out at the last minute when her friends invited her to watch *Cocktail*. When Daddy discovered her plans, he'd made Sloan cancel with her friends and keep her word to Ridge. She'd sulked the entire party, angry she was at a Transformers birthday and not watching Tom Cruise. She wished she'd known her time with Ridge was about to run out and that those so-called friends wouldn't even speak to her one year later.

Noah cleared his throat.

"Yeah, I'll try," Sloan said. She loved being around Noah, but it was the idea of the other party guests that gave her pause. The only advantage of being locked up with her mom all summer was avoiding her classmates. "What do you want for your birthday?"

"I want you to come," Noah said softly.

"Fine." Sloan nudged him off the path. "I'll be there."

Sloan woke up Saturday in a restless mood. Despite barely sleeping, she wanted to be out of this bed, out of this house, out of her own skin.

She stared at a closed dresser drawer. The second copy of Keith Whitley's new tape was inside. Daddy's copy. Sloan had been first in line Tuesday and had been listening nonstop. The album was incredible, but knowing this was the last music Keith would ever make made every note he sang bittersweet.

Sloan was scheduled to visit her dad next Friday, but that seemed too long with that tape inside the dresser, so she decided to call Anna. She sometimes wondered if she was bothering her father's friend, but Anna had promised to take Sloan anytime she wanted, and she wanted to go today. She'd have to come up with something to tell Mom, though. Noah's party didn't start till 3:00, and just last night, she'd told Sloan she was spending too much time with the Dawsons, echoing Walt's words.

Sloan found her mom reading in the living room. "Can I go to the mall?"

"What do you need at the mall?" Caroline's eyes didn't leave the book.

"Noah's party is today. I wanted to buy him a shirt from Gadzooks."

"Fine," Mom said. "But I'm expecting a call from Libby, so it will have to wait."

Sloan was about to suggest riding her bike, but the mall was too far. She should have said Hastings instead.

"Remember Jenny? My friend from school? She wanted to hang out this summer, so I planned to invite her. Her mom can probably drive us."

Caroline sighed. "Fine, whatever. But make the call quick. I'm expecting—"

"A call from Libby. Got it." Sloan pulled the number from her pocket and dialed. She wished there was a phone in her bedroom. Privacy would make this easier.

"Hello." Sloan recognized Anna's voice.

"Hey, Jenny."

"You must have the wrong number."

"Yeah, this is Sloan. I was wondering if you wanted to go to the mall today?"

Sloan looked at her mother. Her eyes were still on the book, but the fact that she hadn't turned a single page hadn't escaped Sloan.

"The mall? Sloan, are you okay?"

"Yeah, yeah, great. Can your mom drive us? My mom's right here, but she's expecting a phone call."

"Oh. Did you want to visit your dad?" Anna whispered as if Caroline could hear her on the other end of the line.

"Yes, please. I can meet you at the end of the street," Sloan said.

"That should work. Can you be ready in half an hour?"

"Yes, half an hour is perfect. Thanks!" Sloan hung up the phone with too much force. "Jenny's mom will take us. Said she'd give us money for lunch and the arcade and can drop us back off at Noah's." Sloan spoke too quickly and wondered if she'd said too much, made the fake plan too detailed. More details than could have been ironed out in a one-minute conversation.

Caroline lowered the book. "Have I met Jenny's mother?"

"Yes." Sloan's voice rose. "The first time I went to her house."

Caroline nodded. "Okay, yeah. What was her name?"

Sloan swallowed. "I'm not sure. I call her Mrs. Robertson."

Sloan jumped at the sound of the phone's shrill ring. She grabbed it in case Anna was calling back. "Hello. Oh, hi, Libby. Mom's right here." Sloan extended the phone. "It's Libby. So, I'll see you tonight after Noah's party?"

"Alright," Caroline said." Have a nice time."

Sloan exhaled as her mother took the phone. If Mom suspected anything, she wouldn't pass up a call with Libby to discuss it. Those unending phone calls with her best friend seemed to be Mom's only hobby nowadays. Sloan didn't blame her for not wanting to watch the crows at the creek anymore, not after everything that had happened. The creek was no longer the scene of Sloan's childhood summers or her mother's research; it was a crime scene.

"Sloan!" Her father lifted her off the ground in a hug.

"I was supposed to come Friday, but I couldn't wait."

"I'm so glad you didn't." He sat her down. "You can come any visiting day. Sometimes there's a wait, so it's always best to come early."

"Yeah." Sloan looked up at the clock. "The line was long, and there was a mix-up with paperwork. Anna got mad."

"I bet. I'll make sure everything is cleared up for next time. Are you hungry? There are some vending machines."

"I'm okay." Sloan pulled the Keith Whitley cassette out of her pocket and handed it across the table. "It also took longer because they had to check this."

He took the tape and grinned. "Those guards probably just wanted to listen to it before me."

"It's really great," Sloan said.

"This isn't your copy, is it?"

"No. I bought two. Almost bought the CD too. I don't have a CD player yet, but Noah does. Do you have a stereo here?"

"Yep, and I'm going to play this till it wears out." Daddy pulled out the tape's insert and spread it out on the table. "Man, I can't believe he's really gone."

Sloan leaned over the table and pointed at the lyrics. "*I'm Over You* was the first single released. I think it's my favorite too."

"Can't wait to hear this. Every time I listen to these songs, I'm going to think of you, Lo." Daddy folded the insert back up. "Say, do you remember how much you loved the moon when you were little?"

"The moon?" Sloan shook her head.

"You were an itty-bitty thing. Wanted to see the moon every night. One night, we walked down to the river for a better view. You were so sad because I had to leave the next day for work, so I told you that no matter where I was, we could look up at the same moon."

Sloan didn't remember that night, but something struck her now. Her father probably wasn't going to work the next day. He was going back to his family.

"So," he continued, "this is sort of the same. I can play this tape and know you're in your room playing it too. It's even called *I Wonder*

*Do You Think of Me*. And we'll always think of each other when we hear it. Music has always been a part of us, a part of our bond. We can feel songs in our souls."

Sloan crossed her arms. "Do you think of Ridge too? Do you miss him?"

He flinched backward. "Of course I do."

"You never talk about him."

"It's just hard." Daddy scrubbed a hand over his face. "But we can talk about Ridge. We can talk about any—"

"It's fine, Sloan said. She didn't really want to talk about Ridge either, didn't want to be sad, but sometimes, she felt like everyone was forgetting him. "Anyway, you can tell me your favorite song on the album when I come Friday."

"Of course." He forced a smile, but Sloan saw sadness in his eyes. "How's your mother, Sloan?"

Sloan cringed. She hated when he asked about Mom. It was a topic that always ruined a pleasant visit.

Sloan shrugged. "She mostly reads and talks to Libby. She's looking for a job, I guess."

"I wish she'd talk to me. It's killing me. I've written a few letters. Has she gotten them?"

Sloan shrugged. "She's never said anything. Have you written me any?"

"No, I didn't want you to get in trouble. Since you're still calling Anna, I assume your mother doesn't realize you're visiting?"

Sloan slid down the chair. "I'm scared to tell her. She got mad when I first asked to visit."

"She'll come around. Give her a little time. And if you two ever need anything, call Walt. Promise?"

Sloan noticed the guard walking back toward their table. Seeing him approach gave Sloan the same feeling as when *Just the Ten of Us* ended on Fridays. That meant the night was over. Daddy had an erratic schedule, but he always tried to be home Friday evenings for pizza and two hours of television shows they loved. Television shows that would be off the air when Daddy was out of this place. The realization brought tears to Sloan's eyes.

"Hey, don't cry." He stood and hugged her. "I'll see you Friday. We'll talk about the new album."

Friday. They'd still be together Friday night. It wasn't exactly the ABC lineup and Pizza Hut, but it was better than nothing.

Sloan cried the entire way home. Anna stayed quiet but kept the tissues coming. She glanced in the rearview mirror every few miles.

Sloan was so upset, she didn't notice Anna pull onto her street. "Stop!" Sloan screamed.

"What is it? "Anna asked, slamming on the brakes.

"Mom's home. You can't pull up."

"Oh gosh." Anna brought her hand to her forehead. "Sorry." She reversed and pulled to the side of the street opposite Sloan's home. She reached behind and took Sloan's hand. "I'm so sorry. For all this."

"Thank you." Sloan let go and wiped her eyes. "Thanks for helping my dad. You've been a real friend to him."

Anna raised her eyebrows. "Has your father not explained who I am?"

Before Sloan could process the question, she spotted movement from the corner of her eye. Mom was standing in the front yard. "Shoot, I gotta go," Sloan said, climbing out of the car.

Sloan walked toward her mom but noticed Caroline's gaze travel past her to Anna. Sloan hoped Mom didn't remember what Mrs. Robertson looked like or wonder where Jenny was.

"Hi, Mom!" Sloan made her tone bright as she approached. She turned back toward Anna's car and waved. "Bye, Mrs. Robertson. Thanks for the ride." Anna didn't even look confused. She stared back at Sloan's mother, matching the intensity of Caroline's glare.

"That's Jenny's mom." Sloan stepped into the house, relieved her mom followed.

Mom cocked her head. "No, it's not." Sloan's legs wobbled. She'd been caught. Mom gestured to the couch. "Sit down. Let's chat."

"I'm sorry, Mom. I didn't think you'd understand."

Caroline held up a hand. "I'm not mad you wanted to see your father. You're only a child. There's so much you don't understand."

Sloan wanted to argue, but Mom was calm, and Sloan wanted her to stay that way. "Do you really believe Daddy killed Ridge?"

"Yes," her mom said without hesitation. "You witnessed the violence."

Sloan tensed her shoulders. "Only when he was dreaming."

"Well, maybe that's what happened at the creek."

"Then it was an accident."

Mom gave a curt nod. "Yes, but people have to pay for accidents, for mistakes."

"But twenty years for one mistake?"

"Oh, Sloan. It wasn't just one mistake. Can't you understand that? Jay made a mistake every single day he refused to get help, every day he lied to us."

Sloan stared down at the thick carpet. She couldn't argue with that.

"Are you even a little mad? About all the lies?"

"Yes," Sloan admitted. She looked up and saw tears streaming down her mom's face. Doreen was right. There were stages in grief, and this meant Mom was out of denial. "I'm sorry I lied."

"Sometimes it feels like no one cares about me. I lost my son, the only man I've ever loved, and now, I'm losing you."

"But you're not," Sloan said.

Mom grabbed a tissue from the table to wipe her face. "That's how it feels when I see you with your father's other family."

Sloan narrowed her eyes. "What?"

"Well, Anna, of course. Every time Jay left, he was going to be with her. And now you are leaving with her too and keeping it a secret. Just like he did."

"Wait. Anna is Daddy's wife?" Sloan's mind raced, searching for answers. How had she been so stupid?

Mom's hand flew to her chest. "They didn't tell you?"

"No. He mentioned his wife, but I didn't realize it was Anna." Sloan felt dizzy. "He said Anna was his friend. I thought she was his secretary, the one he talked about sometimes who scheduled his meetings."

Caroline smirked. "No, sweetie. *Angela* was his secretary. *Anna* is his wife."

"But she's so nice," Sloan said. "She doesn't even seem mad."

"Some women are weak." Disapproval gleamed in Mom's eyes. "Some women can't live without a man."

Sloan remembered the little redhead in the back seat at school that day. Was that her sister?

"I get what he's doing." Mom stood and walked toward the window. "He wants you to be a part of his family with Anna. And if that's what you want, I can't blame you."

"Mom . . ."

Caroline closed the curtains and turned towards Sloan. "But you've got my blood running through you. You're a Hadfield, yes, but you're just as much a Radel."

Mom was crying again. Sloan had wanted to see her cry for so long, and now, she only wanted to stop it. She wrapped her arms around her mother. "You're my family, Mom. I won't go back with Anna."

Mom kissed the top of her head. "I'm sorry I haven't been here for you, but from now on, I will. I promise it's me and you, Lo. Me and you."

"I promise too." Sloan felt terrible for how awful she'd been to her mom. How she'd blamed her and let Daddy off the hook. He'd tried to turn her against her own mother, tried to make her bond with Anna. Sloan should have known not to trust him.

"It's going to be hard, Sloan, but we can let him go together. Ridge would want us to be strong."

Sloan nodded. "I don't want to be weak."

"No matter what you decide, I want you to promise me no more secrets. If you decide to stand with your dad and Anna, be honest. No sneaking around."

"I'm with you," Sloan said. "I'll always be with you."

"Noah . . . Noah!" Sloan hissed from outside his window. She hadn't been in bed long when she jolted up, realizing what she'd forgotten in the day's chaos—Noah's party.

"Sloan?" Noah walked toward the window, rubbing his eyes.

She motioned for him to open the latch, and he did. "Noah, I'm sorry. Can we talk?"

"No," he whispered. He started to close the window, but Sloan put her hand under it, forcing him to stop. "Go home. It's late."

"You're mad. I get it. You have every right to be. But I can't handle it, Noah. I don't care who else in the world is mad at me as long as you aren't."

"We'll talk tomorrow." He glanced behind him at his open bedroom door. "My mom will kill me if I let you in this late."

"Then come outside. I had an awful day."

"That makes two of us."

Sloan averted her gaze. "Just let me explain."

"Fine." Sloan watched him close his door and slip on his shoes before climbing out the window.

They walked for a while in silence. Moonlight splashed them in silver as they followed a well-worn path toward Crow's Nest Creek.

"We waited an hour to start the party." Noah broke the silence. "I tried calling, but the line was busy."

"Mom was talking to Libby. I wasn't home."

Noah turned his head toward her. "You promised."

"I'm sorry. There's no excuse, but I visited my dad. There was an issue with the paperwork. I got home late, and Mom caught Anna dropping me off."

"Anna?"

"Anna, who takes me to see Dad. Anna, who I thought was his secretary or friend, but turns out, she's much more than a friend." Sloan kicked a rock.

"You mean . . . ?"

"Yep, she's his wife."

Noah shook his head. "Wow. You *did* have an awful day."

"Pretty much. And I don't plan to visit again for a while. Mom says it's up to me. I think I've gotta let him go. I want to be a strong woman."

Sloan expected Noah might try to change her mind. She sorta wanted him to—wanted him to tell her it was possible to stand by her mom and still love her dad, but he didn't. Instead, he paused on the path. "We should go back."

Sloan stopped too. The smattering of trees from the creek was visible now. She hadn't been this close to the creek since the search parties ended. She shouldn't want to go back, ever, but something in those trees called to her. "I'm going to walk to the river."

Noah blew out a breath. "You said you didn't want to go back there."

"I've got to move on. Let it go. I don't want to be weak."

"Come on, Sloan. You're the toughest girl I know. You've got nothing to prove. Not to me."

Sloan kept walking. "I need to prove it to myself. Ridge loved the creek. He wouldn't want me to spend my life avoiding it." She turned back to Noah, still frozen on the path. "Thanks for talking. I'll call you tomorrow."

Noah hesitated, but only for a second before jogging toward Sloan and taking her hand.

# Chapter 13

*Mallowater, TX, 2008*

"Sorry for texting so late." Sloan waited till Noah closed his office door to apologize.

"No big deal," Noah said, but even as he sat behind his desk, facing Sloan, he avoided looking at her.

"Was Vickie upset?"

Noah shook his head. "I'm a cop. She's used to my phone going off at all hours."

"Good. I didn't want to get you in any sort of trouble."

Noah finally met her eyes. "You realize this information I'm getting for you could get me in trouble, too, right? Bigger trouble than you could ever get me in with Vickie?"

Sloan sat up straighter. So, he *had* found something. "I'd never tell anyone you're helping me."

"Well, there's nothing on file about an attempted kidnapping in Mallowater in or around August 1989," Noah said.

Sloan threw up her hands. "You said you had information."

Noah smirked. "Are you going to let me finish?"

Sloan put her hands on her lap. "Sorry, go ahead."

Noah opened a file folder on his desk. "Eddie Daughtry was arrested on August 20, 1989, for contributing to the delinquency of a minor. He supposedly offered drugs to a fifteen-year-old boy, but the case was thrown out."

"That's how he got Dylan, with drugs," Sloan said.

"Dylan Lawrence? What do you know about that case?"

Sloan twisted her watch. "We had dinner with him."

"We?"

"Felicity and I," Sloan said.

"Wow, Dylan Lawrence *and* Felicity Hadfield? Seems I've missed a lot." Something bitter dripped from Noah's tone. "Anyway, I tracked down Leo Jackson. I called and asked him if he remembered somebody trying to take you that day at his store."

Sloan leaned forward. "And?"

"And he does."

Sloan felt a rush of relief at having been validated.

"He didn't remember the year, but he remembered the day," Noah explained.

"The day?"

"It was his birthday. He was so bothered by what happened, he and his wife didn't go out to dinner that night."

"And his birthday is?"

"August 20th."

"It had to be Eddie then," Sloan said.

"Now, hold on." Noah raised his hand. "Leo knew Eddie Daughtry. He doesn't think it was him."

Sloan stood, pacing in front of Noah's desk. "Did he actually get a good look at the man's face, though?"

"I don't know. All he said was Caroline was adamant that the police not be involved. She claimed she was taking you away soon—somewhere the bad men couldn't find you."

Sloan stopped pacing. "Bad men? That's what she said, bad men?"

"According to Leo."

"So, she knew?" Sloan plopped down in a chair. "She knew Eddie was after me? Did she know he took Ridge? Noah, what's going on here?"

Noah crossed his arms. "I'm not sure, but this proves nothing about Ridge. There was an investigation. There was evidence against Jay. The D.A. and twelve jurors agreed he killed Ridge."

"I'm well aware of that." She spat out the words. "But has anyone even asked Eddie about this?"

"I'm not on that case. I have no clue what they've asked Eddie Daughtry."

"And you're not going to find out?" Anger like sharp barbs formed on her words. "Some best friend you turned out to be to Ridge."

"And some friend you turned out to be to me, Sloan." Noah's voice rose an octave. "You just drove away and never looked back. Now, you want my help." He picked up the folder. "This is me helping you, but it's still not enough! Everything has to be on *your* terms. It's always been all or nothing with you." Noah slammed the folder back down on the desk, sending a few papers inside flying.

Sloan bent down to gather the papers and her composure. Noah was right; she had no room to talk about being a lousy friend. "Sorry," she said, rising up to put the papers back in the file. "I have no right to ask you for anything, but something's going on here. Can I get a copy of the report of Eddie's arrest that day?" Sloan wanted to read it herself. Wanted to try to put a timeline of the day together.

"This is an active case. I can't do anything to undermine the investigation."

Sloan sighed. He hadn't earned the nickname Noah the Noble for nothing.

"The FBI is in this," Noah said. "I shouldn't be discussing any of it with you. The best I can do is to give you our records about Ridge's disappearance." He reached under the folder and held out a manila envelope. It hardly looked thick enough to hold the contents of an entire investigation.

"Thanks." Sloan's hand shook as she took the envelope.

"This won't turn out like you hope," Noah said. "This isn't like those detective novels you used to like. You aren't going to read these files and find some smoking gun. Read them. Then, let this go."

"Will you read through them too?" Sloan asked.

"I did. Nothing points to Daughtry. Just your dad."

"Then who tried to take me? What bad men were after me?"

"Ask Caroline," Noah said. "It's a long shot, but it's worth a try. And . . ." Noah rubbed his hands over his face. "I'll pass Ridge's file to the chief; tell him it was around the same time as Logan and Dylan. See if he thinks it's worth looking into."

Sloan closed her eyes, letting the relief set in. "Thank you." She reached across the desk and placed her hand on top of Noah's.

He lowered his eyes to their hands as if he wasn't sure what to make of the gesture. Just as Sloan was about to retract her hand, Noah rotated his own until their palms touched. His skin was clammy and cold. His touch still made every nerve ending stir.

He raised his eyes to meet hers. They stared at each other, hands touching, but neither holding on. They were kids again, silently daring each other to make the first move.

It took a knock on the door for them to separate. Noah retracted his hand as if Sloan were a hot stove he'd accidentally touched. "Come in."

Sloan grabbed her purse and pretended to be searching for something when the receptionist entered, but she felt the old woman's eyes on her.

"Sorry to bother you, Mr. Dawson, but Vickie is on the line. Didn't want to interrupt um . . . *this,* but she needs you to get Hudson from preschool. She texted you."

Noah patted his pocket and pulled out his cell phone. "Crap. Yeah, I can get Hud. Put Vickie through if she's still holding."

"Yes, sir."

Sloan wrestled her purse over her body and stood. "Sorry, I didn't mean to keep you."

Noah stood too. "No, it's fine. Good to see you again. I'd walk you out, but . . ." he gestured to the phone. As if on cue, it rang.

"Yeah, yeah, of course. Give Vickie my best."

"Will do." Noah smiled, but it didn't quite reach his eyes.

Sloan knew he wouldn't mention her to Vickie. That exchange was just an attempt by both of them to relieve guilt. *Nothing to hide here.*

Not that there was anything to hide. It was only a touch. Nothing else happened. Nothing else *would have* happened. Even so, Sloan couldn't bring herself to make eye contact with the receptionist as she left the station.

Sloan waited till Caroline was asleep to find Leo Jackson's number. She had to hear his version of events herself.

He told her he couldn't remember much about the would-be kidnapper's appearance. Just that he was average height, thin, and wore a black hoodie. Eddie Daughtry was average height and thin, but Leo was certain he would have recognized him.

And though Leo had set off the alarm, he called off the cops at her mother's pleading. He said Caroline had been hysterical and practically got on her hands and knees to beg, claiming involving the police would only put Sloan in more danger.

"She said she had a plan to get you to safety, but when I saw her a few months later and asked, she seemed to have no idea what I was talking about." Leo sighed into the phone. "She already had those mind troubles then."

Mind troubles. That was an awfully nice way to put it. But it made Sloan wonder if this was the event that set her mom off. When Sloan remembered those days . . . Ridge's disappearance, his funeral, and Daddy's trial, she recalled her mom's strength, her strange calmness. Something had stolen that strength. Sloan had always assumed it was a gradual change, but what if it wasn't? What if this event was the tipping point?

"I was always worried about you after that, Sloan," Leo told her. "But you were always with the Dawsons, so I figured you were in excellent hands."

She *had* been in excellent hands with Noah and his family. Sloan wondered why she'd never told them about what happened at Leo's. What other memories from those difficult days had Sloan blocked out?

Sloan turned on her laptop and googled Eddie Daughtry. A slew of newspaper articles appeared, but all with the same information.

Sloan needed to talk to Dylan Lawrence again and ask him more questions. But his number was unlisted, and she wasn't up to going through Felicity right now.

Sloan stared again at Daughtry's mugshot. But this face was unfamiliar; it unearthed no repressed memories, just a burning sensation in her gut at the thought of what he'd done to Dylan, to Logan, possibly even to Ridge.

Sloan pushed the computer away and pulled out the copies Noah had given her from Ridge's file.

A grainy photo of her brother on the first page took her breath away. This was the picture plastered all over town those first few days when Ridge was still considered a missing person. It wasn't the last picture they had of him, but a good close-up of his face—his missing front tooth, the scar above his left eyebrow, and the blond hair creeping past his ears. This was the image America saw, the only Ridge Hadfield they'd ever know. They'd all forgotten about that gap-tooth grin and shaggy hair, but Sloan never would. A few tears dripped onto the page as she pushed it aside and flipped through the court records.

First was a statement from Caroline detailing the morning of the disappearance. Sloan didn't like remembering that day, but she owed it to Ridge to read everything, to analyze it until she found the truth.

*Detective Peterson: Thank you for agreeing to meet, Mrs. Hadfield.*

*Caroline: It's Radel, actually. Caroline Radel.*

*Detective Peterson: Sorry, Ms. Radel. Can you tell us a little about the morning of November 6th?*

*Caroline: The boys were going fishing, so I got up early to pack a lunch. We ate breakfast. It was all very usual.*

*Detective Peterson: Can you describe Mr. Hadfield's disposition that morning?*

*Caroline: Well, Jay wasn't thrilled about going. It had all been my idea. Something I put together. God, this is all my fault.*

*Detective Peterson: No one can blame you, Ms. Radel. Would you like to pause the interview for a moment?*

*Caroline: No, I'm okay. Sorry. I just keep remembering that Ridge didn't want to go. Jay and Ridge were never close, so I hoped this would be good for them.*

*Detective Peterson: You say they weren't close. Can you elaborate?*

*Caroline: Ridge was a mama's boy. That bothered Jay. He just wasn't the son Jay hoped for. Not athletic or adventurous. He was a smart and gentle boy. That's what they were fighting about that morning. Ridge wanted to throw the fish back because he didn't want to hurt them.*

*Detective Peterson: I'm going to back up here a bit. There was a fight that morning? You said earlier it was a normal morning.*

*Caroline: Oh, well, it was a normal morning. I can't recall many mornings when there wasn't some sort of disagreement between Jay and Ridge.*

Sloan stopped. She didn't remember a fight that morning. In her memories, Ridge was mopey, but their father had been in a great mood. There had been no fight that morning and certainly not every morning.

"Whatcha looking at?" a voice boomed behind her.

Sloan barely caught herself from falling out of the chair. "Mom! What are you doing up?" Sloan realized the answer. She'd been so distracted, she'd forgotten to give Caroline the Doxepin.

"I'm just thirsty."

"Okay, let me get you some water." Sloan filled a glass and glanced over her shoulder before digging the pill bottle from the back of the cabinet. Caroline was staring at the computer in an almost trance-like state.

Sloan used her body as a shield as she broke open the capsule and shook the powder into the cup.

"Here you go." Sloan twirled the cup around a few times before handing it to her mother.

But instead of taking the cup, Caroline knocked it out of Sloan's hand. Glass shattered across the tile.

"What the hell are you slipping me?" Caroline asked.

Sloan's muscles tensed. "Just something to help you sleep."

"You mean something to tranquilize me?" Caroline jammed a finger into Sloan's chest. "I don't want any meds."

Sloan stepped back. "I'm sorry. Just go to bed, and I'll clean up the mess."

"No, I got it," Caroline said, stepping into the pile of glass.

"Mom, stop!" Sloan yelled, but Caroline didn't seem bothered by the shard of glass that stuck into her foot as she stepped forward to grab Sloan's laptop off the kitchen table.

Sloan held up both hands. "Mom, you've got glass in your foot. Let me—"

But before she could finish, Caroline raised the laptop over her head and slammed it down. Bits of plastic and keyboard flew across the kitchen floor.

Sloan bent down to survey the damage. "What the hell, Mom?"

"I saw what you were looking at. I don't want to see that man's face ever again."

"Eddie?" Sloan asked. "Eddie Daughtry's face?" She stood and met her mother's eyes. They had gone wide, with the white showing all around the iris. "How do you know Eddie Daughtry?"

"It's all over the news. Everybody knows who he is and what he did," Caroline said.

"I don't believe you." Sloan fought to keep her voice steady. "I think you knew about Eddie Daughtry a long time ago."

Caroline pounded her hands on the table. "I recognize him from the news!"

"Did he take Ridge?"

Sloan shrieked as Caroline grabbed a clump of her hair and pulled. "Don't talk about Ridge!" Caroline screamed. She released Sloan's hair, causing her to stumble forward. "And why are you reading this?" She picked up the police interview from the table.

Sloan smoothed her hair down. "Because the police missed something."

"Your brother is fine." Caroline lifted her foot and pulled out the broken glass. "I talk to him at the creek."

"I understand," Sloan lowered her voice, choosing words that might calm her mother. "And if he's alive, Dad didn't kill him. It means something else happened. Why don't you sit down, and we can talk about it?"

But Caroline didn't sit; she stared down at the laptop. Miraculously, it was still on. The glass hadn't shattered, but a big black shape like an inkblot covered half of the screen. All that remained visible was the face of Eddie Daughtry.

"Did you know crows never forget a face?" Caroline asked quietly.

Sloan shook her head. This was good. Nothing calmed her mother like crows.

"Captured crows remember the faces of their abductors forever." Caroline's eyes left the broken laptop. "A group has been studying this up in Seattle. They had two masks: caveman and Dick Cheney. They wore the caveman ones to trap the crows." Caroline's voice grew louder and her gestures more demonstrative as she continued. "The crows left the researchers alone when they were in the Cheney mask, but when the birds saw that caveman face, they howled, Sloan. They screeched, dive-bombed, and attacked. Months later, even."

"Sounds like they have excellent memories," Sloan said.

"It's not just their memory. Some crows that harassed the researchers in the dangerous masks were not even present during the initial trapping; some weren't even born. Crows not only hold grudges; they tell others; they pass their grievances down to their offspring."

Sloan wondered what her mother was trying to tell her. Just another random fact about crows or something deeper? She took a chance.

"Do you remember that face, Mom?" Sloan pointed down at the computer. "Is Eddie Daughtry your man in the caveman mask?"

"What are you talking about?"

"He took Ridge. He tried to take me. Didn't he?"

When Caroline's hand met her cheek, it transported Sloan back to her teenage years. This was all familiar. The burning cheek, the burning rage inside of Sloan. Before she had time to react, her mom stomped over to the computer, raised her foot, and brought it down onto the screen, shattering it completely this time.

"That's enough!" Sloan grabbed her mother's arm, but she shook free.

Caroline moved around the kitchen, tearing up the police report, knocking dishes off the table, and breaking the flour canister into the sink.

"I'm calling the cops!" Sloan pulled out her cell phone. "They will readmit you to the hospital."

But Caroline was undeterred. She pushed past Sloan into the living room, knocking pictures from walls and tossing throw pillows off the couch, her voice growing hoarse from screaming. Sloan expected her to run when she reached the front door, but she sat and banged her head against the frame. Harder and harder until drops of blood splattered on the white door.

Sloan's hands shook as she began dialing Noah's number. She stopped halfway through, remembering his warning. *Don't contact me this late again.* She cleared the number and dialed 911 instead.

Sloan's eyelids kept involuntarily closing, so she went to bed without cleaning up the mess. The hospital couldn't keep her mom long; psychiatric holds were seventy hours max but rarely lasted longer than overnight. Sloan was as familiar with that procedure as she was with the burn of a just-slapped cheek.

As she swept the shards of glass and computer parts into the dustpan the next morning, she thought about her mother's reaction to seeing the photo of Eddie Daughtry, about the darkness that had crossed her eyes as she stomped on the screen. There was something personal behind that darkness.

Sloan jumped at the sound of the doorbell. She caught her reflection in the microwave and hoped it wasn't Noah at the door.

She was surprised to see Dylan Lawrence on the porch. He seemed thrown by her rattled appearance but recovered with a smile. "Hey, Sloan. Sorry to just stop by, but I didn't have your number and wanted to talk. Is this a bad time?"

Sloan glanced behind her. It was a terrible time, but with all her questions, she wasn't about to let him leave. "Well, if you think I'm a mess, just wait till you see the living room."

Dylan grinned. "I can come back later."

"No, come in. I've wanted to talk to you too." Sloan ushered him inside.

Dylan took off his sunglasses and glanced around. "Is it okay to ask what happened?"

"Hurricane Caroline." Sloan rubbed her forehead. "AKA my mother. She's . . . um . . . well, she's crazy." Sloan lowered herself onto the loveseat. "We can sit here."

Dylan sat next to her. Sloan expected him to speak first, but after almost a minute, Sloan broke through the uncomfortable silence.

"So, did you remember something or—"

Dylan's cheeks flushed. "Right. Sorry. Before I tell you, please understand it's nothing earth-shattering. But I've been thinking about Ridge's story, and I want to help if I can."

"Go on," Sloan coaxed.

"The FBI has got me going over timelines, and I remembered something. Well, it may be something, may be nothing." Dylan rubbed his hands down his pants legs. "I probably shouldn't even say anything."

Sloan touched his knee. "It's okay, Dylan." Her touch seemed to calm his nervous energy. "I won't share anything you don't want me to. And I won't be angry if it turns out to be nothing."

Dylan smiled. He looked young for his age and especially when he smiled. How he still kept such a sweet smile given all he'd been through was a miracle.

"When Eddie took me, Logan had already been there five years." Dylan leaned forward and held his head in his hands. "This is tough to talk about, but Eddie made a lot of money recording videos and selling them. Early on, he made me watch one of Logan and another boy."

Sloan noticed Dylan's hands were shaking. "You don't have to tell me this if it's too much," she said.

"No, I need to." Dylan raised his head. "This isn't like me, to share personal things. But when they found Logan's remains, something inside me just woke up. I realized I couldn't change what happened to us, but I could make sure Eddie Daughtry was held accountable. Make sure he didn't hurt anyone else."

"You're incredibly brave," Sloan said.

Dylan shook his head. "No. I'm having a moment of bravery after sixteen years of being a coward."

Sloan wanted to tell him a moment of bravery mattered. That it was more than she'd ever had. She'd rarely talked about her childhood with her own husband, much less the media, much less a complete stranger, but she kept quiet, giving Dylan room to speak.

"So, the video . . ." Dylan squeezed his eyes shut. "There was Logan and a younger kid. I asked Logan who the boy was and what happened to him."

Sloan sensed where this was going and felt a sharp pain in her stomach. She didn't want it to be Ridge in that video. The creek was better.

"Logan said the boy had been there about four years ago, and that Eddie sold him to some perv in Louisiana."

"*Sold?*" Sloan pressed her hands against her stomach. "Was that boy Ridge?"

Dylan met her eyes. "I'm not sure, Sloan." His voice was fragile. "Logan told me not to worry. Said the boy only got sold because he was young and that nobody would pay Eddie that much for sixteen and seventeen-year-olds." Dylan leaned forward, resting his head on his hands. "This sounds so screwed up, but in Logan's mind, and eventually my own, Eddie took care of us. We had food, beds, and heroin. So, it was a case of the devil you know being better than the devil you don't."

Sloan put her hand on Dylan's back. "I'm so sorry. I'm just so sorry."

Dylan turned his head toward her. "I hope it wasn't your brother."

"But the timeline fits. Four years before would've been 1988." The air conditioner kicked on. Sloan rubbed at her exposed forearms. "Do they have any other leads on who else it might be?"

"There were no other boys reported missing from this area in that time frame, but the feds have found Eddie had connections in at least three other states. So, the kid could have come from anywhere. Eddie had a lot of victims. He held at least three of us captive; some, he'd pick up off the street and have them home for dinner. Others came to him, knowing he kept bags of quarters for the arcade in the kitchen drawer and willing to do whatever it took to get them. He never got caught. Eddie's smart. Smart enough to set up your dad."

"Did you tell the FBI this? That the boy in the video could be Ridge?" Sloan asked.

"Not yet, but I will. They say the simplest explanation is usually the answer. So maybe your brother really died in the water that day. But it's best to assume nothing is simple when men like Eddie Daughtry are in this world."

"Are they looking for that video?"

"Yeah. As much as I hope it's been destroyed, if it hasn't, then we'll know."

"We'll know," Sloan repeated.

"I looked at Ridge's picture again online, but I just don't remember. I'm sorry."

"I've been doing the same with pictures of Eddie Daughtry," Sloan said. "Me obsessing over his picture . . . that's what caused all this." She motioned around the demolished room.

"How so?"

"I'm not sure," Sloan said. "Something's going on. When a man tried to abduct me, Mom didn't want to call the police. She told the shop owner bad men were after me. That she was going to take me away; only, she never did."

"You think she knows what happened to your brother and was worried it could happen to you too?" Dylan asked.

"I don't know. My mom's a fighter. She wouldn't have let it rest if she found out what had happened or even had an inkling."

"Maybe she had to. I know that sounds crazy, but Eddie has this way of keeping you scared. She might have been worried for your life."

Sloan shook her head. "She wouldn't sacrifice Ridge for me. She probably didn't want to see Eddie's picture for the reason the rest of us don't—because he's a sick pedophile."

"It's possible," Dylan said. "But this," he gestured around the room, "seems a little personal."

"I wish I could just ask Eddie. I mean, they've already got enough to put him away for life, right? So, he might tell the truth about Ridge, especially if he got something out of the deal."

Dylan's face went white. "Please don't contact him. He's an animal." Sloan noticed Dylan fidgeting again, dry-washing his hands. "Leave this to law enforcement."

"Right. Bad idea." Sloan glanced at the clock. "I hate to cut this short, but I'm expecting a call anytime to pick up my mom, and I'd like to get the house cleaned up before."

Dylan stood. "Yeah, sorry."

"No, I'm so glad you came." Sloan rose to meet him. "I've been wanting to talk to you again but didn't want to go through Felicity. That probably sounds horrible, but I don't want a relationship with her."

Dylan pushed his hands into his pocket. "Yeah. I wanted to talk to you without her too, so I found your address."

"Really? Wow. I'm horrible at reading people because I sorta thought you liked her."

Dylan's cheeks reddened. "Liked, liked her? No way. I mean, I'm sure she's a great person, but she's just too, I don't know, too happy."

Sloan laughed. "Well, this is a first. My dismal disposition has made me a preferable companion."

"Hey, we unhappy people need to stick together," Dylan said, his smile contradicting any claim of unhappiness at that moment. He bent down to retrieve a throw pillow from the floor. "Mind if I help you clean up a little?"

"Oh no, you don't have to do that," Sloan said.

"This is going to sound like a lie, but I enjoy cleaning. My therapist says I use cleaning and organization as coping mechanisms—a way to gain control of certain aspects of my life." He shrugged. "Makes sense. I mean, if you can't organize your thoughts, organize your sock drawer."

Sloan smiled as she handed him the broom. "All right then. Let's get to work."

# Chapter 14

*Mallowater, TX, 2008*

When Sloan's phone vibrated with a text notification that afternoon, she hoped it was Dylan. He'd left only an hour earlier, but she missed his company.

Maybe it was those River Phoenix vibes he gave off to blame, but Sloan couldn't get Dylan Lawrence out of her head. The last thing she needed was a crush on a man in the center of a media storm. A crush on a man who was only beginning to come to terms with the horrific trauma and abuse he'd endured. What a screwed-up pair they'd make.

But when Sloan checked her phone, she saw Liam's name. It still stung. Another reminder that the last thing she needed right now was a crush on anyone.

*Good news! House sold for asking price. Closing in July, and you'll get your half. You'll have to be here to sign. Final Decree's filed. Community property sold. Lawyer will send you a check for your half. Hope you are having a nice summer!*

Sloan threw her phone on the pillow beside her. She was glad the house sold, but Liam knew *a nice summer* was impossible, given why she had come to Mallowater. Though Sloan bet *he* was having a nice summer shacked up at Megan's.

Sloan opened the phone book to the yellow pages and found the ad for *Hadfield and Espinoza, Attorneys at Law.* She looked at the tiny picture of Brad Hadfield in the advertisement.

Brad Hadfield, her brother. Brother. The word echoed through her head as she dialed. Would Ridge have looked anything like him? *Did Ridge look anything like him?*

"Hadfield and Espinoza Attorneys at Law. Can I help you?"

Sloan cleared her throat. "Yes, I need to speak to Brad, please?"

"May I ask whose calling?"

"This is his sister." The word left a nasty taste in Sloan's mouth.

Sloan's hands began to sweat as she waited for Brad. She didn't want to do this, but she didn't know who else could help.

"Felicity?" A hint of worry laced Brad's voice.

"No, sorry. It's Sloan."

There was the briefest silence before Brad spoke. "Sloan. Wow. Thanks for calling. Felicity told me she met with you, and I hoped you might reach out."

"Felicity doesn't know I'm calling," Sloan said. "But long story short, I found out some more information that makes me question everything I thought happened to Ridge."

Brad lowered his voice. "Do you want to meet somewhere and talk? Come up with a plan?"

"I already have a plan. I just need help."

"Oh . . . yeah, okay. Whatever you need."

"I need to see Eddie Daughtry," she blurted.

"You what?" Brad's voice lost its professionalism.

"I just want to ask him a few things."

"There's no way his lawyer will allow that. Daughtry's awaiting trial."

"You're a lawyer. Talk to his lawyer. Figure out a way."

Brad chuckled. "I'm an estate planning lawyer, Sloan."

Sloan felt a headache coming on. She unclenched her jaw to speak. "Well, you must have connections, right? I need you to call them in. I realize Dad's getting out either way, but we have a chance to find out the truth."

"So glad to hear you want to clear Dad's name." Brad's voice turned friendly again. "Have you visited him?"

Sloan tipped her head back. She somehow suspected the conversation might go here. Whether or not he committed murder, there was no clearing that man's name. "Not yet."

"But I'm assuming you will? I have to tell you, Sloan, it's broken Dad's heart not to see you. Not that he blames you. I mean, he and my brother were estranged for years. But Kyle's come around, and I sort of hoped you had too."

Sloan didn't know what to say. Why didn't she want to see her dad again if she believed he was innocent? Guilt, awkwardness, and still anger. Fierce, fiery, anger. The anger had never been about whether her father killed Ridge, not really. If he'd done it, Sloan understood it had been an accident. But having two families, well, that was no side effect of anything Jay Hadfield saw in the hostile jungles of Vietnam.

"Sloan? Are you still there?"

"Sorry, yeah. I'll see him. Work out whatever."

"Great!" Sloan heard papers shuffling. "I'll get your email address and send you the paperwork as soon as I get it from the prison."

"Sounds good . . . now, about Eddie. I realize seeing him won't be easy. Maybe this is unethical, but I have some money coming in, and if that's what it takes for Eddie to talk, I'm willing to use it for our advantage."

"So, you really think Eddie took Ridge?" Brad asked.

"Yeah, I do." Sloan straightened her back against the hard kitchen chair. "I can fill you in if it's a lead you want to pursue with me. Felicity wants to help, but it's probably best not to bring her into Eddie's world."

There was a good minute of silence. Sloan would have thought they'd been disconnected if not for the hum of the copy machine in the background.

"Brad?" she finally said.

"Okay, I'm in," he said in a harsh whisper. "I'm all in."

Sloan drove to the prison alone, Keith Whitley's tape blaring and the windows down. She wasn't ready for this. But she never would be. Brad was doing his part in trying to set up a meeting with Daughtry; she needed to do what she agreed to do.

She reminded herself that it was better to visit him here in prison. There were rules—spaces and times were defined.

Yet, as soon as she sat in the waiting room, it felt like a terrible idea. All the memories, fears, and confusion she'd experienced on her last visit flooded back. She had promised her father she'd be back Friday. A Friday that never came. Sloan heard a roaring in her ears and lost track of what the guard was telling her. She was eyeing the room for an exit when she spotted her father being escorted into the room.

Sloan froze at the sight of him. He was older, grayer, with deep wrinkles around his eyes. Rectangular glasses sat a bit too low on his nose. His arms were bigger, and his hair was longer—but it was her dad. The sight of him made her angry and homesick at the same time.

"Sloan!" Jay's voice shook. He stepped forward, holding out his arms. Sloan took a step backward. She caught the pained expression on her father's face, but he recovered quickly. "I didn't expect you to come. Bradley told me, but I didn't let myself believe it till I saw you."

Sloan couldn't help but smile at her father's voice. "You may look different, but you sound the same."

Jay laughed as they sat. "I've even got my Jersey cellmate speaking with a southern drawl."

"Well, I'd recognize your voice anywhere."

"I know what you mean." Her father leaned forward as if he were going to tell her a secret. "I was a little worried I wouldn't be able to spot you when they brought me in. It's been a long time, but my eyes moved right to you, like a magnet." He adjusted his glasses. "Those eyes, I could pick 'em out of a lineup. They're your mother's eyes."

Sloan pushed her tongue into her cheek. "This is hard. I don't know how to let it all go."

"Understood." Her father's voice came as soft as his blue-eyed gaze. "I never expected you or your mother to forgive me. Nor Anna and the other kids. Kyle and I didn't speak for years. He even changed his last name."

Blood rushed to Sloan's head at the mention of Anna and her children. She leaned away from the table. "How could you do that to us all?"

Jay raised his hands and let them fall. "I was selfish. Young. Stupid. I loved Anna, but your mother . . ." He smiled as though remembering. "Instant electricity." He snapped his fingers. "I told myself it was only an affair, but I couldn't let Caroline go."

"And you thought you could keep two women, keep two families forever?"

"No. It was always my plan to leave Anna. I swear, I tried. But she's a saint. I couldn't hurt her."

"In retrospect, don't you think it would have hurt her less if you left her then? Before all that came after?"

"Probably." Jay raised his chin. "But despite everything, we've been happy together. We are *still* happy. I'm sure that's difficult for you to hear, but Anna is my wife, and till death do us part, she will be."

Sloan crossed her arms. "And so, Mom was what?"

"The love of my life," her father answered. "I think of Caroline all the time."

"Wow." Sloan heard the edge in her laughter. "Do you realize how selfish you sound?"

"Of course I do." Her father scrubbed his hands over his face. "Try to put yourself in my shoes. That last letter you sent said you were getting married. Well, imagine that today somebody walked into your life, and you connected." He snapped his fingers again. Right person, wrong time. Could you just let him go?"

Sloan's mind went to Dylan, and her cheeks burned. "Yes, I could." She held up her left hand, displaying her empty ring finger. "Not that I'd have to."

Jay inflated his cheeks like balloons. "Sorry. I didn't know."

"You'd relate to him." Sloan's tone was scathing. "Liam met someone else, and there was just a connection." She mockingly snapped her fingers. "At least he had the decency to divorce me instead of attempting some sort of polygamist lifestyle."

Jay brought a hand to his chest. "I make no excuses for anything I've done. I've considered a million times how different my life would be now if I hadn't taken that business trip."

"You should have divorced Anna—given us all a chance at normal lives."

He scooted his chair closer to the table. "I've learned there are two kinds of love. There's the kind that sets the world on fire, and there's the kind that walks with you *through* fire. As sorry as I am, I can't wish either of them away. Look, Sloan. I was far from perfect, but I tried to do my best for all of you."

His best? Sloan stared at her father. What a flawed, selfish man. What a stark contrast to the image she'd held of him during her childhood. Yet, he'd always been this flawed man, even then. She just hadn't known.

He reached across the table, placing his hand on hers. "Penny for your thoughts?"

*Pennies, Blockbuster Video, Pizza Hut, Friday night sitcoms, camping at Crow's Nest Creek, dancing to Keith Whitley.* The memories brought Sloan to tears. "It seemed so real."

"What did?"

"Our family."

He squeezed her hand. "It *was* real. Every second was real. Don't you ever doubt that."

Sloan shook her head. "But—"

"But nothing." He raised his voice. "Jay, Caroline, Sloan, and Ridge. That was real. We *were* a family. We still *are* a family. Yes, your mother hates me, and yes, Ridge is gone—"

"What if he's not gone?" Sloan blurted out. "I mean, he's gone, but I'm not sure he's dead." Sloan released her father's hand to blow her nose into a Kleenex.

"Yeah, Bradley filled me in. I still can't remember what happened that day." He poked his forehead with his thumb. "I've tried therapy, hypnosis, everything. But I can't remember." His chin quivered. "I should've gotten help back then. Caroline told me I needed help. But nobody knew much about PTSD in the eighties."

"That's clear from the verdict. I've been reading through your trial transcript. Your lawyer did a terrible job. Why didn't you ever appeal?" Sloan asked.

"No way I was spending money on a better lawyer when it could go to you kids."

Sloan leaned back in her chair. "*All* of us kids?"

"Anna tried, Sloan. We didn't have much, but when money started coming in from the community, I wanted your mother to have some of it. Caroline refused to even speak to Anna." He tugged at his earlobe. "Not that I blame her."

Sloan cleared her throat. "So, did Brad tell you my theory?"

"Yeah, Eddie Daughtry." He looked over his shoulder. "He's here, you know? Daughtry. They've got him away from the general population, so I can't talk to him."

"Working on that," Sloan said. "Well, Brad is."

Jay leaned forward. "Seven years ago, I got a letter from a man doing time in Huntsville. Claimed that his cellmate, a guy named Reid Hunt, confessed to kidnapping Ridge. I turned the letter over, but they said his claims were unfounded. He never lived in Mallowater, and he had a history of false confessions."

"But why confess to a crime that's already solved? And so many years later?" Sloan asked.

"The *People* magazine article. Not sure if you saw, but *People* interviewed Anna and the kids in 2000."

An accidental laugh escaped Sloan's lips. "Yeah, I saw it."

"Right, of course you did. Anyway, a friend has some connections on the outside and heard Reid Hunt is being questioned in the Pruitt abduction. They think he may have been Daughtry's accomplice."

"Reid Hunt," Sloan repeated, cementing his name into her mind. "I'll ask Dylan about him."

"Don't get your hopes up," Jay said. "Stories like Dylan's, they're rare. Bradley says stranger abductions are unusual, and when they *do* happen, the child is almost always . . ." he stopped and blew out a breath . . . "always killed within a day."

Sloan remembered the torn piece of Ridge's shirt, his blood, and the shoe recovered from the water. All the evidence suggested he'd been killed and dumped in the creek. But maybe that's what Reid or Eddie wanted everyone to assume.

"Even if they realize I'm innocent, it won't bring your brother back."

Sloan drummed her fingers on the table. "We know Eddie took Logan and Dylan and that he abused others. I don't think it's reaching to assume he had something to do with Ridge's disappearance. But whether Ridge ended up like Dylan or Logan, that's what I am going to find out."

"I want Ridge to be alive too. But if he's alive, where is he?" Jay asked. "Why has he never visited your mother?"

Sloan grimaced. "Mom claims he has. Claims he's come back to her as a crow. She's probably out at the creek right now talking to some poor bird."

Jay shifted in his chair. "It's a shame what's happened to your mother. Once I get out, I'll help you figure something out for her."

"I can take care of Mom," Sloan said.

"Maybe you can, but that doesn't mean you *should*. Doesn't mean it's your responsibility. It *is* possible to be loyal to a fault." He pointed to her shirt. "That's why you're a Detroit Lions fan."

Sloan looked down at her faded blue and gray t-shirt, washed so many times that you could barely see the outline of the lion. "This is old."

"Ah. So, you've given up on them? Realized it's a lost cause?"

Sloan crossed her arms over her chest. "They actually started strong last year. Were 6-2 at the halfway mark. Just had a rough end to the season."

Jay smacked the table and pointed at Sloan. "That's my girl. Loyal."

"Okay, okay. But I've been more loyal to the Lions than Mom. I don't want to stay here, but I hoped I could convince her to return to the treatment facility. Kinda like I've been *hoping* Ridge is alive." Sloan rubbed her forehead. "All this hoping is out of character for me. There's a better chance of Ridge being a crow than alive."

"Hey, now." Jay held up a finger. "I'd never tell you not to hope, Lo. Hope might as well be my middle name, but being *too* hopeful and not living in reality can get you into trouble. Just ask me and my literary namesake, Jay Gatsby."

Sloan grinned. "That green light's a bitch, isn't it?"

Jay's eyes crinkled at the corners as he laughed. "Sometimes, yeah. But occasionally, hope pays off." He reached into the chest pocket of his orange jumpsuit and pulled out a familiar cassette. "You promised you'd be back on Friday, and we'd talk about this here Keith Whitley album." He raised his eyebrows. "Well, it's a Friday, and we've still got time."

"Twenty years later," Sloan said.

"Hell, that's alright. Keith Whitley don't go out of style." He set the tape between them. "Now, let's talk favorite songs on Side A."

When Sloan returned to the car, she was met with Keith Whitley singing just where he'd left off before she went into the prison. She turned the music up. For the first time, the lyrics didn't fill her with overwhelming sadness. She'd left the meeting cautiously optimistic about a future relationship with her father. The anger had always been a boot on Sloan's chest, slowly suffocating her. Though she still felt it, the heaviness had lifted just enough for her to catch a breath.

Sloan needed to get home. The sun would set soon, and Caroline would return from the creek. Then it would be up to Sloan to measure her words and actions to keep from setting her mother off. Even sleep didn't give Sloan a reprieve as it once had. It was harder to slip the pills to Caroline now that she knew about them, so neither of them was sleeping well. Every groan of her mom's bed or creak of the bathroom door awoke Sloan. She imagined this is how it must feel to be a mother of a newborn—one who might sneak off to Crow's Nest Creek in the dark of night.

So instead of going home, Sloan drove in the opposite direction. She'd listen to the entire tape and then turn around. She needed to sort out her thoughts after a whirlwind few days.

Sloan had driven an hour outside of Mallowater when her phone rang. *Mom*, she bet. Home from the creek, wondering what was for dinner. Sloan should have turned around when the tape ended, but driving with no destination in mind had been therapeutic. When Sloan picked up her phone, a much more welcome name flashed on her screen.

"Dylan." Sloan tried to temper her voice. "Hi."

"Hey, Sloan." Something about the way he said her name made the hairs on the nape of her neck rise. "I just wanted to call to see how things were going. I mean, with your mom and everything."

"Mom's okay." Sloan spotted a gas station and pulled into the parking lot. She wanted to focus on Dylan, not the road ahead. "Maybe okay is the wrong word, but it's been three days and no broken flour jars in the sink."

"Well, if it happens again, just remember not to rinse it down the drain with water."

Sloan groaned. "Yeah. I almost made Elmer's Glue. Thank God you were there."

"Yeah." Dylan's voice softened. "I'm glad I was there."

Sloan leaned forward onto the steering wheel. "I'd invite you back," she said, "But well, my mother."

"That's why I'm calling. I mean, not your mother, but . . . sorry. Let me start over." Dylan took in a sharp breath. "I was wondering if you'd like to go to dinner sometime. And not to talk about Ridge. I mean, we can, but we don't have to."

Sloan bit down on a laugh. He was so adorably awkward. "Yeah, for sure. Tell me when and where."

"Um, well, I noticed you ordered pasta at Applebee's, so does that mean you like Italian food? I heard that new place, L'Ultima Cena, is good."

"That sounds great."

"Should I pick you up or . . . ?"

"I'll meet you there." Sloan was nowhere near ready to explain Dylan to her mom nor introduce them.

"Great!" Dylan's voice sounded giddy. "Is tomorrow night too soon? At 7:00?"

At that moment, tomorrow night didn't seem soon enough. Sloan wanted to see Dylan now, to share about the meeting with her dad and to talk through her mixed emotions. But given that she'd only been legally divorced a few weeks, this was the very definition of a rebound. She needed to keep her head. "Sure. See you at 7:00."

Sloan hung up and slumped against the seat. Despite her sense that a date with Dylan Lawrence was not what she needed, she couldn't calm the fluttering in her chest.

"Coffee," she said aloud. Coffee ought to sober her up. Remind her that she was not a lovesick teenager, but a woman who knew better.

She was almost to the door of the By and Buy convenience store when she stopped in front of the commercial ice freezer. It used to be on the other side of the door, and there was a payphone here instead. Sloan wondered how she knew that. Had she been here often as a child? She couldn't imagine why she would have been. They rarely left Mallowater.

The inside of the store was familiar too, but no different from any other convenience store. It smelled like Lemon Pine-Sol and grease from the hot dog machine on the counter. She passed the aisles of pain relievers, snacks, and impulse buys on her way to the self-serve coffee area, unable to shake the strangest sensation of déjà vu. As she prepared her drink, she stared at the wall of built-in coolers in front of her.

*Lunchables*, she remembered. There had been Lunchables there, and she'd bought one. A ham and cheese Lunchable, a bag of Cool Ranch Doritos, and a Slice Soda. How was she remembering this? *Why* was she remembering this?

Sloan overfilled her foam cup, and coffee spilled over, burning the top of her hand. "Shit!" She jerked her hand back and blew on it. Suddenly, the shop was loud. Next to her, someone tapped a straw on the counter to break the wrapper, while ice clanged into his cup. The slush machine roared as a small child pleaded for the big cup, not the small one. The vacuum seal on a refrigerated case broke open as a woman pulled on the door handle, then reached in for a drink, causing other bottles to slide forward.

Sloan stepped back, leaving her coffee on the counter. Her throat tightened, and her hands wouldn't stop shaking. Then, for no discernable reason, she started to cry.

Sloan ran out of the store, gulping in the night's fresh air. A sharp pain permeated through her chest. She stumbled into her car and reached for her cell phone.

*The payphone. The Lunchable and bag of Doritos, ice strewn across the concrete.* She realized why she felt a strange familiarity here. Suddenly, she understood her sense of panic. She remembered this place.

She remembered everything.

# Chapter 15

*Mallowater, TX, 1989*

Sharp white light stung Sloan's eyes as she fought to keep them open. "Come on!" Mom shook her harder. "Get up and get dressed. Wear something comfortable."

Sloan sat up in bed, disoriented. Through a crack in her curtains, she saw the darkness outside. She rubbed her eyes. "It's the middle of the night. Turn my light off."

Mom pulled a pink vinyl suitcase from the closet and threw it onto the floor. *Going to Grandma's* was written on it above a cartoon girl with two pigtails. Sloan had never liked that suitcase, even when she wasn't too old to be carrying it. The girl on it had bright blonde hair, the kind everyone in the family except Sloan had. Besides, it wasn't like Sloan ever had a grandma to visit.

"Pack it," her mother said. "Clothes only. Anything else you want needs to fit in your backpack."

Sloan threw her legs over the side of the bed. "I'm not going anywhere unless you tell me what's going on."

"Have you forgotten what happened at Leo's? Get packed!" Before leaving the room, Mom grabbed Sloan's blanket off her bed and Ridge's beloved stuffed animal off his.

"Why are you taking Blue?"

"Because we may not be back," Mom snapped. "Now get moving. You have ten minutes."

Sloan kicked the stupid pink suitcase back into the closet and reached up to grab a plain black duffle bag that had belonged to Ridge. She put on a pair of sweats and stuffed what she could into the bag. Her mother's words echoed in her head as she stared at the Christian Slater poster above the dresser. *We may not be back.*

She turned her school backpack upside down and shook it, emptying her Trapper Keeper, broken pencils, and several elaborately folded notes from her classmates the year before. She replaced them with her pink cassette player and some tapes, grabbing all her favorites—Michael Jackson, New Kids on the Block, Reba McEntire, Tiffany, and of course, Keith Whitley.

There was still some room, so she grabbed her makeup bag, piggy bank, and the tattered paperback copy of *The Firebrand* from her nightstand. She pulled open the bottom drawer of the nightstand and retrieved a few birthday cards from her grandpa, trying to ignore the ones from her dad. Underneath the pictures, she glimpsed a photo album, a picture of her and Noah displayed through the circle in the front. Noah. Was she really going to leave without saying goodbye?

"Earth to Sloan!" Mom poked her head into the room. "Why are you just sitting there? Five minutes." She held up five fingers as if Sloan needed a visual.

Four minutes later, Caroline shoved Sloan's things in the back of their Ford Escort as Sloan situated herself in the passenger seat. Behind her, stacks of boxes were nestled among their suitcases and a small safe Sloan had never seen. Her mother must have been packing all night. When was she going to explain what was going on? Sloan thought about the man at Leo's and pushed down the lock on the passenger door.

"Birth certificates, social security cards, water, blankets, cash . . ." Caroline recited a long list to herself as she climbed into the driver's seat. "Am I forgetting anything?"

"That depends on where we're going." Sloan's voice was brittle.

Caroline reached over and pushed Sloan's bangs out of her face. "I'm not trying to scare you, but we're in danger. We can't involve the police."

"Why? That's what the police are for. To help people in danger."

"They can't help us. Not with this. I have a plan." Her mother started the car. "You don't need to worry."

"What about the rest of our stuff?" Sloan asked.

"I may come back and get it, but it all depends." She sighed. "I understand this is difficult, but you are going to have to trust me."

Sloan stared at the small, white-paneled house through her tears. Was this the last time she'd sleep in her bed? Sit on that brown, fuzzy, wood-framed sofa, and watch nightly sitcoms? The last time she'd get up and eat cereal on that well-scratched kitchen table?

"But what about Noah?" Sloan asked as the car reversed.

Caroline put her foot on the brake. "You can call him when it's safe."

"He'll wonder where we are. You didn't let me talk to him at all yesterday. He'll assume something terrible happened to us."

"I've got it all handled. I couldn't let you talk to him because you'd tell him about what happened Sunday at Leo's. Trust me. In one hour, everything is going to make more sense. Deal?"

*No deal,* Sloan thought, but it didn't matter what she said. She was a kid and had always known she didn't get a vote. She wiped her tears on the arm of her sweatshirt. "Okay."

Caroline reached in the back for Sloan's blanket. "We'll stop for gas in about an hour. Go back to sleep."

*Like that was possible.* "Can we turn on the radio?"

"Sure." Caroline lifted her foot off the brake. "You be our deejay."

Sloan clicked on the radio just as the clock changed to 12:16. Mom looked over her shoulder to back up, but Sloan stared straight at the driveway. The driveway where Daddy taught her to ride her bike, where she and Ridge had drawn with sidewalk chalk, where she stood in her pink dress the first day of kindergarten as her mother snapped pictures.

She faintly heard George Straight's voice coming through the speakers, "Baby's Gotten Good at Goodbye." The song seemed fitting, so she turned it up louder. Even though the song was sad, Sloan felt strangely comforted hearing about someone having as rotten of a day as she was.

The parking lot of the By and Buy wasn't as empty as Sloan expected it would be at this hour. Were there this many people in the world running from something?

Sloan assumed they were getting gas and leaving, but after her mother filled up the car, she drove to the side of the gas station and parked. "We're a little early," she said.

"For what?"

Caroline grabbed her purse. "Are you hungry?"

"Why would I be hungry at one in the morning?"

"Fine." Her mother pulled out a twenty-dollar bill and put on one of Daddy's ball caps. Sloan had never seen her wear one. "I'm going to grab a coffee. Come in if you change your mind."

Sloan locked her door and reached across the steering wheel to lock the driver's side. If Mom was concerned for Sloan's life, why was she acting so flippant about her safety? Why was she getting snacks? Sloan thought again of Noah. It was their last week of summer break. In about six hours, he'd probably be at her front door.

"So, when can I talk to Noah?" Sloan asked when her mom returned.

"Noah, Noah, Noah." Caroline set her coffee in the cup holder. "You'll talk to him soon enough, but I suspect things may look different in the light of day. Things that feel so important right now may not soon."

Sloan rolled her eyes. Nothing that happened could make her not want to talk to Noah.

"Go to sleep, Sloan. When you wake up, everything will have changed."

Sloan woke up, and nothing except the time had changed. The clock on the dash read 2:56, but they were still parked at the gas station.

"Mom?" She looked to her left and found the driver's seat empty except for a few cigarette butts. The window was rolled down, which explained the chill in the vehicle. Sloan reached over to her mom's seat to crank up the window and pulled the sleeves of her sweater over her hands.

Sloan wiped the condensation off her own window and looked out toward the gas pumps. An old man finished filling up his 18-wheeler and climbed into the cab. He saw Sloan watching and smiled, tipping his hat. Sloan's Grandpa Radel had been a truck driver. She remembered playing in his truck with Ridge when Grandpa's route brought him to Texas. He was going to retire and be a fly fisherman, but instead, he'd had a heart attack during his last week on the job.

Sloan thought about her grandad as she watched this old trucker pull away from the diesel pump. Before he left the parking lot, he and Sloan made eye contact again. She bent her arm, raised it above her head, and pulled it down. She was too old for something so silly, but she couldn't help herself. The old man smiled again and honked his horn. For some reason, the exchange left Sloan teary-eyed.

Between the resounding honk and her own memories crashing around in her brain, she didn't notice her mom until she opened the door.

"Mom, why are we still—" Sloan stopped when she turned and saw her mother. Her face was red and splotchy, with smears of mascara under her eyes. Her hands shook as she fumbled to open a new pack of cigarettes.

"Mom? What's wrong?"

"I don't know, Sloan. I don't know what's wrong," Mom said, still fighting with the cellophane. "Dammit!" she threw the cigarettes against the dash window.

Sloan reached across the vehicle to retrieve the package and unwrap it. "Here you go," Sloan said, handing her mom a single cigarette.

"Thanks." Mom's hands still shook, but she lit it. She took a quick inhale and sunk back in her seat.

"I need to use the bathroom," Sloan said. "And I'm thirsty."

"There's money in my wallet." Sloan's mother waved the cigarette toward her. "Get whatever you want. This is all a misunderstanding. It'll be okay. We'll be on the road soon," she said, her voice monotone.

Sloan used the restroom and then took her time wandering the store. She got a drink, a bag of chips, and a Lunchable. It wasn't often that her mom gave her free rein over her wallet in a store lined with wall-to-wall junk food.

As she stood in the checkout line, Sloan noticed her mom out of the vehicle again, pacing from the commercial ice freezer to the payphone, smoking. She looked like a crazy person.

When Sloan exited the store, her mom had the payphone receiver pressed against her ear. Her eyes were squeezed close, and she was tapping her foot on the concrete. After a minute, she slammed the phone down and cursed.

"Who are you trying to call?" Sloan asked gently.

"It's a misunderstanding. It'll be okay. We'll be on the road soon," her mom repeated as if in a trance.

"It's cold, Mom. Come to the car and wait. I got a Lunchable; we can split it."

"I could call the police," Caroline said, then shook her head. "No, no, I can't."

Sloan put her arm around her mother. "Come on. Let's get you in the car and warmed up. We'll call again in fifteen minutes."

"Sloan! Sloan, wake up! I need more change," Caroline said, shaking Sloan's shoulder.

Sloan rubbed her eyes. "I already checked all the seats, Mom. There's no more change."

Caroline pulled a ten-dollar bill from her purse. "We won't have time to stop. We'll have to drive all day. Go get two more Lunchables.

And tell them you want your change in coins. Quarters, nickels, and dimes only. Got it?"

"I'm not hungry."

"We won't have time to stop," her mother repeated. "We'll have to drive all day. Quarters, nickels, dimes only."

Sloan noticed a broken bag of ice scattered on the concrete in front of the store. "Mom, did you break that bag?" she asked. When no answer came, Sloan touched her mother's arm. "The clerk inside asked me about you last time I used the bathroom. I'm worried she might call the police."

Caroline rubbed her hands over her face. "I can't believe this happened. How could it happen?" She looked at Sloan as if she had given her daughter any information about how this strange night should have panned out.

"I don't know, but it's almost morning. We can figure this out later, but let's go home, please."

Caroline's chin quivered. "Yes. I guess there's nothing we can do but go home."

No matter how many times she asked, Mom never explained that bizarre, cigarette and Lunchable-filled night to Sloan. But Sloan realized that whatever had happened—or didn't happen—at that gas station changed everything. Her strong mom cried uncontrollably, quit eating, and refused to leave the house.

"I told you the grief would get her," Doreen said. "It's a sneaky thing that sadness."

Was that all this was about? Grief? Had her mother broken? Snapped?

Sloan didn't like keeping secrets from Noah. She wanted to tell him about that day at Leo's, wanted to tell him about the night at the station, but Mom said anyone they told would be in danger—that the only way she and Sloan would be safe is to forget all about it.

Forget, like that was possible.

# Chapter 16

*Mallowater, TX, 2008*

When Sloan arrived at the restaurant, Dylan was already at a table waiting for her. He stood as she approached. He wore an untucked white button-down shirt with a skinny black tie and dark blue jeans. As soon as they made eye contact, he looked at his shoes, shoving his hands into his pockets. He always seemed so unsure.

The restaurant was low-lit, with vibrant paintings covering the walls, like small windows to faraway places. Sloan hoped she wasn't underdressed; she was never sure what to wear on dates, or what to wear to certain restaurants. She'd started in jeans and a lace cami top before deciding it looked too much like lingerie and changing into a white shirt and black cropped vest.

Dylan moved around the table to pull out her chair. "Is it still okay to do this?"

"Okay with me." Sloan sat in the seat and pulled it forward to the table.

"You look amazing," Dylan said.

"Thanks." Sloan watched him walk back to his seat. "Same to you."

"We match," Dylan noted, lowering himself into his chair.

Sloan tugged at her vest. "I couldn't find anything to wear, and I realized that ninety-nine percent of my wardrobe is black. Guess I'm more prepared for funerals than dates."

"Well, you've got to be more prepared than me. I don't want to confess how long it's been since my last first date, but it would be measured in years, not months."

Sloan unrolled her silverware from the cloth napkin. "I'll take your years and see you a decade."

Dylan cocked his head. "No way."

"I met my ex-husband in 1998. So that was my last first date. We were married from 2000 till . . . well, two weeks ago."

Dylan tugged at his collar. "Two weeks. Wow. Is this maybe too soon?"

"No, not at all," Sloan said, even though she wasn't sure it was true. "We've been separated for a while." She took a sip of her water. "But I actually don't think you're supposed to talk about your exes within five minutes of a first date."

Dylan's grin was lopsided. Like the two sides of his face couldn't agree on a particular expression. "I don't think you're supposed to date someone you bonded with over shared stories of trauma either, but here we are."

"Here we are," Sloan repeated, raising her water glass in a mock toast.

As if on cue, a server arrived with the wine list. Sloan looked at Dylan to decide, but he pushed the menu toward her. "You pick."

She ordered red wine, then opened her menu. "So, what are you ordering?"

"The Sicily Special looks good."

"It does. But it seems like too much food."

"We can share it," Dylan said. "I mean, not like *Lady and the Tramp* share it, but two plates share it."

"Perfect."

"If you want your own, that's okay. I'm not trying to be a cheapskate or anything."

Sloan smiled. "We're teachers. Of course, we have to be cheapskates."

The server returned with the wine and showed Sloan the label and cork before pouring her a taste. She swirled it, sniffed, then drank. If she'd learned anything from her decade with Liam Bevan, it was wine etiquette. The wine was rich, with notes of black cherry, vanilla, and clove.

After nodding her approval, the server filled the rest of her glass and turned toward Dylan's.

"None for me." Dylan put his hand over the glass. "Just a Dr. Pepper, please."

"You don't drink?" Sloan asked after the server had left.

"I'm an addict. I've been clean for years, but I'll always be an addict. I doubt wine would be an appetizer for heroin, but I don't like the feeling of not being in control."

"Of course, you don't. I should have known," Sloan said, sinking further into her chair.

Dylan reached across the table and touched her hand. "Drinking in front of me doesn't bother me. Really."

His touch caused Sloan to forget the wine, to forget her embarrassment. Dylan pulled his hand back quickly and opened his menu again, even though they'd already decided what to order.

"That looked like quite the process, though," Dylan said. "The wine."

"Oh, gosh." Sloan covered her face with her hands. "Wine tasting was my ex's hobby, so I picked up on some etiquette. You must think I'm so pretentious."

"It was interesting." Dylan nodded at the server as he set a Dr. Pepper in front of him, on the way to another table. "Really, it is. I'd ask you to explain it to me, but it sounds like it was your ex's hobby, not yours."

"Yeah. Let's add that to our list of things not to talk about on a first date."

"Right. So, we've got exes, our ex's hobbies, and heroin addiction." He held up three fingers. "Did I miss anything?"

Sloan raised her glass to take a sip. "I don't think so, but the night is young."

As she drank, she thought about her newly recovered memory from the gas station. She thought about Reid Hunt, the man who had written her father, confessing to kidnapping Ridge. She decided to mentally add both of those to their "no talk" list, at least for the night.

This was not the time to bring back memories of the worst time in Dylan's life.

Dylan picked up his Dr. Pepper and reached across the table to clink it against her wine glass. "Better yet, here's to talking about whatever the hell we want to."

An hour and a half later and well past dessert, Sloan's throat was scratchy from talking, and her cheeks hurt from smiling. She tried to calm herself. She'd ridden the clouds home after her first date with Liam and look how that had turned out. Men were liars. But even though blind optimism went against her nature, she couldn't help but hope Dylan was different. Her thoughts were interrupted by her phone vibrating from inside her purse.

"If you need to answer that, it's fine."

"Let me make sure it's not Mom. She was asleep when I left, but you never know." Sloan rummaged around in her purse. By the time she found her phone, she saw the missed call was from Brad. He had to be calling with information about her request to meet with Eddie. She sent him a text. *Sorry, can't talk. What did you find out?*

"Everything okay?" Dylan asked.

"Yeah, sorry. What were we talking about?"

"That tree where your dad carved your names. I was asking if it's still there."

"Probably. I haven't been to that area in forever. I spent *a lot* of time there during high school." Sloan's throat tightened.

"Because of your mom?"

"Yeah. When she was in her manic state, she wouldn't sleep, and if she didn't sleep, nobody did. So, I'd take my tent and sleeping bag to the creek. Then I'd wake up, get ready in a gas station bathroom, or . . ."

*Gas station bathroom.* Sloan's eyes wandered past Dylan to the jars of decorative oils, dried noodles, and hot peppers lining the wall behind him. She remembered again the night at the By and Buy. *What were we running from? Who were we waiting for?*

"Sloan?" Dylan leaned forward. "You okay?"

Sloan shook her head, clearing the cobwebs out of her mind. "Sorry, but yeah, a gas station, or sometimes Noah's house if his parents were already at work."

Dylan slid his chair closer to the table. "Forgive me for asking, but Crow's Nest Creek, that's where Ridge disappeared, right?"

Sloan smoothed the napkin in her lap. "Yes."

"How were you able to go back?" Dylan asked.

"Not sure," Sloan answered. "I avoided it awhile but then realized I didn't want to stay away forever. Ridge loved it there."

"You're very brave." Dylan rubbed the back of his neck. "I try to steer clear myself."

"Was that where Eddie picked you up the night you went for drugs?"

Dylan shook his head. "It's where he brought me. That Halloween when I was a kid."

Sloan's stomach turned. "How are you still a decent human being after all you survived?"

"God." A flicker of a smile passed Dylan's lips. "Well, God and music. Both can save you."

"Is that when you started playing guitar?"

"Yeah. It became an outlet for me. Music is a miracle, really. The way it heals. Even the saddest songs can bring some sort of twisted comfort. People always say music is a way to escape their pain, but for me, it's always been a way to *face* the pain."

Sloan thought of her Keith Whitley tape. "Yeah, I actually know what you mean. What kind of music do you like?"

As Dylan shared his musical favorites, Sloan glanced at her phone. Brad had responded. *No luck with Eddie's lawyer. Plan B time. You mentioned money. How much did you have in mind? I'll help.*

Sloan figured it would come to this. She fought the urge to text Brad back with an amount. She was already being rude to Dylan.

"I listened to music when Eddie had me, too," Dylan continued. "It was a song that made me decide to get clean. *The Man in The Mirror.* I'd heard it before. What '80s kid hadn't? One morning, I needed a fix, but I couldn't find a spoon or lighter. I caught my reflection in the dirty mirror that hung in the attic. I didn't recognize myself." Dylan lowered his eyes back to the tablecloth. "I remembered Dad. Remembered home. Right then, the song came on." Dylan drummed his fingers on the table to the beat of the Michael Jackson hit. "This sounds simplified and cheesy, but the lyrics spoke to me. They kinda saved my life."

Sloan shook her head. "Wow. That's incredible. I'd love to hear you play sometime." She raised her eyebrows. "I don't guess you know any Keith Whitley?"

Dylan brought his hand to his chest in mock offense. "You don't think *I* know any Keith Whitley? I love Keith Whitley. Easily my second favorite musical Keith."

Sloan cocked her head. "Second?"

"Well, yeah, behind Keith Urban. Obviously."

"No way. Urban is great, but Whitley is a legend."

"Excuse me?" Dylan flashed a grin. "If you want to talk about legendary, listen to Keith Urban's guitar solo in *Stupid Boy*."

Sloan was about to suggest that he play it for her sometimes when her phone vibrated again. The vibration continued, indicating it was a phone call rather than a text. "I'm sorry." Sloan reached into her purse to silence the call.

"What about you?" Dylan asked. "What do you do for fun?"

Sloan laughed thinly. "Well, not much these days. I used to draw, but I haven't in forever. Now I mostly watch TV or read."

"What's your favorite book?" Dylan asked.

"Hmm, tough call. *The Iliad* maybe? I love Greek Mythology. I actually minored in it." She swirled her straw around her water glass. "I always squeeze a unit in for my fifth graders. I was offered a job teaching it full-time at a college last year, but I enjoy this age group too much."

"Me too," Dylan said. "It's a chance to really make a difference at a pivotal time in their lives."

"I agree." Sloan rested her forearms on the table. "I used to struggle in school. My sixth-grade teacher turned it all around for me. She really took an interest after my home life fell apart and started tutoring me after school. By the end of the year, I—"

Sloan stopped when her phone began vibrating again.

"I'm so sorry," she said, pulling it out of her purse this time. She was about to turn it off when she saw it wasn't Brad calling; it was Noah. Sloan rose from her seat. "I need to get this," she said without looking to see Dylan's reaction. She walked toward the exit and answered.

"Sloan? Where are you?" Noah sounded angry.

Her defenses rose. "On a date. Why?"

There was a brief pause before Noah spoke. "Oh. Well, I'm sorry to bother you, but I got a call about your mom. She's out at the creek. I realize she's there a lot, but it's pretty dark now. She's getting loud, walking on the water's edge like it's a tightrope."

Sloan brought her hand to her forehead. "She was asleep when I left. I'm about twenty minutes away. Can you bring her home?"

"I can't make her leave. It's not illegal to walk close to the water." Sloan didn't even recognize Noah's voice, cold as a tomb.

"I thought maybe you would go as a friend, not a cop, but obviously, that's asking too much. I'll handle it."

"Sloan, wait." Noah sighed. "Let me . . ."

"I said I'll handle it." Sloan ended the call before Noah said anything else.

Dylan stood as she came back to the table. "Something wrong?"

"My mom." Sloan grabbed her purse. "She's at the creek. I hate to cut this short, but I need to bring her home."

"Yeah, of course. I'll go with you."

"No, you don't need to do that." Sloan choked back tears. She was thirty-two years old, and her mother still had the power to ruin her night. "I'm just sorry I have to leave. I was having a great time."

"Then let's keep having a great time. I'll help you with your mom, and we can all watch a movie or something."

Sloan's eyes filled with tears. Both at Dylan's kindness and because of how little he understood about her mother. Caroline wasn't a mom you could sit and watch movies with. She wasn't normal.

Dylan pulled a few bills from his wallet and threw them on the table. "At least let me help you; then, I'll go home."

"Fine." Sloan turned away from Dylan, staring again at the vibrant paintings, now blurred by her tears. She wished she could jump into one and take Dylan with her to some faraway place, to a beautiful villa in Italy, but as long as her mom was alive, she'd never even get to leave Mallowater. She couldn't even leave home, apparently. "My mom ruins everything." She spat out the words through gritted teeth. "I guess if you're going to be in my life, you better get used to it."

# Chapter 17

*Mallowater, TX, 1995*

Sloan stared at the pile of unpaid bills. Mom always stacked them at her dad's former place at the table, a move Sloan suspected wasn't accidental. There was no way Dad could pay them sitting in jail. No way Mom could pay them without a job. So that meant they were Sloan's responsibility—a nineteen-year-old's responsibility She had been working for Doreen at her salon since she was thirteen, sweeping up hair, cleaning toilets, making appointments, and counting back change. At sixteen, she added a paper route, and two days after her graduation last month, a third job, a cashier at Blockbuster Video. But it still wasn't enough. The bill stack always grew.

Walt and Doreen helped. They'd paid bills, set Caroline up for public assistance, given Sloan unwarranted bonuses, and even bought her first car— a used but reliable Honda Accord. They'd bought Noah one too, but Sloan wondered how much nicer his would be if his parents felt no obligation toward Sloan. If Sloan had parents, she could count on for things everyone else her age counted on their parents for—cars, college, food on the table.

Sloan grabbed the bills and sorted them by priority. She hadn't paid electricity last month, so she'd better get caught up. Nope, never mind. Car insurance was due this month. That meant nothing else would get paid.

The phone interrupted her sorting. The stranger on the other end of the line asked for her.

Sloan knew it wasn't a bill collector since she hadn't asked for Caroline. No big anniversary of her brother's death was coming up, so it probably wasn't a reporter. She took a chance.

"This is Sloan."

"Hello, Sloan. This is Roberta Perry. I'm a recruiter at LeTourneau University in Longview, Texas."

Sloan slumped against the wall. She'd considered LeTourneau. But even with three jobs and financial aid, paying the tuition would be impossible.

"I mailed an application to your residence yesterday. Once you receive it, please send it back along with your high school transcript and admissions essay as soon as possible. All the instructions are —"

"Mrs. Perry," Sloan interrupted, "thanks, but I'm not interested in attending your university." She caught the sharpness of her tone and tried to soften it. "It's just not in my budget."

"That's why I'm calling, Sloan." Roberta's voice grew chipper. "I have some wonderful news. A donor contacted us, and they would like to pay for your education."

Sloan's entire body tensed. "Very funny. Who is this?"

"This isn't a joke. Of course, you'll have to go through the admissions process, but if you are accepted, this donor will pay one hundred percent of your educational costs, plus a dorm room and basic meal plan, as long as you maintain passing grades."

Sloan's legs shook beneath her. She pulled out a chair from the kitchen table and stretched the phone cord so she could sit. "Who's paying?"

"They wish to remain anonymous. I'll leave you my number in case you have questions filling out the application."

Sloan sat in the chair, frozen with the phone still in her hand for several minutes after the call ended. She was afraid to hang up. Afraid the phone would ring again, and Roberta Perry would say she'd called the wrong number.

Who would pay for her college education? There is no way Walt and Doreen could afford it. No way they'd want her to leave Mallowater and go to Longview, even if it was just an hour away. Doreen had been pushing her to fill out applications to Mallowater Community College's beautician program since the beginning of senior year.

"What are you doing just sitting there?" Caroline shuffled into the room, eyes half-closed and still wearing her pajamas. "Hang up the phone. That costs money. You're wasting electricity."

Sloan sighed. How was this woman and the brilliant scientist her father always talked about the same person? She hung up and walked to the fridge. "How many eggs do you want?"

"None." Caroline poured water into the coffee pot.

"You need to eat something. You keep losing weight."

"Okay, fine. Get me a bowl of cereal." Caroline rubbed her hands through her disheveled hair. "If you keep making me eat like this, I'll look like Anna Hadfield."

"You mean healthy?" Sloan opened the pantry door. "That's how Anna looks because she takes care of herself."

"And how do you know what Anna Hadfield looks like?" Caroline sneered. "You sneaking off with her again?"

"Stop. The last time I saw her was the same time you did." Sloan realized immediately it was a mistake to bring up that day. Nothing made Sloan's mother happier than recounting that incident.

"That's right," Caroline said. "That bitch had the audacity to show up on my property." She chuckled. "You should've seen her eyes when I stepped out on the porch holding your grandpa's old pistol."

Sloan *had* seen Anna's eyes, though she doubted they were as wide as hers. Because when Sloan saw her mother with the gun, she was sure she would fire it right into Anna's chest. Sloan didn't know why Anna was at their house that day. Nor why Anna still tried to call a few times each year. She didn't want to see or talk to her father's wife, but she didn't want her dead.

"How about those Frosted Flakes?" Caroline asked over the gurgling of the coffee pot.

Sloan moved around a few boxes in the pantry. "Looks like we're out of cereal."

"Well, why did you ask me if I wanted some?"

Sloan rested her head against the pantry. "How about some eggs instead?"

"I'll just go to the store," Caroline said.

"I don't get paid till Friday," Sloan reminded her.

"What happened to my money? All the money my daddy left me?" Caroline asked.

"I wish I knew." Sloan grabbed her own coffee mug and poured a cup. "You told me how much you inherited, but by the time you gave me access to the account, there was less than five thousand dollars."

"Well, what the hell did you spend five grand on?"

Sloan clenched her teeth. "Mortgage, utilities, Frosted Flakes."

"And that haircut?"

Sloan ran a hand through her shaggy bob. "Doreen doesn't charge me."

"Well, good. I wouldn't pay a dollar for a cut that makes it look like I just rolled out of bed." Caroline set her mug down too hard, and a trail of black liquid dripped down the white porcelain. "I'll finish my research soon and write my book. That money will set us up for a while."

*Us. A while.* Sloan didn't like the sound of those words together. She thought about the call from the recruiter. Her expenses would be paid, so whatever she made working could go to her mom. That, together with the welfare, ought to be enough for Caroline to get by. "Speaking of the future, I've been planning for college."

"Did I ever tell you crows have regional dialects?" Caroline asked.

Sloan threw up her hands. "Are you even listening? I want to go to

LeTourneau. Longview is close enough that I can still come home and help when needed."

"What's wrong with the community college here?" Caroline asked.

"Nothing," Sloan said. "But I was offered a full scholarship to LeTourneau." It wasn't a lie, she figured. Not exactly.

Caroline's laugh was joyless. "Who gave *you* a scholarship? Daughters of Convicted Killers?"

"Not funny." Sloan kept her eyes on her mother's coffee cup. *World's Best Mom*, it boasted. Sloan had bought it as a Mother's Day gift when she was five. Back when she still thought it was true.

Caroline cleared her throat. "As I was saying, the sounds crows use to communicate with other birds are different depending on where they live. If a crow moves to a new area, he'll learn to mimic the tone of the dominant crows in the region."

"Okay, Mom, but about college—"

"So that's what you want to do?" Darkness crossed Caroline's eyes. "You want to fly off to Longview and attend a fancy private *Christian* school. You want to try to fit in with the cool crows?"

"Come on, Mom. How could I turn down a free ride?"

Caroline raised her coffee mug to her lips. "You'll never fit into their flocks. You can change the way you caw, but they will see right through you."

Sloan knelt, pretending to sort pans in a cabinet by the stove. She didn't want her mother to see that she'd gotten to her, but Caroline was right. Sloan would never fit in at LeTourneau. She squeezed her eyes shut, wondering how the hollowness in her chest could somehow feel this heavy.

"Mallowater Community College is a good school, Sloan. Cheap, too. We'll figure out a way to pay for what financial aid doesn't," Caroline said.

Sloan blew out a long breath and lowered her head. She noticed a penny nearly pushed under the stove. She remembered her last breakfast with her dad and smiled despite herself. "We could make washers."

"Huh?"

"Nothing." Sloan closed the cabinet and stood, accidentally kicking the penny underneath the oven. "You're right. I'll finish my application to MCC after work."

"Good girl." Caroline lowered her coffee cup and smiled. Sloan searched her mother's smile, trying to find a glimmer of the bright, nurturing, and generous woman she'd once been. It was no use. Caroline Radel was lost. Lost like Ridge at Crow's Nest Creek. Lost like Jay Hadfield after Vietnam. Lost like the penny underneath their oven. Lost like Sloan's dream of a new beginning.

The night air was unusually chilly for June. Sloan pulled her hoodie over her head as Noah added another piece of wood to the crackling fire.

"Everything okay?" Noah asked. "You seem quiet."

Sloan looked up through the rustling trees at the black sky, so clear she could detect hints of colors in the stars. "Which stars are the hottest again?"

Noah sat next to her on the gravelly ground and looked up. "Blue's the hottest, followed by white, yellow, and orange. Red's the coolest."

"Sounds like you are enjoying your astronomy class. Sloan took a deep breath. It was now or never. "I hear LeTourneau has an excellent science program."

Noah laughed. "Maybe so, but you know I'm going into the Academy."

"But why? Is that what you want?"

Noah brought a shoulder to his ear. "I guess."

"You guess? Come on; you don't have to do what your dad wants. This is your entire life you're talking about."

"And that's why you're headed to beauty school?" Noah asked.

"Well, actually . . ." Sloan picked up a pinecone and tossed it into the fire. The sap popped and hissed.

"Well, actually what?" Noah's back straightened.

"I'd like to study education."

Noah smiled warmly. "I can see you as a teacher. You can get your basics at MCC and transfer somewhere else."

"That's the thing." Sloan grabbed a pine needle and twirled it around in her fingers. "I don't want to go to MCC."

Noah's face fell the slightest bit. "Okay. Where do you want to go?"

"LeTourneau," Sloan said. "Someone's offering to pay my tuition and living expenses if I do."

"What? Who?"

Sloan shrugged. "Anonymous donor. I realize I'd be dumb to throw that away, but I'm not sure I can leave Mom."

"Oh, come on, Sloan." Noah playfully punched her shoulder. "Didn't you just tell me I don't have to do what my dad wants? That it's *my* life?"

Sloan huffed. "It's not the same, and you know it."

"We'd help with your mom," Noah said. "And it's close. Close enough to drive home every weekend."

Sloan squeezed her fists, forcing her fingernails into her palms. "I wouldn't come back *every* weekend. The whole point would be to get away."

An owl hooted in the distance. "You wouldn't want to see me every weekend?" Noah asked.

Sloan looked away, sifting the words in her mind like sand, trying to soften a blow she didn't want to administer. "I just think I'd be lousy at long distance. I mean, aren't most people?"

"You wouldn't be lousy at it. I could go there on the weekends. We would make it work." A line etched between Noah's eyebrows. "Unless you're telling me you don't want to make it work."

Sloan wasn't sure what she was trying to tell him. She loved Noah. Always had. A part of her wanted him to follow her to school because he'd always been a safe place for her. But another part of her craved a new place. A new life.

But when she looked into Noah's eyes, wet with tears, she couldn't say any of it. "I *do* want to make it work. I'm sorry. Everything just feels turned upside down right now."

Noah scooted close, putting his arm around her. "We'll figure it out, Sloan," he said, rubbing her back. "That's what we do. Figure things out."

Over the next month, Sloan completed her application to Mallowater Community College. She completed her FAFSA, chose her classes, and visited the campus.

Without telling anyone, she did the same for LeTourneau. Sloan had told her mother she was staying; she'd told Noah she was staying; she'd even told herself she was staying, but she couldn't bring herself to tell LeTourneau.

The tour of the LeTourneau campus only solidified her mother's words—she would never fit in. These students had money, family, and faith. Arguably, the three biggest deficits in her own life. Yet, it was hard to close the door on a free education. Noah didn't seem to grasp that, and why would he? His parents were paying for him to go to college. For Noah, college would just be an extension of childhood. One where he could practice adulthood without having to foot the bill.

She glanced at the clock. One more hour until her shift at Blockbuster ended. At least she didn't have to close tonight. She'd get home in time to catch *Friends* and *Seinfeld*.

Sloan was ringing up a customer when her manager, Danny, came behind the counter. "I'll take over. You've got a phone call in the back."

Sloan squeezed her eyes shut. "Is it about my mom?"

Danny bit his lip. "It's Officer Dawson, so maybe." He touched her shoulder. "If you need to go, just go. It's slow tonight."

It wasn't slow. Customers were everywhere. Danny was just being nice. Nicer than Sloan deserved. Noah claimed Danny had the hots for her, but Sloan never got that vibe from him. He was just a nice guy. As glad as she was for the flexibility, she hated being unreliable. Hated that he pitied her.

Sloan jogged to the employee area in the back of the store and picked up the phone.

"Walt? What's wrong?"

"Caroline's in Tyler."

"Tyler!" Sloan tugged at her hair. "Why?"

"At Anna's house. She tried to kick in their door. When Anna called the police, your mom climbed up on their roof. She's refusing to come down."

Vomit burned the back of Sloan's throat. This was her fault. She shouldn't have mentioned the day Anna showed up at their house. It must've got her mom thinking about her again. Obsessing again. "What should I do?"

"Nothing. I'm heading that way now. I just wanted you to have a heads up before it's on the news."

"The news? They already got wind of this?" Sloan asked.

"Noah's on his way to get you and take you home."

Sloan hung up the phone with shaky hands. She realized she should go with Walt. But she couldn't bear the embarrassment of seeing her father's family out in the street watching along with the rest of the neighbors and the journalists. Word would reach her dad by morning, and he'd shake his head and think, *Poor Caroline. What's become of her?* As though it wasn't all his fault.

Sloan felt dizzy. She closed her eyes but only saw the flashbulbs of cameras just like the ones she'd seen when her dad was arrested. The news would have a field day with this. Every detail was going to be dug up again. No hole was deep enough to keep her past buried.

She searched for a trash can, but it was too late. She threw up all over the break room table just as Danny entered. "Sloan, Noah is—" he stopped when he saw the mess.

"Sloan?" Noah came in right behind Danny and put his arm around her. "Are you alright?"

Sloan wiped her mouth with the back of her hand as Danny filled up a cone-shaped paper cup with water. Noah spotted a few paper towels and reached for them.

"I got it," Danny said, handing Sloan the water. "I'll clean it up; you just get her home." He picked up the small trash can and handed it to Noah. "In case she gets sick again on the drive."

Caroline was taken off the Hadfield's roof and into the mental health unit of Mallowater General Hospital. Because she had a gun in her car and threatened to jump off the roof, a judge ordered her to be admitted for a month of observational institutionalization. For the first time in years, Sloan could breathe easily. Someone else made sure her mother ate, made sure she didn't sneak away. And though Sloan had been on the receiving end of a few hate-filled rants when she called or visited, it was mostly the medical staff having to listen.

Still, Sloan wasn't able to completely enjoy her newfound freedom. Not with the future so uncertain for her and her mom.

That's why she was sitting in the office of district attorney Miles Johnson. Sloan had no idea involuntary commitment would involve all this. It felt wrong—like her mom was a criminal facing trial—but what other options did she have?

Walt and Noah sat on either side of her as the attorney read through reports the hospital's attending psychiatrist had faxed over. Sloan's body tensed as Miles looked up from the fax.

"This is good news." He removed his glasses and set them on the mahogany desk. "Forgive me; that's not the best choice of words. This is good news for making your case."

"What do they say?" Sloan asked.

"Ms. Radel's been diagnosed with bipolar disorder, post-traumatic stress, and borderline personality disorder. This diagnosis and the police records solidify my confidence that we need to apply for an extended commitment."

"What do you need from us?" Walt asked. "This has been a long time coming. We should have done something sooner."

"It usually takes something big, like this incident, to make a case strong enough, so this is the exact right time to do it," Miles said. "I'll call several witnesses, including you, Mr. Dawson." He turned to Sloan. "And you too, Ms. Hadfield, if you agree."

Sloan swallowed. "What would I say?"

"The truth." Miles put on his glasses again and stared at the papers. "The doctor's notes mention several past incidents that you included in her intake history. Incidents of physical abuse, neglect, self-harm, and so on. Have you kept a diary or notes regarding these events?"

Sloan shook her head.

"Go home and write anything you can remember; dates can be approximate. Bring it by here, and we'll talk." He pushed the papers aside. "And another thing—you graduated last year. Will you be leaving for college?"

Sloan kept her eyes straight ahead, but out of her peripheral, she saw Noah's head turn toward her. "I'm not sure."

Noah released her hand. "You said you decided on MCC."

"Well, I had." Sloan's voice cracked. "That was when I didn't have an option because I needed to take care of Mom."

Miles nodded. "It's none of my business, but it might help the state's case if you were going away to college. It would mean your mom has no caretaker. Couple that with the fact that she can't find gainful employment, and we've got even stronger arguments for a long-term commitment."

"How long-term are we talking?" Sloan asked.

"The order expires after a year. At that time, we'd have to reapply, or you may choose to look at other options, depending on your mom's progress."

"Would Medicaid pay for this?" she asked.

Walt put his hand on Sloan's back. "That's something we'll worry about later. Right now, let's focus on getting Caroline the help she needs. Whatever it takes."

Sloan nodded. "Whatever it takes," she repeated, then looked at Noah.

He was bent over, staring at the carpet. "Guess you got your wish," he said, his voice low and cold. "An excuse to go to LeTourneau."

Things weren't the same between Sloan and Noah after that. He called less, came over less. Sloan wondered if he realized his coldness wasn't making a good case for her to stay. But with the trial and college preparations, she had little time to concern herself with Noah's fragile feelings.

She told him it helped their case to finish the admissions process for LeTourneau, and that she still had everything in line for MCC if she changed her mind, but she somehow knew she wouldn't change her mind.

The court date was set quickly. After hearing the testimony, the judge ruled in favor of committing Caroline to a treatment facility for one year.

Caroline laughed when the verdict was read, further solidifying to the judge that he'd made the right decision. But the laughing ceased there. Anytime Sloan tried to visit her mother in the hospital, she'd only screamed.

After the third failed visit, Sloan sat in her bedroom, realizing it would be a long time before she'd ever speak to her mother again. Realizing that she and Noah wouldn't last no matter where she went to college. His recent immaturity and selfishness were proof of that.

Sloan was ready to leave them both behind. To leave behind this town that judged her for the sins of her parents. Everything suddenly seemed urgent. Waiting would only give her time to change her mind.

She jumped up from her bed and pulled her duffle bag from the closet. Then she grabbed the legal pad off her nightstand. The one with her notes on how to answer questions on the stand. She ripped off the top three sheets and threw them into her wastebasket, then tried to write a letter to Noah.

When the trash can was full, she gave up and wrote a letter that felt much less complicated.

*Walt,*

*I'm sorry I'm not brave enough to say this in person, but I'm leaving tonight for Longview. It's still a few weeks before classes start, but they said I can move into the dorms early. The offer of free college was too much to pass up, and every minute I stay in Mallowater is a minute I might stay trapped forever. I hope you can understand, and if not, I hope you can forgive me.*

*What should I do about the house? Quit paying and lose it? Try to sell it? If you aren't too angry with me, I'd really appreciate your advice.*

*I'll call when I'm sorted. I know you would have helped, but I need to do this alone.*

*I love you, Walt. Thanks for the car, for the money, and mostly for the chance to see what a normal family is like.*

*Love,*
*Sloan*

*PS: Look in on Mom, please.*
*PSS: Tell Noah I'm sorry.*

# Chapter 18

*Mallowater, TX, 2008*

Sloan rode with Dylan to the creek to look for her mom. She hadn't wanted to leave her car at the restaurant, but Dylan insisted she was in no state to drive. He was right. Tears poured from her eyes as she told him more about her mother's mental history, about the night she'd driven to the Hadfield's with the pistol, about everything.

"I realize it's hard, but you've got to cling to the good memories of her," Dylan said. "You can't forget the bad, but you can focus more on the good. That's the only power we have."

Sloan knew he was right. Since the visit with her father, she'd focused more on the happy memories, the ones she'd tried to forget her entire life. The ones that had hurt too much to remember. It was helping a little.

Dylan reached across the center console and took Sloan's hand. "It's going to be okay."

"Sorry for ruining the date," Sloan said.

"How could it be ruined? I'm still with you instead of being at home, trying to forget the entire night happened like I do with most of my dates."

"Well, the night is young. Don't count that out yet," Sloan said as they arrived at the creek.

"Think we should split up?" Dylan asked.

A light tapping on Sloan's window made them both jump. A flashlight shone in the car. Once Sloan's eyes adjusted, she recognized Walt behind it. Sloan couldn't believe how old he looked, so frail and gray. But he had those same kind eyes. The ones he'd given Noah.

Walt backed away as she opened the door. "Sloan? I almost didn't recognize you."

Sloan stood to hug him. Though she'd communicated with Walt many times, she hadn't seen him since her mother was committed in 1995. "Great to see you, Walt."

He pulled back to study her. "Your hair's longer, and I like the wave in it."

Sloan brushed her hair off her shoulders. "Yeah, that Meg Ryan look really didn't work for me."

Walt laughed. "It looked just fine. I think you got taller too."

Sloan lifted her foot. "It's the boots."

"Well, it's sure good to see you. Doreen and I keep hoping you'll visit, but we understand how busy you must be."

Sloan averted her gaze to the ground. She didn't realize Dylan was out of the car until he was beside her, extending his hand to Walt and introducing himself.

"Are you here for the same reason we are?" Sloan asked. Walt was retired, so he wasn't here patrolling the area for kids drinking.

"Yeah. Noah called about Caroline. He was tied up at the office and wanted me to check."

"And?"

Walt shook his head. "No luck so far. Nobody around here saw her or called it in."

Sloan looked down the long, winding river. "I tried to call her twice on the way over, and she didn't answer. Not that there's great reception here." She looked up at the moon, barely visible behind the clouds. "The dark's going to make it hard to search." A memory surfaced— hundreds of people walking down this river looking for Ridge. Hundreds of voices, hundreds of flashlights. Goosebumps covered Sloan's arms despite the humidity clinging to the air.

"I'm going to grab a flashlight and head downriver." Dylan opened the door of his jeep. There's a place off the beaten path where kids hang out. They might've seen her."

"Good idea," Sloan said. "You lead the way."

Dylan shot her a glance from over the jeep's hood. "Come here a sec."

Sloan stomped over to Dylan as Walt turned away, pretending to look at his phone. "What?" she asked.

"The type who hang out there, they wouldn't appreciate me bringing a cop."

"Walt's not a cop anymore."

"Come on, Sloan. Remember how I said once an addict, always an addict? It's sort of the same for cops. If he comes out, everyone will leave. I taught a lot of these kids, so they trust me."

Sloan tipped her head back and exhaled. "Okay. I'll ask Walt to come with me to check the old campsite. Mom might've gone there. That's where she claims Ridge the crow lives."

Dylan put his hands on her shoulders. "Thank you." He leaned forward and kissed her forehead. And for the second time tonight since arriving at the creek, Sloan got goosebumps.

"Almost there." Sloan used her cell phone for light while Walt followed behind with his flashlight.

"If Caroline made it this far, she's in better shape than me," he huffed.

"Mom comes a lot, but usually not after dark," Sloan said.

"Reliving better memories?"

"No." Sloan laughed uncomfortably. "She thinks Ridge talks to her up here."

"Sorry. The lucidity seems to come and go."

"Yeah," Sloan said. "I'm sorry I left you alone to deal with her."

"You didn't leave me alone to deal with her. You left for college, as is a normal course of life. Caroline was hospitalized. They took care of her."

"Come on, Walt. You guys visited her and brought food. Your

family cleaned out the house, rented it out, and managed the money from it. You did a million jobs that should've been mine." Sloan stopped. "Here we are."

Walt shone the flashlight around the campsite. "Somebody's been here. Still embers in that fire pit."

Sloan wasn't looking at the firepit. Her eyes moved straight to the swamp chestnut oak tree and the list of names still etched deep into the trunk. *Jay, Caroline, Sloan, Ridge*. Like most monuments, it honored something long dead and gone.

"I've gotta take a break before we go back down." Walt lowered himself onto a log. Sloan sat beside him and tried to dial her mother's number again, but there was no signal. "She's probably gone home," Walt said. "If not, I can call it in as an endangered person and get some officers here."

Sloan closed her eyes. "I'm not sure if I can do this, Walt—live with her forever."

"We need to get her back into that home or hire a caretaker," Walt said. "You go back to work in August, right?"

"That's the plan."

"Then we've got a little time."

Sloan pushed the button on the side of her watch, lighting it up. "We shouldn't stay long. No reception, and Dylan may try to call."

"Right." Walt smiled. "That Dylan Lawrence seems like a nice young man."

Sloan grinned. "It's our first date, but I like him a lot."

Walt nudged her shoulder. "So why the long face?"

Sloan chewed on the inside of her cheek. "Dylan and I both have so much baggage. My ex-husband said something once when we were fighting. He said he couldn't carry both of our baggage any longer, so he had to put mine down." Sloan shook her head. "I don't even know what baggage Liam Bevan ever had. His life was pretty perfect. So, if someone with so little baggage couldn't carry mine, how is Dylan going to when his hands are full of his own?"

"What bullshit."

Sloan flinched backward. She had known Walt Dawson her entire life and this was only the second time she'd ever heard him curse. "Walt . . ." She grinned.

"Well, it's true. Liam probably read that in some self-help book, not to carry someone else's baggage, but in the Bible, the word is burdens, and it says we are supposed to carry each other's."

Sloan shook her head. "I'm so screwed up, though."

"No, you're not," he said. "You're the same screwed up as the rest of us."

Sloan laughed. "I miss these talks."

"Me too, baby."

"I'm sorry for leaving like I did. I've never apologized. You must have been so angry at how I hurt Noah."

Walt waved his hand dismissively. "Doreen and I weren't mad. We never really expected you and Noah to grow up and get married. People change. Lives change. Noah ended up just fine, and so did you."

"Maybe so." Sloan stood. "I'm going to get back down and keep looking, but if you need to wait—"

"I'm good," Walt said, but he seemed to struggle to stand. "Let's find your mama."

Sloan and Walt were halfway back to the road when her phone sounded with notifications. Three missed calls, two text messages, all from Dylan. She called him back without reading the texts.

"Dylan, we're on our way back. What's going on?"

"She's hurt, Sloan." Dylan sounded winded. "But she's gonna be okay."

Sloan moved the phone away from her ear so Walt could listen.

"She hit her head, and there's a lot of blood, but she's conscious. I'm driving her to the hospital now. She's not saying much, but she's awake."

"I'll meet you there."

Sloan ended the call, and she and Walt continued. She fell near the end, ripping a hole in her jeans, and Walt struggled to catch his breath, but they made it into his truck and the hospital in record time.

Dylan jumped up as soon as he spotted Sloan and Walt jogging through the automatic doors. "The nurses just took her back."

"Can I go?" She turned to the front desk. "That's my mom back there. Can I go?"

The woman behind the plexiglass stood. "Fill out this paperwork, and I'll check."

Sloan plopped down on one of the beat-up plastic green chairs next to Dylan and started filling out the first page. She stopped at medical history. "This will fill up at least ten pages with all her mental diagnoses," she said, tossing the clipboard on the seat next to her. "What was she doing out there?"

"One of my students saw her balancing on the edge—said she almost slipped several times before disappearing out of view. We found her about a quarter mile away. From the shoe prints, it looked like she slipped in the mud and hit her head on a rock." Dylan shook his head. "She was so close to the water; she could have fallen in."

"Write this down, Sloan," Walt said. "Write everything down like you did before." He glanced at his watch. "I'm going to step outside and call Doreen."

Sloan looked at Dylan. "Thanks for finding her, for bringing her here. If you need to go home, you can. It's late."

Dylan loosened his tie. "I want to be here with you. Unless it would make you more comfortable if I left."

Sloan leaned her head back on the chair. "Are you always this nice, or is it a first date thing?"

"Guess we'll have to plan a second date so you can decide."

If they weren't sitting in an emergency waiting room that smelled of antiseptic and vomit, Sloan might have kissed him right then and there. Instead, she reached out and took Dylan's hand.

As if the action had somehow summoned him, the electronic doors slid open, and in walked Noah.

Sloan released Dylan's hand and jumped up. "Noah."

"Hey," Noah said, finally peeling his eyes away from Dylan. "Is Caroline okay?"

"Not sure. They won't let me back there."

"Come on." Noah placed his hand on the small of her back. "I'll take care of that."

"It's okay that I left her, right?" Sloan asked two hours later as Dylan drove her home.

"Of course. She's going to be fine," Dylan said. "They're only keeping her for observation."

"She told me to go," Sloan explained. "I wasn't going to, but after she fell asleep, I figured it was a safe time to slip away. To slip out of these boots."

Dylan pulled into the driveway. "I like your boots; they're nice."

"Well, that's good because they aren't comfortable. Had I known I'd be running down an embankment at Crow's Nest Creek, I would have worn sneakers."

Dylan placed his hand on Sloan's skin where her jeans had torn. "And some sturdier denim." He kept his fingers there and rubbed against her knee. She felt the contrast of the calloused fingers of a guitar player against her smooth skin. Dylan leaned forward, and she did the same, keeping intense eye contact. She closed her eyes in anticipation just as her phone rang from inside her pocket.

"Sorry." A flush spread across Sloan's cheeks, but Dylan just laughed.

"Par for the course tonight, right?" he asked.

"Yeah." Sloan looked at Brad's name on her phone and sent the call to voicemail.

"Should you answer? Might be the hospital."

Sloan turned the phone to silent and threw it into her bag. "No. It's Brad."

"Brad, your brother?"

"Ugh. Don't call him that, please," Sloan said.

"Why was he calling?"

Sloan opened her mouth, then closed it. Dylan didn't need to hear that she was trying to get in touch with Eddie Daughtry.

Dylan moved his hand from her knee and put it back on the wheel. "Felicity said you'd never even talked to Brad or Kyle. That you hadn't even reached out to her since that night we met for dinner."

Sloan's muscles tensed. "You talk to Felicity?"

Dylan shrugged. "She's called or texted a few times."

"Has she?" Sloan scooted to the edge of the seat.

"Oh, come on. Felicity had more questions, just like you did. She's trying to help your dad."

"Just like me, huh? Did you take Felicity out to **dinner too?**"

Dylan thumped his fingers against the steering wheel. "That's not what I meant."

"And apparently, you've done more than answer a few questions if you've talked about me." Sloan bit down on the side of her cheek. Dylan was a liar. Just like Liam, just like her father. "It was pretty clear during our dinner at Applebee's that she liked you," Sloan continued. "I mean, she practically held your hand. I don't blame you for liking the attention or even liking her, but that's why I mentioned it that day you came over."

Dylan lowered his head. "I'm not and have *never* been interested in Felicity. I was uncomfortable when she took my hand and when you left us there alone. I was interested in you. *Am* interested in you. Where's this coming from? I asked an innocent question about Brad calling. How did it turn into this?"

Sloan let out a long breath. "Okay, fine. Brad's calling me because we're trying to set up a meeting with Eddie Daughtry."

Dylan's face twisted at the mention of Eddie Daughtry, and though Sloan realized she had gone too far, a part of her was glad it had stung. "Are you happy now?" she asked. "You know why Brad called me. Now, tell me why Felicity is calling *you.*"

Dylan squeezed the wheel and stared into the distance. "I think it's time for you to go inside." He didn't raise his voice, but it was thick with anger.

"Yeah, I'd say it's past time." Sloan grabbed her purse and climbed out of Dylan's Jeep, slamming the door behind her.

Sloan woke up on the couch the following morning wearing the previous night's clothes and having the kind of headache born from hours of intermittent crying mixed with hours of incessant drinking. She had overreacted last night. She realized that now in the fresh light of a new day.

It hurt to imagine Dylan and Felicity talking about her. Even if it was as innocent as Dylan claimed, this proved Sloan wasn't ready for a relationship—that she'd never be able to trust another man again. If she wanted someone trustworthy, she should have never broken up with Noah Dawson.

At the thought of Noah, fuzzy memories of the night before crept in. Sloan had texted him after her third or fourth glass of wine. She reached for her phone on the arm of the couch, but it wasn't there. She dug into the cushions until she found it, quickly opening her messages to survey the damage.

*Thanks for coming 2night Noah. I always feel stronger when you're with me.* 🖤

Sloan cringed. She wasn't sure which was worse. The spelling of tonight or the heart emoji. She scrolled down to read Noah's response.

*Welcome. Sorry I wasn't able to help find her.*

Miraculously, Sloan hadn't responded to that text. The next message in the thread was from Noah again, almost an hour later. Sloan read it and the ensuing conversation.

*So, what's with you and Dylan Lawrence?*

*Nada*

*Well, that's good.*

*Oh yeah? Why's that?*

*Because to use the poor man to get the information you want is low.*

*And what if I'm using him for sex?*

Sloan brought her hands to her face, letting the phone fall to her lap. She didn't want to read the rest of the texts; she wanted to curl up on the sofa and die. But she had to read them all, so she could do damage control.

She picked up the phone and looked at the last message from Noah. *Goodnight, Sloan.*

She had let the conversation die there and thankfully hadn't texted Dylan or Felicity. She needed to put some kind of lock screen on her phone, a puzzle she could only solve sober.

Sloan stood from the couch. She needed to take a shower before visiting her mom. She needed to return Brad's call, then text an apology to Noah and Dylan too. But in Dylan's text, she needed to clarify that an apology didn't mean she wanted a relationship because she didn't. Well, she sort of did, but she certainly didn't need one. Not with these trust issues.

But Sloan wasn't up for any of that, so she grabbed her keys. She needed to clear her head and knew just where to go.

She drove to the creek and hiked back to their old campsite. She was huffing by the time she made it. Hangovers and steep terrain didn't mix well. The two-person black tent close to the fire pit caught her off guard. She had no claim to this land, but it felt sacred. Like whoever camped here was walking over her grave. As much as Sloan wanted to rest under that old swamp oak that bore her family's names, she didn't want to disturb whoever was inside that tent. She turned to leave when she saw something shiny behind the tent. A cage. She stepped closer and saw a sleek black crow resting on a wooden perch.

As Sloan approached, she expected the bird to be frightened. That he would beat his feathers, squawk, and begin a frantic flight around the cage. But he only turned his head, looked at Sloan, and muttered one word. One word over and over and over. "Ridge. Ridge. Ridge," the crow echoed in a voice that sounded too much like a man's.

Sloan stumbled backward into a shrub. A branch scraped against her skin. Blood dripped down the back of her leg, but she didn't take her eyes off the bird.

She must have misheard. There was no way. She was still drunk, dreaming, or as crazy as her mother.

As if to refute the thought, the crow opened its beak again and repeated the haunting mantra. "Ridge. Ridge. Ridge."

Tears as warm as the blood dripping down her leg fell from Sloan's eyes. "What's going on?" she asked as if the crow might explain. "What the hell is going on?"

Suddenly, there was movement from behind her, leaves and sticks crunching underneath someone's weight. The hair on her arms rose as she turned toward the woods.

She noticed the shoes first. Nikes as black and slick as the crow. She looked up slowly until she met the stranger's eyes. But it wasn't a stranger. Twenty years had passed since she'd looked into those gentle blue eyes, but she recognized them. She noticed the tiny scar above his left eyebrow. Her chest tingled. Her breath caught. She finally exhaled in a series of short choppy breaths.

"Ridge," she managed.

With an uneasy smile, he took another step forward. "Hey, sis."

# Chapter 19

*Mallowater, TX, 2008*

Sloan took a step back and closed her eyes. This wasn't happening. This man was not Ridge. She opened her eyes, expecting him to vanish like the ghost that he was, but Ridge was still standing there, flesh, bone, and blood. Her own blood went cold. "Who are you? Why are you doing this?"

He held up a hand. "You know who I am, Lo. I understand this is confusing."

Sloan was dizzy. She took another step back and lowered herself onto a moss-covered log. "I'm going crazy."

Ridge took a few tentative steps forward. "You aren't."

The campground spun; the caged crow cawed. Sloan put her head between her knees and took deep breaths. When she looked up, Ridge had knelt on the dirt next to her. "Are you okay?" he asked.

"Am I okay? I'm talking to my brother who died when I was twelve years old."

"I didn't die, Sloan."

Tears filled her eyes. "Obviously." She reached to wrap her arms around him. He squeezed tight, and Sloan felt his tears on her shoulder.

She pulled back and looked at him. His once blonde hair was now chestnut brown. He had perfectly straight teeth, muscular arms, and a strong jawline covered in stubble.

"You're so grown up. So handsome." She wiped mascara from under her eyes. "Where have you been, Ridge? Where *the hell* have you been?"

Ridge's chin dipped to his chest. "I'm not ready to talk about that."

"No." Sloan sprung to her feet. "You don't get to show up after twenty years and not want to talk about it."

Ridge rose to meet her. "I came back because I wanted Mom to know I was alright. But when I saw you up here, I couldn't stay in those bushes. I had to see you."

Hundreds of thoughts bounced in Sloan's brain like tiny rubber balls. She tapped the sides of her head as if she could force them still. Mom. She'd claimed to talk to Ridge. "Have you been talking to Mom?"

"No. Well, not exactly."

He stepped behind the tent and pulled out the cage. "Ridge," the crow said. "Ridge. Ridge."

"You trained a crow?"

Ridge opened the cage. "Step up," he said, and the crow flew up and landed on Ridge's arm. "This is Crawford."

"He's your pet?" Sloan stared at the crow's bony, sharp claws twisted around Ridge's arm.

"Just a bird I studied back at home. Now that Mom knows I'm okay, I'm training him to fly free." Ridge looked around the creek. "This will be a good home for him. A good place to find a mate."

"How does a crow saying your name tell Mom you're okay?"

"I get this makes no sense to you, but I knew it would to Mom," he said. "Crows are kind of a language we share."

Sloan huffed. "Mom doesn't think you're alive; she thinks you're the crow."

Ridge shrugged. "Okay. But either way, it's brought her peace."

Sloan looked back at the tent. "And you've been living here?"

"Not exactly. I've got an RV parked at the campground down the way, but I hike up here to camp sometimes. Just makes me happy remembering our trips here." He smiled at Sloan, but she couldn't return it. "I was glad to see Mom still visited this place, too," he continued. "Made it easier than bringing Crawford near the house."

Sloan rolled her head between her shoulders, but it didn't ease any tension. "So, you've been living out here with a crow, stalking us?"

Ridge shook his head. "I told myself not to do this. Not to make contact."

The dizziness was back, so Sloan lowered herself down on the log. She considered everything Dylan had been through. Maybe Ridge had too. And if so, how could she blame him for not wanting to discuss it? For being scared to come home? "I'm glad you came out to see me," she said. "It's just a lot to process."

Ridge put Crawford back in the cage and sat beside Sloan, placing a hand on her knee. A gesture that filled her with overwhelming comfort.

"Thank God you're okay." She put her hand on top of his. "You can't leave, Ridge. You can't. Not ever again."

"Well, I have to leave eventually, but it won't be till Crawford learns to fly free."

"How long will that be?"

"Hard to say. Depends on when his natural instincts kick in as far as finding food and avoiding predators. But you can't tell Mom I'm here—can't tell anyone." His voice had a frantic edge. "I can't answer questions. I won't."

"You realize Dad is in jail, right?"

Ridge rose, walking away from Sloan. "He's getting out soon. What's done is done."

"You're not going to contact him? Let him know you're okay?"

Ridge kept his back turned, but Sloan noticed his posture straighten. "No," he said, an unmistakable indifference to his tone. "I'm not telling that sonofabitch anything."

"Are you sure this is a good idea?" Ridge asked, sliding lower in the passenger seat.

"I wouldn't bring you to the house if Mom were there. Did you not just hear me on the phone with the hospital?"

"I'm not worried about Mom being there." Ridge pushed his ball cap down. "What if someone sees me?"

"It's not far, and the entire town thinks you're dead. Not to mention, they haven't seen you in twenty years."

"Fair point. Sorry. I guess I'm a little paranoid."

Sloan gripped the wheel tighter. "Are you still in danger?"

"Sloan." Ridge's voice hardened. "I'm not talking about that."

"Right, sorry." Sloan turned onto their street. Silence, heavy as baled cotton, fell around them as Sloan pulled into the driveway. She killed the car, and it became quieter still.

"Wow," Ridge said, exhaling a heavy breath.

"Yeah," Sloan leaned back against her seat. "I hadn't been back since I left for college. Not till this summer."

Ridge looked at her. "You're kidding."

"Nope. Mom was in the institution and then a residential treatment facility. Walt handled pretty much everything. I never came back. Couldn't bring myself to after running away. Not to mention, I didn't want to see Noah."

Ridge unbuckled his seat belt. "Why not?"

"We were sorta high school sweethearts."

Ridge's mouth dropped. "What! For real?"

Sloan laughed. "He was my first kiss, first boyfriend, first love, first . . . *everything*."

"Ew!" Ridge punched her arm. "You and Noah. Who would've thought?"

Sloan shrugged. "Like most things, it worked till it didn't. Well, it wasn't working for me, at least."

"Did you break up with him to be with Liam?"

Sloan's skin tingled. "How do you know about Liam?"

It was Ridge's turn to shrug. "I kept up with you. On the internet."

That hardly seemed fair, but Sloan knew better than to say so.

"So," Ridge fidgeted with his watch, "does that mean you haven't seen Dad in that long?"

"I hadn't," Sloan said. "I did recently. There had been some . . ." she searched for the right word, "some developments that led me to believe he was innocent. Obviously, I was right."

Ridge's face reddened. "Just because he's not guilty of murder doesn't mean he's innocent. Dad had another family, Sloan. Plus, the way he hurt you. Why would you ever consider seeing him again?"

Sloan's mind raced, searching for answers. "Hurt me? What are you talking about?"

"Mom told me," Ridge said. "About the abuse."

"Abuse?" Sloan moved back slightly. "You mean during his episodes?"

"Come on, Sloan. You told Mrs. Evans you were being abused."

"Wait, what?" Spit flew from her mouth. "Dad *never* laid a hand on me."

Ridge touched the base of his neck. "What if you forgot? Blocked it out?"

Sloan thought about the recent memories she'd recovered. Was this another one? "No," she said aloud. "I would absolutely remember if that happened. If I told my teacher about it." The sound of a car door slamming made them both jump. Sloan looked in the rearview mirror. "It's Dylan."

"Dylan?" Ridge folded his body over, and sweat appeared instantly on his forehead.

"It's fine; he doesn't know you. Just go inside. The door's unlocked."

Ridge jogged to the house as Sloan walked in the opposite direction toward Dylan.

Dylan stood outside his jeep, hands shoved into his pockets. "Hey," he said to Sloan, but his eyes were on Ridge. "Is this a bad time?"

"No, not really," Sloan lied.

Dylan rocked on his feet. "Who's the guy?"

Sloan looked at her shoes, formulating a lie when all she wanted to do was tell the truth. "Just a friend."

"Oh." Dylan shifted his weight from foot to foot. "I came because I'm sorry how last night ended, but it looks like you're busy." He walked around the vehicle, back to the driver's door.

"Dylan, wait. I'm sorry about last night too. It's just that you hit a nerve with Felicity—a nerve my dad exposed by daring to have a daughter that wasn't me."

Dylan let go of the handle. "I get that. I know how it feels when someone rubs against an exposed wound. I mean, I kinda feel it now. I came to apologize, and you're sneaking another guy into your house."

"It's not just another guy, Dylan." Sloan raked her fingers through her hair, wincing as she broke through a painful knot. "I want to explain, but I can't. Not yet."

Dylan narrowed his eyes. "Is that Brad? Is this about Eddie Daughtry?"

"It's my brother, but it's not as simple as that."

"So, your dad's other family is some big sore spot unless you need them to get information about Eddie Daughtry? You've got to stop. I told you he's dangerous."

"Dad didn't kill Ridge. I know it for a fact. For a fact, Dylan!" She stomped on the concrete.

"How?"

Sloan bit her lip. "I can't tell you."

Dylan threw up his hands. "I've tried to help you. I've let you into this investigation, into this nightmare of memories for me. But it's not enough. You go behind my back and try to get information from this monster. You've got to trust the legal process. You've got to be patient."

"Why should I have to be patient?" Sloan asked.

"Because if I'm being patient, so can you," Dylan raised his voice. "So can anybody. I'm a victim here. Logan is a victim."

"And so is Ridge," Sloan said. "I can't explain it yet, but I'm onto something big. Just trust me, please."

Dylan blew out a few breaths. His body relaxed. Maybe it was going to be okay. Maybe he would trust her, be in her corner.

But Dylan didn't so much as look at her again as he climbed into the jeep and sped away.

Sloan found Ridge in their old bedroom when she returned. "So, who's Dylan?" he asked as Sloan lowered herself next to him on the bed.

"We had our first date last night, and it went to hell."

"Sorry. Guess seeing me didn't help."

"No, it really didn't," Sloan said.

"You didn't tell him anything, did you?" Concern marred Ridge's features.

"Of course not."

Ridge relaxed and leaned back on a pillow. "Man, this is a trip, being back in this room. All I need is Blue."

Sloan smiled. "Oh, Blue. Wonder where Mom put him. The last time I saw him was—" Sloan stopped, remembering the night at the By and Buy. "I'll have to check in the attic. That's where most of our stuff was stored when mom went into the hospital."

Sloan looked over her shoulder at Ridge as if she might see scars, might see a clue that hinted where he'd been all this time. He seemed so happy, healthy, and confident. Escaping Eddie Daughtry to make a good life was possible. Dylan was proof of that, but why had Ridge never come home?

Sloan took a chance.

"It may not work with Dylan." She pivoted her body to face Ridge. "He's got a lot of trauma, and so do I. It's probably a recipe for disaster."

Ridge sat up on his elbows. "What's this guy's story?"

"He was a victim of Eddie Daughtry," she said, staring at Ridge without blinking.

There were a few seconds of silence, where Sloan watched, wondering what Ridge would say, or at the very least, what his face would say, but it remained blank, slack, unaffected. He looked up at her. "Who's Eddie Daughtry?"

# Chapter 20

*Mallowater, TX, 1988*

Caroline thought about crows as she tried to fix the broken kitchen sink handle. All she wanted to do was stand outside, watch the sunset, and listen to the call of the crows. She loved watching them this time of year, as they forsook their spring and summer homes for the protection of a roost. It was beautiful, the sense of community crows had in fall and winter. How they'd band together and chase away predators, keep warm, and find food.

Of course, spring always came again. The crows separated, fought over territories and mates, then would go quiet, building hidden nests and protecting eggs. Caroline enjoyed finding the nests and observing the daily life of each crow family, but something about those fall and winter night roosts stirred her soul, made her long for a different life.

She followed Jay to Texas, fueled by dopamine and dreams after a chance meeting at a Fuller Brush conference, where she was waitressing. Those raging hormones had long since subsided, and her foolish fantasies had been squashed, but she still loved Jay deeply. Loved their children, loved the life they made.

But at times, like the beginning of fall roosts, Caroline felt an unexplainable sadness. She would watch crows soar by and wish she could fly away somewhere too. It's not that she wanted to leave her family but sometimes daydreamed about what another life would have looked like. A life where she'd followed her dreams. A life with a community of colleagues who understood her and appreciated her contributions. A life where she'd never waited on Jay Hadfield's table.

Not that Jay hadn't been supportive, but being a scientist meant being dedicated and consistent. It was difficult to monitor a community of crows when Sloan was sick. No time to analyze her collected data when Ridge had a science experiment due. And it seemed it was always something with kids. She loved them. She did. But it was always something, even now that they were older. Jay being gone so often didn't help.

Caroline heard the screen door open, followed by Ridge calling to her. "Mom, Libby's here!"

Caroline tossed the screwdriver into the sink and wiped her hands on her denim shorts.

"Did you bring us something, Libby?" Caroline heard Ridge ask as she stepped into the living room.

"Ridge!" Caroline scolded.

"Oh, it's fine, Caroline." Libby reached into her purse, then put both hands behind her back. When she brought them back out, they were in fists. "Pick a hand, any hand."

Ridge bounced up and down, looking from one hand to the next before settling on the left. "This one," he said, tapping on her knuckle.

Libby opened her fist to reveal a grape Push Pop, Ridge's favorite. "Yes!" he put his hands up in the air, "I knew it was in the left!"

Libby opened her right hand, revealing an identical treat. "Take this one to your sister."

"Thanks!" Ridge was unwrapping the paper as he ran out the door calling for Sloan.

"You're spoiling them," Caroline said, leading Libby into the kitchen. "Want some coffee?"

"No thanks." Libby took a seat at the table. "And with no children of my own, I've a right to spoil somebody's."

Caroline sat across from Libby, trying not to be jealous of her perfectly curled hair and expensive cashmere sweater. "Some days, I'd give them to you, to be honest."

"Oh, come on. They're good kids."

Caroline nodded. They were. But sometimes she envied the life of her best friend. Libby had a housekeeper. She slept late and still had time every day to curl her hair *and* her eyelashes. She ran charities to benefit her community. She got to watch *Days of Our Lives* uninterrupted every day.

"So, I'm here with news, and I'm just going to say it." Libby's rings clinked as she clasped her hands together. "Vince has accepted a job at Louisiana State."

"What?" Caroline pushed her back against the seat. I thought he was happy at MCC."

"He is. But LSU reached out to him. Offered him Dean of Mathematics. This is a dream for him."

"And what about you?" Caroline heard the hard edge to her voice. "What about the Women's League or the domestic violence hotline?"

Libby raised her hands and shrugged. "They'll go on without me."

"Will you at least be here for the Christmas Toy Drive?"

"No. We'll leave by the end of October. You should run it this year," Libby said.

"No, thanks." Caroline stood and made her way to the coffee pot. She needed a cigarette, but if she wanted to avoid a lecture from Libby, caffeine would have to do.

"Okay. Why not do something else? You could organize Earth Day activities."

Caroline grabbed a coffee mug from the cabinet and set it down too forcefully on the counter. "No one in Mallowater cares about the environment. Not after eight years of Reagan convincing Americans that protecting the only planet we have is some sort of radical idea."

"Well, change their mind," Libby said.

Caroline finished pouring coffee and faced her friend. "Reagan said trees cause more pollution than automobiles, Libby. He actually said that. He removed the solar panels Carter had installed on the White House. Yet, you people worship this guy."

Libby waved her hands. "Okay, okay, I get it. It was only an idea." She stood and approached Caroline at the counter. "I worry about you sometimes. It's okay to do something outside these four walls that feeds your soul."

Heat flushed through Caroline's body. "You don't think I want to?" She slapped the counter she leaned against. "Someone's always hungry. Something's always broken. I don't have time! I can't even finish my observations, can't write my book. I damn sure can't find the time and energy to plant trees on Earth Day!" A single tear fell from her eye as Libby enveloped her in a hug.

Libby, as always, smelt of Christian Dior's Poison, Oil of Olay face cream, and Doublemint gum. A strange combination that Caroline was unsure how she'd live without.

Caroline's entire body shook. "You're only doing this for Vince. One day you'll wake up and realize it was a mistake. That he got everything, and you got nothing."

Libby pulled back from Caroline and looked her in the eye. "I'm not *only* doing it for Vince. I'm going back to school so I can counsel domestic violence victims."

Caroline wiped her eyes on her sleeve. "You've always wanted your degree. I'm sorry. I'll just miss you so much."

"Oh, honey." Libby tilted her head. "We'll talk every day."

Caroline turned away when the screen door scraped open again. The kids didn't need to see her like this.

"Come on," Libby said. "Dry your eyes. Let's feed the kids, and we'll open up a bottle of wine."

Jay seemed distracted, and Caroline couldn't figure out why. Maybe the transition into fall made him restless too.

"Did you get Ridge signed up for soccer?" he asked as Caroline sat in bed reading.

*Not this again.* Caroline glanced up from her book. "Ridge doesn't want to play soccer, Jay."

He pulled his shirt off. "Well, he needs to do something."

"And I can't find his birth certificate," Caroline added, staring up at him. He was getting soft around the middle, his stomach bulging over his jeans. "Signups are Tuesday, and we'd need it."

"So, go to the clerk and get a copy tomorrow."

Caroline took off her glasses. So much for reading. "He isn't interested in sports. He's interested in birds."

"And you're fine with him growing up to be antisocial?"

Caroline sat up straighter against the headboard. "Am *I* antisocial?"

"Yeah, a little." Jay slipped off his jeans and threw them toward the hamper. He missed, but he didn't seem to care. "I mean, you're depressed because Libby's leaving. I've told you all along you spend too much time with those birds and not enough time with people. If you'd listened, you'd probably have more friends."

Caroline slammed her book closed. "Well, that's a shitty thing to say. My father died, and now, I'm losing my best friend. Forgive me if I'm a little sad."

Jay slipped into bed. "Fine, be sad. But instead of spending hours out with the crows, try actual people. Join a church, volunteer for one of Libby's charities, and meet some of her other friends."

Caroline heard a pounding in her ears. "What's this about? I hardly spend any time at the creek. You'd realize that if you were ever around."

She looked Jay in the eyes, daring him to say something else, but he remained silent. He switched the lamp off on his side of the bed and reached toward her. She pulled the covers up to her chest, wishing she hadn't chosen her thin silk nightgown. She had nothing in mind when she put it on and certainly had nothing in mind now.

But Jay didn't try to touch her; he just stretched past and turned off her lamp.

"Hey," she said. "I was reading."

"Goodnight." He rolled away from her. "Don't forget to pick up the birth certificate tomorrow."

Caroline left the house before anyone else was awake. She didn't want to deal with Jay when he woke up. He told her to get the birth certificate, which meant driving to Tyler. She took her time, stopping for breakfast and a coffee. Jay could feed the kids and get them ready for the day. He probably didn't even know what time school started.

At least she only had to put up with him for the afternoon. Jay would leave after dinner to drive wherever he had to be for the next morning's sales calls.

She and Jay rarely fought. And they'd never fought about how much time she spent at the creek. Something else had to be bothering him, and he'd taken it out on her. Still, that knowledge wasn't enough to quell her anger.

By the time she made it to the public health office, she was fuming. When she got home, she was going to the creek. If Jay needed more clothes washed for work, he could handle it. If Ridge needed help with fractions, Jay could handle that too. As Caroline saw it, if she was going to be accused of being an absentee parent, AWOL at the creek, she might as well be one.

"Good morning." Caroline set her purse on the counter. "I called about a birth certificate for my son."

"Oh, yes, ma'am." A young woman in a business suit stood, handing Caroline a clipboard. "There was static on the line, but you said Hadfield, correct?"

"That's right." Caroline pulled cash out of her wallet and handed it to the woman.

"And the year of the child's birth?"

"1978," Caroline answered.

The woman held up another paper. "I accidentally printed a copy of the Certificate of Live Birth issued by the hospital. Would you like it too?"

Caroline shrugged. "Sure." The woman slipped both papers into the envelope and put it on the counter before Caroline had even finished the paperwork. Caroline signed the final line and pushed the clipboard back across the desk. "Thanks. Have a nice day."

Caroline made it out to the car before it occurred to her that she ought to ask them to make a copy for the soccer registration. That way, she could keep the original.

She walked back to the door, pulling the certificate out of the envelope.

Caroline stopped dead in her tracks when she noticed the mother's maiden name section of the certificate. *Anna Elliott.* They'd given her the wrong damn one. Even right after asking her. She took another step but stopped shy of pushing the door open. The mother's name was wrong but the father's wasn't. *Jay Hadfield.* Caroline released the door handle and turned back to her car, eyes scanning the rest of the certificate. Ridge's name wasn't on it at all. She opened her car door and fell into the driver's seat, staring at the name until the letters blurred.

Who the hell was Bradley Hadfield, and why was Jay listed as his father?

# Chapter 21

*Mallowater, TX, 2008*

Sloan listened to the wind carrying away the song of the crickets as she waited for Dylan.

She checked her watch. Almost 11:30. This could have waited till morning, but Dylan mentioned on their date that he was a night owl—that he stayed up late and wrote songs. But when she called him, it was clear from his raspy voice that he hadn't been up writing a song about her.

Sloan stood as he approached. His messy hair and wrinkled t-shirt further evidence that she'd woken him. "Hey, thanks for coming. Sorry it's so late."

"No problem," he said with a voice that definitely suggested there was still a problem.

"Here, sit down." Sloan stepped out of the way so he could sit in one of the folding chairs. She sat next to him and wiped away sweat from her forehead. Sticky humidity and stony silence hung in the air. "Sorry we have to stay outside," she said. "Mom's sometimes a light sleeper."

"How is Caroline?"

"She's fine," Sloan said. "Thanks to you. The hospital released her today."

"That's great." Dylan rubbed the hair on the back of his head, flat from where he'd slept on it. "But I assume that's not why you asked me to come over?"

"No." Sloan wiped her hands down her jeans. "I want to be honest with you; it wasn't Brad yesterday in my car."

"Oh." Dylan's shoulders slumped. "I figured."

"But it *was* my brother," she added. "It was Ridge."

Dylan rubbed his eyes. "What?"

Sloan wiped her forehead again. "I realize it sounds crazy, but he's alive, and he's back. Yesterday morning, I hiked to our old campsite. Ridge was there."

Dylan raised his eyebrows. "And you're sure you're not the one who hit her head?"

Sloan laughed. "I wondered that myself, but it's real, Dylan. He's real."

"Wow. I'm sure it's a long story, but did Eddie have anything to do with his disappearance?"

"It's actually a very short story in that Ridge won't say anything. He looks great, seems like he's been taken care of, but he's made it clear he won't discuss what happened. He came over today when Mom went to the creek, but he was on edge. Constantly looking out the back door for her."

"He doesn't want her to know?"

"He doesn't want *anyone* to know, but I need to talk about it with someone." She twisted her watch. "And I don't want to keep secrets from you. I know it's soon, but you're special to me."

The corner of Dylan's lips quirked up into a nervous smile. "You're special to me too, Sloan. That's why I came back yesterday. I wanted to apologize for flipping out about you and Brad wanting to talk to Eddie Daughtry. Instead, I see you with another guy and have a second flip out to apologize for." He shuffled his feet against the concrete. "You ever see a smudge on your bathroom mirror and try to wipe it away, but in the process, you just keep making more and more smudges? That's sort of a good analogy for my never-ending ability to make things worse."

Sloan shook her head. "I should have listened to you about Daughtry—should have thought about how that would hurt you. I'm done with all that. I wanted to talk to him, to find out what happened to Ridge. But now that Ridge is here, it doesn't matter." Even as the words left her mouth, Sloan wasn't sure she meant them. She still desperately wanted to understand what had happened to her brother.

"Still, I had no right to demand answers," Dylan said. "I'm still working through some stuff."

"That makes two of us." Sloan tapped her fingers on the lawn chair's armrest. "Sorry for being a psycho about Felicity. It was a first date, and I acted like I had some claim on you. It's just that . . . well, I can't stand her."

Dylan laughed. "Felicity is a nice girl, but you have just as much reason to worry about me and her as I did to worry about you and Ridge yesterday."

Sloan reached for his hand. "Thank you."

"So, are you going to see him tomorrow?"

"As long as Mom goes out to the creek. I mean, I hate her going back after what happened, but at least it buys me some time with Ridge. Not like I can lock her in her room, anyway."

"Do you think she'd stay here with me? Then you can meet Ridge at the creek?"

Sloan tilted her head. "Maybe. She did ask about you today, about that nice boy who rescued her. But I don't want you to have to do that."

Dylan stretched his legs out in front of him. "I don't mind. Maybe some new company is just what she needs. Let's give it a try? What time tomorrow?"

"Um, 3:00? I'll meet Ridge at the RV park just in case you aren't successful at keeping her away from the creek. You know, maybe Ridge will be okay with you knowing about him if it means there's someone to watch mom. He was so nervous today about her catching us."

"Yeah, hopefully so."

"You really are too good to be true, you know?" Sloan turned her body toward him. "Just be careful. Don't slip up and say anything about Ridge."

"Don't worry. I can keep a secret." Dylan mimicked zipping his lips, turning a key, and throwing it to the ground.

Sloan knelt down to the concrete to pick up the imaginary key, used it to unlock Dylan's lips, and leaned in for a kiss.

"You definitely have a type," Ridge said after Dylan drove away. "He reminds me of Noah."

"Really?" Sloan considered the similarities. "Yeah. I guess you're right. They're both the quiet, gentle types, but Noah's practical, and Dylan's a dreamer."

"And you're sure we can trust him?"

"Come on; you just said he reminds you of Noah. Plus, now, we don't have to worry about Mom. You should have seen her face fall when I said Dylan had to drop me off for an appointment before they could hang out. But I wanted y'all to have a chance to meet."

Ridge took a drink of his soda. "So, what about Liam? Same temperament as Noah and Dylan?"

"Ha!" Sloan set her drink on the table in front of her. "No way. Liam Bevan is as bold as brass."

"Did you meet him at LeTourneau?"

"Yeah. Sophomore English. I was so surprised someone like him could be into—" Sloan stopped. "Wait. How did you know where I went to college?"

Ridge's eyes widened. It was brief, but Sloan noticed. He got up and turned toward the cabinets above him. "You must've told me."

She hadn't. They hadn't talked at all about college.

"Or I might've seen it online somewhere." Ridge opened a cabinet and pulled out what appeared to be a scrapbook. "Wanna see my college days?"

"You went to college?"

"Yep," he said.

Sloan huffed. "Ridge, you've really got to tell me what happened . . . why you disappeared . . . where you've been."

His face darkened. "I told you. I don't want to talk about it. Now, do you want to see these pictures or not?"

Sloan scooted over to make room for her brother. "What school did you attend?"

"Cornell."

Sloan rubbed the cover of the scrapbook. The words *Freshman and Sophomore years* written in black Sharpie. "Cornell," she repeated. "Same as Mom."

"Yeah." Ridge reached over and turned to the first page. "This is the campus."

Sloan saw that it wasn't her brother's handwriting below the picture. It was tiny, neat, and decorative. She turned the page and saw a photo of a younger Ridge, sitting in his dorm room surrounded by boxes. *Big man on campus, day one*, the caption read.

Sloan's brain felt waterlogged. This was a book a mother would make. She lowered her eyes down the page and noticed a photo was missing. All that remained were the four corner tabs and a caption: *We were so proud.*

Sloan stared at the page until her vision blurred. Whoever was in that missing photo had likely taken Ridge and raised him as their own. "What happened to this picture?"

Ridge shrugged. "Must've fallen out somewhere."

Her eyes bounced to the adjoining page, searching for more clues.

Pictures of the dorm room were decorated with Chicago Bulls posters, signed jerseys, and ticket stubs. Whoever raised her brother had money—an expensive college, tickets to Chicago Bulls games. "Since when do you like basketball?"

Ridge scratched his cheek. "I got into it around middle school."

"I see." Sloan's stomach tensed. None of this made sense. Ridge had developed a relationship with his captors. They were obviously terrible people to take a child, but not as terrible as Eddie Daughtry. These pictures, these captions, this life Ridge had lived, proved that.

Sloan turned page after page, looking at pictures of birds, football games, bonfires, and Ridge with various friends. Each photo captioned in the same loving handwriting. *Ridge and Tracy,* one caption read above a picture of Ridge with a pretty blonde.

"Girlfriend?" Sloan asked.

"She was. Didn't stick."

Sloan turned the page. There was a picture of Ridge wearing a suit and American flag tie, standing in a group of other well-dressed students, hands all clasped in front of them. Next to it, Ridge in the same suit and tie, holding a stack of blue "Dole/Kemp" yard signs. *Hard at work with the Young Republicans,* the caption read, a peeling American flag sticker above it.

Sloan pushed down the sticker's edges. "You were a Young Republican?"

Ridge gave a curt nod. "Yeah, so?"

Sloan laughed. "Don't tell Mom and Dad."

Ridge joined her, but his was a nervous laughter. Did he even know their parent's political beliefs? He'd left so young and been gone so long, probably not. He probably didn't even consider them Mom and Dad.

A few pages later, Sloan found a second spot with a missing picture. *Home for Christmas*, it read, a hand-drawn string of lights looping through the words.

Ridge flipped the page before Sloan had the chance to comment. "Check out the snow we got that January."

Sloan pressed her back against the couch. This felt just the same as finding out about her father's secret life all those years ago.

"This is a lot to take in," she said. "Mind if I take it and look at it later?"

"Oh yeah, you bet." Ridge closed the book for her. "Be sure you put it somewhere Mom won't see it."

"Yeah, of course." Sloan picked up her drink, downing it in one guzzle.

"What about you?" Ridge asked. "Do you have any pictures?"

"I have some with friends and stuff," she said. "And Mom has a few scrapbooks of us when we were kids somewhere."

"I'd love to see them."

Sloan picked at the tab on her empty can. "I'll check the attic."

"Thank you," Ridge said. "And if you come across Blue, it would be cool to have him again too."

*And it would be cool to know what the hell happened to my brother,* Sloan thought.

"I should go." Sloan pulled the phone out of her pocket. "I don't want to overwhelm Dylan on day one." She glanced around the RV. "Is there anything you need from the store?"

Ridge stood. "Nah, I'm stocked up. Need a ride home?"

"No thanks. Dylan and I are going to pick up some dinner and eat with Mom. What are your plans for the evening?"

"Gonna head out to the creek and work with Crawford. He seems to be adapting well on his free flights. Probably won't be long before he finds a mate and doesn't come back."

Sloan understood the implications of that. Once Crawford flew away, Ridge would do the same. "I'll dig around for the pictures tonight too."

Ridge smiled. "Digging up bones."

Sloan understood his meaning immediately: their dad loved Keith Whitley, but Randy Travis came in a close second. And "Diggin' up Bones" was one of his very favorite songs. Sloan had been reluctant to bring up their father again after Ridge's first reaction, but maybe this was a sign he was willing to talk about him, evidence that he was remembering better times.

"Yep," Sloan said. "Resurrecting memories indeed. I'll bring whatever I find tomorrow."

# Chapter 22

*Mallowater, TX, 1988*

Caroline marched back into the health office. "You gave me the wrong certificate."

The young clerk who had helped her stood, her eyes wide. An older woman from an office with gray hair pulled in a tight bun walked up to the counter. "The wrong one you say?" She shot a glare at the other clerk. Caroline felt bad for the poor woman. She didn't mean to get her in trouble.

"Yes, this one is for a Bradley Hadfield. The father has the same name as my partner."

"Didn't you check her ID, Susan?" the woman turned to the younger clerk.

"It's not a big deal," Caroline said, pulling out both papers. "If you can just get me the correct one, there's no harm done. Ridge Hadfield, date of birth May 2, 1978." She pushed the documents across the counter and noticed the signature lines on the Certificate of Live Birth for the first time.

"Ma'am?"

Caroline realized she was still hanging on to the papers. "I'm sorry." She released them, bringing a shaky hand to her throat.

It couldn't be. But it had looked so much like Jay's signature. The big full capital letters, the largeness of the loop in the y, the upward slant from the line he was supposed to be signing on.

"Would you mind printing the other certificate for Ridge well?" Caroline asked. "The one from the hospital? It would be nice to have for his baby book."

"Of course," the older woman said. "Just one moment."

Caroline paced across the room, a storm of questions brewing. Did Jay have an illegitimate child? Caroline caught the hypocrisy of thinking of this child as illegitimate when Sloan and Ridge were technically illegitimate as well.

"Here you are." The older woman held up another envelope. "We are so sorry about the—"

Before she could finish, Caroline snatched it out of her hands. "Thank you," she managed, already opening the envelope as she walked out the door.

Her eyes went straight for the line on the Certificate of Live Birth where Jay had signed. There was the oversized J, the Y with the ridiculously large loop, and the signature that steadily rose above the line. Her entire body went numb.

She climbed into her car and drove home too fast, questions buzzing around in her brain. *Who was Anna Elliott? What did she look like? Was it just one time? Did she know about me? Did Jay meet his son? Have a relationship with him? Has he been paying child support? Is that why we never have money?*

Jay had really cheated on her. That sonofabitch. Pressure built in her chest until she realized she was holding her breath. Hopefully, it had just been once. A horrible mistake. She'd almost made one of those. Three years ago, with Sloan's third-grade teacher, Mr. Brewer.

Frank Brewer was ten years older than Caroline, tall with salt and pepper hair and a strong baritone voice. There had been an instant attraction between them. They were friendly all year, flirty even. Mr. Brewer always wanted to talk to her about Sloan, even when there was nothing much to say. They'd always end up discussing politics, science, books, and films. Frank always smelled of just-applied cologne. Caroline thought about him on nights she laid in bed alone, even on a few she didn't. She listened to "You're the First Time I've Thought About Leaving" over and over, finally understanding what Jay meant when he talked about songs you could feel in your soul.

But she hadn't left. Nothing had even happened between her and Frank. They were both in committed relationships; they were both good people. Maybe they'd fantasized about it; Caroline certainly had, but that was as far as it had gone. When Ridge entered third grade, Caroline didn't even request that he be placed in Mr. Brewer's class. Now, she wished she had.

*No*, she told herself. Even if she knew Jay cheated, she wouldn't have done anything differently. She'd never sleep with another woman's husband, no matter the sparks that flew. And if she had, well, she wouldn't have been stupid enough to get pregnant. This Anna woman might have been trying to trap Jay.

When Caroline returned home, Jay was sprawled out on the couch watching a news program detailing the Bush/Dukakis debate from the night before. He jumped up when she walked in. "Hey baby," he said, looking especially contrite. "Did you get the certificate?"

"Yes. There was a bit of a mix-up, but I got it."

"Listen, if Ridge doesn't want to play sports, it's okay. Sorry I was a jerk about it. There's just a lot of stress at work. Can you forgive me?"

*Never.* "We all have bad days," she said coldly. "I'm sort of in the middle of one myself."

"Yeah, I'm sorry about that." Jay pulled her close to him.

Caroline remained stiff in his arms. He must have noticed because he leaned in and pressed his lips against hers. She didn't kiss back.

He broke away from her, seemingly perplexed that she would still be angry with a kiss like that. He could be such an arrogant bastard sometimes. "And I'm sorry for what I said about you spending all your time at the creek," he added, stroking her hair. "The opposite is true. But Sloan's twelve now. She's old enough to cook dinner and help around the house. That way, you can spend more time there. Treat it like a job, keep office hours, and I'll support you however I can."

*How about by being faithful?* Caroline thought. But she wasn't brave enough to match her words with her internal dialogue. Couldn't force Bradley's name off of her tongue.

"Kids are at school." Jay pressed his body against Caroline's. "I'm here all day."

Caroline pulled away. "I've got a headache."

Jay pursed his lips. "Did you sleep crooked again? I can give you a neck massage; that might help."

Caroline clenched her teeth. A massage. She understood what that meant. She wanted to tell him that there would be no massages, that there would be no *post* massages until he came clean about everything, but instead, she found herself agreeing.

As she lay on her stomach and Jay kneaded her shoulders, she allowed a few silent tears to fall onto her pillow. Why was she doing this? She should be confronting him. Maybe she just needed to feel close to him, needed to assure herself they still had a connection. That one night over ten years ago didn't undo everything.

But when the massage ended and she rolled over, she only felt disgust. Disgust as he kissed her neck, disgust as he ran his hand down the side of her leg. Is this the way he'd touched Anna Elliott? Caroline looked into his eyes, such a brilliant blue. *My Blue Jay*, she used to call him. But now she understood he wasn't a blue jay at all. Like crows, blue jays mated for life.

Caroline couldn't stomach looking into his eyes, so she closed her own. Closed them tight enough to pretend it was Frank Brewer on top of her.

Jay left following dinner. He always did, but for the first time, Caroline wondered why. He wasn't going to Beaumont or even Frisco. Tyler was less than an hour away. Why the rush to get on the road?

Did he just need to unwind before a busy day of knocking on doors, or was Anna Elliott meeting him at his hotel?

Caroline tried to distract herself by playing Uno with the kids, but during the third hand, she threw her cards down.

"What?" Sloan asked. "That bad a hand?"

Caroline stood up and slipped on her shoes. "Jay left his paperwork."

"No, he didn't. He had his briefcase." Ridge laid down a wild card. "I change it to red."

"It wasn't in his briefcase." Caroline spotted a manila envelope on the shelf under the phone. She knew it was empty, but they didn't. "It's in here," she said, grabbing it.

"You'll never catch him," Sloan said. "He left like thirty minutes ago."

It had been eighteen minutes, actually. Each one more torturous than the one before. "I'll take it to his hotel then."

Caroline called Doreen and repeated her made-up story. Sloan and Ridge would be fine alone for a few hours, but she didn't want Ridge to be afraid.

Caroline grabbed her purse. "Doreen and Noah are coming over. Be good for her."

Caroline was already in her car when Sloan charged out the front door, holding something in her hand. The envelope.

"Forget something?" Sloan asked in that know-it-all voice she said everything in nowadays.

Caroline took the empty envelope without saying a word to Sloan and peeled out of the driveway.

Caroline drove twenty miles per hour over the speed limit, praying that Jay hadn't done the same. She wasn't even sure what the name of the hotel was where he stayed. Jay said the company put him up wherever they got the best rate.

Simultaneous relief and dread filled Caroline when she spotted his truck five minutes outside of Tyler. She followed him, being careful to stay far enough back where he wouldn't notice her in his rearview mirror. Once in town, he turned down a road called Brookhaven Drive, a neighborhood of two-car driveways, piles of raked leaves, and an occasional campaign sign.

Jay wasn't going to a hotel. Caroline's car was suddenly stifling. She turned off the heater and cranked down her window, letting in the cool fall air that smelled of pumpkins and chimney smoke.

There had to be a reasonable explanation. *Please*, she thought. *Be lost. Be visiting your boss. Be doing anything but seeing Anna Elliott and your son. Your son. You have a son who's not Ridge.*

Jay pulled into one of those two-car driveways. Caroline parked a few houses down and across the street, glad at least to be no longer moving. She needed to be still, needed her stomach to settle.

Even with the window down, the car was too hot, and Caroline felt trapped. She opened her door and stood, watching Jay retrieve his suitcase from the truck's bed. The suitcase she'd packed full of underwear she'd washed. A gust of wind swept by. Secrets and fall leaves swirled around her.

Seconds later, the screen door of the house on Brookhaven Drive flung open. A little red-haired girl ran out and straight for Jay's arms. "Daddy!"

The wind carried the word. Jay dropped his suitcase and fell to his knees, letting the child rush into his arms. Caroline's own knees loosened, and she grabbed her door for support.

Like passing a terrible car accident, she didn't want to watch, but she couldn't turn away. Two boys came out. One looked to be Ridge's age, one older. Jay put an arm around each of them and squeezed. "Where's your mother?" Caroline heard him ask.

On cue, a short woman with strawberry blonde curls sashayed out the door and into Jay's arms. She spoke, but her voice was too soft. Caroline couldn't make out the words. But Jay was loud. He was always so damn loud.

"I missed you, darlin'," he said, then lifted her off the ground and right out of her white high heels before pressing his lips against hers.

"Ew!" The little girl screamed, charging against Jay from behind. "Stop!"

Caroline lowered herself back into the car, no longer able to stand. *Yes, stop, stop. Please, God, stop.*

They eventually did. Jay scooped the little girl onto his shoulders and took the woman's hand. The older boy grabbed the suitcase, and they all walked inside together—closing out the dark night, the chilly air, and the woman watching from across the street.

Caroline sobbed the entire way home. Sobbed and screamed. Screams that came from somewhere deep inside of her. Some dark place she didn't even know existed.

*Anna Elliott.* The name clanged inside Caroline's head. But then, realization struck her. It probably wasn't Anna Elliott, anymore. It was probably Anna Hadfield. After ten minutes of sitting in her car, Caroline had unstuck herself and driven by the house. "Hadfield Family" boasted the carved sign mounted to the yellow brick. The porch light above it acted as a spotlight, illuminating it in an almost holy glow. Caroline fantasized about grabbing a rock and shattering the porch light. That sign should be in the shadows, not her. But she had no strength left in her body. No strength to get out of the car, no strength to pick up a rock, no strength to confront them.

Caroline thought again about the boys. The younger had to be Bradley. The girl was a few years younger. Seven or eight? Caroline hadn't gotten a good look at the other boy. He was older than Bradley, that much she could tell by his height, but how much older?

Not that it mattered much either way, but if he was older than Sloan, that meant Anna was Jay's wife before he met Caroline.

If Jay had a wife, Caroline was his mistress. She'd pursued nothing further than friendship with Frank Brewer because she didn't want to be the other woman. But she already was. She'd always been Jay's other woman.

Caroline didn't remember getting home. Didn't remember making the turns or stopping at traffic lights. She wasn't even sure how long she'd been sitting in the driveway until her own porch light came on, and Doreen Dawson stepped outside.

There was no hiding that she'd been crying, but Caroline wiped her eyes anyway. As soon as she stepped out of the car, Doreen jogged toward her. "Caroline, are you okay? What happened?"

Caroline started crying again. It was cruel how tears never ran out. How the body was capable of producing them forever and ever and ever. "Jay and I just got into a silly fight. I don't want to talk about it."

Doreen gave an understanding nod. "Men can be damn fools, can't they?"

Caroline nodded, too, even though she knew *she* had been the damn fool.

"The kids fell asleep about ten minutes ago. Oh, and Ridge slipped in the kitchen. Running in his socks. He's fine but is gonna wake up with some bruises."

Caroline rubbed her head. "That boy. I've told him to stop running on the floor after I wax it. And I'm sorry I got home so late. Noah can stay the night if he's already asleep."

"It's fine, honey. He's just watching TV. We'll be home in time for him to get plenty of sleep. You try to get some too. Call me tomorrow and let me know you're alright."

As soon as Doreen and Noah left, Caroline checked on the kids. Sloan had burrowed under her quilts, and Ridge was snoring gently. Her poor babies. Thanks to their father, life as they knew it was ending.

Caroline wanted a drink. Something hard that would make her stomach burn like her throat, but she hadn't eaten since breakfast. She needed to get some food inside her so she could drink herself to sleep without throwing it all up.

She entered the pantry and pulled the cold metal chain attached to the lightbulb. The light clicked on, illuminating Caroline's perfect pantry just as the porch light had illuminated that Hadfield Family sign. She looked around the orderly storeroom. A place for everything and everything in its place. That's something her mother had always said about her own pantry when Caroline was growing up. Caroline thought it was stupid to care about something like that, but as soon as she became a mom, she surprised herself by following in her own mother's sensible heels. There was a lot about domestic life that didn't come naturally for Caroline, but her mother had taught her how to cook, and by cooking, Caroline could nurture her family. She often felt like a fraud, but food was a need she could meet. And so, she attended Tupperware parties and bought the latest storage containers. She actually asked Jay for a label maker for Christmas back in '78. She labeled and arranged, then rearranged, when she decided that perhaps the cereal should be on the low shelf because when the children grew older, they would need to reach it.

Standing in the pantry now, Caroline felt pathetic. Pathetic that she'd spent so much time and energy here. Pathetic that she'd forgotten who she was and what she liked to the point of asking for a goddamn label maker for Christmas. Pathetic that she'd ever believed that these stupid Tupperware containers made her a good mother. Pathetic that she'd always longed for Jay to acknowledge how much easier she made his life by shouldering this fundamental need of nourishing him and his children. Pathetic, pathetic, pathetic.

She swung her arm against the shelf, knocking over rows of canned goods. It felt good, watching them topple like dominoes. Standing on her tiptoes, she shook the shelf above, knocking over the canisters of flour and sugar. But their labeled containers did what they were designed to do, kept their contents contained and prevented a mess. But Caroline wanted to make a mess. She stood on the step stool to reach the sugar, then pushed open the spout on the lid and sprinkled it all over the floor, like snow. She started laughing, and it somehow improved her mood. Like she was releasing some of the chaos inside of her. She grabbed the flour container next. This time, she took the entire lid off and slung the container back and forth until it was empty. It still wasn't enough.

She broke jars, tore open boxes, and stomped on chip bags. The noise she was making never occurred to her until she caught movement out of the corner of her eye. She turned and saw Sloan standing wide-eyed in her pajamas, watching her mother lose her mind.

"Sorry I woke you, Sloan." Shame instantly replaced the strange and manic joy Caroline had just experienced.

"What's wrong, Mom?" Sloan's voice shook.

Caroline bit her lip and squeezed her eyes shut. "I'm just missing my daddy." She wiped her flour-coated hands on her jeans and put her arm around her daughter. "Come on, let's get you back in bed."

# Chapter 23

*Mallowater, TX, 2008*

Sloan smelled mold and damp wood as she climbed the ladder into the attic. "Need a push?" Dylan asked from below.

"I've got it." Sloan pulled herself up into the dark, dank room. Dylan followed closely behind. Sloan used her shirt to cover her nose. "Ugh. Sorry it stinks."

"No worries," Dylan said, but even in the dark room, Sloan saw a green tint to his face.

She took a few more steps before finding the string to the light. She pulled it, and the bare bulb flickered on.

Sloan glanced around the room. Spider webs drifted off exposed wooden beams and straddled an old rocking chair in the corner. The floorboards were dusty and littered with dead moths and mouse scat. Stacks of mildew-stained cardboard boxes lined the walls. Some were labeled in her mother's handwriting and others in an unfamiliar script. Probably Doreen's, Sloan realized, since she and

Walt had been the ones to prepare the house to be rented when Sloan left for college.

"Mind if I let in some fresh air?" Dylan kicked a box out of the way that blocked a small window. He pulled to open the window but struggled. Struggled with the latch. Struggled with his breathing.

"Here, I got it." Sloan unlatched the window, disturbing a layer of grime and dead flies on the sill. She pushed it open, and Dylan brought his head closer, taking in a deep breath. Sloan rubbed his back. "Are you claustrophobic?"

"A little." Dylan backed away from the window as his breathing resumed normal patterns. "Sorry."

"I can handle this. Why don't you keep Mom company?"

"No, it's fine with the window open." He turned toward a pile of boxes. "Any idea where to start?"

"None," Sloan said. "Some boxes are labeled, but it looks like most aren't. We're looking for pictures and albums. Oh, and a stuffed bluebird, if you can find it."

"Pictures, bird. Got it."

"Or if you find a stash of money somebody hid up here, that would be great too." Sloan unfolded a step stool to reach a high box. Dust showered down on her and produced a coughing fit.

The box Sloan found was full of Christmas decorations. It wouldn't contain what she was looking for, but she couldn't resist. She tugged out a container of red, green, and gold-colored satin balls. Sloan held one in her palm and scratched her thumbnail against it, remembering doing the same as a child when they hung on the tree.

She continued digging into the box, pulling out strands of thick silver foil tinsel and glass bulbs shaped like tops.

Sloan took her time unpacking napkin-wrapped ornaments commemorating special memories. An engraved brass pair of bells reading *Jay and Caroline's first Christmas 1975*, a baby's first Christmas silver spoon from 1978, a gingerbread man missing one leg that still miraculously smelled the way their kitchen had the day she and Mom made him.

"Oh my gosh!" An excited flutter filled Sloan's stomach as she pulled out a small Hallmark box.

"What? Did you find something?" Dylan stepped behind her.

"This was my favorite ornament!" She pulled out the appaloosa rocking horse for Dylan to see. "Mom took us to the mall to pick out our own ornaments this year. I got the horse, and Ridge got this little rabbit inside a roller skate. I've got to find it and show him."

"No luck for me yet," Dylan said. "So far, just clothes."

"At some point, I've got to clean this place out. Sell some of it, toss more of it. But this box stays. If I'm here for Christmas, I'd like to put up our tree again."

"You should," Dylan said.

"It must have looked atrocious. Mom flocked it with white every year. New flock over the old. Hodge podge ornaments with clashing colors, but it always made me so happy. Ridge and I would lie under it and look up at the flashing lights."

"Dad and I always cut down a real one." Dylan leaned up against a stack of boxes. "By Christmas, it would sag under the weight of the ornaments, leaving pine needles everywhere, but it made me happy too."

"We should put up Christmas trees more often," Sloan said. "Maybe Christmas trees are the secret of life."

Sloan resumed looking for Ridge's roller-skating rabbit, and Dylan tackled another box.

"This must be the Halloween one." Dylan held up a sheet of mummy and vampire window clings.

"Oh! I wonder if any of our old costumes are in there."

Dylan brought his nose closer to the box and sniffed. "For sure. I can smell the plastic already."

Sloan stood, dusted off her jeans, and looked into the box. "Rainbow Bright!" She pulled out the plastic mask with eye holes right in the middle of the character's blond hair. Sloan stretched the elastic strap over her head and turned to Dylan. "Well?"

"That's terrifying," Dylan said. "Truly. They at least could have put the eye holes over her actual eyes and not in the middle of her hair."

"Right?" Sloan removed the mask. "And look at the rest of the costume. A plastic smock with a picture of Rainbow Bright. I mean, could they not have made it look like the dress she wore?"

"I think you're asking too much from a costume made from a trash bag."

Sloan laughed. "True. I'm going back to my box, but tell me if you come across my Jem costume."

"Rainbow Bright? Jem? Wow."

"Yeah." Sloan knelt in front of the Christmas box again. "I was much more colorful as a child."

"There's a Casper one in here too. Is that yours?"

"That was Ridge's. Leave it out. He'll get a kick out of seeing it again." Sloan heard the mask hit the floor as she continued digging around in the ornament box. "Here it is!" she said, pulling out the roller-skating rabbit.

When she turned to show Dylan, she noticed he had stopped searching in the box. He'd stopped moving altogether. He stared at the ground, taking quick, shallow breaths.

Sloan stood. "Hey, are you okay?"

When he didn't respond, she placed a hand on his shoulder. Dylan spun around, his eyes wide and his hands trembling. He looked frantically around the cramped attic as though searching for an escape.

"Dylan, what's going on?" Sloan asked, her own pulse picking up.

He opened his mouth, but then he crumpled to the ground right beside the mask.

"What was that?" Caroline called from below. "Everything okay up there?"

Sloan knelt beside Dylan. He pulled his knees into his chest and put his head down. His breathing still sounded labored. "Let me help you downstairs," she said. "Can you stand?"

When Dylan raised his head, his skin was flushed, and his forehead was drenched. He held out a fluttery hand for Sloan to take. She helped him stand and called for her mom.

Caroline stood at the bottom of the stairs, and they helped Dylan down. "He must have gotten too hot," Sloan said, but as she was lowering herself down the stairs, she saw what had caused Dylan's reaction. It wasn't the Casper mask he'd dropped to the floor; it was another one.

"I'm so sorry." Sloan scooted her patio chair closer to Dylan's. "I forgot about Ridge dressing as Luke Skywalker. You told me about Eddie wearing that mask."

"Not your fault." Dylan seemed fixated on a line of ants that marched across the porch. "I felt it coming on as soon as I got into the attic. Eddie kept Logan and me in his attic."

Sloan pinched the bridge of her nose. "You told me that, too. I wasn't thinking. I've had panic attacks before. I should've realized what was going on."

"Once I got the window open, I thought I'd be okay. But when I saw that mask," Dylan clutched his hands together, "it was like I was a kid again . . . like it was all happening again."

Sloan rubbed his back. "What can I do to help?"

"You helped. By getting me out of there, by helping me calm down, by giving me time." Dylan turned his head toward the front door. "I just wish your mom hadn't seen me freak out like that."

Sloan swatted a mosquito on her arm. "Mom can hardly talk to anyone about freak-outs, now, can she?"

"Come on, Sloan. Caroline's been through a lot. The human spirit isn't indestructible."

"Well, no need to stay with her today." Sloan lowered her voice. "My plans can wait till tomorrow if you're up for it then."

"I'm up to it now," Dylan said. "Go. Your mom and I are going to watch *America's Funniest Home Videos* and *Desperate Housewives*, okay? Don't crash our plans."

Sloan smiled. "Okay, but only if we get our date when Mom goes to bed. You can control the remote."

"How about we look at a different kind of star?" He pointed up to the sky. "We can spread out a blanket and count the stars. And if the mood strikes, I've got my guitar out in the jeep."

Sloan leaned closer to Dylan, touching her forehead to his. "Most guys would have bowed out of my crazy life a long time ago."

"And most girls would have bowed out of mine today." He unstuck his forehead to move his lips to hers. Their kiss was interrupted by a bang on the window behind them.

"Come on, Dylan! Funniest Videos is starting." Caroline motioned him inside.

"On my way," he said, rising from the chair. He smiled at Sloan. "I'd like to stay, but then I'd miss videos of kids falling off trampolines and cats meowing strangely."

Sloan rubbed her forehead. "Sorry. Mom has always had the most annoying taste in television."

"It's fine," Dylan said, opening the screen door. "These days, I'll take laughs however I can get them."

Brad called as Sloan was driving to the RV park. "Still no luck with Daughtry," he said. "I bet he'd talk for the money, but his lawyer won't let us anywhere near him. May have to bribe a guard or something."

"Well, thanks for trying," Sloan said.

"I won't give up. It's important we get to the bottom of this. There's something to it. I'm sure of it."

Sloan grimaced. He had no idea.

She realized she should call the whole thing off now, but she couldn't bring herself to. She still had too many questions. "Well, keep me posted, okay?" she said.

"Yeah, I will. But hey, that's not the only reason I called. Dad gets out Thursday."

Sloan slouched in her seat. With everything going on with Ridge, she'd forgotten.

"And I was wondering . . . " Brad continued, "The media's going to be buzzing like flies. It would be nice if you were there with us. In a show of solidarity for Dad."

"A show of solidarity?" Sloan sat up straighter. "Why would I do that?"

Brad cleared his throat. "I just assumed that since you saw Dad, since you agreed with me about Eddie that—"

"I'm not some PR puppet. I'm an actual human being with feelings," Sloan practically screamed into the phone.

"Okay, okay." Brad lowered his voice. "I just thought you were all in for Dad."

"Well, you thought wrong." Sloan ended the call without bothering to say goodbye.

Sloan and Ridge sat outside his RV, drinking beer and watching the darkening sky. "Sorry I wasn't able to get the pictures. But I'll bring them tomorrow, along with a few other things that will make you smile," Sloan said.

"You coming here makes me smile," Ridge said. "Man, I wish it was fall, so we could head out to the creek and watch a roost. Remember the last time we did?"

"Yes. Flying crows, flying stars." Sloan brought the beer bottle to her lips but lowered it before taking a drink. "You wanted to stay longer. I promised you I'd bring you back. You said I wouldn't." Sloan froze, and goosebumps suddenly covered her arms. "Wait. How did you know we wouldn't go back?"

Ridge picked at his beer bottle's label. "That was just me being an annoying little brother. And you must admit, it's not like you enjoyed taking me anywhere."

Sloan relaxed and took a drink. She was reading too much into everything. She swatted at an ant on her ankle. "The ants are bad tonight."

"That will make the crows happy."

"Oh yeah?" Sloan turned her body towards Ridge. "How so?"

"Anting," he said. "You know what anting is, right?"

"Do I look like Mom?"

Ridge studied her. "Yeah, kinda. You have her cheekbones."

Sloan rolled her eyes. "Okay, so what's anting?"

"Well, crows and some other birds will sometimes take ants and crush them against their bodies," Ridge explained. "Scientists aren't exactly sure why it happens. Most believe it's for protection against parasites, but some think that the formic acid excretion of the ant gives the birds a pleasurable sensation."

Sloan wrinkled her nose. "So, like a sexual thing?"

"No, more like a getting high thing. Sometimes birds dance around afterward. It probably feels like being stoned."

Sloan laughed. "And how would you know how getting stoned feels, Mr. Young Republican?" Sloan thought again about the scrapbook. *Who was in those missing pictures, Ridge?*

"Oh, I smoked a time or ten," Ridge said.

Sloan took another sip of her beer. "Well, that's ten more times than I've done it." *Where are those missing pictures, Ridge?*

"You're kidding."

"I hung out with Noah Dawson in high school. Do you think he'd ever in a billion years smoke pot? Noah the Noble?"

"Good point," Ridge said. "But college? With your life of the party, Liam?"

Sloan shook her head. "Nope. He was a wine kind of guy." *They could be inside the camper.*

Ridge picked up an ant and squeezed. "Here. Rub it under your armpits and see what you think."

"Stop." Sloan slapped the ant out of his hand and excused herself to use the bathroom. She had to at least look for the picture. Once in the RV, her eyes went straight to the cabinet under the television where the scrapbook had been.

Sloan glanced out the window to ensure Ridge wasn't approaching, then darted to the drawer. She pulled it open, wincing when it creaked. She looked inside. Empty. *Dammit.* She tried the drawer above it, but it was filled with DVDs, mostly old westerns. Ridge didn't like westerns. Not the Ridge she knew anyway. *This isn't his RV,* Sloan thought as she searched the bedroom area. Though some of Ridge's clothes hung in the closet, so did a leather belt with a gaudy brass buckle shaped like the United States. A pair of bifocals sat beside a paperback copy of Sue Grafton's *T is for Trespass* on the bedside table.

Maybe this belonged to his parents . . . his fake parents. *Find something with their names.*

She walked back into the living area and glanced around. She wasn't even sure what exactly she was looking for. Maybe a magazine with an address label or a Christmas letter they'd received on the fridge, but every surface was clear.

Sloan stole another gaze out the window. Ridge was standing now, stretching his lower back. Time was running out.

She rushed into the bathroom to flush the toilet when she noticed the medicine cabinet. She tugged it, and it opened with a pop that made her jump. Aspirin, contact solution, Rolaids, cold cream—no prescription bottles.

Sloan closed the cabinet and decided it was time to leave. Ridge was surely getting suspicious. She was about to walk out the door when it hit her. *The registration.* If this RV belonged to Ridge's parents, their names would be on the registration.

The glovebox stuck when Sloan tried to open it the first time. She pulled harder, and it popped open, sending a piece of paper flying through the air. *Dammit.* Sloan turned to grab it just as she heard Ridge yell, "Everything okay in there?"

"Be right out!" She picked up the paper from the floor and realized it was actually a picture. And not just any picture. A picture of a family in front of a Christmas tree. And it wasn't just any family—it was Ridge's family. His *new* family. This was one of the missing pictures from the scrapbook.

Sloan's hand shook as she brought the photo closer to her face. It couldn't be. It couldn't.

But it was. Her entire body shook. The camper spun.

Sour beer sloshed in her empty stomach and rose in her throat. She turned and grabbed the trash can just in time to vomit.

"Sloan?" She heard Ridge climbing the steps.

She shoved the photo into her pocket and coughed loudly to hide the glove compartment's sound when she pushed it closed.

Ridge pushed the door open and stepped inside, nose wrinkling at the sight and smell of the trash can. "Are you sick?"

"Yeah, sorry." Sloan wiped her mouth with the back of her hand. "Told you I'm a lightweight."

"Wow, yeah." Ridge rubbed the back of his neck. "Let me drive you home."

"No, I'm good." Sloan stumbled down the steps. "I'll see you tomorrow." She patted her jean pocket to make sure the picture was there. Its sharp corner dug into her skin.

She waited until she was almost home before pulling over to the side of the road to look at the photo again. The faces had not changed. Sloan stared at the three of them until she started to cry. The crying soon gave way to screaming. She screamed until her throat was raw and her fists hurt from pounding on the steering wheel. Then she put the picture back in her pocket and drove home.

# Chapter 24

*Mallowater, TX, 1988*

"Are you sure?" Libby asked again. "I mean, are you *really* sure?"

Caroline wrapped her trembling hands around her coffee cup. "I know what I saw."

Libby shook her head. "This doesn't sound like Jay. He adores you."

"I'm his mistress." Caroline's eyes burned again. "I stopped by the library this morning. Found their wedding announcement in the Tyler Tribune. He and Anna married in 1970, five years before we met." Caroline recalled that night in New York where she'd waited on his table. Jay was married; he had a child. Her relationship with Jay Hadfield had been a lie right from the start.

"Why didn't you call me last night?" Libby reached across the table to touch Caroline's arm. "How did you face this alone?"

Caroline wiped her eyes with the sleeve of her sweatshirt. "I destroyed the pantry."

"What?" Libby asked.

"I destroyed the pantry. I need to clean it up before the kids come home."

Libby waved her hands. "I'll do it. Don't worry about anything. I can stay a few days and handle the kids."

Caroline bent forward, laying her head on her arms. How was this her life?

"When does Jay come home?" Libby asked.

Caroline lifted her head. "Friday."

"Okay. That gives you some time to figure things out."

"What is there to figure out, Libby?" Caroline's voice shook. "I'm leaving him."

Libby nodded. "You'll need a lawyer to sort out child support and custody issues. I'll ask Vince who he recommends."

"What custody issues? I'll keep the kids. Of course, I'll keep the kids."

"It won't be that simple," Libby said. "The court won't take away all Jay's rights because he's an immoral man. He's still their father. And you weren't legally married to him, so I don't think bigamy laws apply."

An edgy, twitchy feeling crawled up Caroline. "He's not taking them to *her* house. To Anna's house."

"I'm sure he won't. Anna will leave him too, don't you think?"

"And if she doesn't?"

"Well, either way, when you calm down, you'll realize that keeping the kids from their father is not healthy. Sloan and Ridge love Jay, and he really is a wonderful dad."

Rushed breathing made Caroline's throat dry. A wonderful dad? A wonderful dad wouldn't do this. Any judge would see that.

"Jay's not a good dad," Caroline spoke through clenched teeth.

"Okay, okay." Libby pursed her lips. "These are things you can deal with later and—"

Libby stopped when the front door swung open. Caroline glanced at the microwave clock. "It's the kids." She didn't want to see them. Not still wearing last night's clothes with last night's black mascara smeared all over her gummy eyelids.

Libby dashed out to meet Sloan and Ridge in the living room. Caroline listened to her tell them that their mom was sick, so she'd be staying a few days to help. The news elicited cheers from her children. Cheers that Caroline was ill, cheers that they'd have a better mother for a few days. They were so ungrateful.

"Let's get a coke from Sonic and some Pickle-O's too. We'll eat them at the park. Call and invite Noah," Libby said.

More cheers. Caroline realized she should be thankful for a friend like Libby, but she only felt betrayed. How could she still consider Jay a good father? How could she believe that Jay deserved to see the children? Jay Hadfield deserved something alright, but not taking her children into Anna Hadfield's house like they were some big happy family.

Caroline knew what she deserved; she deserved to go back in time and never wait on Jay Hadfield's table. She deserved her internship and a chance to earn her Ph.D. She deserved to study crows at a prestigious lab, not some dirty creek in Podunk, Texas.

She deserved her entire life back.

Libby and the kids returned two hours later. Caroline heard them come in but didn't move from her spot on the pantry floor.

Libby's heels clicked as she walked through the small house. "Caroline? Where are you?"

"In here," Caroline said.

The door opened a few seconds later. The suitcase in Libby's hand dropped when she saw the mess. "What are you doing?"

Caroline pressed her hand into a pile of flour. "I was going to clean it up, but I just don't want to." She raised her flour-coated hand and touched the wall, depositing a handprint. "I sort of like it better like this."

Libby sniffed the air. "Have you been drinking?"

*Had she?* Caroline wasn't sure, but judging by the warm and cozy feelings rushing through her body, she might have had a glass.

"Come on, get up. I'll get this cleaned up while the kids do their homework. Take a shower and go to bed."

Caroline tried to stand, but she slipped on the remnants of a turned-over bottle of wine. She held up the bottle and laughed. "Guess I had a drink."

"Here." Libby reached for her hand. Caroline made it halfway up when she hit a pile of brown sugar and slipped again. Libby stepped back and rubbed her forehead. "Oh, for goodness' sake, Caroline."

Caroline picked up some brown sugar and sprinkled it on her chest. "What's that song that was so popular last year?"

"I don't know, but we need to get you out of here."

Caroline tried to snap her fingers, but the flour made it impossible. "*Pour Some Sugar on Me.*" That's the song." She lowered her voice. "It's about sex, you know?"

Libby crossed her arms. "Yeah, I got that."

"Jay and I had sex right here." Caroline slapped the floor. "Right on this frigid linoleum. I bet he and Anna never had sex in *their* pantry."

Libby bent down. "Caroline, your kids are down the hall. They don't need to see you like this. Pull yourself together, and let me help you up."

"Dammit, I'm trying." Caroline attempted to suppress a laugh. "I waxed the floor a few days ago, so it was already slippery before all this spilled. I mean, I assumed that's what good housewives did. Waxed the floors, had sex with their husbands on waxed floors, etcetera, etcetera."

"Yeah. Ridge told me he fell too. He's really banged up."

Caroline tried to remember Ridge falling. "Ridge didn't slip on the floor." Caroline felt like she was speaking in slow motion, like a cassette getting chewed up by a boombox.

"What do you mean? What happened to his face?"

Right as Libby asked, Caroline remembered. Doreen had told her last night that he'd slipped. But before she could explain, Libby's words came to mind. Jay would get to see the kids. Caroline couldn't let that happen.

"Well, actually," she said, forcing the smile off her face, "Ridge didn't fall. Jay did that to him."

Caroline woke with a start the next morning. The sun shining through her curtains meant she had overslept. She needed to wake the kids and get them ready for school.

She sat up and immediately regretted it as blood rushed to her already pounding head. "Ow," she groaned, falling back onto her pillow.

"Are you awake?"

Caroline raised her head and saw Libby standing in the doorway, wearing an apron and holding a wooden spoon. "Did the kids get on the bus?" Caroline asked.

"Yes. Now get up. I'm scrambling eggs."

Caroline pulled the pillow over her head. "My brain is scrambled eggs."

"You had a lot to drink," Libby said. "Do you even remember?"

Caroline tried to recall the night before. The details were foggy, but she remembered flour, handprints, spilled wine, and a lie. "A little," she answered, sitting up in bed. She noticed her clean pajamas. "Thanks for hosing me off."

"Pantry is cleaned up, too. Not much was salvageable, so we'll have to make a grocery run before the kids get home." Libby flipped the light on. "Get up."

Caroline didn't argue. She dragged herself out of bed and to the kitchen table. "Coffee." She made the word a sentence.

Libby pushed an already-filled cup toward her, along with two aspirin. Caroline put the pills in her mouth and let them dissolve for a second on her tongue before taking a sip of her coffee. The pills tasted bitter; the coffee tasted bitter; everything inside Caroline was bitter.

"So . . ." Libby sat in the chair across from Caroline. "What really happened to Ridge?"

*He slipped on the floor.* Caroline should just say it. Tell the truth. She was drunk last night. Libby wouldn't hold anything she'd said against her.

Caroline, however, held something against Libby. She'd defended Jay. Defended his right to see Sloan and Ridge when he'd voluntarily missed half their lives. How many times had he claimed to be away on business when he was actually going back to his real family in Tyler? And now, he'd want to take her children with him. If her best friend thought he deserved to see Sloan and Ridge, so would a judge.

"Jay did it," she said, looking Libby in the eyes. "Jay hurts him a lot. Still think he's some polygamist dad of the year?"

"He did it in one of his flashbacks." Libby made it a statement rather than a question. Libby's blind faith turned Caroline's stomach. Jay hadn't only charmed her; he'd charmed everyone into believing he was a good man. He'd cast a spell on them so strong that even when faced with proof that he was a terrible human being, they justified and defended him.

"No!" Caroline slammed her palms into the table. "Not a flashback. Jay doesn't have flashbacks."

"But—"

"I made that up," Caroline said. "I knew you'd notice the bruises and had to think of something."

Libby's gaze clouded. "Jay's been abusing you? All this time?"

"Yeah," Caroline said. And he had. Emotional abuse was abuse, maybe the most dangerous kind.

"I'm so sorry." Libby covered her mouth. "I never suspected. When did this start?"

Caroline tucked her hair behind her ear and looked Libby right in the eye. "Well, for Ridge, it all started a few weeks ago when Jay got angry and threw him against the wall . . ."

When the phone rang late that night, Caroline knew who it was. When Jay called, it was always late, long after the kids had gone to bed, sometimes even after Caroline had. She always imagined him lying in his hotel bed, fighting off sleep just long enough to make sure hers was the last voice he heard. But now she realized he was probably sneaking out of Anna's bed to call Caroline. And if he was sneaking away from Anna to call her, he was sneaking away from her to call Anna.

"I can't talk to him," Caroline said.

"Okay, should I just let it ring or—"

"He'll keep calling. Answer and come up with an excuse."

Libby sighed but answered the phone. Caroline listened as Libby explained that she was staying over to help with the kids since Caroline wasn't feeling well. Caroline could hear the concern in Jay's voice on the other side of the line. It was almost convincing.

"Thank you," she said when Libby hung up the phone.

Libby retied her robe and sat back down next to Caroline on the couch. "Okay, so as I was saying, Vince called his friend from college who's a lawyer. He said the abuse would be hard to prove since you took no pictures nor called the police."

"I've called Walt," Caroline said.

Libby held up a finger. "That's good. He's probably had to keep records."

Caroline bit her lip. "I've lied, though, saying Jay hurt me during a flashback." *And he's seen Jay having flashbacks*, Caroline thought.

"Well," Libby continued, "the good news is that the judge would probably talk to Ridge and Sloan."

*Shit.* Caroline might convince Ridge to lie if he believed this was for the greater good, but Sloan would never play along. She worshiped her dad.

"I don't want the judge talking to them. How traumatizing! I don't want anyone talking to them about it, including you or Vince. I've spent so much time trying to convince them that the times their Daddy hurt us, he was having a bad dream. They'd tell the judge that too."

Libby pinched the bridge of her nose. "Well, I'm not sure what other options you have here, Caroline. We have to protect you; we have to protect the kids. Sloan and Ridge need to hear the truth. All of it. The other family, the story you made up to justify Jay's violence, everything."

Caroline's guts felt knotted together. Sloan and Ridge were not toddlers that she could sell bullshit to. Sloan especially. "There's got to be a safer, more sure-fire way."

Libby folded her legs underneath her. "Okay, so let's brainstorm. Vince already said we'd pay for your lawyer and do anything we can to help you. What else can we do?"

That question—What else can we do?—kept ringing through Caroline's mind. It was that question that planted the seed for everything that was to come.

"It would have to be after we leave," Libby said. "If he disappears when we move, it will raise red flags, don't you think?"

"Yeah, you're right," Caroline said. It was 2:00 AM, and Caroline had to pinch herself every so often to be sure this wasn't a dream. Libby had gone from shock and outrage at Caroline's plan to putting the finishing touches on it. Half of Caroline thought this was all just crazy talk—that they'd both wake up in the morning and laugh at the silly fantasy their exhaustion and anger had cooked up. But the other half of her thought it was crazy enough to work.

"I can tell Jay he needs to plan a fishing trip with Ridge. I can crush some sort of pills in his drink. Once he's out, Ridge can walk to a set location, and you and Vince can be there."

"That all sounds well and good, but they'll assume someone took Ridge. They won't stop looking."

Caroline chewed on her fingernail. "What if we made it look like Jay killed him?"

"Caroline!" Libby pulled away from her. "The plan was getting Ridge to safety, not to frame Jay."

"It's like you said, unless they believe Ridge is dead, they'll never stop looking. They might find out what we did. I'd lose the kids forever. And Jay has to pay, Libby."

"I want him to pay, but not with life in prison for a crime he didn't commit."

"We can't prove the domestic violence, but we can prove this."

Libby stood up. "This is going too far."

"Come on, Libby. You work with domestic violence victims. These abusers don't change. Jay will keep hurting Ridge. And you know what happens to boys who grow up with an abusive father." Caroline slapped her hand on her bare leg. "You know! You talk about it all the time. Children of abusers often grow up and become abusers. The cycle continues."

Libby sat back down. "Even if we helped you, how are you going to convince Ridge to go along with this? No, he shouldn't have to grow up with an abusive father. But he shouldn't have to conspire with his mom to frame his father either."

"I'll figure out Ridge. You talk to Vince and see what he—" Caroline stopped when the motion porch light outside flickered on. Libby noticed it, too, and looked back at Caroline, eyes wide.

"It was probably a cat. I didn't hear a car door or—"

Before Caroline could finish, the doorknob turned. She jumped up, then froze, staring at the handle twisting like she was in the middle of some horror movie. Who else had a key but . . . ?

"Jay!" She screamed. "You scared me. What are you doing home?"

Jay looked at her and then at Libby, clutching her robe and trying to hide behind a throw pillow.

"I came home to take care of you. Libby told me you were sick. I figured I could take off a few days." His face scrunched. "But you seem to be feeling just fine."

Caroline swallowed, wondering how long he'd been standing out on the porch. How much he'd overheard.

"She's been throwing up all night," Libby said. "But I think she's finally okay to go back to bed."

Jay's face seemed to relax, and so did Caroline's heart rate. He hadn't been out there. The light would have come on sooner.

"Ah well, let's get you in bed, darlin'." He put his hand on her back. "I figured it had to be bad for you to ask Libby to come over. You can always call me when you need me. Family comes before work."

Caroline had to stop herself from laughing at that one. She wondered what lie he'd told Anna. Emergency broom sale at 2:00 a.m.?

"Thanks, Libby," Jay said. "I'll take it from here."

"It's so late, I don't mind crashing out on the couch. I can get up and help with the kids."

"I can take care of my wife and my children." Caroline caught the annoyance in Jay's voice.

"It's fine, Libby." Caroline looked into her friend's eyes and tried to convey that leaving was okay. Libby didn't look convinced, but she picked up her suitcase behind the couch.

"All right," she said quietly. "I'll call in the morning to check in on you, but if you need anything before—"

"Good night, Libby," Jay said loudly. "Go home."

# Chapter 25

*Mallowater, TX, 2008*

Sloan stared at the picture. Libby, Vince, and Ridge standing in front of a bright, beautiful Christmas tree. None of them were looking at the camera, and they'd all been caught mid-laugh. It was the kind of perfect picture that you couldn't plan. One that captured genuine happiness.

They looked like a family out of the Sears Christmas Wish Books Sloan flipped through each year as a child, circling Barbies and paint-by-numbers books, knowing that no matter how tight money was, several of these gifts would somehow end up under the tree. She tried circling items as a teen, but it never worked. Sloan gave up wishing for CD players and watercolor paint sets but still flipped through the pages longingly each year, wishing she had a happy family who wore matching Christmas pajamas.

Why would Libby and Vince Turner kidnap Ridge? The question pinged back and forth between the walls of Sloan's skull. Libby was her mom's best friend. And why would Ridge go with them? How could he accept them as his family?

She wanted to call Ridge now. Wanted to demand answers, but it would only push him away. Still, she realized she couldn't contain a secret this vast. You couldn't fit the ocean inside a vase.

*Dylan,* she thought. She needed to call Dylan. She'd told him she had thrown up and needed a raincheck when she'd returned from seeing Ridge. He had been understanding, but he might have taken it personally. She needed Dylan to help her make sense of it. And he's the only one who knew Ridge was alive. There was no one else to call. Sloan pulled out her cell phone. But rather than go to her contacts and find Dylan's name, she dialed a number she had memorized years before. She called Noah.

"What's this about, Sloan?" Noah tugged his baseball cap down lower as he walked toward Sloan's porch.

She pushed the screen door open. "Come inside."

Noah looked back out at the street as though he'd been followed.

"Oh, come on. You didn't want to meet in public because it could look bad. Now you don't want to come in my house for the same reason? Get over yourself."

Noah shook his head. "You've got some nerve, you know? The last time I heard from you, you said you were using Dylan Lawrence for sex.

Then you call tonight, frantic, demanding that I come over, refusing to say why. I'm off tonight. I had to lie to Vickie, and it's not worth it. *You're* not worth it. If you need something, call the police department."

Sloan watched him stomp back to his car, but even after such cruel words, she couldn't let him drive away. She charged toward him, gripping the picture in her right hand. "I may not be worth it to you, but is Ridge?"

Noah clicked his key fob, unlocking the doors of his cruiser. "What are you talking about? Is this still about Eddie Daughtry?"

"No." She held up the picture. "It's about Vince and Libby Turner."

Noah squinted at the photo, then grabbed it out of her hands. "What the hell is this?"

She snatched the picture back. "Still want me to call 911, or do you want to come in and help sort this out?"

Noah clicked the fob again, locking the doors, and followed Sloan inside the house.

Sloan filled Noah in on everything. On the talking crow, on Ridge appearing from behind the bush, on the scrapbook. She whispered, frequently breaking to glance down the hallway and make sure her mother's door remained closed.

Noah rubbed his eyes. "I can't believe this. If they moved the same time Ridge disappeared, why weren't they looked at?"

"They left before. Libby came to stay with us for the funeral."

"Did she come back again? After that?" Noah asked.

"I don't think so. Mom would talk on the phone with her for hours. Then, it just stopped. I assumed mom's deteriorating mental health was to blame."

Noah stared at the picture again. "You shouldn't have told me this, Sloan. As an officer, I have a duty to report it."

"But you're not going to," Sloan said. "Because I didn't call Noah the cop over here. I called Noah, Ridge's best friend."

Noah stood and paced in front of the couch. "Your dad is in prison, Sloan."

"And he's getting out Thursday. I'm not asking you for justice for my father; I'm asking for support for me." Sloan's voice shook, and tears filled her eyes. "I want to get to the bottom of this, but I don't want to push Ridge away, and I sure as hell don't want to face it alone."

Noah sat back down next to her but stared straight ahead. "You aren't alone."

Sloan sat still, letting the relief sink in. It filled her entire body, pushing the tears out of her eyes.

"Hey, don't cry." Noah put his hand on her knee, and Sloan's own fingers tingled with the need to touch his skin. She placed her hand on top of his. "I want to see him." Noah's voice was barely audible. "I can't believe he's alive."

Sloan turned her head towards him. "Maybe I can convince Ridge it's safe to see you. If not, we can arrange an accidental meeting."

Noah looked at her. "I'm sorry for what I said. About you not being worth it."

"And I'm sorry for the crude text about Dylan. I was drunk."

"So, you're not having sex with him?"

"No," Sloan said. "But we *are* dating."

Noah pulled his hand off her knee and scratched his face. "Well, I'm sure he's a nice guy. Sorry for assuming it was all about Eddie Daughtry."

"And I'm sorry you had to lie to Vickie. I wish it didn't have to be like that. I want us to be friends again."

Noah's eyes locked on hers. "Is that really *all* you want?"

Sloan closed her eyes. No, it wasn't all she wanted. She wanted to sneak Noah into her bedroom like she had those nights a lifetime ago. She wanted to be held in his now considerably stronger arms. She wanted to feel like a teenager in love again, but with the experience of a grown woman. Just one time. At least one time.

But Noah was too sturdy to fall, too rooted. He would never. And even if he did, then what? He'd be so wracked with guilt he'd never look at her again. Yes, she missed the passion she shared with Noah, and she was still riding the high of his touch. But a deeper intimacy is what she really craved. She missed her best friend; she missed their talks and his complete understanding of what she'd been through. His complete understanding of her.

She opened her eyes to find he was still staring at her. "Yes," she said. "That's really all I want."

"Good." Noah stood and dug his keys out of his pocket. "That's all I want too. Let's not act like we have anything to hide. I'll talk to Vickie about having you and Dylan over for dinner sometime."

Sloan's mouth went dry. "Um, yeah, sure, if she wants, but no pressure." She stood and walked Noah to the door. "And you'll look into what happened to the Turners after they left Mallowater?"

"Yeah, and you'll ask Ridge about seeing me?" He held up a finger. "Seeing Noah, the friend, not Noah, the cop."

"Absolutely." Sloan held up three of her own fingers, a nod to her Girl Scout days. "Noah, the *friend*," she said, making it a pledge to herself as well.

"Where's Crawford?" Sloan rubbed her fingers along the bars of the empty cage behind the tent.

"Pretty sure he's gone for good." Ridge looked up to the sky. "Hasn't returned in a few days."

"So that means . . ."

Ridge picked a piece of lint from his sleeve. "Yeah, time for me to go, too."

Sloan rocked slightly. "Well, you can't leave before I show you the old albums I found."

Ridge clapped his hands together. "Hell yeah, let's see 'em."

"Well, there were a lot, plus some other old things you might remember. Why don't you come over tomorrow night and look?"

Ridge's posture stiffened. "What about Mom?"

"Well, she's been drinking a glass of wine every night. If I give her a sleeping pill with it, she's out. I'm not proud of drugging her, but you don't know what she's like now."

Ridge grimaced. "I'm sorry, Lo. For what happened to her."

"Well, it wasn't *your* fault," Sloan said. "Whoever took you is to blame."

"What's that supposed to mean?" There was tension in Ridge's voice.

Sloan looked him in the eye. "I assume you didn't run away?"

Ridge jumped to his feet. "I said we weren't going to talk about this."

Sloan stood to meet him. "You owe me an explanation. Why can't you tell me what happened?"

"Because it could get people that I care about in trouble."

The folded picture of Vince, Libby, and Ridge in her pocket poked against Sloan's leg. She took a deep breath and then took a chance. If Ridge was getting ready to leave anyway, what did she have to lose? "Libby and Vince, you mean?"

Ridge took a few steps backward and leaned against the giant tree that bore his name. Even from a distance, Sloan saw the sweat dripping from his brow. "What are you suggesting?"

"I'm not suggesting anything." Sloan pulled the picture out of her pocket. "I found this."

Ridge stepped forward. "Give it back," he said.

"You can have it." Sloan tossed the picture toward him. It fluttered in the air and fell at his feet. "I'm not trying to get them in trouble, Ridge. If I wanted to do that, I could have done it already. I just want answers."

"So, all this time, you've been snooping through my stuff? Why wasn't I enough?"

"Why weren't we enough!" Sloan yelled.

"I don't know what you're talking about. You're crazy. Like Mom."

Sloan felt a flush of heat in her face and neck. "Don't you dare talk about Mom. You don't even know her."

Ridge covered his face and lowered himself to the dirt. "It wasn't my fault."

Sloan forced herself to calm down. "I know that. You were a kid."

"Libby and Vince aren't bad people. They did it for you. We *all* did it for you."

For her? Sloan took a few steps closer to Ridge and knelt down to get on his level, just like she'd done when he was young and frightened. "What do you mean?"

"Dad was hurting you, Sloan. You've blocked it out, but Mom wouldn't have lied about that."

Sloan shook her head. "Dad never hurt me. I didn't forget."

"But—"

"Think about it, Ridge. If Dad abused me like Mom said, why would she tell you? A ten-year-old? And what does that have to do with Libby and Vince taking you away? Why not me?"

Ridge looked up at the sky. "They were going to bring me back.

They were *supposed* to bring me back. That was the plan. I'm sorry, Lo."

"Start from the beginning."

Ridge raised his head till his red eyes met Sloan's. "Dad would have gotten custody, and it would never stop. The only way we would ever be safe is if he were in jail."

Sloan felt a prickling along the back of her neck. "So, it was a setup? Libby and Vince framed Dad for your murder?"

Ridge shook his head. "*Mom* framed dad. It was all her idea."

# Chapter 26

*Mallowater, TX, 1988*

Jay suspected something. Caroline was sure of it. He was overly kind and nurturing, insisting on staying home until Caroline was completely better. That was the last thing she wanted.

So, after two days of sleeping, Caroline emerged from her room Friday morning. "You can go back to work today," she announced, sitting in front of a piece of toast she knew she wouldn't be able to eat. She'd left her appetite, like so much more of her, on Brookhaven Drive.

Jay set the paper down. "I don't mind staying. I'm supposed to be coming home today, anyway. Sloan won't be happy if I miss our Friday night shows."

"You've wasted two vacation days." *Go home to your wife.* "Sloan will live. You've missed your busiest days of sales. Make up for it this weekend. I have a lot of housework to catch up on." *Because by the looks of this place, you certainly haven't lifted a finger.*

"Well, alright." Jay took the last sip of his coffee and stood. "But not without one dance."

He turned up the radio. The chorus of "Eighteen Wheels and A Dozen Roses" filled the kitchen.

Jay extended his hand. Caroline loved this song. It had seemed so fitting for her and Jay. A sweet ballad about a couple separated by work being reunited. Now the sappy lyrics made her nauseous. Whatever happened to those good ole cheating songs?

She waved his hand away. "I'm not up to dancing."

Jay pressed his hands down on the back of the chair. "What's going on, Caroline?"

She shrugged. "Do you often feel like dancing after you've been sick in bed for two days?"

Jay sat. "If you aren't up to dancing, how are you up to housework?"

Caroline's fingers retracted, became claw-like. "Well, some things have to be done, don't they? Housework, caring for children, selling cleaning products door to door to provide for your family. Then other things, well, they are extra, and frankly, I'm not up to extra."

Jay shifted in his seat. Watching him squirm made Caroline feel oddly powerful. She couldn't explain the shift inside, but she wasn't even sad anymore. She'd felt like she was dying the past two days, but she woke up today different. Perhaps she'd cried all her tears out. But she felt stronger now, like she'd risen from her own ashes.

"Are you sure everything's okay? This is me, Caroline. You can talk to me."

"I'm just sad about Libby," she said, avoiding Jay's eyes.

She heard him sigh, and she hated him even more. *If you think I'm dramatic now, just you wait.*

"Alright. I'll catch up and be home Thursday night—make it a long weekend." He leaned in for a kiss, and she turned her head, offering her cheek.

"I'm still a little warm. Don't want to get you sick."

Jay's face and neck flushed, but he said nothing, just planted a tiny kiss on her cheek. His stubble rubbed up against her face. That had once driven Caroline wild, but now she felt nothing.

He broke the news to Sloan, waved the kids off to school, and gave Caroline a last hug. "Don't overdo it," he said, kissing the side of her head. "Call Libby if you need help cleaning."

Once he was gone, Caroline did exactly that. And as soon as she hung up with Libby, she raised the heavy phone in her hand and slammed it against her eye.

Time to clean house indeed.

"Oh, honey!" Libby wrapped her arms around Caroline. "I've been so worried. Every time I called, Jay claimed you were asleep." She moved Caroline's hair away from her face. "Did this just happen?"

Caroline lowered her head. "I wouldn't give him a kiss when he left."

"That sonofabitch!" Libby's heels clicked as she entered the kitchen and retrieved a bag of frozen vegetables from the freezer. "He didn't hear us talking that night he came in, did he?"

Caroline shook her head. "I don't think so."

"We need to call the police?" Libby asked.

"No," Caroline said. "We already have a plan."

Libby swayed slightly as she wrapped the vegetables in a towel. "You still want to go through with this? It's something you really need to think about." Caroline flinched backward as Libby touched the vegetables to her eye. "Hold it," Libby instructed. "You need to get the swelling down."

Caroline took the makeshift ice pack and held it against her throbbing eye. "This is the only way. Even if they did arrest him for this, it's only a matter of time before he gets out and kills one of us."

Libby bit her lip. "Alright. Vince suggested these." She pulled a pill bottle out of her purse. "He takes them for narcolepsy."

Caroline took the bottle in her free hand and studied it.

"It's called GHB," Libby said. "It's safe. Bodybuilders use it because it induces weight loss, but it also induces sleep. It's really regulated Vince's sleep cycle, helped him sleep at night and have fewer episodes during the day."

"Okay." Caroline stared at the words on the amber-colored bottle till her vision blurred. They were really doing this.

"It's untraceable on most drug tests. Even if they took a blood sample, GHB only stays in the system for eight hours. If you give him enough, he'll pass out and won't remember a thing. It's like being drunk, but without the hangover."

"How much do I give him?"

"That's what we aren't sure about. You'll have to try a few different doses and see how long he takes to pass out and how long he stays asleep."

"Okay." Caroline set the bottle down. "He's coming home next Thursday for a long weekend. I'll try. What else?"

"We leave October 24th," Libby said. "So, this needs to happen sometime after."

Caroline stood and lifted a page of the calendar by the stove. "What about November 6th? I can tell Jay he needs to take Ridge fishing."

"Are you sure you want to risk it in public? Why not set something up here?"

"Because I want it to be clear it was Jay. It's turning cold. There won't be many people fishing. And if someone sees them there at some point, that's even better. They'll know Jay was alone with Ridge. Plus, we won't need a body."

Libby nodded. "So, we make it look like Jay passed out and drowned Ridge during an episode?"

"Or better yet, that he killed him in an episode, realized what he'd done, and then dumped him in the creek to cover it up. I mean, I'd love to make it look like it wasn't accidental at all, but then we'd have to establish a motive and that might be tougher to convince a jury of."

"Right. PTSD is an easier sell for sure, but I worry a judge wouldn't put Jay away for life for manslaughter."

"Whatever he gets will be enough." Caroline expanded her chest with a full breath and held it in. The media would cover this. The truth would all come out. Anna would find out. His kids would find out. Jay would be ruined forever, just as Caroline had been. Yes, it would be enough.

Libby cleared her throat. "So, when are you going to talk this out with Ridge?"

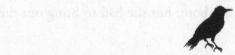

Sitting down with Ridge at the kitchen table a few weeks later was the closest Caroline had come to guilt since devising the plan. It was hard to look into those blue eyes and lie, but this was for the greater good. She couldn't let Ridge grow up with the influence of Jay Hadfield. He'd ruin everything good and pure about their boy.

"Remember last month when I told you I fell and hit my eye?" Caroline asked.

Ridge nodded.

"I was lying. Daddy hit me."

Ridge froze, eyes wide like he was struggling to comprehend.

"He's hit me a lot, hurts me a lot. There are two sides to your father. I was okay living with both until he started hurting your sister."

Ridge shook his head. "Dad never hurts Sloan. She's his favorite."

"He does." Caroline pressed her lips into a thin line. "I've noticed little bruises here and there, but she always makes up stories."

"Then how do you—"

She told her teacher," Caroline interrupted.

Ridge's chin quivered. "Then why doesn't Mrs. Evans tell the police?"

"She doesn't believe your sister. She told me to speak to Sloan about telling lies. Your dad is a very influential man, Ridge. That's why Mrs. Evans won't believe Sloan. Why no one will believe us."

Caroline's mouth felt suddenly dry. She stood and filled up a glass of water. This was nothing to lie about, but she had to bring out the brother crow in him somehow.

"I need your help, Ridge. She finally said. Sloan needs your help." Caroline took his tiny hands in hers. "Remember that crows don't fly away when they grow up like other birds; they care for their siblings. Sloan needs you to take care of her. But you can't tell her we know. Do you understand that this is our secret?"

"Yes." Ridge's voice was loud, resolute. "What do I do?"

After Caroline explained the plan to Ridge, she realized she was past the point of no return. Looking into his scared and sad eyes for a moment, she almost told him to forget all about it. But of course, he could not have forgotten, just as she could never forget what Jay had done to her. Just as a crow never forgot the face of who wronged them.

When all was said and done, Ridge only had one question, one small objection. "But I thought crow families were forever. Isn't Dad part of our nest too?"

"No," Caroline had told him. "He's a part of somebody else's. I'll explain all that to you later."

On the eve of the camping trip, Caroline was unable to sleep. She'd managed one last time to avoid Jay's advances. Between his erratic schedule and a few well-constructed excuses, October had been mostly sexless. She had given in a few times. No need for Jay to suspect anything. Not when it was so easy to close her eyes and imagine another man's face.

"Tomorrow," she'd promised him right before he had fallen asleep tonight. "I'm exhausted."

Caroline watched the rise and fall of Jay's chest as he snored. Looked at his disheveled blonde hair that hadn't yet thinned. She tried to remember how much she loved him thirteen years ago, how much she loved him six weeks ago. If her plan were successful, that man she loved would go to prison. He would leave behind two women and five children. But then she remembered how it had felt to watch him kiss another woman and scoop up another little girl in his arms. She didn't know Jay Hadfield at all. The man she had loved had never even existed. The thought was black enough to make her consider picking up her pillow and smothering him right then and there.

Caroline realized there were less permanent ways to exact revenge than what would happen tomorrow. Ideas had swirled in her head like tornado debris during those early days. She could take a crowbar to his truck or a baseball bat to Anna Hadfield's windows. She could record her and Jay having sex and leave the VHS in Anna's mailbox. She could sleep with Frank Brewer. Or she could simply show up at Jay and Anna's doorstep and enjoy watching the horror and panic overtake him. She fantasized most about that. What would he say? What would he do?

But no matter what came out of that meeting, whether he passed out, sobbed on his knees, or pissed his pants, it wouldn't be enough. It wouldn't last long enough. Their relationship had been his long con, and now, it was time for hers.

She climbed out of bed and walked across the hall to Sloan and Ridge's room. She knelt beside Ridge's bed and stroked his sweat-soaked hair. "I'm sorry, baby boy," she whispered. "Sorry I lied to you, but someday you'll understand."

She must have been louder than she intended because Ridge opened his eyes. "Mom?"

"Sorry to wake you." Caroline kissed his forehead and stood. "Go back to sleep."

Ridge sat up. "I'm nervous about tomorrow."

Caroline turned to make sure Sloan was still sleeping, then knelt beside Ridge again. "It will be okay. Remember the plan."

"Blue thermos," Ridge said. "I only drink from the blue thermos."

"That's right," Caroline whispered. "Dad has two. One is green, and one is red. Green is water, and red is sweet tea. You keep the sweet tea in your little cooler and give it to him around 3:30. He won't turn down sweet tea. The medicine will make him tired right away. He may act silly and out of it for a bit, but soon enough, he'll fall asleep. And what are you going to be doing while he sleeps?"

"Playing in the mud," Ridge whispered. "Only that's not really what I'm doing."

Caroline nodded. To anyone watching, he would look like a boy playing in the mud, but Ridge was really building the crime scene, a scene of struggle.

"I slide around in the mud, cut myself a little with my pocketknife, make sure blood is in lots of places."

"But not too deep." Caroline paused. This was like an out-of-body experience. She was telling Ridge to cut himself with his pocketknife. A pocketknife she'd argued he was too young to have.

"Not too deep," he repeated. "Make sure the bleeding stops."

"Right. There's a band-aid in your bag. Don't leave the trash on the ground. What else do you leave there? In the mud?"

Ridge pointed to his hair.

"That's right. And when no one is watching, you need to scratch your daddy's arms a few times, or even his face. Take his hand and scratch yourself too. That way, they will find skin under his nails."

"What if he wakes up?" Ridge's voice shook.

"He won't," Caroline said. "I've practiced this. He doesn't wake up."

Ridge scrunched up his face. "Why can't I give him the tea first thing? Why do we have to be there all day?"

"It's too risky for Vince to show up before dark. There's less of a chance of anyone seeing him once the sun is down. I tried to talk your dad into leaving after lunch, but you know how he is about fishing."

"What if people are around when Vince comes?"

Caroline bit her lip. This was the only part of the plan that gave her pause. People came to watch the crow roost at night, but not typically where Jay and other fishermen frequented. "It's going to be cold tonight. And most of the people who like to fish near Big Rock leave before dark. But you leave that to Vince. He's going to be watching and waiting for the perfect time. He'll pull up next to Dad's truck. He's borrowing a car. It's one you haven't seen before. He'll flash the lights two times when it's safe for you to come. Do *not* go until you see the flashes."

"Then I throw my beanie and shoe into the creek and leave with Vince."

"But you forgot to take the tea thermos. That's the most important part of all, that you take it, nothing else. Leave your cooler, backpack, and fishing pole. But take the red tea thermos. Vince will remind you."

Ridge picked up his stuffed blue jay. "Where will Vince take me?"

"You're going to stay with them in Louisiana."

"For how long? Will I go to school there?"

"Not long. No, you won't go to school there. Libby will teach you at home, and guess what? They bought you a Nintendo."

"How long?" Ridge asked again.

"A few months probably," Caroline said, even though she had no idea how long a trial would take.

Ridge squeezed his stuffed animal. "What about Blue?"

Caroline put her hand on Blue and lowered him. "He's going to stay with me. Dad won't let you bring a toy to the creek. But I'll keep him safe. Once things are sorted out here, you, me, Sloan, and Blue are moving."

Ridge cracked a small smile for the first time in days. "Will I like New York?"

Caroline brushed his bangs back. "You're going to love it. You'll see where I went to school, and we'll study the birds together. And Daddy will never hurt me or Sloan again."

Ridge squeezed his eyes shut. "Okay."

"And after a few days, you can call and talk to me."

"And Sloan?" Ridge spoke the two words with such hope.

"Um, yeah. Eventually. You better get to sleep." Caroline stood and walked to the door before pausing and looking back at Ridge. "One last thing," she whispered. "I've been thinking about what you asked me. About why we would abandon Dad when he was part of our nest. Well, like any rule, there are exceptions. Crows look out for their own, but when one of their own is injured, sick, or acting strangely, the rest of the family will often turn on it."

"Turn on it how?"

"Kill it," Caroline said. Her voice was firm.

Ridge gasped.

Caroline approached the bed. "I realize that sounds harsh, but think about it. That injured crow would attract predators. The laws of nature understand it's better for one crow to die than to jeopardize an entire family. We aren't killing your father. We are leaving him here and flying to a new nest where he won't destroy us all. That's better, don't you think?"

"Yeah." Ridge yawned.

Caroline pulled up the covers to his chin. "Sleep tight, my very brave crow."

Caroline only slept a few restless hours that night and woke up before anyone else. Thank God it wasn't raining. It had rained on and off for two weeks, but there was no chance of precipitation in the forecast today. Almost like this was meant to be. Caroline had her coffee and then started her preparations. She was really doing this. If she got caught, she would be the one in jail, not Jay. Everything had to go according to plan. Everyone had a part to play, and she'd assigned the hardest and most critical part to a ten-year-old. There was so very much that might go wrong.

But Ridge was smart, and he understood why he was doing this. He'd never even been close to his father. Unlike his mother and sister, Ridge had probably always seen Jay Hadfield for the fraud he was.

Jay woke up next. He came up behind Caroline and wrapped his arms around her. "Good morning, sunshine. How does a big breakfast sound?"

Sunshine. Caroline remembered their first date. He'd called her sunshine, pure sunshine. The memory brought unexpected tears to her eyes. She blinked them back. *Think about Anna. What pet name does he have for her?*

At the breakfast table, Ridge was quiet, Jay read his paper, and Sloan did what Sloan did best nowadays, bitched about *everything*. Bitched that she couldn't go, that she'd miss watching TV with her dad. This would be the hardest for Sloan. But it would be better in the long run. She'd discover her mother was strong, and she'd learn not to make the same mistakes Caroline had. Sloan Hadfield would never give up so much for any man.

Jay told Caroline to sit. Told her she should order a pizza tonight. Like he was some malevolent lord, allowing her to order out. She *would* order pizza. And from now on, she would order one anytime she damn well wanted to.

While Sloan and Jay carried out the ice chest, Caroline pulled Ridge aside and went over the plan one last time before wrapping her arms around him. "It's going to be okay," she promised. "See you soon."

Caroline let go as Sloan pushed past them, slamming the door of her room.

"Goodbye, Sloan." Ridge looked down the hall.

"Don't worry about her," Jay said, pulling his Texas Rangers' cap down on his head. "You ready to go, big man?"

"I'm ready," Ridge said. He turned back to Caroline and repeated the words in too strong of a voice for her sweet ten-year-old. "I'm ready."

Caroline distracted herself most of the day by building a fire in the living room and feeding it thirteen years of cards, love letters, and gifts from Jay.

Sloan stayed in her room, only coming out for meals. At dinnertime, they sat watching TV, the pizza getting cold. Each stroke of the clock darkened them both. Sloan growing angrier, Caroline growing more nervous. Jay still hadn't returned. Caroline was sure he'd be awake by now. She wanted to call Libby, but that wasn't part of the plan. Too many phone calls might look suspicious.

Caroline tapped her foot to the bouncy rhythm of the *21 Jump Street* theme song. She grabbed a piece of pizza but couldn't take more than a bite. Had Jay gone straight to the police? She decided to give him until the end of the show. If he wasn't back, she'd go looking.

Caroline didn't have to wait that long. She heard a truck door slam outside as the first commercial break began. She sat up straighter and held her breath. Seconds later, Jay burst through the front door. He looked terrible. Sweat was dripping from his face, and his eyes were glassy and unfocused.

"Jay?" Caroline jumped up, letting her uneaten pizza fall to the floor.

He ran past her looking down the hallway. "Is Ridge here?"

*It had worked. It had all worked.* "What do you mean is Ridge here?"

"Oh, God," Jay cried. "Call the police, Caroline."

*Scream at him, make a scene. Make it real.* "Where's Ridge, Jay?" she yelled. "Where is he?"

Jay fell to his knees, grabbing at his greasy hair. "I don't know," he sobbed. "He disappeared."

Caroline had thought this part would be hard. Seeing Jay in so much pain, so worried about their boy. But it made her happy to watch him come undone. Happy she'd brought him to his knees just like he had brought her to her own outside Anna Hadfield's home. Karma. Karma. Karma. Things always come full circle. You get what you deserve. And this is what he deserved. He'd begun their relationship with a lie, and she was ending it with one.

# Chapter 27

*Baton Rouge, LA, 1989*

Libby Turner smiled as she finished grading Ridge's math test. "One hundred percent!" she said.

"Yes!" Ridge held both hands in the air. "Ice cream tonight!"

"That's right," Libby said. "I knew you could do it."

"Do you think we can go to Baskin-Robbins? Instead of Vince bringing home ice cream?"

Libby sighed. She couldn't blame him for wanting out of here. What eleven-year-old child wanted to stay home all day? Ridge should be at the ice cream shop or the arcade with friends.

"Soon, sweetie. It's not safe for you to be seen right now."

"When will I go back with Mom?"

"Not till your dad's trial is over." Libby knew this was a lot for a child to take in, but she would not lie to him. He had already been through enough lies. "Would you like to call your mother tonight? Tell her about this A+?"

Ridge looked at his hands. "Not really."

Libby's brow furrowed. "Why not? It's been a week since you talked to her. She loves you very much."

"Do you love me too, Libby?"

"Of course, I do."

"Will you still love me as much after I go home with Mom?"

"I'll love you always, forever, and no matter what." She angled her chair toward him. "But we were talking about your mom and why you haven't wanted to call her."

Ridge began wringing his hands. "She never lets me talk to Sloan."

Libby frowned. "I think she's worried Sloan won't understand. That she'll tell someone she shouldn't."

"But Mom promised I could talk to Sloan. I'm doing this for her, and I can't even talk to her."

Libby cocked her head. "When you say you did it for Sloan, what do you mean?"

Ridge looked up at her, his face ashen. "Mom didn't tell you?"

"Tell me what?" Ridge stared past her at the kitchen wall. Libby swept his bangs away from his eyes. "What did your mother tell you, Ridge?"

"Daddy was hurting Sloan. She told Mrs. Evans, but Mrs. Evans didn't believe her because she liked Dad so much."

A lump formed in Libby's throat. Why hadn't Caroline told her this? "So, your father was abusing all three of you?"

"No. He was nice to me. I'm not sure why he hurt Mom and Sloan."

Libby pressed her back against the kitchen chair. This boy needed counseling, and soon. He was confused about so much.

"Nice? But he was hurting you, Ridge. That's not nice. Hitting isn't nice."

Ridge looked confused. "That time he was sleeping and threw me off of him? That kinda hurt."

"Yeah. I bet it did. And remember how you had those bruises on your face and arm? How did you get those?"

"Oh, when I slipped? I was running in the kitchen with my socks on. Doreen told me not to, but I did anyway."

"You don't have to lie anymore. We know your father hurt you."

Ridge gave a slight headshake. "Just that one time, but he was asleep, so it was an accident."

He was in denial, Libby realized. He wanted to pretend he was the lone family member who was not a victim.

"Did you ever witness him hurt your mom? Or Sloan?" Libby wondered if Ridge would give his own stories to them. That way, he could share but still not paint himself as weak or victimized.

Ridge shrugged. "Well, that time I jumped on his back. He was on top of Mom, but he was asleep. He had been on top of Mom before shaking her, but Walt pulled him off her. Those were the only times I saw him try to hurt her. Mostly he screamed in his sleep. It's from the war."

"Your mom got a black eye after you got your bruises. Do you remember that?" Libby asked.

Ridge brought the collar of his t-shirt to his mouth. "Yeah. She told me Daddy hit her."

"And how did it make you feel to know that?"

"Surprised. Because Daddy was real nice to her. Noah said sometimes Walt and Doreen yelled at each other. But my mom and dad never fought. I didn't know he was hurting her."

Libby heard the stress in Ridge's voice. She needed to let it go for tonight. "Why don't you go play in the backyard? I'll call Vince and tell him to pick up ingredients for ice cream sundaes."

Ridge opened his mouth, letting the soggy shirt collar fall out. "It's nice how Vince comes home *every* night."

Tears filled Libby's eyes. This poor kid had never known a normal family. "It sure is," she said, turning away so he couldn't see her cry.

Libby waited till Ridge was in bed and the dishes were washed before calling Caroline. "How are you?" she asked, trying to keep a pleasant tone, even as Ridge's words gnawed at her. He was a child, and children lied. Caroline was her best friend. She could trust her.

"I'm great." Caroline's voice was light and bubbly. "How's our boy?"

"He's good." Libby dried the final bowl. "Already asleep. We had a busy night."

"No problem. Tell him to call whenever he's free. So, listen, I talked to the D.A. today. We've got this, Libby. Ridge did everything right. We hit a home run."

The excitement in Caroline's voice disgusted Libby. Made her feel like she'd just accidentally dipped her sleeve into dirty dishwater. It shouldn't have. This was her plan, too. She wanted Jay to go to jail. He shouldn't be free to hurt Ridge or Caroline. But to be this excited about the destruction of a family didn't feel right.

"Anna's still the media's sweetheart," Caroline said. "She's so pathetic. People eat it up, though. I heard her church set up a fund for the kids' college. Must be nice. Maybe I should take one of those interview offers for my side of the story."

"Don't," Libby said. "People would pick apart every word you say. Something might slip. And the more out there you are, the more they will follow you. They'll keep looking for you after you leave."

"I know. It would just be nice if I got *something* out of this. Something for the kids' futures, I mean. Has anyone set up a college fund for Sloan? Of course not."

"How is she?" Libby asked.

"She's good."

"Good? Really? Vince and I have worried about Sloan. I thought it would be difficult for her."

"Um, yeah, it's been a bit rocky. She wanted to visit her dad, but I put an end to that. She hasn't asked again and spends most of her time with the Dawsons."

The sleeve in dirty dishwater feeling was back. Hate Jay, that was fine, but Caroline's complete lack of compassion for her own daughter was astonishing. "She needs someone to talk to. She needs you, Caroline."

"Sloan won't talk to me." Caroline's voice suddenly had an edge. "She's a teenager."

"Have you gotten her an appointment with a counselor?"

Caroline groaned. "What's the point of doing that here? We'll be gone in a few months. I'll find them one in New York."

"Scars from abuse run deep, Caroline. She needs to talk to a professional, and soon. It would probably even help the case against Jay," Libby added. If Caroline wouldn't do it for her daughter, she might for her own vengeance.

"Did Ridge tell you that?" Caroline's voice had lost its animation.

"Yeah. Why didn't you? You told me Jay was abusing Ridge."

"Well, he was," Caroline said.

"But you didn't feel the need to tell me he was hurting Sloan too? And that she told her teacher? My god, Caroline, that's huge. She could have been a witness for you. Judges believe teachers. We didn't have to do any of this."

"She didn't believe her. Jay has her fooled like everyone else."

"Are you serious?" Libby paced as far as the cord would allow, silently convincing herself they had done the right thing. What kind of teacher would just dismiss claims like that from a child? "You still should have told."

"You're right, sorry," Caroline said with no emotion. "I had a lot on my mind back then."

Libby heard movement from Ridge's room down the hallway. "I need to get off the phone. Vince doesn't think we should talk much till the trial is over. He's worried they bugged your house."

Caroline sighed into the phone. "How do you live with such a paranoid conspiracist? No one has bugged anything. The police haven't been to my house since Jay was arrested. If they'd bugged it, we would have all been arrested months ago."

Libby knew that. But they were putting their entire lives on the line for Caroline and the kids. And did Caroline even realize that the paranoid conspiracist was currently reading her son another chapter of *Hatchet* before bed? Libby felt her blood pressure rising. She affixed her pleasant voice and told Caroline it was good talking to her. But she couldn't help slamming down the phone when she finished.

"What was that about?" Vince stood in the hallway, leaning against the wall.

"Caroline."

He stroked his gray beard. "I told you not to talk to her. She hasn't messed up, has she?"

"Legally, no? As a mother, yes, I think so."

Vince walked toward the kitchen. "Come on, have a seat. I'll make you another bowl of ice cream, and we'll talk."

Libby plopped down at the kitchen table. "Is Ridge asleep?"

"Yeah, he passed out before I finished reading." Vince looked up from the ice cream carton. "It's nice to have a chance to do these dad things."

A much-needed warmth expanded in Libby's chest. "You would have made such a good father. Why did we never try to adopt?"

Vince set a bowl of Rocky Road in front of her. "Shoulda coulda woulda. I'd say we've had a good life, a fulfilling one, wouldn't you?"

"Yeah, of course. But it does feel good to do this. To take care of a child, to nurture him."

"He's so resilient," Vince said, scooping a bite out of his own bowl. "He's a tough kid. I guess he had to be to survive all that abuse."

Libby set her spoon down. "That's what led to my phone call with Caroline tonight. Ridge told me earlier his dad never abused him. He seemed shocked that I thought otherwise."

"Ridge is a child. I think you forget that sometimes because he's so smart. You saw the bruises."

"Yeah, but he said his mother told him Sloan was being abused by Jay. That Sloan even told her teacher. Don't you think it's strange she never mentioned that to me?" Libby asked.

"Sloan?"

"No, Caroline. Why would she tell Ridge that but not me?"

Vince tapped his spoon against his chin. "Ridge lived in that house. He probably heard or saw things. Probably realized what was happening, and Caroline just confirmed it."

"It's possible," Libby said. "But something seems off. The way Caroline is acting, the things Ridge said."

Vince sat down his spoon, rubbing a hand over his prominent belly. "Let me talk to Ridge tomorrow. He'll shoot straight with me."

Libby reached out and touched her husband's arm. "Thank you. I'm sure I'm just emotional after learning that about Sloan."

Vince put his own hand on top of hers. "Don't worry. They'll both be safe with their mother."

Libby smiled and nodded, but honestly, she wasn't so sure anymore.

# Chapter 28

*Mallowater, TX, 2008*

Sloan drove home in a daze. What did Ridge mean it was her mother's idea? Why would Mom hatch a plan for Ridge to be kidnapped? He was lying. Covering for the Turners.

"How was she?" Sloan asked Dylan, hating that she sounded like a parent quizzing the babysitter.

"Pretty good," Dylan said. "How did it go for you?"

"Pretty bad." Sloan plopped down on the couch next to Dylan. "He'll probably be gone by tomorrow. But I don't wanna talk about it."

"Okay. So, what *do* you want to talk about?"

"I don't know." Sloan rubbed her forehead. "Dad's getting out tomorrow. Brad asked me to be there for his homecoming."

"Are you?"

Sloan leaned away. "Why would I?"

Dylan shrugged. "I thought you had a good visit with your dad. Thought you wanted to build a good relationship."

Sloan crossed her arms. "The only reason the Hadfields want me there is PR. Because they want the media to see that I'm supporting Dad now."

"And you don't want the media to know that? That you support him?"

"I don't know if I support him. And the Hadfields just want to play like we're some big happy family. It would be so awkward."

"Understandable," Dylan said. "But if you want to be there and don't want to do it alone, I'll go with you. Unless that would make it weirder."

"As much as I'd like to see Felicity's face when I walk up with you, I'm not up for the rest of it."

Dylan groaned and threw his head back against the couch. "So, you'd only want me there to make Felicity jealous and not for moral support?"

"A little of both."

"I really don't get the thing with Felicity."

"Sibling rivalry." Sloan smirked.

"But you didn't even grow up together."

"But she got the best of Dad. She was his little girl. She was his real family."

"That's really not a healthy—" He stopped and shook his head. "Sorry," he said. "You need a boyfriend, not a shrink."

Sloan leaned forward till she was inches from Dylan's lips. "You're right. I don't want a therapist, just you." Sloan inhaled Dylan's woodsy cologne and saw the tiny flecks of gold in his deep brown eyes. She needed to forget about last night, about tonight, about Noah, about everything. She pressed her lips against Dylan's, anchoring her hand to his belt, then slipping a finger beneath the waistline fabric. She deepened the kiss before pulling away. "Come on," she whispered, standing and offering him her hand.

Dylan hesitated only a moment before he took it and let her lead him into her bedroom. His skin felt hot, feverish.

Sloan closed the door as he sat on the bed. She couldn't help but notice he looked uncomfortable.

"Everything okay?" she asked.

"Yeah." Dylan tapped his foot. "Can you turn the light off?"

"Sure." Sloan flipped the switch before taking a few steps toward her bed. She kissed Dylan again, pushing him gently onto the silk comforter. But when Sloan tried to raise his shirt, he seemed to tense. He stopped kissing back. "Is this about my mom? The door's locked." Sloan laughed; it was like she was in high school again, sneaking Noah into her room. *Ugh. Stop thinking about Noah.*

"It's nothing," Dylan said, pulling his shirt off, revealing another T-shirt underneath. "Sorry." He laughed and removed that one too.

Sloan ran her hands down his chest and brought her lips to his neck. He moaned softly, reaching past a gap between the buttons on her blouse to touch her skin. She fumbled to unbutton her shirt, tossing it behind her.

But when she reached for his belt, Dylan jerked away, pushing his back against the headboard. "I'm sorry," he huffed. "I can't." He reached around him on the bed. "Where's my shirt?"

Sloan stood and turned on the light, trying to make sense of his rejection. She felt her neck and ears reddening.

When she turned around, she caught sight of Dylan's back just before he pulled his shirt over it. It was littered with scars. Round ones like cigarette burns and long thin ones like he had been whipped. Dylan picked her shirt up off the floor and handed it to her, keeping his head turned. "I'm sorry," he said again. "This part is hard for me."

Sloan slipped her arms into her blouse, holding it closed in front. "Don't apologize. I didn't mean to push you. I thought you wanted this."

"I did want this. I *do* want this. Please don't take it personally. Intimacy is just hard for me. I've had positive sexual experiences, but my mind mostly goes to the negative, no matter how much my body fights against it."

Sloan sat beside him, putting her hand on his back, staring at his other shirt still on the floor. It made sense now, why he wore layers even in the heat of summer. "I'm fine with waiting."

Dylan kept his eyes on the carpet. "I get it if this is a deal-breaker."

Sloan laughed. "Come on, Dylan. A wife in another town—deal-breaker. Going slow—not a deal-breaker."

"It's not that I don't want to. It's hard to explain. I should have talked to you about this before now."

"And I should have considered it from your side." She began buttoning her shirt. "Let's stop feeling bad and go watch a funny movie."

Dylan didn't move from the bed.

"Come on. Really, it's fine."

He exhaled. "There's something else that's been bugging me. The other night you said you'd gotten sick and weren't up to hanging out."

"Yeah."

"Then why did Noah come over?"

Sloan froze. "How did you know that?"

"Caroline told me. I think she was trying to make me jealous." He stood. "Should I be?"

Sloan's heart thudded against her chest. Her mom had been awake. What all had she heard? "No. There's no reason to be jealous."

Dylan rocked back on his heels, stuffing his hands into his pockets. "I'm trying not to assume the worst."

"There's really nothing to worry about there. Noah's just helping me look into some stuff about Ridge."

"So, you felt up to talking to him about Ridge, but you won't talk to me?"

Sloan tapped her fingers against her jeans. "It's complicated. Intimacy is hard for me too. I mean, not this kind," she motioned to the bed, "but the sharing stuff."

Dylan swallowed. "But it's easy with Noah?"

"That's not what I meant. He's a detective and has access to the information I need. That's the only reason I told him." It wasn't the entire truth, but it was hard to explain her and Noah's shared history, their shared history with Ridge. She wanted to talk to Dylan, but it didn't come as naturally.

"Okay." Dylan managed a small smile. "Let's just forget about intimacy of all kinds for tonight and go see about that movie."

"What did you find out?" Sloan asked Noah when he called the following night.

"Vince worked at LSU for less than a year," Noah said. "They left Baton Rouge late in August of 1989, and it looks like they spent the rest of the year in El Paso. In 1990, Vince began working as a math professor at New Mexico Junior College. He retired in 2004, but they still live in Hobbs, New Mexico."

Sloan stepped outside to the back porch. "But he moved to Baton Rouge to be a dean. Why would he trade a dean's job for a professor's?"

"Change of pace?"

"Or he was running," Sloan said. "Ridge made a comment that they were supposed to bring him back." *The gas station*, Sloan realized. "I remember this night at a gas station. Mom said we were leaving Mallowater. We packed and waited there. Waited all night for someone that didn't come. That was when Mom lost it. They were supposed to bring him back."

"Calm down, Sloan. We aren't sure this was your mother's idea."

"Ridge said it was."

Sloan heard papers shuffling. "Kidnapped children sometimes eventually take the side of their captors," Noah explained. "We can assume they were hiding him out for a while, homeschooling maybe. There was no record of your brother until 1992, when a Ridge Turner was registered for school. He attended Hobbs schools from ninth-twelfth grade."

"Ridge Turner? They changed his name?"

"Likely got him a new identity altogether," Noah said.

"How do you do that? How does no one question a ninth grader just popping into existence?"

"Possibly black-market papers. But there are a few other ways too."

"Vince and Libby didn't change their names?" Sloan asked.

"No. That surprised me too."

"Then Mom could have found them. If she knew they had Ridge, why didn't she hunt them down when they didn't return him?"

"My hunch is that she never knew they took him."

"Then explain the gas station, Noah." Sloan caught her voice rising. "Do you have a number for Vince and Libby?"

Noah hesitated for a minute before saying no.

"Don't lie to me. What's their number?"

"I don't have it," he said. "Unlisted."

"And you don't have a way to get it?"

He sighed. "Talking to them is a bad idea. If they took your brother, they need to be prosecuted. They will run if they realize we are on to them, and it's all over."

Sloan leaned against the house. "Fine. But you've got to keep looking into this."

Noah promised he would, and they ended the call. As soon as Sloan stepped back inside, she heard a soft rap on the front door. It caught her off guard. Who would be here this late?

She opened the door, leaving the chain latched. She was surprised to see Ridge standing in the shadows. "Can I come in?" he asked.

"Of course." Sloan undid the chain and opened the door again.

Ridge stepped inside. "Mom's asleep, right?"

"Last I checked. She had her sleeping pill, but her sleep seems restless tonight."

Ridge seemed restless too. He walked circles around the room, stopping to pick up the lone picture off the mantle—one of Caroline and Sloan her senior year.

"What's going on, Ridge? I haven't heard from you all day."

He sat down on the couch. "I slept most of the day and couldn't fall asleep tonight. I just wanted to see you. I wanted to see the pictures you found. Maybe I even wanted to see Mom."

Sloan sat beside him. "I'm glad you came. Dad got out of jail today."

"Did you see him?"

Sloan shook her head. "Just on TV. I couldn't bring myself to go. I didn't even let Dylan come over today. I wanted to be alone with it all. With my memories."

"Didn't mean to crash your party," Ridge said.

"It needed crashing. I was just about to get another beer. Want one?"

"Absolutely." While Sloan was in the kitchen, she heard Ridge turn the TV on. "Think they'll replay Dad getting out?"

"I'm sure." She handed him the beer. "Turn to channel five. Local news comes on at 10:00."

"Well, at least it's just *local* news."

"Yeah, until the Hadfields do another *People* magazine interview."

Ridge used his class ring to twist the lid off his beer. "I saw that." He took a sip. "Well, I did more than see it; I bought it and tripped out a few weeks."

Sloan laughed. "Years for me. Not proud to admit this, but I brought it back out today."

"It's just hard to imagine that Dad had this whole second life with them," Ridge said.

Sloan took a drink of her own beer. "You should talk."

Ridge gave a shallow sigh. "Yeah, I guess you're right, but—"

"Shh!" Sloan grabbed the remote and turned up the volume as the news played footage of their father walking out of prison. Felicity and Anna ran, wrapping their arms around him. Kyle, Brad, and their families close behind.

"Wow." Ridge moved closer, sitting on the coffee table. "Dad has gray hair."

Sloan folded her legs up beside her. "And grandkids."

Ridge stared transfixed as the reporter spoke. "Jay Hadfield was released today after spending almost twenty years in prison for the murder of his son, Ridge Hadfield, back in 1988. Jay, a Vietnam Veteran, was Texas's first, and perhaps most famous, use of the PTSD defense, claiming he killed his son in a dissociative flashback. The jury ultimately convicted Jay Hadfield of manslaughter. The body of Ridge Hadfield was never found."

Ridge scrubbed his hands over his face. "What a trip."

"During the investigation into the child's death," the reporter continued, "it was discovered that Jay Hadfield had a secret. He had two families. A wife and three children living in Tyler and a long-time girlfriend in Mallowater who had two children with Hadfield. Neither family had any knowledge of the other. Today, when Jay Hadfield was released, only his legal wife and their three children were present. Ridge's mother, Caroline Radel, could not be reached for comment, but our records show she has spent most of her life in various mental hospitals and living facilities."

Ridge turned back to Sloan. "They tried to call Mom?"

"I unplugged the house phone right after I came home," Sloan said.

"Such a fascinating case," the balding reporter back at the news desk said. "This is the second time in recent weeks that Mallowater has made the news."

"You're right, Ralph," the chipper woman sitting on his right said. "Recently, former Mallowater resident Eddie Daughtry was arrested for the murder of Logan Pruitt after another of his alleged victims, Dylan Lawrence, came forward."

"Geez." Ridge shook his head. "Talk about the news hitting close to home."

"Yeah." Sloan muted the TV. "Thus, the beers."

"May need something harder."

Sloan unfolded herself from the couch. "On it." She emerged from the kitchen with two gin and tonics, and a bag of Chex Mix. "Slumber party?"

"Hell yeah." Ridge took one of the drinks and sat back on the couch. "Man, that never stops being weird. Hearing about my death."

"I bet," Sloan said.

Ridge kicked his shoes off. "Seeing Dad is the weirdest of all. To say I have mixed feelings about him right now would be an understatement."

"Yeah." Sloan took her first sip, and the gin burned her throat. "Dad didn't abuse me, Ridge."

"I believe you. Nothing adds up. Mom told me he hit her a lot, but wouldn't we have known?" I mean, I never even heard them fight."

"The only time he was violent was during the flashbacks," Sloan said. "He wasn't faking that."

"How can you be sure?" Ridge asked.

"Oh, come on, Ridge. You were there. You saw his eyes. He was out of it. You heard him all the times he'd wake up screaming. Don't try to justify what Mom did." Sloan ran her fingers through her hair. "Why did she do this? Why did she lie to you to frame Dad?"

"A crow never forgets," Ridge said. "I bet she found out about Anna. Remember how distant and strange she got? Remember the night with the pantry? I think she used me to make him pay."

"Surely not," Sloan said, but she couldn't exactly put it past her mother. "You should ask Libby if you're right."

Ridge leaned against the couch. "I plan to call her tomorrow. I just hope she'll be honest with me."

Sloan downed the rest of her drink. "What about Dad? Do you want to see him?"

"Yes and no. I'm so mad at him about the other family, yet I've got all these good memories of him, too. One day at Hastings, I came across that Randy Travis album he loved, *The Storms of Life*. I bought it and listened to it over and over. It was the closest to home I ever felt."

"It was the same for me with Keith Whitley." Sloan jumped up. "I brought down Dad's old tapes in the attic. Let me see if the Randy Travis one is in there."

She returned to the room a few seconds later, holding a shoebox of old photos, Ridge's beloved stuffed animal, and the Randy Travis cassette.

"Blue!" Ridge emerged from the kitchen, where he'd mixed a few more gin and tonics. "I thought I'd seen the last of him."

Sloan plugged in her old cassette player. "Let's hope this still works." She placed the Randy Travis cassette in the tape deck and pressed down the slightly stuck play button. "On the Other Hand" began to play softly. "Wow," she said, "This song certainly takes on a different meaning now."

"Right?" Ridge sat on the floor beside her with the box of photos. "No wonder Dad loved country music. His life was a country song."

"Aren't all of ours?" Sloan asked.

"Well, my girlfriend broke up with me six weeks ago, so I left New York for Texas. But I drove an RV here instead of a truck, and I had a pet crow instead of a dog."

"You stayed in New York even after college?"

"After college?" Ridge laughed. "What's that? I'm still trudging through my Ph.D."

"So, you don't work?" Sloan asked.

"Writing a dissertation *is* work. But no, I got a research grant, and Mom and—I mean Libby and Vince—still help me out."

Sloan tried to ignore the fact that he'd just called Libby his mom. She bumped her shoulder against Ridge's. "I'm impressed. My little brother's gonna be a doctor."

"I'm studying crow families." Ridge pulled out a picture from the box and stared. "Specifically, bonds among sibling crows and how they affect social skills and eventual survival and reproductive success."

Sloan couldn't stifle her giggles.

"What?" Ridge sounded offended, "What's so funny?"

"I'm sorry." She held her lips together, but a burst of laughter escaped. "Maybe that explains all my problems. If sibling relationships are as important to human success as they are to crows, no wonder I haven't found any social or reproductive success in life."

Ridge tried in vain to suppress a smile. "You're terrible."

"Nah, just a little past my alcohol limit." She leaned over to look at the picture Ridge was holding. It was one of them opening presents in front of the fireplace. "Oh, do you remember the year we got to pick out our ornament?"

Ridge pointed a finger at her. "Rabbit in a roller skate?"

"Yes!" Sloan jumped up too quickly and felt light-headed. She lowered herself back to the floor, making a mental note to slow down on the drinks. "It's in the attic!" She kicked the box of pictures away from her brother. "Go get the Christmas box, please."

"Hey." Ridge reached for the shoe box. "You go get them."

She fanned herself. "Come on, Ridge. I'm a little tipsy. You're going to freak out when you see this stuff. Honestly, the ornaments brought back so many good memories, it made me want to put the tree up this year. Go get them, please. I'll tell you right where they are."

"Oh geez." Ridge stood. "I remember where they are. Dad and I had to bring them down every year."

"Yay! Thanks!" Sloan ignored her own inner voice and drank the rest of her second gin and tonic as she looked at old pictures and listened to old country songs.

A few minutes later, Ridge emerged from the attic carrying the Christmas tree box.

"What are you bringing that down for?" Sloan asked. "I said the ornaments."

Ridge began climbing the attic stairs again. "Yeah. You also said you wanted to set the tree up."

Sloan laughed. Maybe Ridge was a little drunk, too. "I meant I wanted to put it up at Christmas."

"I won't be here for Christmas. Let's put it up tonight."

"It's July, Ridge."

"And? If putting up a Christmas tree will make us happy, let's do it."

"You know what? You're right." Sloan retrieved a pair of scissors from the kitchen to cut open the box. "We haven't put up a tree together in twenty years. I'd say we waited long enough."

Ridge brought down the box of ornaments, and Sloan pieced together the tree as Randy Travis sang in the background.

"This feels like something Dad would do," Sloan said, stepping back to admire their work. "Christmas in July."

"I thought the same." Ridge straightened the crooked star on top of the tree. "He was always an outside-of-the-box kind of thinker. Remember those weird questions he'd ask?"

Sloan grinned. "Do you think leprechauns are related to gnomes?"

"Or how about, is cereal soup?" Ridge added.

"Oh!" Sloan slapped his shoulder. "If peanut butter wasn't called peanut butter, what would it be called?"

"We had some good times, didn't we?" Ridge collapsed on the carpet. "I remember we used to lie under here and look up at the lights." His words were slightly slurred. He scooted under the tree and laughed. "Come on; it's even cooler when you're drunk."

"Isn't everything?" Sloan lay beside him and had to admit it was still pretty magical to stare at the twinkling lights through the branches.

"Merry Christmas," Ridge said, taking her hand.

"Merry Christmas." Sloan squeezed his hand, then laughed. "What's mom going to think when she wakes up to this?"

Ridge pushed himself up. "Speaking of, I better get back to the RV. It's late."

"You can't walk all the way out there this late. You're drunk."

"And you're not? I'll get some coffee on."

"Don't bother." Sloan sat up too quickly and saw twinkling lights all around the living room. "Just sleep in our old room. Lock the door. I'll sleep out here on the couch."

"And how am I supposed to get out in the morning?" Ridge asked.

Sloan grinned. "The same way I snuck out to meet Noah for five years—through the window."

"Alright. I am pretty beat." He rose to his feet and stumbled forward a few steps. "Night, Lo."

Sloan stood up. "Hey! You almost forgot something." She tossed Blue at his stomach. Ridge caught the stuffed animal and smiled—the same little boy smile she remembered.

Sloan realized she could have asked her brother anything she wanted tonight, and the alcohol would have loosened his tongue enough to answer. But she didn't care. Her heart was full for the first time in forever. Maybe remembering was more important than knowing.

# Chapter 29

*Mallowater, TX, 1989*

Attending Jay's trial became Caroline's favorite pastime. She enjoyed the smell of the treated wood in the courtroom, the clack of the prosecuting attorney's shoes across the polished floor, and the way Jay squirmed in that uncomfortable seat every time he saw Caroline.

She would never forget the look on his face when she walked in the first day. She shoved the swinging doors open and clicked her heels loud enough that everyone, including Jay, noted her entrance.

The proceedings had not begun, but Jay was already seated with a young public defender to his right.

When Jay saw her, his entire face softened, his eyes glistening with tears. He rose to his feet and pulled in an expansive breath. She saw the hope in his expression as she approached. What did he expect her to do? Kiss him in front of his wife? He was so pathetic.

Caroline stopped in the middle of the courtroom, locking her gaze with Jay's. She pressed her lips into a thin line, making sure her face remained emotionless. Then she pivoted and sat behind the prosecutor. A front-row seat to Jay's destruction. What more could any woman scorned ask for?

She faced the front of the courtroom but glanced at Jay in her peripheral. His entire face had fallen, like a boy who had just watched Santa Claus skip his house. It took all the composure Caroline had to keep herself from smiling.

Caroline never testified against him, even though the District Attorney had discussed it with her. In the end, he didn't feel it necessary. Jay's attorney wasn't denying the murder per se; the only question was whether PTSD would work as an insanity defense. Caroline's witnessing of past episodes would only help Jay's case.

Caroline sometimes wished she would have lied to the police like she had to Libby and told them Jay was abusive. She had no idea that defendants had been acquitted using PTSD as a defense until Jay's lawyer cited two cases from other states. The D.A. assured her just as many had been convicted when trying this new defense and that the media storm around Jay's lifestyle would make the jury less sympathetic. Not to mention, this was only the second case this public defender had tried, and it showed.

Jay had started writing Caroline letters again when his trial began. Letters begging her for a chance to talk. Letters asking why she sat on the State's side. Because no matter what he'd done to her, she had to know he'd never purposely hurt Ridge. A letter for almost every day of the trial. She had a letter for him too, but she was saving it for today, for after the verdict. Walt would deliver it to his cell. She scribbled it on her yellow legal pad while waiting for the jury.

> Jay,
> *A crow never forgets, and neither do I.*
> Caroline

The judge entered the courtroom, then the jury a few minutes later. Jay stood. Caroline noted how the jurors looked past him or down at their laps. That was a good sign.

"We, the jury, find the defendant, Jay Greggory Hadfield, guilty of murder in the second degree."

Jay's knees buckled, Anna cried out, and the bang of the gavel echoed throughout the courtroom. Anna's father had to drag her out. Jay's eyes filled with tears as the bailiff secured his cuffs. The idiot public defender put a hand on Jay's back, shaking his head as if the jury somehow got it all wrong.

Caroline looked up in silent prayer. *Guilty, guilty, guilty.* It was over. She was free of him. Free of him forever. Now her life, the life that Jay Hadfield had hijacked, could begin again.

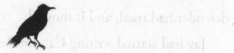

"I swear, she sounds happy about all this, Vince. It's sick."

"What did you expect? That she'd be angry that her plan, that your plan *together*, worked out?"

Libby pulled a mug out of the cupboard. "Well, not angry, but I just expected this would be difficult. Instead, she's relishing in his fall."

"And you aren't?"

Libby slammed the cupboard. "Of course not. I mean, I hate what he's done, obviously."

"*If* he's done it." Vince crossed his arms. "Ridge is holding his story."

Libby swallowed but seemed to have a permanent lump in her throat these days. If Jay hadn't been abusive, then her best friend had used her.

"Hopefully, now that the trial is over, Caroline will put her children before her own bloodlust," Vince said.

"Yeah." Libby bit her lip. The trial was over. That meant they didn't have much time left with Ridge. "I'm going to miss him so much."

"Me too," Vince said. "He's a good boy. And so smart. Let's set something up for college for him."

"We can't very well do that for him and not do the same for Sloan."

"Okay." Vince took his glasses off. "Let's do the same for Sloan."

Despite her husband's generosity, Libby still felt a hollow feeling in her chest. College was important, but a stable home life more so. Maybe Caroline just needed time. With the trial behind her, she could focus on Sloan, focus on finding them a place in Ithaca. Still, Libby couldn't shake the feeling that none of this had ever been about Sloan and Ridge.

Now that Jay was sentenced, Caroline knew she should make some phone calls about apartments and jobs in Ithaca. She doubted she would get hired at the Cornell Lab with only a bachelor's degree, but she could work on her master's and get a job teaching high school science or something.

She just wasn't in the mood to make phone calls today. She was in the mood to go to the creek. There was nothing about Mallowater she would miss when she left, except for the crows. Sure, there were roosts in New York, even bigger ones than this, but they were city roosts. The birds gathered near courthouses, prisons, or traffic lights. In some towns, they made such noise and left such a mess that mayors tried to get rid of them—air cannons, silver mylar balloons, lasers, plastic owls. Caroline guessed most people only liked their own noise and their own mess. Not that crows were treated much better here. She remembered Jay telling her last year that a hunting magazine had encouraged its readers to take up crow shooting to cure cabin fever. Caroline wondered now just where he'd seen that magazine. Probably at Anna's house. Anna Hadfield seemed like the type to have an extra freezer in the garage stuffed with a dismembered deer. To think Jay lived a life with each of them was mystifying.

Once she arrived at Crow's Nest Creek, Caroline made her way to a tree that held a large nest. The last time she'd been here, she'd seen four speckled blue eggs but couldn't get close to them with the mama crow around. Caroline understood that, understood the fierce instinctual need to protect your offspring. That's why she'd done all this for Sloan and Ridge.

The cry of the baby crows filled the air before Caroline got close. She climbed a nearby tree to get the best view of the large bowl-shaped nest. Two crows, likely a mother and father, were feeding their nestlings. One noticed Caroline but didn't seem bothered. *They know my face,* she realized. *They remember me.*

Caroline watched the parents feed their babies what looked like chunks of roadkill. She understood that the red gape of young birds was a stimulus that turned on the feeding behavior of adult birds. So much so that the chicks became anonymous mouths to feed. When she was in college, a scientist had swapped chicks from different broods, and the adult crows didn't seem to care, if they even noticed. They would later recognize their own fledglings by voice, but apparently not their nestlings. When there were screaming red mouths open, you fed them, whether they were your chicks or not.

The instinct wasn't so different for human females, really. That's how Caroline knew Libby would help her once she heard Sloan and Ridge were in danger. No, they were not Libby's flesh and blood, but when children were screaming, you did what you could to soothe them. It was innate.

Eventually, the feeding ceased, and the baby crows grew silent. The smaller adult, likely the mother, stayed in the nest, but the other flew away. Probably to forage for more food. These sleeping baby birds would be hungry and screaming again within twenty minutes. Papa crow didn't have time to go to another nest; that was certain.

Crows could do two things at the same time. Their two-sided vocal organ made them able to sing two songs at once. They could sleep with one eye open, keeping half their brain active to detect approaching predators. But they didn't build two nests with two mates. Not even the cleverest of crows were that duplicitous.

Caroline realized she had to let it go. Jay had been caught and caged. She had to think about herself now . . . and the kids. They would get out of this town, out of this trap, while Anna and her children would remain chained, too weak to fly free.

"Sometimes I'm not sure if she's going off with Noah or sneaking back with Anna to visit her father," Caroline said.

Libby held the phone in the crook of her neck as she folded laundry. "I'm sure Sloan's not seeing Jay. But if she is, would it be the worst thing ever?"

Caroline huffed into the phone. "Whose side are you on?"

"Ridge and Sloan's," Libby said. "You realize it's August, right? Shouldn't you be in New York before the new school year starts?"

"Working on it. Don't you think I want my son back?"

No, sometimes Libby didn't think she did. Jay was sentenced in May, and there was still no plan for exchanging Ridge.

"How's Sloan doing?" Libby picked up another towel to fold. "She always sounds so sad when she answers the phone."

Caroline laughed. "She's sad when anyone calls that's not Noah. I wonder if she's developing a bit of a crush on him. She's been lightening her hair, wearing makeup, dressing differently."

Libby smiled. "All normal for her age. Noah's a nice boy."

"What's not normal is where she's getting the money for this stuff."

"Are you not giving her any spending money from what we've sent?"

"No, Libby, I'm sorta using that to feed us."

"Well, maybe Walt and Doreen are buying it for her."

"I bet it's Anna," Caroline said, switching to a conspiratorial tone. The kind they used to adopt when sharing tidbits of gossip. That seemed like a lifetime ago.

"How would Anna get money? She's in the same boat as you."

"Not really," Caroline said. "The entire city of Tyler is rallying around them."

Libby noticed she'd been folding the same towel repeatedly since she got on the phone. She threw it back in the basket with the others and stood. "Anna is a victim in this too, Caroline. I don't expect you to have warm feelings for her, but if anyone knows what she's going through, it's you."

"Oh, don't feel sorry for her. She was at the mall yesterday with Felicity and was all smiles. Bought new perfume and makeup, two My Little Ponies for Felicity, and a Sega, I'm assuming, for her boys. A Sega, Libby."

"How do you know this?" Libby asked. "Did you follow them around the mall?" Caroline's momentary silence was the only answer Libby needed. "Why would you do that?"

"Curiosity. I wanted to get a good look at Anna. She's not all that pretty. No wonder Jay couldn't keep his hands off me."

Libby's skin crawled. "Do you follow them a lot?"

"No!" Caroline raised her voice. "I'm not obsessed. I just don't think they should have a higher standard of living than we do."

"Listen, Caroline. Stop worrying about them. You need to—" Libby stopped talking as Ridge entered the room. "Hey, Ridge just came in. Want to talk to him?"

"Yeah, sure," Caroline said. "Put him on."

"Ridge, it's your mother." Libby couldn't help but notice how Ridge's face dropped when she handed him the phone. Couldn't ignore his one-word answers as she pretended to fold towels. It was like he and his mother had nothing to talk about. "How was your talk?" she asked when he hung up the phone.

"It was okay," Ridge said. "When can I talk to Sloan?"

Libby squeezed the towel in her hand. "Probably not until your mother picks you up. Sloan still doesn't know you're here."

Ridge's eyebrows shot up. "Lo still thinks I'm dead? Why? That's so mean."

"I agree," Libby said.

"But the whole thing is pretty mean. It was mean of Mom to make me lie—and mean of you and Vince too."

Libby couldn't disagree with him. "You're right. It wasn't nice. But we all had our reasons, right? You and your mom wanted to protect Sloan. Vince and I wanted to protect you."

"I didn't need to be protected. Dad never hurt me. Why didn't Mom just tell the police Dad was hurting Sloan? Why didn't Mrs. Evans? It would have been the same! He would have gone to jail the same."

"You have every right to be angry. None of it was okay. Vince and I had good intentions, but intentions don't determine if something is right or wrong. I'm sorry, but I can't be completely sorry because I'm glad for the time I've spent with you. Vince and I will miss you very much when you go."

Ridge's gaze pinged around the room. "I don't want to go."

Libby walked toward him. "Yes, you do, Ridge. You and your mother have always been very close."

"I don't want to go to New York. I don't want a new name. I'm sick of being dead."

Libby felt something inside her break at the sight of Ridge's tears. She wrapped her arms around him. He fought her off but eventually gave in, collapsing in her arms and sobbing.

"What *do* you want," Libby asked, pulling away from Ridge after the worst of the crying was over. "Do you want to go back to Mallowater and tell the truth?"

Ridge shook his head. "I don't want to get any of you in trouble."

Libby sometimes couldn't believe so much intelligence and heart fit in such a small boy. She was about to offer him some ice cream and control of the remote when he spoke again.

"I want to stay with you and Vince."

Libby's breath caught. "You what?"

"I'm happy here. Why can't I just stay?"

Libby didn't know what to do, what to say. "Go get some ice cream," she managed. "As much as you want. We'll talk about this later."

While she waited for Vince to come home—and while Ridge ate his Rocky Road straight from the carton—Libby went into her room and called Doreen Dawson.

"What a nice surprise, Libby. How are things in Louisiana?"

"They're good." Libby tried to sound upbeat. "I just called because I'm worried about Caroline."

"I spoke with her earlier," Doreen said. "She seemed fine."

"Yeah, that's what I'm worried about. She seems a little too okay."

"Grief comes in phases," Doreen said.

"I guess so. I just worry about Sloan. Caroline seems to have left her to fend for herself."

"Yes," Doreen's voice lowered. "Walt and I, we've been trying to help all we can. We love having Sloan over, but we're trying to encourage her to build up that relationship with her mom too."

*That's not a child's job,* Libby thought, but instead asked, "Is Sloan there now?"

"Yep. Out on the trampoline with Noah. Would you like to talk to her?"

"Please. And don't mention this to Caroline. I'm not implying she's a bad parent. I don't want to upset her."

"I understand. Let me get Sloan."

"Hi, Libby." There was a sadness in Sloan's voice. Not the voice of a child who'd just been jumping on the trampoline with a boy she liked.

"Hi, sweetie. You've been on my mind, and I wanted to check in."

"I'm fine."

"And how's your mom?" Libby asked.

"She's been weird," Sloan said. "I wish you could come stay with us like you did before."

"I do too. I just can't right now."

"Yeah, I figured."

"Your mom tells me you're spending a lot of time with Noah. That's great. I always liked that kid. Is he your boyfriend?"

"No," Sloan said, but her voice lightened.

Libby laid back on her bed. "Well, he'd be crazy not to like a pretty girl like you."

"I think he might," Sloan whispered. "He held my hand last week when we walked to the creek."

"Ah, I'd say he does like you then," Libby said. "Have you gotten to visit your dad recently?"

Sloan groaned. "Did Mom tell you to ask me? I haven't seen him again since I promised her I wouldn't."

"Okay. But if you wanted to, that would be normal. He made some awful decisions, but he was a good dad, wasn't he?"

"Yes," Sloan said. "I really miss him. I shouldn't, but I do."

"You know the trial is over. Nothing you say about your dad will change his sentence, so I have to ask you. Did your dad ever hurt you, Sloan? Did he abuse you?"

"No!" Sloan answered immediately. "The police already asked me that."

"Did you ever see him hurt your mom? Or Ridge?"

"Yeah," Sloan said. "He tried to hurt Mom a few times during his nightmares. Once Ridge jumped on his back, and Dad threw him off."

Libby squeezed her eyes shut. This was the same story Ridge told. "But what about when he was awake?" she asked. "I remember Ridge had bruises right before we moved."

"Daddy didn't do that," Sloan said. "Ridge was running around in his socks even after Doreen told him not to." Sloan laughed. "Sorry, it's funny to remember the way he slid."

"It's okay to laugh," Libby said. "It's okay to remember."

"Hey, Doreen, do you remember that? When Ridge slid across the waxed floor?" Libby heard Sloan ask.

Doreen chuckled in the background. "That boy was something else, wasn't he?"

"Well, thanks for calling," Sloan said. "Doreen's finished cooking dinner, so I should probably go. Love you, bye!"

"Love you too, sweetie." Libby sat frozen with the phone in her hand.

It had been lies, all of it. No, her best friend's partner wasn't who she thought he was, but turns out, neither was her best friend.

Libby was about to push the switch hook and call Caroline. Call her and call her out, give her a real piece of her mind, but she hesitated. Just because Jay hadn't hurt Ridge that particular time didn't mean he never had. And she'd often seen kids lie for abusive parents during her time at the shelter. She needed to be sure and knew how she could be.

Libby sat on the bed and continued explaining her afternoon to Vince. "So, I got the number of Sloan's teacher, the one she supposedly told about the abuse."

Vince stopped his pacing. "Tell me you didn't call her, Libby. Not her and Doreen Dawson in the same afternoon. You realize you calling and snooping around like this raises all sorts of red flags."

"I said I was with CPS," Libby said. "Told her there had been an anonymous call about Sloan Hadfield being abused last year, and we were just doing some final checks before closing it out."

"And?"

"And nothing. She never saw a single sign of abuse on Sloan, and they were very close that year. After Jay was charged with Ridge's murder, she even asked Sloan point-blank about abuse, and Sloan denied it. What's more, Mrs. Evans never even met Jay. Caroline told Ridge that Sloan's teacher didn't believe her because she didn't think Jay was capable, but turns out, she didn't even know Jay Hadfield from Adam."

Vince began pacing again. "We should have never trusted Caroline."

"She was my best friend," Libby said, wiping black smudges of mascara from her eyes. "What reason would I have not to trust her?"

"So, what do we do?" Vince asked. "Go to the cops?"

"No!" Libby said. "Are you crazy? We'll all be in jail. Then what would happen to the kids?"

Vince tapped his foot. "So she's vindictive, so she lied. That doesn't mean she won't take care of her children. We just have to go along with the plan and monitor Ridge and Sloan as best we can. There's nothing else we can do."

"Yes, there is." Libby bit the side of her cheek until she tasted blood. "Ridge wants to stay with us."

Vince stopped walking and put his hands on his hips. "He what?"

Libby began bouncing a knee. "He doesn't want to go back to Caroline."

"You've lost your mind!" Vince yelled. "I worried this would happen. You always get attached. Why would you put that idea into his head?"

"I didn't!" Libby jumped up. "He told me on his own."

"Oh, come on! Why would he want that?"

"Why don't you ask him yourself, Vince." Libby spat out his name. "Ridge!" She called, opening the door. "Come back here for a second."

"Yes?" Ridge stood in the hallway looking at them, a ring of chocolate circling his lips.

"Earlier, you told me you wanted to stay with us. Now, we won't be mad if you've changed your mind. But—"

"I haven't changed my mind. I want to live here."

Vince sat on the bed and patted the space beside him. "Come sit down. Tell me why."

Ridge shuffled over beside Vince. "Because this feels like an actual family. Like the way my family used to feel. But dad was lying then. He had another family. You don't. You guys love me. We have fun. Mom doesn't even care about me anymore. She wanted me to lie, and now, she wants me to change my name. I don't want to change my name. I like being Ridge."

"Those are all good reasons, bud. But this is something we need to really think about."

"I *have* been thinking about it, and I'm sure. Do you guys not want me?"

"Of course, we want you." Libby knelt in front of him. "We love you. Always, forever and no matter what, remember?"

Ridge shrugged. "Okay. Then, it's decided. But two things. First, can I get Blue? And second, can we ask if Sloan wants to live with us too?"

Libby turned to Vince. He rubbed the beard on his chin. "I can't make any promises," he said, "but we'll see what we can do."

# Chapter 30

*Mallowater, TX, 2008*

Sloan woke with a buzzing head to a buzzing phone. It took a few minutes to orient herself. She was on the couch, and a gaudy Christmas tree stood in the corner of the living room. Her brain felt slushy. The blurry details of the night before came into focus just as the lights of the Christmas tree did. She silenced the alarm on her phone and noticed a text she'd missed from Noah the night before.

> *How about tomorrow night for dinner? Vickie will make barbecue sandwiches.*

It was too early to respond. Sloan needed longer to sleep this off, but her mom would wake up soon. That's when Sloan realized she hadn't heard Ridge leave.

The headache behind Sloan's eyes intensified as she trudged down the hallway. Both doors were open. She glanced into her room and noticed the bed was rumpled and unmade, but the window remained locked from the inside.

"Mom?" She walked across the hallway to Caroline's room. A small cardboard box sat on the bed—the box of ammo Sloan had found in the attic with Grandpa Radel's gun. It was open, and a few bullets were scattered across the comforter. Sloan didn't need to check the attic to know the gun was gone.

The room spun. Sloan grabbed the headboard for stability. Where had Mom gone with the gun? Where was Ridge? Sloan checked outside, expecting to see Caroline's car gone, but it was still parked on the curb. *The creek*, Sloan guessed. She grabbed her keys but threw them right back down. She was too dizzy and disoriented to drive, so she ran, calling Noah on the way.

"Good morning." Noah's voice was scratchy in that just woke-up way. "Did you get my text last night about dinner?"

"Noah, get to the creek now!"

"What? What's going on?"

"Mom has Ridge." Sloan gasped for air. "She took a gun, but her car is here, so they walked somewhere. I don't know where else she'd be but the river."

Sloan heard drawers opening and closing on the other side of the phone. "Meet you there."

334 | A RIVER OF CROWS

Sloan arrived at the creek first. The low morning light rose like smoke from the night grass. Where would she go? Sloan started the trek up to their camping site but stopped short. Big Rock, she realized—the scene of Ridge's fake death.

She turned and ran through the trees, stumbling across uneven terrain. Her lungs seemed near collapse, but she couldn't stop. She heard her brother's deep voice first, echoing in the valley. "Come on, Mom. You don't want to do this."

"Who else has seen you?" Caroline's voice was bitter as the morning air.

Sloan was close enough to see them now, Ridge on his knees at the water's edge, Caroline behind him, gun drawn.

"No one else." Ridge's voice sounded hoarse. "Sloan only knows because I showed up last night," he lied.

"Mom, stop!" Sloan screamed as she stumbled down to the water. When Caroline cocked the hammer, Sloan stopped running and raised her hands. "Calm down." She took slow, small steps forward. "Ridge is alive. This is good news."

"You shouldn't have come back!" Spit flew from Caroline's mouth. "You lost the chance to come back a long time ago."

"It wasn't Ridge's fault," Sloan said. "He was just a kid."

"Who else saw you?" Caroline yelled now, the gun shaking in her hand.

"Nobody, I swear."

"I'll go to prison." Caroline's voice shook along with the gun. "Jay will be a martyr. It will be in all the magazines."

"No one else knows." Sloan continued to edge closer. "Put the gun down, and let's make a plan. You won't go to jail. If Ridge wanted that, he would have gone to the police already. But if you shoot him now, they will find his body, and the truth will come out."

"He's already dead," Caroline mumbled. "As far as the world knows, Ridge Hadfield already drowned in this creek. This won't change anything."

"Caroline!" Noah's voice boomed as he stepped out of the grove of trees opposite of Sloan. "Drop your weapon."

The interruption disoriented Caroline. She turned to look in Noah's direction, moving the gun slightly away from Ridge's head. Sloan took her chance. She charged at her mom, knocking her to the ground. While Ridge stood, staring at the water, seemingly paralyzed, Noah flung himself between Sloan and her mother. He wrestled the gun away and handcuffed Caroline.

"I'm not going back to the hospital!" Caroline screamed. "I'm not!"

"Ridge?" Noah looked up at his best friend. "What the hell happened, man?"

Ridge finally turned away from the river. "It's kind of a long story."

Ridge, Sloan, and Noah settled on a lie. They couldn't tell the truth about Caroline trying to kill Ridge—not when the world thought Ridge was dead. Noah would claim it had been a suicide attempt, and that would be enough to initiate a seventy-two-hour psychiatric hold. Long enough to get Ridge the hell out of Mallowater.

Sloan knew how much it pained Noah to do anything dishonest, especially regarding his job. This was a testament to how much he loved them. Noah Dawson was the truest friend Sloan had ever known. Who else would stay loyal when asked to resurrect ghosts just to bury them again?

"Maybe we should have told the truth." Ridge sat in front of the Christmas tree. In the light and sobriety of the afternoon, it didn't look as magical. Several branches were still clumped together, leaving gaping holes throughout the tree. Ornaments were concentrated on one side, and a strand of lights had completely burned out. "Mom needs to be in jail. She's dangerous."

Sloan pulled out her phone. Where was Dylan? Why hadn't he responded to her three texts? She looked back at her brother. "Mom doesn't need to be in jail. I can handle her."

"What's with your constant defense of her? She lied to us both."

"She had her reasons," Sloan said.

"So did Dad, but I don't see you over at his house pretending like nothing happened. Mom almost killed me."

Anger spiraled from the pit of Sloan's stomach. "Then why did you leave me with her?"

Ridge jumped up. "Because I saw a normal life. Mom's plan was sick. *She* was sick. She didn't care about us, just getting back at Dad. He spent twenty years in jail for something he never did."

"Oh, poor Dad; he was a real saint."

Ridge threw up his hands. "No, not a saint, but he didn't deserve all he got."

"So, you're telling me you *wanted* to stay with Libby and Vince?"

Ridge's body relaxed; his voice softened. "Yeah, but I wanted you to come too. They told me they asked, and you said no."

"No one asked me anything." Sloan choked back tears. "Ever."

"I know." Ridge's chin dipped down to his chest. "They came clean recently. There was a plan. Someone was supposed to talk to you, bring you to us if you wanted to come, but it all went wrong."

Sloan's heart banged against her chest. "Is this the guy who tried to take me? I remember that. It terrified me, Ridge."

"I swear that's not how they meant for it to happen," Ridge said. "I didn't even know about any of this. Not till a few weeks before my trip here. I've been wanting to see you and Mom for a while. I wasn't sure how much you knew, so I asked the Turners. They told me the truth."

Sloan chuckled. "How big of them."

"Libby and Vince made mistakes, but they were great parents," Ridge said.

"Oh, because they spoiled you? Because they have money? Because they gave you a life where you've made it thirty years without a job?"

The darkness that crossed Ridge's eyes told Sloan she had hit the mark. "Oh, shut up, Sloan."

"No, you shut up, Mister 'I lived a life of privilege while my sister barely survived!'" Sloan's breathing pounded in her own ears.

"They paid for your school, too," Ridge said. "They've always looked out for you."

Sloan was momentarily stunned into silence. She'd never dreamed Vince and Libby were the anonymous donors. They had been long out of her life at that point. She tried to hold on to her anger. Paying for her college excused nothing they'd done.

"The only thing they didn't tell me is that Mom lied about your abuse. They didn't want to turn me against her. Like good parents, they've only ever wanted to protect me."

Sloan raised a hand to her throbbing temple. "They are *not* your parents, Ridge. Caroline Radel is your mother. Nothing can change that. Libby Turner is the woman who kidnapped you."

"She didn't kidnap me. She raised me." Sloan saw ligaments bulge in Ridge's neck. "Libby Turner gave me a normal life."

"She manipulated you."

"She loved me!" Ridge threw his hand backward, hitting the tree and knocking a few ornaments to the floor.

"Then why are you here?" Sloan stomped her foot. "If they're your family, go back to them!"

"Great idea," Ridge sneered. He grabbed his jacket from the chair, accidentally stepping on an ornament before walking out the front door.

Sloan looked down at the shattered ornament. It was the roller-skating rabbit, and both of its ears and one wheel were severed victims of the fall.

Given everything that had happened, a busted ornament should have been the least of her worries, but it brought her to her knees. She held the broken bunny and sobbed deep, gut-wrenching sobs for all she had lost.

Dylan called back at 5:00. "Where have you been all day?" Sloan asked, bitterness dripping from each word.

"I had a meeting with the district attorney and depositions. I told you about this."

He had. But Sloan hadn't realized that was already today. "That's right." She slumped into a chair. "I'm sorry, it's been a terrible day. Can you come over?"

"I'll stop by the house and change, then be right there. Want me to pick up dinner for you and Caroline?"

"Mom's back in the hospital under observation."

"Uh oh." He lowered his voice. "Should I pick you up some wine?

"No." Sloan rubbed at her still-pounding forehead. "Never again."

Sloan rearranged ornaments on the Christmas tree while she waited for Dylan. As stupid as it was, she couldn't leave the tree like this.

She had just replaced the burned-out bulb when Dylan knocked at the door. He was still dressed for the deposition in the same shirt and tie he'd worn on their first date, tucked in this time, and accompanied by a jacket. He was carrying an overnight bag.

"Wow, look at you." Sloan pulled him into the house and into her arms.

Dylan sniffed her hair. "You smell . . ."

"Horrible." Sloan pulled away. "Like sweat and gin."

"I was going to say pears," he said. "Some sort of pear-scented shampoo, but yeah, I detect the gin too. Do I even want to know?"

"Long story."

"Well, we've got all night." Dylan held up the bag. "I mean, since Caroline's gone, I thought I'd stay here. But only if it's okay with you."

"Of course." A fluttery sensation filled Sloan's chest. "That's more than okay. I don't want to be alone."

Dylan leaned in for a kiss but stopped short, looking across the living room. "Sloan? What's with the tree?"

"Another long story." She ran a hand through her sweat-soaked hair. "Tell you what, if you don't mind making a pot of coffee, I'll get a shower, and then we'll talk."

Sloan took a quick shower and put on some yoga pants and a t-shirt. She wasn't sure what Dylan had in mind by staying the night, but regular pajamas seemed too intimate. She didn't bother with makeup but couldn't bring herself to go back out without at least blow-drying her pear-scented hair.

Dylan was sitting beside the tree when she came back in. He took a big breath. "Now you really smell like pears."

Sloan glanced back at the tree, noticing a gift underneath it, wrapped in newspaper with a bow made of a coffee label. "What in the world?"

Dylan picked up the present and shook it. "Catch." He tossed it to her. "Merry Christmas, I guess."

"Yeah, about this," she waved a hand at the tree. "Ridge came over. We got drunk and decided to decorate." She held up the present. "But how did you know to bring a gift?"

"I've had it a few days," Dylan said. "I didn't plan on wrapping it, but when I saw the tree, I improvised." He stood. "Open it."

Sloan tore into the paper, revealing two sketchbooks and a set of professional-colored pencils. A sudden thickness in her throat left her speechless.

"You said you used to draw," Dylan said. "I wondered if you might like to try again. Thought it might be like music for me. That it could help you heal."

Sloan swiped at tears falling on her cheek.

Dylan's eyes dulled. "Did I mess up?"

"It's perfect." Sloan's voice cracked. "I'm a crappy girlfriend, is all. I've never even heard you play guitar. I forgot about the depositions. I haven't even asked how the case is coming along."

Dylan swept her into a hug. "Hey, it's okay. You've got a lot going on. I haven't wanted to overwhelm you with more."

"I'm so sorry. Can you fill me in tonight?"

He wiped a strand of still-warm hair out of her face. "You bet. And hey, I brought my guitar with me today to help me relax during my breaks. So, it's still in the jeep if you want to listen later. But first, tell me what happened today."

Sloan motioned to the couch behind him. "We better sit. And a cup or two of that coffee wouldn't hurt."

Half an hour later, they had filled each other in on everything. Despite the intensity of the conversation, Sloan felt lighter just for having shared with Dylan.

She stared at the tree across the living room. "Will you help take it down?"

"Sure, but if you want to leave it up, leave it up."

Sloan looked away from the tree. "I used to love Christmas, but I haven't enjoyed one since Ridge disappeared. He took away all my Christmases, Dylan. Putting this tree up with him seemed like redemption, but it wasn't."

"I get that," Dylan said. "It's the same for me with Thanksgiving. My dad was an incredible chef. He cooked Thanksgiving dinner but always needed Mom and me to help. He spent the entire day yelling at us to bring him this or that or to chide us for doing everything wrong. It sucked."

"I bet." Sloan leaned in closer. Dylan rarely talked about his parents.

"It just wasn't worth it. We'd end up with an amazing gourmet dinner, but we were on the verge of tears by dinnertime. I would have rather ordered a pizza and been happy with each other. Thanksgiving is a holiday for being thankful for what you have, not for yelling at the people you are supposed to be thankful for."

Sloan remembered her last Thanksgiving. She'd spent it with Liam's family, like always. Two days later, she'd discovered a text from Megan on Liam's phone. Three weeks later, he'd filed for divorce. Sloan wondered where she'd be next Thanksgiving. Unnerving how much could change between Novembers.

"So," Dylan continued, "when I was twelve, I decided that when I grew up and had my own family, I'd never be unhappy on Thanksgiving."

Sloan smiled. "I like that. There are enough unhappy days in life. Thanksgiving shouldn't be one of them." She turned back to the tree. "I guess Christmas shouldn't either."

Dylan leaned forward and picked Ridge's broken ornament off the coffee table. "Do you think he left town?"

"Yeah." Sloan looked again at the glass bunny's broken ears. "I do."

Dylan set the ornament back down. "Well, I'm glad you got to see him. I'm glad you know. Because even though the truth can really blow, it's always better to know."

"You think knowing the truth is *always* a good thing?" Sloan asked.

"I do. I mean, Logan Pruitt's parents told me the same when I met them. Well, not in those words, but they were glad to learn the truth," Dylan said.

"Wow, you met Logan's parents? You never told me that."

Dylan wiped his hands down the legs of his slacks. "Yeah. They were so great, I assumed they'd hate me."

"Why would they hate you?" Sloan noticed Dylan pull his elbows tight against his sides like he was trying to make himself smaller.

"Because I could have saved Logan." Dylan clutched his hands together. "I should have gone to the cops the night I left, and they could have busted Eddie then. I justified my silence, told myself that Logan was getting too old and that Eddie would let him go soon, but in reality, I was scared to death of Eddie coming back for me. Coming after Dad."

Sloan squeezed Dylan's forearm. "You were a kid, Dylan. One who'd been through trauma. No one can blame you for that."

"Eddie killed Logan soon after I left. They can't say the exact date of death, but by the time Eddie left Mallowater, Logan was in the ground. Eddie probably did it because I ran. Because he figured I'd go to the cops." Dylan pressed a fist against his trembling lips.

"Dylan . . ." Sloan paused, trying to collect her thoughts.

"You don't have to say anything," Dylan said. "There's nothing to say. I only brought it up because you asked if the truth, even the ugly truth, is worth it."

Sloan kicked at the coffee table. "Does my dad deserve the truth?"

"Yeah, I mean, in theory. But that's easy for me to say, right? I never told Dad what happened to me, and I waited till he died to tell the world. I guess I thought knowing would be a burden for him, but now, I think him feeling like he couldn't help me all those years was probably the real burden."

Sloan stared at her feet. "I kinda want to see Dad again. But not with Anna, and definitely not with Felicity."

"So, see him," Dylan said. "On your terms. Go to dinner somewhere. Just the two of you."

Sloan shook her head. "I don't want the media attention."

"Use my house. Don't make excuses; make things happen."

"Man, you're full of quippy bits of wisdom, aren't you?" Sloan nudged him. "Don't make excuses; make things happen. The truth can blow, but it's better to know."

Dylan grinned. "I should make motivational home décor."

"How about you make some music instead?" Sloan tapped her feet against the floor. "I'm dying to listen to you play."

Dylan rubbed at his chin. "Only if you promise to show me one of your drawings sometime."

"Oh, so this is a 'show me yours, I'll show you mine' type of negotiation?"

Dylan's cheeks reddened. He opened his mouth, then closed it as though struggling for words. He finally stood and pulled out his keys. "I'll just go grab that guitar."

Sloan checked her phone for the first time since Dylan arrived. She noticed the voicemail icon, but when she checked the call log, there were no missed calls. That voicemail notification always seemed to put up a fight to disappear. When Dylan returned, a maple-colored acoustic Gibson guitar was strapped over his shoulder. He held a gray pick and strummed a few chords, warming up. Sloan marveled at the change in the Dylan that walked out the door and the one who came back in. His posture was stronger, and he held his head higher. For the first time Sloan had ever seen, Dylan Lawrence looked confident. It was extremely sexy.

He sat down next to her and, with no introduction, strummed the opening to "Making Memories of Us."

Sloan watched in awe as the guitar became an extension of Dylan. He made it look so effortless. His voice was smooth and sweet, perfect for the romance of a song about pledging the best part of yourself to someone. Sloan inhaled deeply, anchoring herself in the moment and taking in the scent of Dylan's cologne. She knew that no matter what became of her and Dylan, the smell of Calvin Klein's Eternity for Men would forever bring her back to this perfect moment.

Goosebumps covered her arms by the time Dylan strummed the last note. She stood and turned toward him to clap.

"Stop." Dylan squeezed his eyes shut and motioned for her to sit.

"That was beautiful. Please play another one."

Dylan stretched his arms out in front of him, interlocking his fingers. "Any requests?"

Before she could respond, a tiny electronic melody filled the room. "Sorry. I thought I had it silenced." She pulled out her cellphone. "It's Felicity."

"Answer it," Dylan said.

"No way." She pressed ignore. "I have no idea why she'd be calling, and I'm busy." She set the phone down and turned toward Dylan. "Since you played Keith Urban, it's only fair you play some Whitley."

Dylan tuned a couple of strings. "I expected this and have been practicing." Sloan sank back on the couch cushion and listened as Dylan began playing, "When You Say Nothing at All."

He was still on the first verse when Sloan's phone sounded again, this time with a text notification. She didn't want to be rude to Dylan, so she ignored it. But when the second beep came, alarm bells sounded in Sloan's head louder than Dylan's gorgeous vocals. She pulled out her phone and turned away from Dylan to check it. Both texts were from Felicity.

*Sloan, your mom is here at my parents' house. Just sitting in her car across the street. Dad is on his way home, but he was in Longview with Brad, so it will be a bit.*

"What!" Sloan jumped to her feet, trying to read the second text through the spots in her vision.

*Should Kyle go talk to her? Or should we wait for Dad? We aren't sure what to do.*

Dylan stopped strumming. "What's wrong?"

Sloan ran to the window. "Mom's car is gone! Was it here when you pulled up?"

Dylan set his guitar on the couch and walked up behind her. "Yeah. It was parked on the street."

Sloan shook her head. "I don't understand. How did she get out of the hospital? How!"

"Are you sure no one stole the car?"

"Mom's in Tyler." Sloan moved around the room till she located her shoes. "At Anna's." She struggled with her flip-flops, accidentally putting the left one on her right foot. Suddenly, Sloan was at Blockbuster Video in 1995, getting the phone call from Walt. She was waiting for Noah to drive her home and leaving her vomit all over the break room table for Danny to clean up.

"Are they sure it's her? How did she get her keys?"

Sloan ran down the hall and into her mother's room, Dylan close behind. Her mom's purse was missing from the table beside her bed where Sloan had put it. And the window was wide open.

"I'm sorry," Dylan said. "I thought I heard something earlier, but you were blow-drying your hair, so I assumed I was hearing things. I should have checked."

*The gun.* Sloan had a moment of confusion, thinking that her mother still had the gun. But of course, she didn't. She'd been in the hospital. Sloan had unloaded the gun and put it back in the attic. Noah was bringing her a lockbox tomorrow. Sloan hated guns, but it was one of their few possessions that belonged to her Grandpa Radel.

Dylan looked around the room. "The noise didn't sound like it came from her bedroom. It was above me."

Sloan shut the window. "Well, she didn't get into the attic. She would have had to walk right by you."

Dylan stepped farther into the room. "There's not another attic entry in here? There's a draft coming from somewhere."

"No," Sloan said. At least she didn't think there was. She scanned the popcorn ceiling. "The draft was coming from the window."

Dylan walked into the closet and looked up. "It's in here. An attic access door. It's open, so she's been up there. I knew I heard something."

Sloan grew dizzy. Black spots clouded her vision. "Come on." She latched onto Dylan's arm to steady herself. "Get me to Tyler and fast."

# Chapter 31

*Mallowater, TX, 1989*

Caroline reviewed the list of everything she needed before she backed out of the driveway. She was rushing this, but a deranged man grabbing Sloan at Leo's Drug Emporium had sped everything up. "Just let Sloan come stay with us awhile," Libby had said. "No need for you to leave town without having a solid plan."

But Caroline couldn't chance it. It was time to get Ridge back. It was time to get the hell out of Texas.

It could have been random, another stranger abduction like that Pruitt boy years ago, but what were the odds? Caroline feared someone was on to her. Just as she'd taken Ridge away from Jay, someone was trying to take Sloan away from her. And she couldn't go to the police. If the cops knew someone tried to kidnap Sloan, they might wonder if someone took Ridge, too. Then, Jay might get a new trial. He might get away with everything.

Caroline had told the kids they'd move to New York. She had an old college friend she'd counted on crashing with, but that was before their story became national news. One of her old Cornell professors had even sent her a sympathy card. She couldn't just show up there with her daughter and dead son. But hopefully, she could show up with them in Columbus, Ohio. She would be able to continue her studies there in avian biology. No, it wasn't Cornell, but she'd read about a large crow roost in a nearby town.

This would not be as easy as she'd planned. They'd all have to change their names. Vince knew a guy who would help with that. And Sloan and Ridge would have to homeschool for a while. Give people plenty of time to forget Ridge's face and story.

She'd call Walt in the morning and tell him she and Sloan just needed to get away—that they were going to sort out her dad's estate in Ohio. Walt didn't need to know that the estate was in Oklahoma and was already settled. In fact, it was the money from the sale of her father's house that sat in the safe in her back seat, along with his pistol.

Caroline would eventually tell Walt that they'd decided to stay in Ohio. Then she'd return to get another load of items and ready the house for sale. But if something prevented her from returning, they had everything they needed and enough money to get by for a while.

Sloan hardly spoke during the first leg of their drive. She just leaned against the window, listening to her sad country songs. Country music made Caroline think of Jay, and thus, she could never enjoy it again. She was glad to kill the engine—and the radio—when they filled up the tank at the By and Buy.

Despite the tough times that lay ahead, Caroline was looking forward to reuniting with her baby boy. Ridge had probably grown an inch since she saw him.

Caroline parked and glanced at the clock on the dash. They were early. She needed coffee for the fourteen-hour drive ahead of her to Ohio. It would be hard, but then they could crash in a hotel tomorrow night, and Caroline would wake up Monday refreshed and ready for apartment hunting.

Caroline grabbed her purse. "Are you hungry?"

"Why would I be hungry at one in the morning?"

Caroline clenched her fists. Leave it to her teenage daughter to suck the joy right out of the car.

Caroline walked inside and bought a large cup of coffee, telling the weary woman at the counter to keep the change. A decision she immediately second-guessed. Caroline didn't want to stand out in anyone's memory, and that gesture may have set her apart from other customers.

She regained her composure. It wasn't a big deal if someone remembered her or Sloan stopping here. As long as they didn't see Ridge getting into her car, everything would be fine.

Why had Libby suggested meeting here? A secluded place might be smarter, but then again, not necessarily. Two cars in a field at this hour might stand out; two cars at a gas station would not.

Caroline wondered if she'd be on edge like this for the rest of her life—thinking through each step, looking over her shoulder? She hoped not, but if this was how it had to be, it was worth it to see Jay punished. Anything was worth that.

They weren't here. Why weren't they here? The Turners were never late to anything and were forty minutes late. Forty minutes. Caroline felt a physical pressure inside her—like she was being squeezed. She grasped the sides of her head and breathed deeply, trying to regain control. When it didn't work, she went back inside for a pack of cigarettes. She didn't let the cashier keep the change this time.

Sloan was awake when Caroline made it back to the car. "Mom? What's wrong?"

"I don't know, Sloan. I don't know what's wrong," she said, fumbling to open her cigarettes. Why did they wrap them up in plastic? It would just end up in a landfill somewhere. "Dammit!" she screamed, throwing them against the dash.

Sloan reached across to unwrap the package. "Here you go." Sloan handed her a cigarette.

"Thanks." She lit the cigarette and took the first puff. Her heart resumed its regular rhythm, and Caroline told herself that this was all just a misunderstanding.

"I need to go to the bathroom," Sloan said. "And I'm thirsty."

"There's money in my wallet. Get whatever you want. This is all a misunderstanding. It will be okay. We'll be on the road soon." Maybe saying it out loud would make it real.

Caroline couldn't just sit in the car and wait. She got out and paced in front of the store, smoking in the cool night air. She saw the pay phone, and it hit her. Libby and Vince had probably overslept. Or maybe their car wouldn't start, and they had no way to reach her. She just needed to call and tell them she wouldn't mind driving all the way to Baton Rouge if she needed to.

Caroline put in her change, dialed the Turners' number, and listened to the phone ring and ring. At first, she thought she must have misdialed. Why else had their machine not picked up? On the second try, by the twentieth ring, every muscle in Caroline's body went limp.

"Who are you trying to call?" Sloan was suddenly standing right beside her. How long had she been there?

"It's a misunderstanding. It will be okay. We'll be on the road soon," she said to herself.

"It's cold, Mom. Come to the car and wait. I got a Lunchable. We can split it."

"I could call the police," Caroline said, but what would she say? That the people she used to help her fake her son's death had kidnapped him? "No, no, I can't."

Sloan put her arm around Caroline. "Come on. Let's get you in the car and warmed up. We'll call again in fifteen minutes."

And Caroline called back every fifteen minutes on the dot. She used every nickel, dime, and quarter she had in her wallet, then tore apart her car to find more. But they never answered, and their car never pulled up beside hers. Adrenaline rushed through Caroline's body. How could they? She picked up a bag of ice and slammed it down onto the concrete.

Even if they'd had car troubles on the way, that didn't explain the removal of their answering machine. Libby had been acting so weird and distant. She hardly ever let Caroline talk to Ridge.

Caroline grabbed a clump of her hair and pulled. They'd taken her boy. Libby was barren. She'd pretended to be her friend when all she wanted was a child, Caroline's child.

"I can't believe this happened. How could it happen?" Caroline's chest ached. Was she hyperventilating or having a heart attack? She recognized she was losing control but wasn't sure how to rein her emotions back in.

"I don't know, but it's almost morning." Sloan spoke in a gentle tone that Caroline had never known her sharp-tongued daughter to have. "We can figure this out later, but let's go home, please."

Caroline started to cry. She didn't want to go home, but maybe a message was waiting on her machine. Better yet, maybe Ridge was waiting there for her. "Yes. I guess there's nothing we can do but go home."

Ridge wasn't at home. There was no message on the machine. "Go to bed," she told Sloan. "Sleep in. If you wake up and I'm gone, it's because I have business in Tyler later today. Call Doreen if you need anything."

"Are you sure you're okay, Mom?" Sloan asked.

"Yes. Now go to bed. Forget any of this happened."

As soon as Sloan climbed into bed, Caroline called Libby's number again and was met with a message that the number had been disconnected. *What is going on?* She didn't know their address, so she dug through an enormous stack of mail, praying she hadn't thrown away the envelope from the birthday card Libby had sent her.

She tossed bill after bill on the floor until she got to the lavender envelope. Yes, this was it! "Thank you, God, thank you, God," she said aloud.

Lavender envelope in hand, Caroline walked right back out the door and drove to Louisiana.

It was nearly noon by the time Caroline made it to the Turners. She held on to the tiniest bit of hope until she spotted the house.

The house was large and red-bricked with a green manicured lawn. Libby's signature rose bushes bloomed right behind a shiny black "For Sale" sign.

Caroline got out of the car and ran toward the neighbor's house. A woman with a baby on her hip answered the door. "Can I help you?"

Caroline tried to steady her voice, but she couldn't hide her breathlessness. "Vince and Libby Turner? Did they live next door?"

"Yes," the woman said, locking the screen door.

"Any idea where they moved?"

"No, sorry. We weren't very close." She attempted to close the door, but Caroline spoke again. "Was there anyone else they were close to?"

The woman bit her lip. "I never saw anyone over. Check with LSU. He worked there."

Yes. LSU. Why hadn't she thought of that? "Can I borrow your phone to . . ." before she finished, the woman slammed the door. *Bitch.*

Luckily the man across the street was kinder. He didn't know where they'd moved, but Vince had mentioned they weren't fond of the area and had been applying for other jobs, so it didn't surprise him to see the sign yesterday morning. Yesterday morning. They must have left right after Caroline had talked to Libby to solidify their plans for that night. *How could they?*

The old man let her use his phone, where she called LSU and spoke to the department head, who had no idea where Vince had moved to.

*They might be anywhere. She would never find them.*

Caroline knew that Vince had connections. Libby had hinted that Vince's father and brother had ties to organized crime. Caroline had always wondered if that's how the Turners made so much money. She wiped a puddle of sweat from her forehead.

Caroline called the realtor listed on the sign next. He told her that Vince and Libby had only been renting the house with plans to buy one of the homes being built in a new subdivision close to LSU. However, they'd unexpectedly decided to move out of town with two months still remaining on their lease and had left no forwarding address. "The owner has had enough of these unreliable renters just skipping out, so he's decided to sell." The realtor had one of those salesman voices, like Jay. "There's an open house next week if you're in the market. It's a great property."

Caroline hung up and wiped more sweat from her forehead. Renting. Caroline knew then that stealing Ridge and leaving Louisiana had been Libby's plan all along. Why else would the Turners do something so beneath them? So "middle class," as Vince would say.

"Forgive me for asking, but is there a reason you need to get in touch with them so badly?" the kindly neighbor asked. "Are you okay? You don't look well."

*Libby stole my Ridge. They kidnapped my son, and I can never tell without implicating myself in his disappearance. Of course, I'm not frickin' okay. I'll never be okay again.*

Caroline stood to leave. "Thank you for letting me borrow your phone." She couldn't even manage a smile. "They just owed me some money is all."

"You found them?" Caroline leaned over the private investigator's desk. Three months of searching, and he'd *finally* found them. "Where are they?"

Mr. Garcia looked down at the folder on his desk. "El Paso."

Caroline couldn't figure out why he didn't look happier about this news. Maybe he had just realized he could no longer bill Caroline an exorbitant amount of money each month with nothing to show for it.

She tapped her foot against her chair. "Do you have an address?"

He loosened his collar. "That's the thing, Ms. Radel. An associate found their house on Friday. He returned Saturday, and they were gone."

Caroline's insides vibrated. "What do you mean gone?"

"The Turners had left, moved out. The owners said they gave no notice at all."

"So, they saw your guy?" Caroline raised her voice. "What kind of PI is dumb enough to be seen?"

Mr. Garcia held up his hands. "These things happen sometimes. I can assure you that he was as careful as possible."

"No!" Caroline slammed her hand on the desk. "He wasn't careful at all, or they'd still be there."

"I understand you're upset. But we found them. I suspect they realize you're looking for them and thus are keeping their guard up."

Caroline sank back in her chair. "Okay, so what's next? Back to square one?"

He closed the folder. "That's all up to you, Ms. Radel. You already put a lot of money into this. I suspect it will cost just as much or more to locate them again. And, of course, there are no guarantees."

Caroline covered her face with her hands. *As much or more?* If she weren't careful, her inheritance would disappear, and then what? How would she pay her bills? How would she take care of Sloan?

"Don't get me wrong," he said. "I'll be glad to continue working the case. You mentioned the Turners owed you money. I guess you have to ask yourself if the amount they owe is worth the amount you are spending to find them." He drummed his fingers on the desk. "Unless you have another motive for locating them. Either way, it's your decision to make."

Caroline's skin prickled. He suspected something. Or else he would if she continued searching. She'd hired this private investigator out of Dallas on purpose, so he wouldn't know who she was—wouldn't know who Ridge was if he found them, but she was kidding herself. Their story had made national news. If she kept this up and one of these detectives recognized Ridge, she was signing her own warrant.

"You're right," she said, forcing her shaky legs to stand. "It's not worth the money at this point. Thank you for your help. I'll mail you your last payment."

Mr. Garcia stood and gave a sympathetic nod. "I'm sorry, Ms. Radel, but sometimes you just have to cut your losses and move on."

# Chapter 32

*Tyler, TX, 2008*

Sloan called Noah on the way to the Hadfield's. History was repeating itself, and Sloan needed Noah now, just as she had then.

"Noah, are you at work?" she asked as soon as he answered.

He hesitated for a few seconds. "I'm with Ridge. Don't get mad. He just—"

"I don't care," Sloan said. "Meet me in Tyler. At Anna's house. Mom is there. Noah, she's there *again*."

"What are you talking about? Caroline is still at the hospital. It was a 72-hour hold."

"She's not!" Sloan yelled into the phone. "The hospital called, and she's gone. They left me a message earlier tonight. My phone didn't ring."

"Alright, calm down. How could she have gotten to Tyler on foot?"

"She didn't!" Sloan grabbed a handful of her hair. "Her car's gone. She must have gotten a ride back to the house and snuck in her window for the keys. Felicity texted. Mom's right outside their house."

"I'll meet you there, but I should call this into the Tyler police."

Sloan thought of the open attic entrance. Her mom had climbed up there for the gun. Yes, the Tyler police needed to be called.

But when she opened her mouth, the wrong words came out. "Please, no. She's just sitting there. I don't want the media there again, Noah. I can't handle this all again. Please, just come."

"On my way." Sloan listened to his car start on the other end of the line.

Sloan ended the call and texted Felicity.

> *Don't go out there. None of you. Text Dad and tell him not to talk to her if he gets there before me. I'm on my way.*

She set the phone in the console before pulling it back out to send Felicity a second text.

> *And just to be safe, lock your doors.*

Sloan let out a steadying breath when she spotted her mother's figure still in the front seat of her car.

"Park there behind her," Sloan said. "You stay in here."

"No way." Dylan angled the car to pull up behind Caroline. "Not when she has the gun."

"Mom's not going to hurt me."

"Fine." Dylan didn't sound convinced. "But signal if you need me."

Caroline stared straight ahead, her face void of all emotion as Sloan approached the car. Sloan tried the door—locked. She lightly rapped on the window. "Mom? What are you doing?"

Caroline rolled down the window and leaned forward on the steering wheel, staring across the street. "This is where I stood when I found out about your father. Right at this spot." Her voice cracked. "This is where my life fell apart."

"Is that why you're here? To feel the pain again?" Sloan understood that. It was why she played the Keith Whitley cassette on repeat, why she couldn't stay away from Crow's Nest Creek.

"I've never stopped feeling the pain." Caroline turned to her. "Imagine giving up everything for a man only to have him betray you."

"I don't have to imagine it. I lived it too. Let's go home," Sloan said. "We can talk about it there. We'll stop at Taco Bell. That used to be your favorite."

Caroline turned back toward the house, but Sloan noticed her wipe away a tear. "I want to talk to him, Sloan. I *deserve* to talk to him."

"Yes, you do," Sloan said. "But will it do any good?"

"It will make me feel better."

"Okay. But why do you need a gun, Mom?"

"A gun!" Caroline jerked her head toward Sloan. "I don't have a gun."

"Don't lie to me."

"Seriously, I don't have it," Caroline said. "I was messed up this morning with Ridge. Out of my mind. I don't want to hurt anyone. All I want is to talk to Jay."

As much as Sloan wanted to trust her mom, she knew better. This was an act, a smokescreen of sanity, a manipulation. "You were in the attic." Sloan crossed her arms.

"I climbed in the attic, but not for the gun. Why would I even think you'd put it back there where I could find it? That would be pretty stupid of you." She reached into the passenger seat. "I was looking for this." She held up a handwritten letter with an old photo attached. "I burned most of the letters and cards from Jay, most of the pictures, but I kept these." She rubbed her thumb across the white border of the Polaroid. "These were special. The first letter he ever wrote me, the first picture we took together. As much as I've hated him all these years, I could never let these burn."

"I'm glad you didn't," Sloan said. "It's a great picture. You both look so happy. And I'd love to read the letter sometime."

"Why?" Caroline wiped away another tear. "Every damn word in it is a lie."

Sloan leaned closer and pointed at the picture. "That smile on his face doesn't look like a lie. It wasn't right what he did. None of it, but Dad loved you, Mom. It was gross how much he loved you."

Caroline shook her head. "Jay has to answer for this. For this and for every year, every lie that followed."

Tires squealed as a car rounded the corner. Sloan turned and saw Brad stop in the middle of the road and let their father out before peeling into his mother's driveway.

"Sloan, is everything all right?" Jay asked, looking into the car.

Caroline threw open her door, pushing Sloan out of the way. "No, Jay. I would say everything is most definitely not alright."

Jay drew his mouth into a straight line. "I'm sorry. I'm just so sorry about everything."

"Dad!" Brad took wide steps toward them. "Should I call the police?" He looked Sloan in the eye as if this were her doing.

"No," Jay said. "We aren't calling the police."

"Come inside," Brad said. "You don't have to . . ."

"Bradley!" Jay thrust his arm out. "Go back inside."

Brad's face tightened, skin stretching into a snarl, but he didn't argue.

"Nice boy you got there," Caroline said, watching Brad walk away. "I remember when I learned about him. Went for Ridge's birth certificate and got his instead."

Even in the dark of the night, Sloan saw her father grow pale. "That's when you found out?"

Caroline charged at Jay, slamming her fists into his chest and screaming. "Did you really think you could keep it a secret forever?" Sloan heard Dylan's truck door open, but Sloan motioned for him to stay. Her father deserved far worse. He could handle himself.

"Caroline, don't do this." Jay's voice was calm. He gently grabbed her wrists. "I know you hate me, but you loved me once. Let's calm down and talk."

Caroline shook herself free from his grasp and stumbled back to her car, crying.

"I'm glad you came." He took a careful step toward her. "I've been wanting to talk to you. I've imagined it for twenty years. I never imagined it out here, like this, but it's okay."

"And I never imagined it would be out here where my life ended."

"Your life ending?" Jay shook his head. "Don't talk like that."

"It already ended. At this very spot." She stomped her foot. "This is where I first saw you . . ." She waved her hands toward his house across the street. "This is where I first saw you with her."

Jay's chin dipped to his chest. "How come you never confronted me? I knew something was wrong. Why didn't you tell me you knew? Were you just going to let me off the hook?"

"No." She crossed her arms. "How could I let you off the hook after you stole my entire life?"

Sloan's fingers and toes went numb. Was her mom going to tell the truth about what she'd done to make him pay? "Mom!" Sloan reached into the car and pulled out the letter. "You said you wanted to show Dad this."

Caroline snatched it from Sloan's hands. "Do you remember this? Do you?" She shoved it against his chest.

Sloan watched her father hold up the letter towards a streetlight before dropping his arms to his side, lifeless. "Of course, I do. I meant every word."

"Every word, huh?" Caroline's voice was rough and thick. "Even the ones that claimed I was the love of your life?"

"You were," Jay whispered. "You *are*. I was going to leave Anna for you." He glanced over his shoulder to ensure it was still only the three of them standing in the street. "I never felt for her—for anybody—what I do for you."

"Right." Caroline sniffled and wiped her nose with the back of her hand. "So, you were going to leave Anna, but in thirteen years, you never got around to it?" She glanced at his hand. "Make that thirty-three years. Nice to see you wear a wedding ring. You never used to."

Jay folded up the letter. "I couldn't leave her, Caroline. But I damn sure wanted to. I was a coward. I wanted to be with you. I wanted to be with you forever."

Caroline knocked the note out of his hand. It blew a few feet, and Sloan jogged to grab it.

"And yet you are still with Anna." Caroline grew in height as her spine stiffened.

"You didn't give me a choice." Jay's voice rose for the first time. "She stood by me."

"Ah well, Anna's a regular Tammy Wynette, isn't she?" Caroline walked slowly toward her car. "But not me. I'm a little more *The Night That the Lights Went Out in Georgia* than *Stand by Your Man*, if you know what I mean."

When Caroline reached into the open car window, Sloan understood what she meant by her comment; she knew what her mom was reaching for. The gun. She *had* brought it.

"No!" Sloan unstuck her legs as she saw her mom pull the weapon from the car, but she felt like she was moving in slow motion. Thankfully, Dylan wasn't. From the corner of her eye, Sloan saw him jump out of the jeep and charge toward Caroline, right as she pointed the gun at Jay.

The wail of a police siren in the distance stole everyone's attention. It seemed to stun Caroline enough for Dylan to pin her against the car. She fought but couldn't break free. "Sloan, grab the gun," Dylan yelled as Caroline raised it toward the streetlight.

Caroline tilted her head back and shouted, "It's the night the lights went out on Brookhaven Drive!"

"Sloan!" Dylan said more forcefully, but Jay was already there. Caroline fought harder, but Jay pried the gun from her hands. He tossed it behind him as both men fought to keep Caroline pinned against the vehicle.

"Stop fighting, Mom." Sloan picked up the weapon. "The police are coming. They'll take you in. To prison this time."

"Get them off me!" Caroline screamed. "Get them off me!"

Sloan looked down at the gun in her hand as blue and red flashing lights filled the street. She ran to the other side of her mother's car and tossed it into the backseat, covering it with a reflective sun visor. She had just shut the door when the police cruiser pulled up beside her.

Noah jumped out, gun drawn. "What's going on?" he asked.

"It's okay," Sloan said. "She only wanted to talk to him."

Noah looked at her incredulously. "Where's the gun?"

"There's no gun," Sloan said. "I was wrong. Mom was getting an old letter out that she wanted Dad to read." Sloan sensed Dylan's eyes boring into her, but she didn't turn to look at him.

"Get them off me!" Caroline screamed again. "They're hurting me."

"Let go," Sloan told them. "She's not going to do anything."

Both men released their grip and slowly backed away. "What happened here, Mr. Hadfield?" Noah asked.

Jay looked at Sloan. "We were talking," he said. "Caroline got a little upset. That's all."

Noah didn't look convinced, but he holstered his weapon.

Sloan looked to her right. A nosy neighbor was peering out her window. The Hadfields had come out and filled their front lawn. "Turn your lights off, Noah, please. Before the entire neighborhood comes out."

As Noah walked back to his cruiser, Sloan faced her mother. "Let Dylan take you home. Go to bed. If you try anything else, I'm telling Noah *everything*."

The street seemed strangely dark after Noah turned off his lights, like the switch had dimmed the streetlight as well.

"It's best you go home, Caroline." Noah's voice was deeper than normal.

"She is," Sloan said. "Dylan's going to take her, and I'll drive her car back soon." She turned back to Dylan with hopeful eyes. He nodded, but his expression was tight.

"Sound good to you, Caroline?" Noah asked.

"Yeah. I'll leave for now." Caroline smoothed down her shirt and tightened her ponytail. "But I assume I can come back; I mean, it's a public street."

"It would be best for all if you didn't," Noah said. "But for now, let's get you home. Get in with Dylan, and I'll follow."

Jay looked at Sloan. "Do you want to come inside for a bit?"

She didn't. Not at all. She didn't want to face the Hadfields, but she had some damage control to do. She also wanted to thank her father for going along with her lie about the gun, for keeping her mom out of jail in Tyler tonight. For keeping their names out of the next day's paper. Hopefully.

"Yeah, sure," Sloan said. "Just let me say goodbye to Dylan first."

But as Sloan walked toward Dylan, she saw the passenger door of Noah's squad car open. She'd been so distracted she didn't notice his partner was with him.

But the man who exited the cruiser was not Noah's partner. Not an officer at all. Ridge. Sloan remembered now that Noah said he was with him when she called.

Ridge glanced at Sloan, then at their mother before locking eyes with their father. Sloan waited for him to speak, but he only stared, opening and closing his mouth like a baby crow, waiting for his parents to feed him.

Jay took a step forward and brought a trembling hand to his mouth. "Ridge?" he whispered.

"Yeah, Da—" Ridge's voice broke. He cleared his throat and tried again. "Yeah, Dad, it's me."

Fifteen minutes later, Sloan sat next to Ridge on the Hadfield's sofa, right under a *Welcome Home* banner, untouched slices of cake on the plates in their hands.

Sloan couldn't understand why Ridge had stepped out of that police car. It had surely sealed their mom's fate. She'd go to prison; they'd all make news again. But as she sat surrounded by her father's other family, Sloan was glad to have Ridge with her.

"I'm going to take the kids home to go to bed," Kyle's wife, Tessa, said as she wrangled two blonde toddlers, mouths stained with blue icing. "Say goodbye to Nana and Pappy."

*Nana and Pappy.* This was bizarre.

"And I'll get a ride home from Tessa," Brad's wife said. Sloan didn't blame them for wanting to run from this family drama. She wanted to run too.

"So nice to meet you all," Tessa said to Sloan and Ridge.

Sloan smiled and nodded. Of course, they hadn't actually all met. "I think you all know Sloan," Jay had said when they came in from outside. "And this is her friend."

But Sloan knew by the look on Felicity and Anna's faces—they realized Ridge wasn't just some friend. Even if they hadn't heard the interaction outside, Ridge had Jay's sparkling blue eyes.

Their father seemed to be in a daze. He hadn't even asked any questions; he had barely spoken at all.

Kyle finally approached Ridge after the wives and kids left. "You want to explain what the hell is going on?"

"Kyle!" Anna yelled. "Sit down. This is good news."

"It is," Brad agreed. "We can finally prove Dad's not a murderer."

Jay put his hand up. "That doesn't matter right now. All that matters is that my boy's alive."

"What happened to you, Ridge?" Felicity asked. "Are you okay?"

Ridge looked at the ground. "I'd rather not talk about it."

"Bullshit!" Kyle crossed the room again. Sloan jumped up too. The big sister inside of her awakened.

"Sit down!" Jay scolded, and they both did. Apparently, Sloan, the daughter, was still somewhere inside her too.

"Was it Eddie Daughtry?" Felicity asked. "I've been talking to Dylan Lawrence, and he said Eddie had other victims."

There was a stiffness in Sloan's jaw and neck. "Well, we've been talking to Dylan Lawrence, too, because I'm dating him."

Felicity flinched. "Well, yes, I heard that."

*Then maybe you should stop texting him*, Sloan thought but settled for an exaggerated eye roll.

"Who's Dylan Lawrence?" Anna asked.

"The whistleblower about Eddie Daughtry," Felicity said. "Sloan and I noticed many similarities between Logan Pruitt and Ridge, so we met with Dylan."

"Then Sloan and I started working on a way to talk to Daughtry," Brad said. "But she seemed to stop caring. Guess I know why now," he said, gesturing toward Ridge.

"Well, Ridge has valid reasons to be afraid," Felicity said. "Dylan's feared for his own life plenty. Eddie has a lot of connections."

"Just stop," Sloan said. "You have no idea what you're talking about, so stop talking." She looked at her brother. "Should we just leave?"

"No." Jay held out his hand. "Please don't go, Ridge. You don't have to talk about what's passed."

"If he doesn't want to talk, why is he here?" Brad asked.

Ridge raised his head. "I don't know. I guess I just wanted to see Dad."

"You saw him out there," Kyle said. "Why are you in *our* house?"

"I figured I should apologize," Ridge said. "For not coming home sooner. If I had, Dad could have come back to you all a long time ago." He stood, so Sloan did the same. "Sorry to disrupt your evening. I'll be gone tomorrow."

"Whatever happened, it isn't your fault." Jay stood and put his hands on Ridge's shoulder. "And I don't care about my name being cleared. Don't leave. Not yet. There's so much I've missed."

"No more than you've missed with any of us," Kyle mumbled under his breath.

"Kyle, that's enough," Anna said.

"Don't compare your life with ours." Sloan pointed her finger. "Don't you dare."

Felicity groaned. "My family didn't have it easy either, okay?"

"Oh, give me a break, Felicity. You didn't live with a mentally ill woman. You didn't have to take care of yourself!" Sloan's yelling had silenced the rest of the room except for her father, who began to softly cry. His tears rubbed her wrong. "That's right, Dad. I worked three jobs. I had to take care of Mom when I could barely take care of myself."

"Until you locked her up in a nuthouse and ran away," Kyle said, standing. "Of course, that was after she spent an evening up on our roof."

Jay stomped over to his oldest son, putting a finger in his face. "Stop right now."

Kyle pushed Jay's finger away. "Stop choosing them over us. Their mom probably had something to do with Ridge disappearing. She's a psychopath."

The slap echoed throughout the room. Anna gasped, but Kyle stood silently, absently wiping at his cheek a few moments before finally speaking.

"This is why I changed my name. Why I tried to get away from this family. You're all crazy."

Anna jumped up from the coach and ran to her oldest. "Don't leave, Kyle. Dad didn't mean it."

Sloan rubbed her forehead. Her mom hadn't been wrong about one thing: Anna Hadfield really was pathetic.

"This is all my fault," Jay said. "But you're all my children, and we are going to have to learn how to be a family . . ."

*Not a chance*, Sloan thought. She continued listening to her father's speech, but her eyes were on Kyle. His pupils had widened, and his breathing was erratic. He pulled out his phone, holding it up in front of him. When Jay stopped talking, Sloan heard the click of the camera's shutter and realized too late what Kyle had done.

Sloan stepped in front of Ridge. "He's taking pictures of you. Go to the car."

Ridge put his head down and hurried out the front door.

"He can run if he wants, but we'll sort this out," Kyle said. "We'll figure out where he's been, and we'll expose it." He turned toward Brad. "Won't we?"

Brad stared down at his feet. "Leave it alone, Kyle. Dad wants to leave it alone."

"Fine." Kyle raised his nose. "If you won't help me, I'm sure the fine people on Facebook will." He turned his phone toward them, displaying a perfect shot of Ridge's face.

Sloan charged for him, but Jay got to him first. He grabbed Kyle by the collar and slammed him against the wall.

"Jay, stop!" Anna cried.

For all his talk, Kyle didn't even try to fight back or resist. "Breaking parole already, Dad?" he asked.

"Give me the phone," their father demanded. When Kyle didn't respond, Jay bounced him against the wall again. "Now!"

Kyle dropped the phone, and Jay kicked it across the floor toward Felicity, but Sloan got to it first. She raised her foot and stomped down with all her weight. The screen cracked. Sloan kept stomping until it was completely smashed into pieces. When she was finished, all eyes were on her. She walked past them all, through the littered pieces of plastic and glass, stopping only to yank down the *Welcome Home* banner before walking out the front door.

Sloan looked down at her cell phone lighting up on the center console. "It's Dad again. Turn it off, please."

Ridge powered the phone down. "That was rough. Seeing Dad chase after us like that."

"It's the least he could do."

"You don't have to play the tough guy anymore, Sloan. You aren't alone."

Sloan's hands tightened around the wheel. "Well, after our last meeting, I felt pretty alone."

"I'm sorry. What you said about Libby and Vince hurt because they raised me. But I get that what they did wasn't right. None of it."

"So that's why you showed up tonight with Noah? So Mom, Vince, and Libby can all go to jail? Because that's what will happen."

"Kyle will calm down," Ridge said. "Don't you think?"

"No," Sloan said. "I don't."

Ridge hit the dash. "I'm so stupid. I didn't think it through. I just wanted to see Dad, so I told myself it would be okay."

"You've always been the eternal optimist, Ridge. I can't be mad about that. But we should probably find Mom a lawyer."

Ridge stared out the windshield with a vacant expression. "Whatever happens, thanks for having my back tonight."

Sloan shrugged. "That's what sisters do."

Ridge turned up the radio, only to turn it right back down. "Anna seemed nice, though. I'll give her that. She's a saint for staying with Dad after everything."

Sloan rolled her eyes. "More like a fool. But it doesn't matter. I'm done with them all."

"Even Dad?" Ridge asked.

"Especially Dad."

"Well, you've got me," Ridge said. "Let's hang out tomorrow before I head back home."

Sloan nodded, keeping her eyes on the road. She was surprised at how sad it made her, the thought of Ridge leaving. "Will you come back for Thanksgiving? Assuming we aren't all in the slammer?"

"Well, in a perfect world, yeah, but I can't very well have Thanksgiving with you and Mom," Ridge said.

Sloan hadn't even considered that. "Yeah, guess not."

"So, what's the plan with her?" Ridge asked. "Are you gonna quit your job and stay here?"

Sloan straightened her arms. "Not sure. I can probably get a teaching job easily enough. There's a social studies teaching position open at Dylan's school. I really don't have anything keeping me in Houston."

"Yeah, I can see you teaching social studies," Ridge said. "You once read a book about the Louisiana Purchase for fun. But really, can you trust Mom at home while you teach?"

Sloan felt an ache behind her eyes again. Why was he bringing this up? Hadn't she been through enough for one day? "I'll work it out."

"Mom needs to be committed. If not, she will cost you your job, your boyfriend, your entire life."

"It's not that easy," Sloan said. "It's a legal process."

Ridge cocked his head. "I'm assuming attempted murder would be enough."

"I'm not going to talk about this right now, okay? Today sucked enough. Leave Mom to me and book your plane ticket back here for Thanksgiving."

"Alright." Ridge leaned back, putting his feet on the dash. "Hope you know how to cook a turkey because I sure as hell don't."

Sloan laughed. "Never cooked one in my life."

"We'll figure it out," Ridge said. "We'll figure everything out."

# Chapter 33

*Hobbs, NM, 2008*

Vince was asleep in the recliner, so Libby took a chance and turned off the television. Surely twelve straight hours of Fox News was enough for one day. She turned off the living room light and headed to the bedroom. She hadn't been sleeping well since Ridge's trip to Texas, but maybe if she spent some time reading, she'd be able to relax and fall asleep.

As soon as she entered the bedroom, the landline rang. Libby dove across the bed to grab it before it woke Vince. "Hello?"

"Hey, Mom."

"Ridge!" Hearing his voice instantly lifted her mood. It had been several days since his last call.

"Did I wake Dad?"

Libby moved the phone from her ear. "Nope. He's still snoring."

"Well, I tried to call your cell phone."

"Did you? I never turn that on unless I go somewhere. There's no point in having it on when I'm home."

Ridge chuckled. "Yeah, there is, if you'd learn to text."

"You know I don't like texts. So, how are you? How's everything?"

"Okay," Ridge said, but Libby had known his lying voice since he was ten.

"No, it's not," she said. "Spill it."

Libby couldn't believe the story Ridge told her. She assumed Caroline would be happy to see Ridge. She understood if Caroline wanted to kill her or Vince, but her own son? Was she so bent on revenge that she couldn't bear to let him expose the truth?

"You need to come home, son. You wanted Caroline to know you were okay, and you wanted to see Sloan. You accomplished both."

"I'm scared it will come back on you and Dad." There was worry in Ridge's voice. "I shouldn't have gotten out to see Jay. I shouldn't have gone inside to meet his other kids. It was stupid."

"That's not stupid. It's natural you wanted to see them."

"But if they start digging, they may find out everything. Are your passports up to date?"

Libby smiled. "They aren't going to find anything out about us."

"And if they do?"

"Then we'll deal with it. Look, your father and I aren't worried about ourselves. We'd never have encouraged this trip if we were. All that matters is you."

There was a brief silence followed by a muffled sob. "I wish things were different, Mom. I want to have a relationship with my family here."

Libby swallowed. *Don't take it personally,* she told herself. *This is normal.*

"Sloan asked me to come over for Thanksgiving. But I can't. Not with Mom around."

"We can get a lawyer." Libby laid back on a pillow. "Caroline tried to kill you. That should be enough to get her committed."

"I can't go to the cops with that. Not unless I want to open a whole can of worms."

"Oh, right, right." Libby rubbed her forehead. "Tell Sloan to take good notes. We can build a case."

"Sloan doesn't want to build a case."

"Why on earth not? After all Caroline has done?"

"She's got this weird guilt thing about Mom. Makes excuses for her. Tonight, when she called Noah, she said Mom had a gun. Later, she claimed she was mistaken, but I saw the gun in the backseat when we were driving home."

"Wow. Did you call her out on that?"

"I didn't. It's pointless to argue with Sloan. Mom will end up killing someone or drown herself in the river."

"Drown herself? Caroline's suicidal?"

"No. Noah said he gets lots of calls about her walking along the rocks, and she fell and hit her head recently. She goes to the creek every day. Stays super late. Sloan's boyfriend has had to stay at the house to make sure she doesn't leave when Sloan is out at the creek with me."

"Goodness. Poor Sloan."

"Yeah. I hate to say this because I know it would be hard on Sloan to lose Mom to prison or the creek, but at least she'd be free. At least we'd both be free."

*Unless you're the one she kills,* Libby thought. If she knew anything about Caroline Radel, it was that vengeance drove her. She had and would continue to do anything in the name of it. "So, when are you heading back?"

"I'm going to stay one more day. The plan is to spend some time with Noah in the morning and Sloan in the afternoon, as long as Mom goes to the creek." He paused. "Does it bother you that I call her Mom? It's just a habit."

"Why would it bother me? She is your mother."

"*You're* my mother," Ridge said without hesitation.

Libby hated to admit how badly she needed to hear that. It was hard not to be insecure, hard not to worry about being replaced, but she'd reminded herself one thousand times that this was about Ridge, not her. It had *always* been about Ridge.

"I'll head back Friday and take the RV to you guys before driving home," Ridge said.

"Dad got the oil changed in your truck. It's filled up and ready for you to take off, but we hope you'll stay a few days."

"You bet I will." He yawned. "It's been a long day. I'm going to let you go. Love you."

"Love you too," she said. "Always, forever . . ."

"And no matter what," he finished for her, reciting what had always been their mother-son mantra.

Libby hung up the phone and went into the bathroom to remove her makeup. She splashed cold water on her face and thought about Caroline. She'd always suspected that her family hadn't seen or heard the last of her.

Libby remembered back to those early days. The decision to keep Ridge, the decision to try to get Sloan too. The memory still made Libby shudder all these years later. How terrible the depths they had to sink to play Caroline's game. Of course, grabbing Sloan like that was not part of the plan, especially in broad daylight. It was supposed to look like she ran away; it was all supposed to be different.

If only Caroline would have let Sloan visit, if only the guy Vince's POS little brother had hired hadn't gone rogue, if only Libby had gone to Mallowater and gotten Sloan herself.

Vince said it was for the best. That if Sloan went missing, Ridge's case would be reopened. That it would jeopardize everything.

Caroline called that night; said she was ready to pick up Ridge. There was no time to try again for Sloan. *It's for the best. It would have jeopardized everything.* Libby still repeated Vince's assurances all these years later.

Libby wasn't completely surprised when Caroline found them in El Paso. Of course, Vince saw they were being tracked. His paranoia had paid off, and they were gone in the night.

Vince and Libby had spent the ensuing years looking over their shoulders. But no strange car ever parked across their street. Caroline never showed up at their doorstep. Libby figured she'd used all her inheritance to find them the first time and couldn't afford to do it again. Vince worried she might go to the police, but Libby knew better. Caroline would never implicate herself, never let Jay go free.

Still, they'd had to be so careful—homeschooling Ridge for a couple of years, keeping a loaded gun under the mattress and a packed suitcase in the closet with up-to-date passports. She and Vince used to stay up at night, imagining worst-case scenarios, trying to stay one step ahead of Caroline, but turns out, they hadn't needed to.

Caroline gave up. Sacrificed her son to keep Jay in prison. They were relieved, but Libby still worried about Sloan.

That's why she started making drives to payphones in other towns to call Doreen. Doreen Dawson was the only window Libby had into Sloan's life. Vince had been so angry at first. Contacting the wife of a cop couldn't be a good idea when they were supposed to be hiding out, but Libby assured him she was careful not to call from their house and that Doreen and Caroline barely spoke anymore.

Libby took a wet washcloth and scrubbed away at her makeup. She had regrets, but she could still face herself in the mirror. They'd given Ridge a better life. Saved a fledgling bird who had been shoved from his nest. And they'd helped Sloan too. They couldn't give her the kind of life they'd given Ridge, but a free college education was nothing to shake your head at. Libby wondered what Sloan thought of them now. She probably hated them, but in time, she might come around.

But according to Ridge, those were all pipe dreams. Caroline couldn't be left alone. They ran into the same problem when looking for a college to send Sloan to. "She won't go anywhere too far from her mama," Doreen had told Libby. So, LeTourneau it was.

Sloan did eventually break free from Caroline, but now, she was back. It made Libby think of Ridge and the terrible case of mono he caught as a child. The symptoms subsided, but the virus was there to stay. It had found a host forever and could resurface whenever it wanted. Caroline, too, was a virus.

Libby reached into her cold cream and slathered it on her dry and wrinkled skin. When had they all become so old? But wrinkles and gray hair didn't much matter. She and Vince still had their health, and they had each other. They had the money for a good lawyer if they needed it, but she was still optimistic that nothing would come back on them.

"And if it does?" Vince had asked when Ridge took off in their RV, Mallowater bound.

"Then it was still worth it," she'd said. Vince had nodded, putting his arm around her and waving goodbye to their son.

It was worth it because they both understood what it meant to be an actual parent. An actual parent didn't sacrifice their children; they sacrificed *for* their children. How had Caroline let her son go so easily?

Libby couldn't imagine it. She had always been a worrier by nature; motherhood only amplified it. And there was always something to worry about with children. She'd read you should always close your child's bedroom door because a closed door would likely save their life if there was a fire elsewhere in the house. But if she closed the door, how would she hear if someone climbed into his window and stole him? The past twenty years had been riddled with panic-inducing games of "Would You Rather." Libby assumed they'd go away as Ridge got older, but their phone call tonight proved otherwise. That familiar crippling fear had once again risen up inside the pit of her belly, but so had that same old mama-bear instinct.

Ridge was a grown man; he could take care of himself now. He had done what he needed to do, and it was over. He would be safe in his bed across the hall in a few more days.

Libby turned the bathroom light off and walked back to the living room, hoping Vince would wake up if she made enough noise. She wanted to tell him what had happened with Ridge, wanted to talk it out as they always did. But he didn't budge, even when she turned the light on. So, she covered him with a blanket, turned the light off again, and retreated back into her bedroom. She guessed she was on her own tonight when it came to lying in bed awake and worrying.

# Chapter 34

*Mallowater, TX, 2008*

The house smelled like breakfast in 1988. Like greasy bacon, burnt toast, sour orange juice, and overly buttered scrambled eggs.

Sloan wasn't much of a breakfast eater, but Dylan was. So, when he said he was picking up McDonald's, she'd offered to cook instead. It was the least she could do after all Dylan had done for her last night—all he'd done for her the past few months. Maybe after Ridge left, Sloan wouldn't have to worry about watching over her mom 24/7. She hid the keys to prevent any more trips to Tyler. Sloan couldn't keep her from the creek, but at least she wasn't a danger to anyone else there. Ridge was wrong. Working would be possible; keeping a relationship with Dylan would be possible. A normal life would be possible. Semi-normal, at least.

Sloan checked the bacon and thought again of her dad. The breakfast was to blame. It was always the smells that took her back.

She remembered the night before and winced. Mom, Dad, the

gun, the awkward family party, the smashed phone. But despite how everything ended up, something amazing happened that Sloan had once thought impossible. She had stood next to her mother, father, and brother. They had all been together again, right there in the middle of Brookhaven Drive.

"Knock, knock." Dylan opened the front door.

"In here," Sloan called.

Dylan walked into the kitchen, "Wow, this smells great."

"Thanks. I'm so sorry about last night. Sorry you weren't able to stay over."

Dylan kissed her forehead. "Best laid plans, right? Is your mom okay?"

"She's still asleep. Probably for the best. But once she's up and at the creek, I'll call Ridge over."

Dylan kneaded her shoulders. "Wish I was free to help with her today. This professional development has been scheduled for months, and we're running out of summer."

"Don't remind me," Sloan said. "Teaching has been the furthest thing from my mind, but since summer is halfway over, I better bring it back to the forefront."

Dylan set his keys and phone on the table. "Need help?"

"No." Sloan pulled out a chair from the table. "You sit."

"Have you thought any more about the position here?" Dylan asked, lowering himself into the chair. "No pressure, of course."

Sloan smiled. "I'm going to apply."

"Really? That's great!" He drummed his fingers on the table. "I guess you don't have much choice with your mom and all, but it's still great."

Sloan flicked off the burner. "I'd stay even if I had a choice." She met Dylan's eyes as she turned from the stove. She didn't realize that eyes so dark could shine like that.

Dylan's phone began to vibrate just as Sloan set a tray of bacon and toast on the table. She wasn't trying to snoop, but the name flashing across the screen was impossible to miss. Felicity. Sloan's breath caught.

Dylan looked at the phone and then back up at Sloan, the sparkle gone from his eyes. "I have no idea why she's calling. We haven't talked in a while."

Sloan wanted to trust him, wanted to force her heart to beat normally again, but Felicity's words from last night looped in her head. *I've been talking to Dylan Lawrence.*

Dylan reached for the phone and answered with an unsure hello. "Oh, hi. Yes, I'm here with her now. Would you like to talk to her?"

Sloan didn't want to talk to Felicity, but it was better than Dylan talking to her. He handed his phone across the table. "It's for you."

"Hello," Sloan said, hoping she'd put enough disdain in her voice.

"Hey, Sloan. It's Kyle."

Sloan looked at Dylan. He raised his hands and shrugged.

"I tried to call you a few times this morning," Kyle said. Sloan patted her pocket. She must have left her phone in the bedroom. "And I had to call from my sister's phone because, well . . . you know."

Sloan poked her tongue into her cheek. "Well, I'd say I'm sorry, but I'm not."

"Can't say I blame you," Kyle said.

"So, why are you calling?" Sloan asked.

"I wanted to apologize to you and Ridge. Is he around?"

"Left last night," Sloan said. No way she could trust Kyle with the truth.

"Shoot. I hoped he'd be willing to see Dad again."

Sloan put a hand on her hip. "So, Dad made you call?"

"Dad asked me *not* to call." Kyle raised his voice. "He said to leave you alone. That you both needed time, but I figured there wasn't much time to spare when it came to Ridge."

"You're right. No time at all."

"Look, I said I was sorry, and I am. I won't say anything. I'm pissed about it all, but my mom means a lot to me, and I don't want to hurt her. She's been through enough."

Sloan gave a harsh laugh. "Haven't we all?"

Kyle sighed. "Mom bought Dad a cell phone. Felicity texted his number to your phone in case you or Ridge want to get ahold of him. If you talk to Ridge, tell him I'm sorry. I'd ask you for his number, but—"

"Not a chance," Sloan interrupted.

"Fine." Kyle cleared his throat. "Well, I tried. Take care."

Sloan hung up the phone, wishing she'd told Kyle to delete her number from Felicity's phone and Dylan's number, too, while he was at it.

She handed the phone back to Dylan. "Sorry for assuming the worst when her name popped up."

"It's okay. You didn't say anything. I mean, your face did, but it's fine. Do you want to talk about the call?"

Sloan set down a potholder and put the skillet of eggs on top of it. "I want to eat with you and not think about anyone with the same last name as me."

Dylan picked up a fork. "Works for me."

But as much as Sloan wanted it to work for her, sitting at her childhood table, eating her childhood breakfast, all she could think about was her family.

"Hungry?" Sloan asked when her mom emerged from her bedroom.

"No thanks." Sloan knew by the faraway stare in her mother's eyes that she was still out of it. That meant it was going to be one of those days. Zombie days, Sloan used to call them, when Caroline roamed around in a dormant-like state.

Sloan pulled out a chair at the kitchen table. "Come on. I actually cooked."

"Okay, okay," Caroline grumbled as she shuffled to the chair and plopped down. Sloan looked into her mom's dull green eyes. Caroline Radel really was a zombie—a shell of her former self. And grief hadn't caused it like Sloan had once believed; revenge had.

Sloan reheated her mother's plate, poured two cups of orange juice, and sat at the table across from her mom. "Do you remember last night?" Sloan asked. "At Dad's?"

Caroline shoveled in a bite of scrambled eggs. "I do."

"I understand how Dad hurt you. He hurt us all. But you're going to have to let it go. I have to trust that you can let it go."

"Did you know that crows hold funerals?"

Sloan rubbed her forehead. Of course, her mom wasn't going to talk about it. Why had she expected any different?

"Some crows will gather around the dead bird. Many more will fly to nearby trees or rooftops. Soon there's a continuous, raucous cawing. Screaming almost."

"Grieving?" Sloan asked.

"No. It probably has more to do with survival than mourning. That crow on the ground, it's dead for a reason. Something got the better of it." She paused, pinching a piece of toast between her fingers. "'What killed that bird?' they seem to scream. 'And how can we avoid it?' Crows are clever, Sloan. If one makes a mistake, you better believe the next one won't." Caroline pushed the chair out. "I'm going to the creek."

Sloan stood and took her mother's plate. "Alright, but we need to talk about this tonight."

"I'm not going into any hospital."

"I don't want that either. And I don't want you to go to jail. That's why we need to talk. So, we can come to an understanding."

Caroline removed her hand from the back door. "Did you know crows are about as intelligent as a seven-year-old child?"

Sloan threw her head back. "Mom, are you even listening?"

"Do you remember how smart Ridge was at seven?" Caroline smiled.

"He's still smart. Ridge attended Cornell; he became an ornithologist, just like you. If you'd talk to him, you'd—"

"The night before we carried out the plan," Caroline continued, "Ridge asked why we were turning on Dad when he was part of our nest. I had to explain that if a crow gets injured, sometimes other crows murder it to protect themselves. But there's another reason crows turn on one another." Caroline met Sloan's eyes. "Territorial transgressions. Sometimes crows venture to a nest they don't belong in. Just like people. Just like Jay, Ridge, even you, Sloan. Even you."

"Well, I'm here now. I'm not going to apologize for going to college or getting married. But when you needed me, I came back. Does that count for anything?"

"Of course, it does. I'm glad you're here, Lo. You've always been a good girl."

The shock of the words nearly brought tears to Sloan's eyes. It was probably the first affirming statement her mother had said to her since October 1988. "Thanks, Mom."

Caroline nodded, then opened the back door. "Just remember that flying off to other nests you don't belong in, whether that be the one on Brookhaven Drive or the one in Hobbs, New Mexico . . . well, it's a dangerous game to play." She smiled at Sloan and stepped outside, leaving the back door wide open. "I'll be home by dark."

Sloan pushed the door shut and sagged against it. Despite the sticky humidity making her shirt cling to her back, a shiver shot through her.

Sloan couldn't fully enjoy the time with Ridge, knowing that her mom might come home any second. The back door was locked, but Sloan looked out the window often.

"Mom doesn't have the gun. Even if she walks in, she's not going to be able to hurt me," Ridge assured her.

"You don't give her enough credit. She knows Libby and Vince are in New Mexico. How would she know that?"

Ridge shrugged. "She must have overheard us talking that night. She's left them alone all this time; hopefully, that won't change." He glanced at his watch. "I do need to get on the road soon."

"Are you driving all night?"

"No, just to Dallas. Gonna find an RV park for the night. I'll drive the rest of the way in the morning."

"Then stay longer. Dylan just texted. He's leaving his meeting and offered to pick up dinner. What sounds good?"

"Okay," Ridge said. "It'll be nice to hang out again before I go. Ask him to grab a few pizzas."

Sloan frowned. "Pizza? Really?"

"Come on, if you wanted to choose, why did you even ask me?"

Sloan stared at her shoes. "It's just that the night you disappeared, Mom had ordered pizza. I was too upset to eat. But the next night, I got hungry and had a piece. I ate one piece a day for a week. Pizza has never tasted the same since."

Ridge slipped off his sandals and folded his legs under him. "Well, that's just sad. Let's crack open a few beers and redeem it."

It was nearly dark, and Caroline wasn't home. Dylan offered to take Ridge back to his RV and then search the creek. Sloan wanted to go, but he reminded her she needed to be here in case Caroline came home. It was just as well; Sloan wasn't sure she could handle another goodbye with her brother.

She pulled out her phone and typed. *Miss you already. Text me when you get to Dallas.* But before she hit send, a call from Dylan came through. "Well, did you talk her into coming home?"

"Sloan . . ."

She heard distress in Dylan's voice.

"What? Are you okay?"

"Come to the creek. Near Big Rock."

Sloan's chest tightened. "Why? What happened?"

"I can't find Caroline. But they've got an extensive area blocked off. There are police. Someone said a woman drowned."

His words and all other sounds in the room were muffled, like Sloan was the one underwater. She grabbed a throw pillow and clutched it to her chest. "It's not Mom. Noah would have called me. Is he there? Give him the phone."

"I don't see Noah. Just come down here, okay? You'll get here easier on foot. They're blocking off a lot of the road."

Sloan threw the pillow across the room and grabbed a flashlight. Her limbs felt heavy, but she ran as fast as she could. *It's not her. Noah would have called. He'd already know by now, and he would have called.*

But when Sloan arrived at the creek, it was Noah's arms that caught her. "Let go of me!" She tried to fight against him, but he held her arms tightly.

"You can't go any farther. I'm sorry."

Sloan leaned to look past him. Police officers. Flashlights. Blue and red flashing lights reflecting off the water. Bright yellow tape. Déjà vu.

"Is it her? Tell me it's not her."

"I just got here. I'm going to check, but I need you to stay here. You can't come any closer."

Dylan must have heard her yelling because he appeared out of nowhere, taking her into his arms. Sloan swatted a single tear. "This isn't where she likes to walk. It may not be her."

But then, a sound echoed through the trees. A crow's caw so loud it made them both jump. Sloan watched the skies as another crow came, and then another. Soon, at least two dozen landed in nearby trees, screeching. It was the loudest, saddest sound Sloan had ever heard.

"A roost?" Dylan covered his ears. "This time of year?"

"No," Sloan shook her head. "It's not a roost. It's a funeral."

Noah was the last officer left in Sloan's living room. "Did you call Ridge?" he asked.

"He's back at the RV park, and Dylan's picking him up now," Sloan said. "We didn't want to bring the RV back here. It would raise too many questions."

Noah nodded. "Between you and me, was Ridge here *all* day?"

"Yes. Right until Dylan left to look for Mom." Sloan spoke through her teeth with forced restraint. "How could you think he had anything to do with this?"

"I don't." Noah scratched his lip. "He made a weird comment to me yesterday, is all. Something about you being unable to live a normal life till she was gone."

Sloan leaned away. "He was just venting. He was here *all* day."

"Okay. Just covering the bases. They sent a few officers to your father's as well. Is there anyone else who may have a reason to hurt Caroline?"

Sloan rubbed her exposed forearms. "You don't think this was an accident?"

"Most likely was. We've got a few witness statements about her walking along the edge today. It was a long way from where she was found, but the body probably floated downstream."

"You identified her, though. Couldn't you tell by looking if there was a struggle?"

"There were signs of struggle. But it might have been with the river. In drownings, the face and hands are often dragged along the rocks. The water washes away a lot of forensics, but we'll conduct a thorough investigation." He took hold of Sloan's hand and squeezed. "I'm so sorry."

Sloan let go of his hand and ran for Ridge's arms as soon as he entered the door. She put her head on his shoulder and cried. A reversal of all those times she'd comforted him as a child.

Noah patted Ridge's shoulder. "I'm sorry, man. I'm going to give you guys some time alone. You can stay here with your sister. I'll make sure no officers come back tonight."

"I can leave too," Dylan said once Noah was out the door.

Sloan reached out for his hand. "No, please stay. Would you mind bringing me some aspirin from the kitchen cupboard? My head's killing me."

"You bet. I'll make some coffee too. The caffeine will help."

"He's a good one, sis," Ridge said as they sat on the couch.

"Yeah, too good for me."

"Bullshit. You're the best person I know, Sloan; you've always been the best."

Sloan looked away and noticed her cell phone on the coffee table. "Dad called. About an hour ago. I didn't answer." She bit her lip. "You don't think he'd do anything to—?"

"No way," Ridge interrupted. "Mom slipped."

"She talked about crow funerals this morning." Sloan looked down at her hands. "Maybe I should have told the police, but I didn't want them to assume she did something on purpose. She wouldn't."

"Right," Ridge said, but he didn't sound as assured. "She fell. It was an accident." He pulled out his own phone. "I better call home. I was supposed to be in Dallas already. I'm surprised Vince and Libby haven't got the National Guard looking for me yet."

Ridge stood and walked a few steps down the tiny hallway. The house was quiet, and Ridge's phone volume was loud enough that Sloan could hear Vince on the other side of the line, his voice thick with sleep.

"Dad, it's me. Sorry to wake you," Ridge said.

"That's alright. Did you make it to the Big D?"

"No. I'm back in Mallowater. You need to get back to sleep, but Mom can fill you in tomorrow. Can you put her on?"

"Yep. She's in the bedroom; give me a minute to get up."

"The bedroom?" Ridge asked. "She's not already asleep, is she?"

"Yeah. We slept on and off all day. Your mother threw up a lot. Some bug's going around."

"Don't wake her," Ridge said. "She must be pretty sick to not wait up for my call. You both get some rest."

Dylan came in with the coffee just as Ridge hung up. If it weren't scalding hot, Sloan would have drunk it in a single gulp. Not that it would fix any of this. She was exhausted, but not in the places coffee could touch. Over the past few months, her life had been one emotionally draining event after the next.

A soft knock on the door made them all jump. When Ridge looked at Sloan, she saw him as a child again, frightened during one of Dad's PTSD-induced nightmares. "Just go down the hall," she said. "Noah said no more cops tonight."

"I'll take care of them," Dylan said, making his way to the door. Sloan stood back as he opened it.

"Sorry to just show up like this but are my kids here?" the voice on the other side of the door asked.

*Dad.* Despite everything that had happened, despite knowing that he had no right to be here, no right to grieve, hearing his voice turned Sloan back into a little girl, waiting for him to walk through that very door. Dylan stepped aside, and Sloan met her father on the front porch, wrapping her arms around him.

"I heard about your mother," he said. "I'm so sorry," Sloan noticed Ridge from the corner of her eye, frozen in the doorway, staring at them. Their father broke the hug, keeping one arm around Sloan and holding the other forward. "I'm so sorry, son," he said.

At first, Ridge looked away, staring down at the concrete, but then he took a few steps forward, reluctantly joining their embrace. They held on to each other underneath the porch light, silently sharing a grief no one else in the entire world could understand but them.

# Chapter 35

*Interstate 20, 2008*

Libby felt herself veering onto the shoulder of the road, so she stopped for coffee. Her sleep last night had been fitful and nightmare-ridden. She'd been awake since 4:00 a.m. and had a plan by 5:00. Vince had tried to talk her out of it, but he didn't put up much of a fight. This was the way of their marriage. She'd get an idea:

"I'd like to donate $15,000 to Golden Oak Elementary for new playground equipment."

"I'd like to go back to school so I can counsel domestic violence victims."

"I'd like to hide my best friend's child away from his abusive father."

"I'd like to keep him."

"I'd like to get his sister too."

"I'd like to encourage Ridge to visit Mallowater."

And finally, "I'd like to kill Caroline."

Vince always put up some resistance:

"$15,000 is a lot to spend on a charity project."

"Aren't you a little old to go back to school?"

"Hide Ridge? Have you lost your mind?"

"You *have* lost your mind! We can't keep Ridge! I worried this would happen. You always get attached."

"We are *not* adding to your laundry list of felonies by kidnapping another child."

"Ridge doesn't need to visit Mallowater. It will only cause more pain. We are his family."

"Your joking, right? Murder Caroline? My god, Libby, tell me you're joking."

But after he let his opinions be known, Vince always came around:

"I suppose it is a win/win. Sloan and Ridge's school gets new equipment, and we get a tax write-off."

"LSU has a great social work program. And since I'll be working there, you can take classes for free."

"I can't believe that sonofabitch is abusing his son. I knew there was something off about Jay Hadfield. We will help Caroline in any way we can."

"You're right, Libby. Caroline is insane. We can't give Ridge back. She lied to us, and that means the entire deal is off the table."

"If Caroline won't let Sloan visit, we'll just have to come up with another plan to get her."

"If seeing Caroline and Sloan will bring Ridge peace and closure, he needs to do it."

"If you're going to do this, Libby, you've got to have a solid plan. You can't make any mistakes."

And she hadn't made any. At least she didn't think so. She'd waited in the rented car at the creek, just as Vince had done all those years ago when this all started. Now she'd finished it. Full circle.

Libby was glad to find Caroline already at the creek when she arrived. She had hoped Ridge wasn't exaggerating when he said Caroline spent all her time there. She waited till the time was right, till the area was empty, till Caroline was distracted, balancing on the river's edge, barefoot, arms out like a trapeze artist.

Libby had rehearsed what she'd say the entire drive, but she didn't have time to say anything. One push and Caroline was submerged. All Libby had to do was hold her down. She had the advantage. She'd taken Caroline by surprise, and Caroline had to fight Libby and the river too.

Had they found the body yet? Libby hoped it would take a while, but the creek was running slow. It didn't matter how slow it was; it would surely wash any potential evidence off Caroline's body.

Libby experienced many feelings as she drove home. She was relieved she'd done it and that it had been so easy. She was proud that she'd kept Ridge safe—that she'd removed yet another obstacle to his happiness. She was scared someone had seen her. She even felt a little guilty. Libby knew she'd probably see Caroline's haunted eyes staring up at her through that murky water every night for the rest of her life.

She adjusted her blonde wig, bought her coffee, then deposited her change into the payphone outside the convenience store.

"Hello," Vince answered. His voice was too chipper for this hour. He hadn't taken his sleeping pill. Sweet of him to be so worried.

"Everything's done, and it went fine," she said. "I'm about to leave Fort Worth. Hope I didn't worry you, but payphones are much sparser than they used to be."

"Ridge called about half an hour ago. He sounded upset. I think they found her."

"Did he ask to talk to me?" Libby asked.

"He did. I pretended to be asleep when I saw it was his number on the caller ID. Said you weren't feeling well and had turned in. Offered to get up and wake you, but he said not to."

Libby laughed. "Well, that was quite the risk. What if he had asked you to wake me?"

"I knew he wouldn't. Ridge knows I'm out of it after I take my medicine, knows it makes me unsteady on my feet. And he wouldn't dare wake you up when you were sick. He's a good boy. He's always been a good boy."

"Yes." Libby smiled. "He sure has. We got lucky, didn't we?"

"We did," Vince said. "Now, get back on the road. Do what you can to ensure our luck doesn't run out."

Libby told Vince goodbye and started her car. She'd been careful. Everything would be fine. Their luck would not run out, but if it did, well, that was okay. Because Ridge would be safe. He had Jay and Sloan. He would be okay. And if he was okay, Libby would be okay too. Always, forever, and no matter what.

# Chapter 36

*Mallowater, TX, 2008*

Sloan, Ridge, and Jay sat around the kitchen table. It was 1:00 a.m.; Dylan had gone home an hour ago, and they were on their third pot of coffee.

They'd all sat at what had once been their seat at that round, scuffed table. Old habits. Every so often, Sloan would glance at her mother's empty seat, and it would hit her again that she was gone.

"Remember when Mom left the price tags on the gifts from Santa?" Ridge asked.

"Yes!" Sloan laughed. "She said sometimes the elves got behind on making toys and bought them at Walmart. That was the year I stopped believing."

"Not me," said Ridge. "I held on embarrassingly long."

"Speaking of Santa gifts." Jay glanced at the Christmas tree. "Ridge, remember that Masters of the Universe play set?"

"Heck yeah, I do. That thing was huge."

"More like a huge pain in the ass to build." Jay chuckled. "I assumed we'd leave it in the box, that you and I would build it later, but Caroline insisted it be built so you could see it. I spent half the night putting together that damn toy." He tore his gaze away from the tree. "After that incident, it's no wonder Caroline was suddenly okay with leaving Santa toys in their boxes."

Sloan smiled. She liked remembering good things about her mom. She had experienced twelve years of good with her mom, and Caroline Radel had lived twenty-five good years before that. Why did the end have to be all there was? Didn't beginnings count for anything? Sloan would try hard to remember her mother by her best moments, not her worst.

And she was going to try it with her father, too. Sloan realized it would never be the same now. There was no turning back time. And she didn't want to be a part of the family he'd made with Anna, but why couldn't she, Ridge, and their father make a few more memories around this kitchen table? Ridge had another family. Dad did too. But for Sloan, this was it. And as they sat together sharing memories, this actually felt like enough.

By 2:00 a.m. Ridge had crashed out on the couch. "I'm not gonna be far behind," Jay said. "I should probably hit the road."

Sloan felt an unexplained pang in her chest. A phantom pain from all those years ago, from all those goodbyes with her father.

"Why not stay the night? You're too tired to drive to Tyler." Sloan looked down at the table. "Plus, given everything, it would be nice to have you here."

He pulled out his phone. "I appreciate the offer. I'll text Anna."

"And what does she think of all this?" Sloan asked.

Jay rubbed his chin. "Anna's a very compassionate, empathic woman. She wouldn't have stuck by me if not. I'm sure she thought she'd had her share of surprises for a lifetime, but they keep coming. Ridge being alive, Caroline being," he raked a hand over his face, "no longer alive. It's been a complicated and emotional few days." He put his hand on top of Sloan's. "But she's always supported me having a relationship with you. In fact, she'd like to have one as well."

Sloan pulled her hand back. "I'm not up for that. This here," she touched the table, "this is familiar; this is us. It's something I think I can handle. But your house, your life with Anna, with the boys, with *Felicity June*, that's not my life. I don't want it to be my life. I'm still so angry."

He nodded. "Fair enough. But don't be mad at Anna or the kids; be mad at me. When I reflect on my life, all I see is this black wintery river of pain I left behind me. Some I loved kept their heads above water; some drowned in it. But everyone's cold; everyone's exhausted from treading water all these years."

Sloan considered his words for a moment. "Yeah. I guess we've all left a lot of pain in our wake. But it's not all we leave. It's not all you left."

Her father reached for her hand again, and this time, she took it. His skin felt different. It was as calloused as their relationship but still brought comfort. She'd lost Ridge, Daddy, and now Mom. It was miraculous that she'd gotten two of them back. She would try her hardest to tread through the pain to keep from losing them again.

He checked his phone. "Anna thinks it's a good idea to stay. Says a big storm woke her up earlier. Guess it's heading this way."

Sloan rose from the table. "I need to make sure my bedroom window is closed, and then we should get some sleep."

"Yeah. Should I wake Ridge up? I can sleep on the couch."

Sloan covered her brother with a blanket. "Nah, leave him. You can sleep in Mom's—" Sloan stopped herself. "Well, in your old room."

Jay put his arm around Sloan as they walked, stopping at the end of the hallway. "Man, this is weird," he said, glancing into the bedroom. "It's hard," he added. "Really hard."

"It is." Sloan looked into her own room. The window was closed, but the blinds were open. It was already raining, fat drops slapping against the glass. The image took her back to hundreds of summer nights like this, hundreds of summer storms she watched out that window, surviving each storm, surviving her life, one day, one memory, one Keith Whitley song at a time. "But we're no strangers to the rain, are we, Dad?"

He smiled just as a flash of lightning lit up the hallway. "Damn right."

# Epilogue

*Mallowater, TX,*
*Thanksgiving Day, 2008*

"This place looks great." Ridge glanced at the old family photos as he carried his suitcase down the hallway. "You've been busy."

"Yeah, it's finally starting to feel like mine." Sloan opened the door to their parents' old room. "I cleaned everything out and turned it into a room for you."

Ridge stepped inside. "Wow, you didn't need to do all this just for me."

"Who else is going to use it? Just be happy we finally get our own rooms in this place."

"For sure." Ridge studied a painting of Crow's Nest Creek above the bed. "Whoa. Did you paint this?"

Sloan looked down at her shoes. "Yeah. Dylan got me some art supplies. It's been good, therapeutic, to get back into it."

"I love it, like really love it. Can I commission one? It would look so great in my apartment. Just like this, but on a three-panel, maybe?"

"Sure, I can do that. Absolutely."

Ridge pulled out his wallet. "What's a fair price?"

Sloan pushed down it down. "Put your money away. I know you think you have to help me, but you don't. I actually make a little more teaching here than I did in Houston."

Ridge bumped against her shoulder. "And you get to make out with your boyfriend in the teacher's lounge."

"You should talk. Did you ever ask out that research assistant you told me about? Liv?"

Ridge set his suitcase on the bed. "Until I graduate, I'm dating my work."

"Next year, then," Sloan said. "Next year, you'll be Dr. Turner and should have no trouble finding a girl to bring home for Thanksgiving."

"And next year, you might be Mrs. Lawrence." Ridge raised his eyebrows. "Maybe with a little Sloan Jr. on the way?"

"Slow down there, Uncle Ridge. Right now, Dylan and I are just looking forward to the Daughtry trial being over. It's scheduled for next May."

Ridge unzipped his bag. "I heard it's going to be televised."

"Yeah. A regular circus." Sloan stepped back. "Well, I'm sure you are exhausted from your layover last night. Take a nap. Dylan and I can handle the cooking."

"Nah, I'm good. May take a quick shower."

Sloan bit her lip. "Well, that's going to have to wait a few hours."

"Why's that?"

"See for yourself." Sloan stepped across the hallway and pushed open the bathroom door.

It took Ridge a minute to notice what she was referring to. When he did, he started laughing. "You forgot to thaw out the turkey."

Sloan pressed her forehead against the door jamb. "Dylan reminded me to take it out four nights ago when he left. I got distracted and totally spaced it till last night. It wouldn't fit in the sink."

Ridge walked to the tub and put his hand on the submerged turkey. "I don't expect we're going to be having this guy today."

"Really?" Sloan touched the turkey. Ridge was right. It was still solid. "Ugh. I wanted everything to be perfect, and I sabotaged the most important part of dinner. Thank goodness Dylan is smoking a ham."

Ridge shook the water off his hand. "It doesn't matter what we eat; at least we're together."

He was right. But it didn't escape Sloan that they weren't *all* together. Dad had invited them to his home for Thanksgiving, but Sloan wasn't ready for that.

"Have you talked to Dad again?" Ridge asked as if he'd read her mind.

"Not in a few days. I don't understand why he can't spend half the day with them and half the day with us. I mean, he split his time between us all those years."

Ridge raised his eyebrows. "I think we can all agree that wasn't the best idea."

"And pretending to be some big happy family is?"

"I didn't say that." Ridge put his hand on her shoulder. "Relax. I get you not wanting to go."

"And you *did* want to go? I'm sorry it's just us. I invited Noah's family, but they went to Dallas."

"Sloan, I don't care who else is here. I wanted to spend Thanksgiving with you, and I am. Now, let me change out of these clothes, and I'll meet you in the kitchen to help."

As Sloan began peeling potatoes, she wondered what Ridge's actual opinion was about having Thanksgiving with their dad. Had she really ever asked him or just assumed he didn't want to?

Ridge returned a few minutes later, changed from his athletic shorts and t-shirt into jeans and a blue button-down shirt. Sloan looked over her shoulder. "Wow, look at you."

"Well, it's a special occasion. First Thanksgiving with my sister in a couple of decades." He sat at the kitchen table. Sloan stifled a laugh. He'd offered to help and was sitting at the table. Still the baby of the family through and through.

"As much as I like the new furniture, I'm glad you kept the table."

"Yeah, I couldn't get rid of it. Too many good memories. It's pretty much the only thing I didn't change."

"And the tree."

Sloan laughed. "Surprisingly, I'm not even sick of it."

"I noticed the roller-skating rabbit was back in one piece. Sorry about that."

"Dylan glued it back together. No big deal."

"Well, stop peeling those and come sit down."

Sloan threw her head back. "Ridge, I need to start this, or I won't finish in time . . ."

"In time for what? The bathing turkey in there? Come on, sit."

Sloan finished the potato and wiped her hands down her apron. "Okay, five minutes."

Sloan saw a small package on the table she hadn't noticed. Ridge pushed it toward her.

"What's this?" she asked.

"Early Christmas gift."

Sloan unwrapped the small box and pulled out a felt crow hanging from a red string. "An ornament?" Sloan smiled. "How perfect."

"Check under the wing."

Sloan lifted the wing and saw a single word embroidered in yellow thread—*Mom*. She held it to her chest. "Let's find a place for it."

They stood in front of the tree they'd put up. Ridge pointed to a hole just right of the center. "We actually left the perfect place for it."

Sloan hung it. "That was probably accidental. We were pretty wasted."

Ridge put his arm around her. "Yeah, we were. But it looks pretty damn perfect, doesn't it?"

"Yeah, it does. Mom would have loved the ornament." Sloan laid her head on her brother's shoulder. "Sometimes I miss her, Ridge. But other times, I'm relieved I don't have to worry about her anymore. I miss her, and I don't. Is that terrible?"

"No," Ridge said. "Not terrible at all. I like to think she's back to her old self again—finally at peace."

Sloan reached out and rubbed the felt crow between her fingers. "She slipped, right?"

"Yeah," Ridge said. "I mean, that's what the police found."

Sloan nodded. "It's just been hard for me to let it go."

"And that's why you don't want to eat with Dad's family? You wonder if one of them was involved?"

Tears pooled in Sloan's eyes. "It's not that big a stretch, is it? Mom pointed a gun at Dad the night before. We all got into that fight."

"It was an accident. Mom slipped before."

"How do I let it go?"

Before he answered, there was a soft knock at the door. Sloan wiped the tears off her face and held the door open for Dylan.

He gave her a quick kiss. "You okay?"

"Yeah, just the normal." She inhaled. "The ham smells delicious."

Dylan carried it into the kitchen. "Can I put it in the oven, so it stays warm?"

"Sure." Sloan opened the oven door. "The turkey's certainly not going in."

"Yeah," Ridge said. "Should I go change its bathwater?"

Sloan touched the side of her forehead. "Ugh. Just drain the tub and put the bird in the fridge."

Dylan suppressed a smile. "We'll cook it over the weekend."

"I know, I know. You told me, and I forgot."

"It's not a big deal." Dylan pushed a strand of hair out of her face.

"So, I get the feeling Ridge wants to go to Dad's," she said after Ridge was out of earshot.

"But you still don't want to?"

"No. I'm too angry."

"So be angry tomorrow."

"Huh?"

Dylan wrapped his arms around her. "Remember? Today's Thanksgiving. No being angry on Thanksgiving."

Sloan pursed her lips. "I should have never agreed to that."

"I get it, I do," Dylan said softly. "But Kyle apologized. Brad and Felicity have always been cool to you. Anna took you to see your dad as a kid. Can you imagine what she was going through, yet she still did that? And I understand you don't want to hear this, but nobody killed your mom."

Sloan pulled away. "You don't know that."

Dylan sighed. "What I do know is you can't let bitterness poison you. Not like Caroline did. You've got to let this go, Sloan."

This wasn't like Dylan to challenge her, but he was right.

Ridge came down the hallway, carrying a turkey wrapped in a bath towel. "You may want to bleach your tub," he said. "Unless you want to soak in salmonella."

"Ridge, what would you say to having lunch at Dad's?" Sloan asked.

Ridge stopped. "Really?"

"Why not?" Sloan shrugged. "You came all this way for a turkey. I'm sure Anna's isn't still dripping with dirty bathtub water right now."

"You sure it's okay?" Ridge asked. "You aren't going to get angry at them?"

She took Dylan's hand and squeezed. "No, not today."

"Well, that was awful," Sloan said as she spread out a blanket at Crow's Nest Creek that evening.

Ridge plopped down. "Not awful, just awkward, but I could tell it meant a lot to Dad. Hey, here they come." He looked up at the sky as a group of crows flew overhead. "Dylan didn't want to join us?"

"He said he was tired, but I think he just wanted to give us some time alone." Sloan looked out at the river. The rough water frothed and crashed—like it was vying with the crows for Sloan's attention. She thought back on all her times here at Crow's Nest Creek. Her earliest memory here came to mind first. Standing in a shallow ford of the river, holding hands with her parents, singing "Ring Around the Rosie." They'd circle, fall, splash, laugh, stand up, and do it all over again.

*Ashes. Ashes. We all fall down.*

When Sloan got older, she'd come here with Dad to fill buckets of water to put out their family campfires. Was there ever a time they both came back dry? As soon as one was crouched over the water, they were a goner.

*We all fall down.*

She remembered hundreds of times when she, Ridge, and Noah splashed in this water, waiting for the crows, rocks on the creek bottom poking into their bare feet. They were too old for "Ring Around the Rosie," but they played plenty of innocent games of Truth or Dare.

Then she thought of being seventeen in the river with Noah. The cold shock of water against her bare skin as the dares became less innocent. A fist full of wildflowers he'd picked for her, shoved into the pocket of her jeans. Jeans she'd shed on the riverbank.

*Pocket full of posies.*

Ridge's voice broke through her memories. "It's been a while since we've been here for a roost. We just need Noah."

"Grape Squeezeits and Fruit Wrinkles, too," Sloan said.

Ridge sat up and unzipped his backpack. "Well, I brought the adult version of Squeezits." He pulled out two beers from his backpack, using his ring to twist off the caps.

"Thanks." Sloan took a drink. "These are a definite improvement."

They took a few sips in silence then she spoke again. "Ridge, you can tell me the truth now. Did you know you were leaving the last time we were here?"

Ridge kept his eyes on the crows. "Yeah. I knew."

Sloan couldn't imagine. To be ten years old and hold the weight of such a secret inside his tiny chest. He must have been so scared. Sloan wished she could go back and change how she'd treated him that night. She wished she could go back and save him, save them all. But what was that saying Grandpa Radel always told her? *The river can't return to its source.*

More crows flew overhead, landing in trees all around them. Minute by minute, the purple sky grew blacker and noisier.

"Just think, amid all that screeching, there's a crow named Crawford saying your name," Sloan said.

"Yeah." Ridge's eyes lit up. "I forgot how cool this is. I mean, we've got plenty of roosts in New York, but not rural ones like this. You can't exactly go lay down on Elmira Avenue like you can here."

"Why are so many roosts in cities?" Sloan asked.

"Hard to say, but probably because cities are a few degrees warmer than rural areas and have more food."

Sloan motioned to the sky. "So why don't these guys move into town?"

"I've wondered. This is one of the longest-running roosts in the country. One of the few in Texas. Something here draws them back year after year."

Sloan leaned back on her elbows. "Guess I can relate. This is the creek I thought you drowned in, yet it was the first place I ran to for sanctuary. I slept out here in our tent hundreds of nights after you were gone. Then, you miraculously rose out of that river, but Mom took your place. Yet here I am—*again*."

"Wow. Yeah. This is the river where I ruined dad's life and destroyed our family. It's where I faked my death, where I sat shivering and crying, waiting for Vince Turner to take me away from a life I loved. Yet, when I came home, this is where I spent my days."

"Maybe it's like visiting a grave," Sloan said. "Respect. Remembrance."

"Speaking of . . ." Ridge reached into his backpack. "Are you ready?"

Sloan pushed herself up. "Ready or not."

Ridge pulled the lid off the cardboard box, revealing the bag of their mother's ashes. "Where should we do it?" he asked.

"I think here is fine. Close to the water, close to the crows."

They stepped beyond the canopy, and Ridge handed her the bag. "You can go first."

Sloan tilted the bag, but Ridge held out his hand. "Wait. Shouldn't we say a prayer or something first?"

"Go ahead." Sloan held up the bag as Ridge said a quick prayer. "Anything you want to say?" he asked when he finished.

Sloan wished it were that easy. What could she possibly say about such a complex life? About such a complex relationship? Tears filled her eyes as she poured. "Goodbye, Mom," were the only words she could manage.

"Goodbye, Mom," Ridge echoed, emptying the bag's contents. "I hope you're at peace."

The wind picked up just as Ridge finished. A stream of ash flew toward the water just under a formation of crows. The flock flew above the ash as if guiding Caroline to her final resting place.

*Ashes, ashes, we all fall down.*

They were both quiet for several minutes, listening to the cawing crows, rushing water, and howling wind. Ridge finally spoke. "Knowing Mom, I half expected a crow would rise from her ashes."

"Guess Caroline Radel was no Phoenix," Sloan said. "She had plenty of chances in her life to rise from the ashes, but she refused to let it all go."

Ridge took her hand. "But we can rise from our family's ashes. We *are* rising from them."

Sloan considered his words as she watched the river flow. Was she actually rising? Some days it didn't feel like it.

No matter how many dinners she had with Dad, how many Detroit Lions games they watched, the fact that he had set everything wrong with her life in motion was never far from her mind.

And as glad as she was to have Ridge in her life, she couldn't accept his invitation for Christmas in New Mexico. She just wasn't ready for that. She couldn't forgive the Turners for their part in ruining her family, no matter how good their intentions had been. The mere thought of them still knotted her stomach.

A similar knot still appeared anytime Dylan's phone beeped. Her dad was a cheater, her ex-husband was a cheater. To be expected to blindly trust Dylan felt naïve. And they were both so broken, disaster seemed imminent. Like two terrible swimmers trying to save each other from drowning.

She hadn't looked at the *People* magazine article in months, but she felt the urge to now. Her mother's obsession with Anna Hadfield and her children had begun with a birth certificate, Sloan's with that damn article. She suspected that even after a friendly Thanksgiving, it would still cut to her core to look at that cover photo. To look at Anna, Felicity, Brad, and Kyle, and understand that despite pleasantries, she'd never really be a part of them.

But then again, six months ago, she'd never imagined returning to Mallowater, and here she was. She was back and allowing herself to reflect on her childhood and remember it all—the good and the bad.

Maybe she'd ultimately failed to protect her mother, but she'd tried. She was grieving Caroline while simultaneously trying to forgive her.

She was trying to forgive her dad too. Six months ago, she'd never believed she would ever speak to him again, but she'd just shared Thanksgiving dinner with him. Things could never be the same, but that didn't mean she couldn't accept a new, different relationship with him.

And as for the Turners, they loved Ridge; she loved Ridge. If she could sit at Anna Hadfield's table, sitting at anybody's felt possible. Another of Grandpa Radel's sayings came to mind. *With enough time, the river can cut through rock.*

And she loved Dylan. The water was rising around them both right now, but they weren't drowning. They were treading water together. Eventually, the Daughtry trial would be over, and sooner or later, Sloan's grief would subside. Their feet would touch solid ground.

And although she couldn't force herself into another family, she could stop obsessing over them. She could stop comparing. She could let it go. She could throw the magazine away; no, she could burn it.

*Ashes. Ashes.*

She pulled her shoulders back and closed her eyes. Ridge was right. She could rise from the ashes. She could. She was.

## Acknowledgements

One highlight of becoming a published author was the relationships I made with other authors. Many thanks to the 2020 Debuts group for saving my sanity and helping me navigate the year that was 2020. You were the first place I turned for so much. I'm honored to be among such talented and kind human beings.

To the many seasoned authors who helped this newbie along the way, thank you. Claire Fullerton, thanks for the phone call full of advice and for connecting me with three inspiring ladies: Kathleen Rodgers, Johnnie Bernhard, and Michelle Cox. Elena Hartwell Taylor, thanks for mentoring me and being the first author to provide a blurb for this book. Also, thanks for the writing workshops during the pandemic that were so often the highlight of my weeks stuck at home. Laura Kemp thanks for everything especially your friendship. Ivy Smoak, I didn't even know how successful you were when I first reached out with a question, but despite being an international bestselling author, you couldn't have been sweeter or more supportive. Allen Eskens, thanks for the early marketing advice and for the blurb. Seeing your name on the cover of my book is truly a dream come true.

To all the book bloggers and bookstagrammers who helped promote my books, I just can't thank you enough. Emily Carter @Emeryreads, you were the first bookstagrammer to feature *Enemies of Doves*. Seeing your post was a moment I'll never forget. Ashley Spivey, thanks for coming to the rescue when my 2020 events were shut down. You do so much for so many and just make the world a better place. Dawnny Ruby, Susan Peterson, Denise Birt, Kathy Murphy, Laura Kemp, Linda Zagon, Mandy Haynes, Chris Davidson, and Kristy Barrett, thank you for connecting authors with readers through your wonderful groups. (Many apologies to anyone I accidentally left off that list). Thank you to the bookstore owners and librarians who put my books on your shelves.

Thanks to the team at TouchPoint Press. You make dreams come true. Stephanie Hansen, thank you for selling the audio rights to the team at Dreamscape Media, LLC. Michael Brusasco, you are such a talented narrator who brought my characters to life so well.

Thanks to my fellow TouchPoint Press authors who have supported me: Kathy Ramsperger for featuring me on your Story Hour Program and Kathy Maresca for choosing *Enemies of Doves* for your book club. Both of you have shown so much kind support to me on this journey. Scott Rutherford, thanks for reading my book instead of studying, leaving a review that is still ranked most helpful on Amazon, and for your friendship. Rob Samborn, thanks for your advice, for pushing me outside my comfort zone, and for sharing your wealth of wonderful ideas with me. You've been a lifesaver. Ty Keenum, thanks for the advice, laughs, and the "good luck crow" hanging on my wall. There are so many other TouchPoint authors who have helped me promote my books, who have shared their knowledge, and who have become true friends. I would list you all, but I would be like those presenters at the Academy Awards still reading off names as the music plays.

To my beta readers, Tammy, Sarah, Dana, Rob, Leslie, and Bri, you saved me a lot of embarrassing mistakes and made this book so much better. To my editor, Kim Coghlan, ditto. Stephen King was absolutely correct when he said, "The editor is always right." (I feel like you would advise me to drop the word absolutely in the above sentence for conciseness, but I'm going to keep it anyway).

I learned a lot about crows thanks to Kaeli Swift's fascinating Twitter feed and the wonderful book, *Bird Brains*, by Candace Savage. Any mistakes are my own.

Thanks to my family for all your support, with a special shout-out to some special aunts. Aunt Mary and Aunt Janet, thanks for blasting my book and posts all over your Facebook pages. Aunt Karen, thanks for the encouraging message to keep writing and for sending me cool Civil War articles. Every time I get one, I want to try my hand at another novel set during that time. Merry Leissa, thanks for telling others about my book and creating fans, but mostly thanks for being my fan my entire life. Thanks to all my cousins, aunts/uncles, brother-in-law/sister-in-law, and mother-in-law who sent encouragement my way. I'm thankful for a wonderful family.

Sarah, Beth, Tausha, Monica, Trisha, and Summer, for being the best friends a girl could have.

To all my readers, thank you. You are the reason I get to live out this dream. Thank you to everyone who chose *Enemies of Doves* for their book clubs. And special thanks to my own book club, Mayra, Sarah, Amanda, Brittny, Trisha, and Summer, for the books, laughs, drinks, and friendship.

Jaleigh and Brandon, thanks for reading *Enemies of Doves* and being excited about it. I remember many long-ago nights making you both read when you saw it as a chore. So, for you to both pick up my book by choice is special. Aidan, thanks for always asking me how the book is going and never complaining if I feed you corn dogs instead of cooking on those nights when deadlines loom. Asa, thanks for saying, "Just write, Mom, I'll cook," every Friday night and for constantly updating me on my YouTube views and giving unsolicited advice on how to get more.

Josh, what can I even say? Thanks for buying me a second computer screen after I swore that I only needed one (in a repeat of the wedding band incident). Thanks for helping with every single plot hole this book had and just accepting that the FBI is surely monitoring everything we do after my weird research. Thanks for being supportive of my writing career and never complaining about the time I spend with imaginary people. Thanks for listening to bizarre serial killer facts, watching true crime documentaries that don't interest you at all, and still believing I'm a good person despite my fascination with these things. We survived quarantine without becoming a Dateline episode, so surely the next forty-plus years will be a breeze. Just let me win a game of cards every now and again, okay?

Uncle Randy, if you've read far enough, you'll see your name is FINALLY in one of my books. (But it's *still* all about me!)

Thank you so much for reading *A River of Crows*. If you've enjoyed the book, we would be grateful if you would post a review on the bookseller's website. Just a few words is all it takes!

CPSIA information can be obtained
at www.ICGtesting.com
Printed in the USA
BVHW071320270423
663156BV00018B/909